Unclear Skies

Born and raised in Upstate New York, Jason LaPier lives in Portland, Oregon with his wife and their dachshund. In past lives he has been a guitar player for a metal band, a drum-n-bass DJ, a record store owner, a game developer, and an IT consultant. These days he divides his time between writing fiction and developing software, and doing Oregonian things like gardening, hiking, and drinking microbrew. He can be found on Twitter @JasonWLaPier and he blogs at jasonwlapier.com.

Also by Jason LaPier

The Dome Trilogy
Unexpected Rain

Unclear Skies

JASON LaPIER

Book Two of The Dome Trilogy

HARPER
Voyager

Harper*Voyager*
an imprint of HarperCollins*Publishers* Ltd
1 London Bridge Street
London SE1 9GF

www.harpervoyagerbooks.co.uk

This Paperback Original 2016

First published in Great Britain in ebook format by Harper*Voyager* 2016

A catalogue record for this book
is available from the British Library

ISBN: 978-0-00-816026-5

Printed and bound in Great Britain

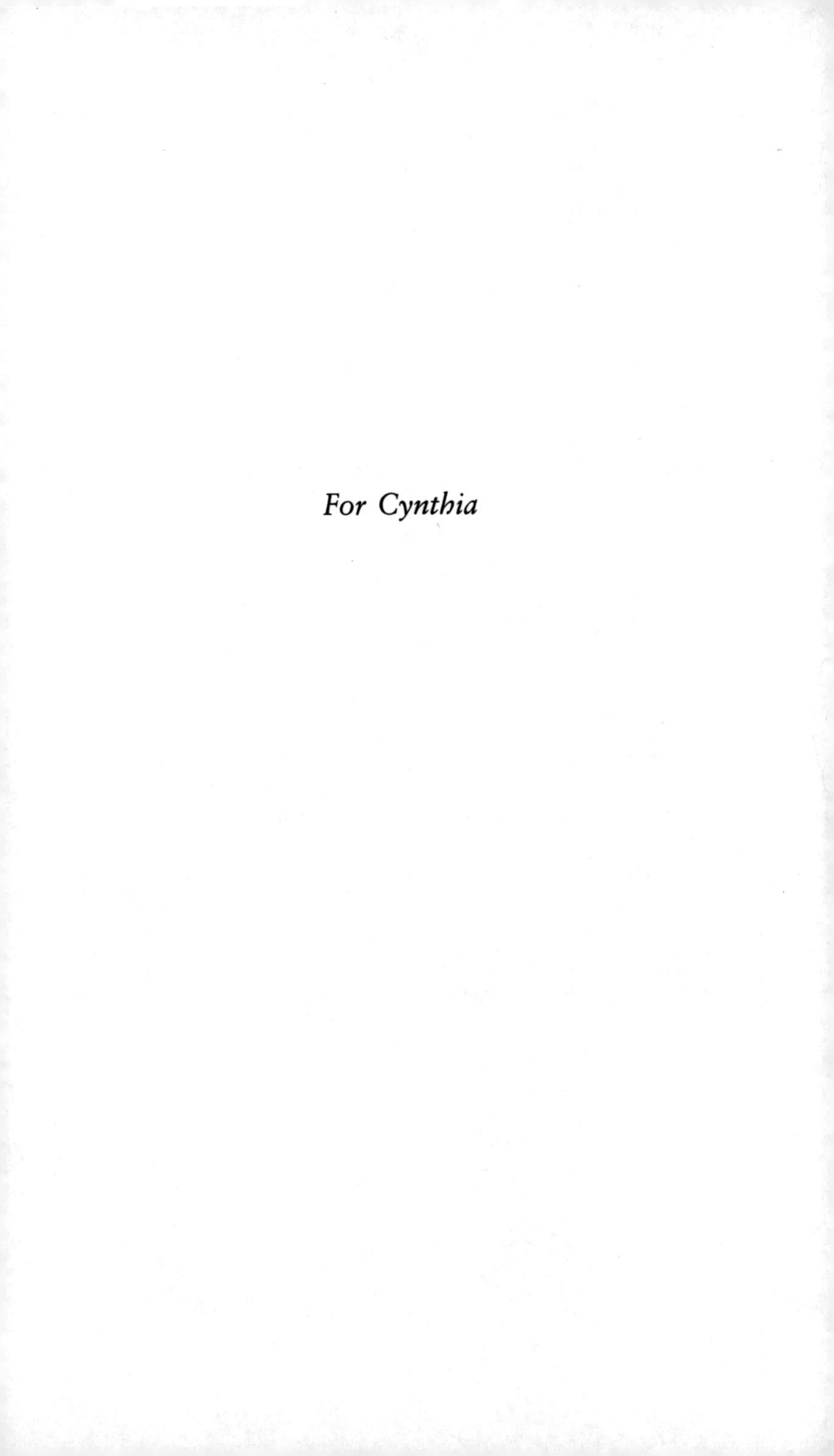

For Cynthia

CHAPTER 1

Jared McManus stared at the hodgepodge of numbers, colors, and stars in his hand. There were no patterns. He'd somehow worked himself into a black hole where no ink printed on cardboard could ever be useful to any other ink printed on other pieces of cardboard.

"Stalling?" Susan Horowitz's eyes didn't leave her magazine. The cards in her hand rested against the table like a comfortable fan. She flipped over a page. "Only thirty minutes until the next bus is in range."

McManus grunted and reflexively glanced at the viewport. The security center of the superliner had a broad window and he could see the burning disc, Barnard's Star, far off to the left, three hundred million kilometers away, give or take. A larger globe of swirling pink and gray encroached on the right.

He turned his attention back to his hand, but he could only feel the hard and cold metal of the table surface under his wrists and not the cards between his fingers. "Gimme two," he said. Instantly, he wished he'd asked for three.

"Only two? You must have something better than I thought," Horowitz taunted. She flipped a pair of cards his way, then one for herself. "One for me."

"I still don't get this game." Kendra Katsumi leaned over McManus, causing him to pull his cards tight to his chest. "What?" she said, pulling her pale face back against her neck. "I'm not playing. What does it hurt if I look?"

"Bad luck," McManus muttered. He directed his attention to Horowitz, who looked at her card and folded it into her hand in one motion. She puffed a long lock of black hair away from her eyes with an idle exhale and turned back to her magazine.

"You guys and your paper," Katsumi rambled as she paced around the table. Her youthful energy grated him. "Seems like you'd play something on holo."

"Can it, jockey." McManus squinted at his cards, daring them to be liars. No matter how hard he stared, they did not budge. If his face was capable of smiling, he might have given himself away. The two cards he'd drawn completed a short star run. Finally he had something he could work with. "One hundred," he said, pushing the last of his chips into the center of the table.

Horowitz grinned. "Jerry, you really want me to take the last of your Alleys?" With a quick toss, she matched his chips before he could reconsider. "Want to push it?"

"With what? That's all I got left."

"Next run."

The words turned over in his head. "What, you mean if I win, you take my run?"

"And if I win, you take mine."

It was tempting, McManus couldn't deny that. He hated the shuttle runs. Docking a patroller with another vessel in mid-space – it was hell on his stomach – to do a passenger check and cargo inspection. And then to rub it in afterward, playing escort to a bunch of rich bastards.

"It's your turn for the run," he said. "So if I win, you still go this time. And you go next time, when it would have been my turn. After that, it's back to your turn again."

"That's right," she said. "That's the bet."

"That's the bet?" Katsumi laughed. "I don't see what the big deal is. I go on every run."

"Can it, jockey. Okay, Horowitz. You're on."

They laid their cards on the table. As McManus registered the hand that his fellow ModPol officer spread before him, he felt the burn start in his chest, spreading quickly to his arms, his neck, his eyes.

"Full ship," she said. "Beats that little run of stars you got there. Hope you had your suit cleaned, Jerry."

"Oh, hey, you guys!" Katsumi called, her face pressed against the viewport. "Look, you can see the shuttle. It's a Polarlys!"

"Damn you all," McManus mumbled. He hoisted himself out of his chair and kept his back to the window as he left the room.

* * *

As the ModPol patroller sped to meet the other vessel, McManus turned to take in the full view of the Royal Starways Interplanetary Cruise Delight Superliner #3 that had been his assignment for almost five months. Assignment, but it felt like a prison sentence, or at the very least a punishment. Whatever the case, it was a sight to behold from the outside. Fantastically large, oblong like a sausage, and covered in domes that bubbled around its surface like welts. Some radiating different colors – lush greens, wet blues, warm yellows – and some just completely clear so that when viewed from the side, the black was visible beyond.

He sighed and turned away. Scanning the field before them, he picked out the ship in the distance. Of all shuttles, it had to be a Polarlys. It was coming from Barnard-3, so it would have to be a big one, and the Polarlys held over seven hundred passengers at full capacity. Plus their luggage.

"Isn't she beautiful?" Katsumi cooed, leaning over the throttle to get closer to the viewport. "What a machine." She leaned back, but kept her back straight as she glanced at McManus. "Not that I would fly one, mind you. It's too big. You can't maneuver worth a damn in something like that."

"No maneuvers, Cadet," McManus said, eyeing his pilot warily. He reflexively tugged at his seat harness, which felt too loose. A bright floral scent tingled in his nose and he looked around the tiny cockpit, trying to find the source. "You got an air freshener hidden around here somewhere?"

"Officer Horowitz is sending the passenger manifest now."

McManus poked at his console with a pair of index fingers and let out a groan as the list scrolled on. "Shit, Katsumi, I'm glad you get such a kick out of sitting in this tin can, staring at that other tin can. You're going to be waiting a while."

"How many passengers, Officer?"

"It's at capacity. Seven hundred and thirty." He sighed. "It's going to take hours."

"Oh yes, at least four. Maybe eight." She turned to him,

her face jumping upward. "I'll be able to practice my maneuvers!"

McManus stared at the distant shuttle that was slowly growing in size. He had not had his suit cleaned since the last run, because he wasn't expecting to go on this run. The last run had not gone well for him, or his breakfast.

"This is all Runstom's fault," he muttered.

"What did you say? Runstom?" She was facing forward again, flicking at switches above her head. "You mean, Officer Stanford Runstom?"

McManus closed his eyes. "Yeah, Officer Stanley. You know him?"

"Everyone knows who Officer Runstom is." Her voice rose and she kicked the patroller clockwise a couple of degrees and McManus gripped the sides of his seat, fearing a spontaneous barrel-roll. "He blew open a ring of corruption inside ModPol!"

"You have got to be kidding me," McManus muttered. He could feel the red in his chest, and he pushed it down, afraid he might end up breaking a window and suffocating them both. "Let me tell you something, Cadet. Runstom ran off with a fugitive. He ran off and hid on one of these goddamn superliners. With a fugitive."

"Yeah, but he had to, right?"

McManus sighed. "He could have brought Jack Jackson right back to ModPol, but instead he chose to hide out on a superliner. And Royal Freaking Starways has a freaking fit about it, but you don't hear about that, no, because ModPol decides to pay them off with some free security. And while I get stuck doing shuttle security, Runstom of all people gets a goddamn promotion!"

As he ranted, Katsumi peered tentatively over her shoulder.

"Officer McManus?" she said in a whisper. "Why are you sitting on your hands?"

"Just can it and fly, jockey."

* * *

As soon as the airlock cleared, McManus fought to detach his helmet. He coughed and sucked in the stale air of the shuttle's service chamber, which was slightly better than the sour insides of his suit.

A pale-skinned security guard wearing a slim, black, silken outfit came through the opposite door. "Officer Horowitz?"

"McManus." He tossed the helmet to the floor and followed with his gloves.

The guard stiffened. "We were told it would be Officer Horowitz."

"Horowitz came down with something," McManus said, unzipping his suit.

"That's unfortunate."

"Buddy, don't talk to me about fortune. Anyway," he waved, then went back to his suit. "You should have received an update."

"Hold on." As the guard lifted his hand to his ear, his biceps flexed large beneath the expensive garb. To most, it would have been impressive, but McManus suspected the clothes were designed to flatter muscles that weren't really there. He lowered his hand. "Okay, you're clear."

McManus thought about challenging the man to a friendly round of arm-wrestling, maybe earn back some of his dignity, but then he got a better idea. "You look strong, Mr., uh..."

"Yernson." The arms folded and the shiny biceps appeared again.

"Mr. Yernson." He gestured toward the cases he'd dragged through the hatch. "Give me a hand with this equipment. Least you can do, seein' as how I'm doing your job."

Yernson frowned at McManus for a moment, then unfurled his arms and walked to the cases. He stared at them, either trying to work out what was in them or trying to work out how heavy they would be. Not that the shuttle's artificial gravity was anywhere near a full G.

"Take those down to the cargo bay," McManus said. "I'm going to start with the passengers. After I get through all seven goddamn hundred of them, I'll do the luggage."

* * *

By the time he'd gotten to passenger #365 – exactly halfway down the list – McManus had been at it for almost two and a half hours. He thought people would be more anxious to get this over with so they could get on with their blessed cruise, but no one was prepared as he came through and asked for identification.

"You should have brought more guys."

"What?" McManus lowered his list to look at #365. A lanky, twenty-something male, red-gray skin, leather jacket, leather pants, and an aural augmentation of some kind that looked like a small, matte-black square where his left ear should be. A top hat on his head and a gold crossbar through his septum.

"This would go faster if you had more guys."

"Tell me about it. You got your—"

"ID, of course, Officer." The young man's eyes sparkled as he presented his biometrics card.

McManus yanked it away and looked at the name, which read Reezer, Frank. He stuck it into his identification unit, tapped a few buttons, and spun the machine around so the hole faced #365.

"Put—"

"My finger in the hole." The young man peered at the device with an unsettling curiosity before sliding his finger in. "I studied this system. Multi-factor. You have my encrypted bios in the box's database. I carry a card imprinted with another encrypted version of my bios. The two are only recognized when hashed together with the bio sample from my finger."

McManus frowned. He knew how the damn thing worked – well, he didn't really know how it worked, but he knew it *did* work – and he didn't need a civilian explaining it to him. He held his tongue; the guy wasn't worth his breath. Instead, he did what he always did when he was stuck on these inspection runs. While he was waiting for the box to do its part, McManus closed his eyes and imagined punching Stanford Runstom right across the jaw.

The box chimed and he gave the card back to #365. "Enjoy your trip, Mr. Reezer."

"Thank you, Officer. If you'll excuse me now, I need to go wash the smell of ID-box off of my hands."

The young man stood, tipped his top hat, and strolled down the aisle. McManus moved on to #366. "ID?"

"Yes, of course, Officer. I have it right here somewhere." After a minute of digging, the old man with wisps of gray hair and a bright white suit produced his bio card from a worn briefcase. "There you go, sir."

They went through the process of slotting the card and verifying biometrics. As McManus closed his eyes to daydream about punching, he heard an alarming buzz. The box jiggled in his hands.

"Oh, goodness." The old man tugged reflexively, but his finger remained. "I'm stuck."

"Just hold on a minute, there, Mister." McManus gripped the box firmly so he could look at the readout on the tiny screen. "Not a match."

"Wh-wh— I beg your pardon? Who does it think I am?"

McManus lift his gaze. "It doesn't think you're anybody, that's not how it works. It's just saying that between my database, your card, and your biosample, something doesn't match." McManus had done twelve shuttle runs and Horowitz had done eleven. They'd never actually found anything. Everyone always matched.

"Alright, sir. I'm sorry to have to do this, but you're under arrest."

"What? Me?" The man gripped his chest with his free hand.

"Just relax, sir." Was he feeling a rare moment of pity? Or was he just afraid of the paperwork that would come if one of the passengers had a heart attack during the ID test? "I'm just going to take you back to the holding room and we'll get this sorted out." He eased a pair of cuffs from a pocket on his belt. "Now I don't want you to be alarmed, but the box won't come off until I get some cuffs on you."

"C-cuffs? Me?"

He slid the cuffs around the old man's frail wrists and at the moment they latched, the box blipped and released his finger.

"I just can't believe this," he dribbled on. "Oh, misfortune."

"Yeah, misfortune." McManus tapped his earpiece. "Katsumi, McManus here. You read me?"

No immediate reply came, so he started escorting #366 toward the hall. The holding room was really just a big closet at the far end of the shuttle.

"Will I still get to go on my cruise?" the old man burbled as McManus shuffled him along.

"Katsumi, where are you?" She was either napping or off doing her useless maneuvers. "Damn it, Cadet. Come in."

He took #366 into the holding room closet and looked around for a good place to stash him. He was worried about just chaining the geezer to a shelf or something without having anything to sit down on. He shut the door and started moving around boxes of towels.

The shuttle had come to a full stop in order for McManus to space-walk over to it from the patroller, so when it started moving again, he fell backwards onto his ass.

"Oh, are we going to the cruise ship now?" The old man had been less fazed by the unexpected acceleration, and was only teetering slightly.

"What the hell?" McManus yanked himself up and yelled into his comm. "Katsumi, what the hell is going on? We're moving. Cadet!"

"Officer McManus. I'm sorry, I'm here. I – I must have dozed off."

He sighed. "Yeah, okay, kid. Forget about it. I would have dozed off if I were you. What's going on? We started moving."

"Yes, I noticed. When the engine fired up, it set off an alarm in the patroller. A-and that's what woke me up."

"Is it already docking with the superliner?"

"Well, it does appear that the autopilot has engaged." Katsumi's voice trailed off.

"Cadet?"

"Yes, sir. The autopilot is on, but the course is – well, it's definitely not locked onto the superliner's beacon."

"What's it locked onto? Where is it going? Can you override it?"

"I uh, uh – no, I can't."

"Okay, just stay on our ass, Katsumi. I'm going up to the control room." He headed for the door. "Don't go anywhere, Mister," he said over his shoulder as he left the room.

He closed the door behind him and considered locking it – the door lock was lit green – and he put his hand into his pocket to fish out his keycard, but then paused. A cold, damp feeling was spreading through his body and smothering the burning heat he was used to. Whatever it was made him decide he didn't want to lock an old man in a closet right at that moment and he turned to head toward the control room.

His momentum shifted in the hallway as the ship turned in its orientation routine and he shuffled his feet in a clumsy dance to stay upright, then he continued to jog to the opposite end. Even at double-time it took him several minutes to reach the other end, the damn Polarlys shuttle was so long, and the artificial gravity was only about a quarter-strength. When he reached the control room door, he stuffed his hand into his pocket for his keycard, and found none. He turned out both pockets. "What the hell?"

A shadow in the shape of a big stupid top hat eclipsed the door lock and McManus spun around.

"Hello, there, Officer. I believe you dropped this." Frank Reezer held out a keycard.

"How did you get this?" McManus said, snatching it away from him.

"As I said, you dropped it. I found it on the floor as I returned to my seat."

McManus eyed the other man for a second, then felt the ship turn slightly. "Shit." He reached for a pair of cuffs. "No offense pal, but you creep me the fuck out."

"Are you going to arrest me?" He put his wrists together in front of him. He wasn't incredulous, more like curious, when he asked, "What charge?"

"No charge yet." McManus slapped the cuffs on. "Just holding you. Officer's discretion."

"I mean the cuffs," Reezer said, pulling his hands closer to his eyes to peer at his bonds. "How much is the electrical charge on these babies?"

McManus closed his eyes and shook his head. "Enough."

He swiped the keycard against the lock, half expecting it to fail for some reason. But the lock went green and he slid the door open. He pulled Reezer into the room with him.

The control room was small and windowless. These shuttles ran entirely on autopilot – they were launched from their home docks with a particular trajectory and course, where they would find the beacon of the superliner waiting to pick them up. Once locked onto the beacon, they would pilot themselves into the massive landing zones along the side of the superliner. As such, the control room was really just a bank of computers with a single maintenance terminal. McManus leaned in close.

BEACON ACQUIRED. IDENTIFYING...
ROYAL STARWAYS SUPERLINER #3.
HOLDING FOR SECURITY CHECK.
...

...

...

BEACON LOST.

...

BEACON ACQUIRED. IDENTIFYING...ROYAL STARWAYS SUPERLINER #3.

...

SECURITY CHECK COMPLETED. ENGAGING AUTOPILOT.

...

...

APPROACHING TARGET.

"What the hell?" McManus muttered. "We're already back at the superliner?" He pushed his earpiece. "Katsumi, is the shuttle at the superliner? There's no windows in this damn thing. Not even a contact map."

"Negative, Officer McManus. You're just drifting. You're drifting away – hold on. Contact ten kilometers out and coming in fast."

"Are you talking to your ride?" Reezer leaned in close, causing McManus to flinch. The younger man's face drooped for a moment, losing its smug expression. "Listen, man. I'm not a killer." His voice was different – the act was dropped – and he continued in a hush. "But they are. If you have a ship out there, tell your pilot to stay back. They won't hesitate to smoke a Pollie."

"Who won't? What the hell are you talking about?"

Reezer's eyes grew cold and he looked at the floor. "I'm just giving you fair warning. They will not hesitate."

"Katsumi, listen to me." McManus turned away from Reezer and headed back into the hall. "Cadet. You have to get back. Go back to the superliner. I repeat, go back to the superliner. That's an order."

"You want me to go back?"

"Yes, dammit. Go back. Don't dock, just keep a holding pattern alongside the superliner."

There was a rumble and a terrible screeching sound then and McManus froze in mid-stride. He looked all around, trying to identify the source of the noise. It was followed by drumming sounds, rhythmic thumping. He crouched and listened, then stalked slowly down the hall. Halfway down, he heard scraping sounds and turned to one of the hatchways that led to the cargo hold.

He leaned against the wall next to the hatch and unsnapped his holster. He drew the stun pistol out slowly with one hand and with the other, held his keycard to the door lock.

The lock went green and the door flew open, and he caught sight of a large, black boot, quickly withdrawn.

"You first," came a voice from the adjoining corridor. There was a yelp and a man dressed head-to-toe in tan leather stumbled through the doorway. His head whipped around, and with it long, black hair. Immediately behind him came another leather-clad, this one in black, with no hair and several dozen face piercings.

McManus decided to forgo introductions and blasted the first one, who stumbled and spasmed down the hall. The pierced one was quick and slapped the pistol away with one hand and clocked the officer in the jaw with the other.

"Sonova." McManus glanced toward where the pistol had sailed, but not for long, as another punch was incoming. This one he blocked and then countered with two solid right jabs to the stomach, followed by a mean left hook to the jaw as Piercings doubled over. The last blow set his target twirling a full circle before crumpling to the floor.

The hallway spun and dipped then as McManus was tackled hard by a third assailant. His head hit the far wall and everything went blurry for a moment. He shook it off and forced himself to his feet, using the wall for support.

"Stun gun, eh?" The voice came from a very large man, whose biceps were not a trick of any fancy clothing, because he wore only a tank-top, jeans, and large black boots. In one hand was McManus's pistol. With an angry wink, he asked, "Do you know how much these fuckin' things hurt?"

McManus hadn't known, but he soon learned.

CHAPTER 2

Dava watched the Pollie spasm and twitch himself into a nightmare-filled sleep. Johnny Eyeball grinned as he hefted the stun-gun. He looked up and down the hallway, seeking more victims.

Freezer strolled down the corridor, top hat on his head and hands behind his back, and approached the unconscious cop. "Told ya you shoulda had more guys." He turned around and crouched so he could reach the cuff control on the officer's belt. With a ding, the bonds popped off.

"Freezer, any other security?" Dava asked.

The hacker was going through the rest of the gear still attached to the cop. "There's a few guards," he said as he rifled. "But I think they're mostly for show. Expensive clothes and flashy muscles."

"Target practice," Eyeball muttered. "Where?"

"Aft. I can show you."

"And Sandiego," Dava said. "Where is he?"

"Ah, yeah." Freezer stood up, tapping at a handypad that he lifted from the Pollie. "He's passenger number 485, so you'll want to go up the stairs and hit the aftmost doors on the starboard side. Assuming the Pollie was doing his passenger checks in numerical order, then he never got to the 400s yet. They should all be sitting quietly waiting their turns."

"Good." Rando Jansen joined them, taking his sweet time. Dava looked the man up and down – he wasn't even wearing armor, just a two-piece gray suit, black dress shoes, and nothing on his neatly trimmed head. To most he would appear unarmed, but Dava picked out the subtle lump in his waistband. "Freezer, your hack will hold?" Jansen asked. "This thing's not going to suddenly turn around and make for the superliner?"

Freezer huffed a laugh. "I reconfigured the nav computer to lock onto our fake beacon. Someone could reset it, but then it will be blank. No autopilot."

"What about a real pilot?" Dava asked.

"I haven't seen any, but it's safe to say someone on board is qualified." He gestured at nothing. "No alarms tripped yet though, so if there are any pilots around, they're probably napping."

"Fine. We'll move quickly," Jansen said. "Johnny, you and Freezer take care of security. Make sure no alarms get tripped. Dava, you find Sandiego. And remember, we want him alive."

"Here ya go, RJ," Freezer said as he handed the handypad to Jansen and walked down the hall, waving to Eyeball.

"What's with that hat?" Eyeball mumbled as he followed.

"It's my disguise. Doesn't it make me look like a rich person?"

"Makes you look like a fuckin' idiot," Eyeball said, their banter trailing off as they went through the door midway down the hall.

"Dava," Jansen said, putting a cold hand on her arm. "Did you hear me? I want him alive. But we don't want him slipping away, so don't let him see you coming."

She pulled her arm away. "They never see me coming."

* * *

The blade went through the man's leg cleanly, but wetly.

The populace jumped in synchrony when he screamed. Rows 470, 480, and 490 cleared quickly, flashing the shine of jewelry and top-thread clothing in the softly-lit comfort of the passenger compartment. All except for seat number 485.

When he was able to form words through the screeching gasps, he managed, "Other leg. Other leg!"

"What was that?" Dava whispered into his right ear. His skin was bright yellow and it clashed with the pale-green shirt he wore. "You stick out like a bloody thumb here, you know that?"

He coughed and gritted his teeth. "The drugs…the pills are in the other leg."

She sighed. No one ever withheld information any more. "I *know* your left leg is the false one."

She yanked the blade free and the man screamed again. His palms went to the wound, instinctively applying pressure. "I'm sorry!" he blurted. "You have to tell Moses I'm sorry!"

"Detach it."

He looked at her, eyes pleading, then at the hole in his real leg, his reddening hands holding back the blood flow, then at her again. She twirled her short, curved blade around her index finger. He quickly forgot his wound and poked at either side of his left thigh until there was the clunk of a release.

"While you're working on that, let's make sure I got your name right."

"S-S-Sandiego." He was crying now, as he tried to angle his body in such a way that he could pull the leg free of his pants. "Mr. Sandiego," he blubbered, mostly to himself.

"Mister, hmm," Dava purred. She jerked the leg out of his hand as soon as it came free from his clothing.

"Are you going to kill me?"

"Do you know who I am?" She bowed slightly into his space, and he reacted by squeezing back into his seat.

"Y-yeah. You're Dava."

"And who is Dava?"

He coughed and swallowed. "Dava is the b-bla—"

"Black?" She leaned closer. Looked into his eyes. Fear. Shock. Pain. Was there repulsion? "You ever see a black woman before, Sandiego?"

"N-no. But—"

"Does the sight of me frighten you?"

"Assassin," he blurted. "The assassin who works for Moses Down." He spouted the words in gasping sentences. "Sposta have been born on Earth. Sposta been an orphan on Betelgeuse-3. Became an assassin. Sposta have killed forty men."

She tracked his eyes and nodded slowly. "Not all at once. And not all were men." She ran the blade lightly across Sandiego's leg. "I don't know if you'll count as a full one. Maybe I'll only make it to forty and three-quarters tonight."

"I didn't take them!" He gripped the arms of his seat, leaning back away from her. "You have to believe me!"

Without looking back, Dava flipped the leg over her shoulder, aiming it at the direction of the clomp of Jansen's dress shoes.

"Are they all there?" Jansen said, taking the leg. She turned her eyes to him and said nothing. He slid away from her gaze nonchalantly. "Hey. Sandiego, right? How do you open this thing?"

"J-just turn that part there, push down that button, and then twist that."

"Ah, there we go," Jansen said, popping the top off the false limb. "Wow, that's quite a stash. So, Sandiego," he said. "Who gave them to you?"

"It was Mr. Joshi. He lifted them. I'm – I was just supposed to sell them."

"And where are you gonna do that, huh?" Jansen lifted his head out of the leg-hole to lean his bronze face close to Sandiego's. "This shuttle isn't going anywhere except to a superliner."

"They're designer. Delirium-K."

"We know what they are, Sandiego," Jansen said evenly. "You stole them from *us*."

"I didn't, Mr. Joshi did!" the dealer stammered. "I'm just supposed to sell them to rich people. That's why I'm going – why I was going to the Royal."

"How enterprising," Dava said, taking a moment to put eyes around the room. The passengers had begun filing into the hallway. The pushing, shoving crowd parted quickly as though a buffer of wind blew them apart, and Johnny Eyeball strode through, a strange dark and flickering cloth draped over one shoulder.

"Look what I got, RJ," he said, spreading what turned out to be a shirt across his chest. The fabric stretched and ballooned cartoonishly. "Pretty awesome, right? One of the guards gave it to me."

"Yeah, that's great, Johnny." Jansen turned back to their victim. "Okay, Sandiego. What happens after you unload all this stuff? Do you meet up with this Joshi guy again?"

"Mr. Joshi." Sandiego's head sank and he mumbled into his chest. "I was supposed to get on the Royal for six months, move the product, and get off at Terroneous."

"And Joshi?"

"Not him, someone else is sposta to meet me there." Sandiego flinched as Dava picked at her fingernails with her blade, and his voice sped up. "Mr. Hill – I'm sposta meet Mr. Hill and give him the cash."

"Where?" Jansen asked. "How do you contact him?"

"No contact beforehand. I'm just sposta go to this bar called Angry Candy. It's in Sunderville."

"What's your cut?" Dava asked, less to know the answer and more to see how much more the man could spill. She emphasized the word *cut* with a quick wrist-turn of her blade.

"No cash," he said, looking down again. "Was going to get a new leg."

"Ooh, a cyberleg?"

"No," he said firmly, raising his head. "A real one."

"Gross," Dava said with a frown.

"Okay, that's enough," Jansen said, touching her arm. "We need to move out."

"Hey boss," Eyeball said, pulling on Jansen's shoulder, causing him to let go of Dava. A good thing, since she had been considering giving their new underboss a scar to discourage his touch-feely behaviors. "I'm thinking we get Freezer to fuck up the life support. You know, cut off the oxygen. That way when they find this piece of shit, everyone will just be lying there dead." He beamed a smile at Dava and nodded slowly. "Subtlety."

She caught herself betraying a rare smile. "I suppose it's more subtle than blowing the whole thing up."

"No," Jansen said, putting his hands out to both of them. "We're sending a message. We leave everyone alive. Johnny, you didn't kill those guards, did you?"

Eyeball sighed. "They'll live. Probably."

"What about him?" Dava said, tilting her blade at Sandiego.

"Is that ModPol officer still alive?" Jansen asked Eyeball.

"Sure is," he beamed, showing all the teeth he still had and winking unintentionally. "I'm going to torture him."

"No, we leave him. We leave them both. ModPol can take Mr. Sandiego here into custody."

"Aww, what?" the one-legged dealer cried. "You can't do that!"

"RJ, you took the drugs back," Dava pointed out. "What are they going to charge him with, being a gimp?"

"Johnny, give me that stun gun you picked up. And give me your shirt. Not the new one, the one that says Space Waste on it."

"Aw, man," Eyeball groaned. "I knew we should have just blown the whole thing up."

* * *

A few minutes later, they were standing outside the door to some kind of closet. Freezer locked it with a keycard. Inside were the unconscious cop, a couple of badly broken guards, Sandiego – who was holding a drained stun pistol and wearing a too-large *Space Waste Summer Camp* T-shirt – and some old man who was already cuffed to a shelving unit, who Freezer described as the poor sap to be scanned after he'd left a droplet of fake DNA in the finger-fed ID machine.

"Well, that oughta do it," Freezer said as the lock went red. "Somebody else's problem now."

"Yeah, Captain 2-Bit?" Jansen said, touching his earpiece. He listened, then sighed. "Yes, this is Underboss Jansen, who else would it be?...Over!...How far away?...Yeah... No, no. We're leaving right now. Let them be. Right, right... over and out to you too."

"Company?" Dava asked.

"Just a single patroller," Jansen said. He waved at the door. "Just in time to find the scene we left behind."

"If you don't mind me saying so, RJ," Dava said, "this seems over the top for a legful of stolen Delirium."

"Hey, this is D-K," he said, waving the false limb, causing the fake hair sprouting from the rubbery skin to flex in the breeze. "You know what the street value of this amount of D-K is?"

Dava huffed. "Street value?" She looked at Eyeball.

"Drugs." He chewed through the word with disdain. "Good for morale. Shit for tactical value. And we don't do street."

"Okay, right." Jansen let the leg drop to his side. "You've got a point. But let me ask you something. Mr. Sandiego. Mr. Joshi. Mr. Hill."

"Was there a question in there?" Dava said, unwilling to back away from the clean-cut man as he leaned in too close.

"Do you know them?"

"No. Do you?"

"Not those names specifically," he said. "But I know the Misters."

Eyeball laughed suddenly and heartily, causing Jansen to flinch and take a step back. "The Misters? The fuck?"

"The Misters are a new outfit." Jansen straightened up, puffing up his chest, holding up his pride. "They've been on the down low for about a year or so. Building a network. This," he said, shaking the leg. "This is them knocking on our door."

"How do you know about these guys?" Dava said.

"I know things," Jansen said firmly. "And I know people who know things. That's why I'm here. Now pack it up. We're moving."

"To hunt Misters?" Eyeball said, grinning.

"No. We'll pick up that trail on Terroneous later. Sandiego said he wasn't supposed to contact Hill beforehand, so our best bet is to check out Sunderville in six months when the superliner makes it up that way."

"And you have something planned for the meantime," Dava guessed.

"We have another target in the Sirius system," Jansen said. He turned and slapped a fist against Eyeball's chest, clad in his shiny new shirt. "A target with *tactical value*. Now let's move out."

CHAPTER 3

Stanford Runstom was lost.

It wasn't that today was the first day of his new job; no, he didn't allow himself to feel lost in the metaphorical sense, lost because of the uncertain, unplanned path of his career. He was the normal kind of lost.

"Can I help you, officer?"

A baby-faced, blue-haired woman sat behind a wide, circular desk in the center of the building. Only it wasn't the center of the building. There were three corridors extending from the space in directions equidistant from each other, which certainly gave the impression of centralization, but Runstom knew better, having wandered the building for over an hour. This was the third such *center* he'd encountered since entering the Modern Policing and Peacekeeping Universal Headquarters and Outreach Center.

"Please tell me this is B-deck."

"I'm afraid not, officer," the young woman beamed. "This is C-deck."

"What? I came into A-deck. Did I somehow pass B-deck?"

The piece of paper that Runstom had jotted down the office number onto was becoming thin from being scrunched into his hand for so long.

"Would you like a map?" The receptionist held out a small, gray stick. When he reflexively reached for it, she pulled back. "I'm sorry, officer. Where is your mate?"

"My mate? Excuse me?"

She cocked her head, then lifted her wrist. She pointed at the four-inch-wide black band that went around her forearm. "You know, your WrappiMate. I need to upload the map to it."

"I don't have one of those. You can't just give me a paper map?"

She stared at him for a few seconds, her eyes narrowing slightly, her jaw slowly sliding from one side to the other, and he got the sense she was trying to work out whether or not he was pulling her leg. "We don't have any paper maps, officer."

"Stanford."

"I'm sorry?"

"My name is Stanford. Stanford Runstom. Look, can you just point me in the direction of B-deck?"

She pointed at him. "Back the way you came. Look for a lavender hallway."

"Lavender?"

"You know," she said. "Kind of purple."

* * *

The changing of the colors in the ModPol HQ hallways was not abrupt; in fact, they changed at such a mild gradient over such a long distance, he hadn't noticed the difference until the receptionist had called attention to it. The walls didn't come down to the floor at nice, neat, ninety-degree angles, but instead just curved, as they did at the ceiling. The whole experience was very disorienting for Runstom.

Likewise, the different sections of the building were named "decks", as though it was a ship, and this made no sense to Runstom whatsoever. They were more like wings, and it wasn't until he was deep into the B-deck wing that he found an elevator that took him to the 97th floor.

When the elevator doors opened, a pale, squat woman – an obvious resident of the strong gravity of Sirius-5 – in a bright-green suit stood before him.

"Stanford Runstom!" she belted, thrusting a broad hand forward. "Victoria Horus. A pleasure to finally meet you in person."

Runstom took the hand and shook it firmly. "Yes, nice to meet you, ma'am." He glanced at the elevator. "Are you on your way out? I apologize if I missed our meeting. I couldn't seem to find—"

"No, of course not." She took a step back and looked Runstom up and down. "I'm here to show you to your office. Come with me, Stan. Is it okay if I call you Stan? Or do you like Stanley?"

"Not Stanley. Stanford. Please. Sir. Ma'am." He cleared his throat. "Stan is fine."

"Great." Horus smiled, putting a hand on Runstom's shoulder. "Stan. And you can call me Vicky – to my face. Behind my back, you'll want to call me Big Vicky if you want to fit in with the rest of these clowns!" she said, her voice burbling into a laugh.

Horus led Runstom down another bizarrely curved

hallway for a minute, then stopped at an open door. "This is your new office," she said, gesturing.

The room was sparse, to say the least. An empty coat rack, a desk, and a terminal, and that was about it. No footlocker, no holovid, no receptacle to charge stun sticks or pistols. There was a window that stretched fully across the back wall, but all that could be seen were thick, white clouds. Their oppressive presence made him look for curtains or blinds, but he saw none.

"It's...great," he said, causing Horus to squeeze him across the shoulders.

"Ain't it though? A beautiful view. But no time to take it in." She tugged Runstom away from the blank office. "I need you to come into my office so that we can talk about your first mission."

Horus's office was just down the hall and much more densely furnished. The walls were lined with fully-stocked bookshelves, and her window was garnished with velvety, lavender-colored drapes. There was a thick, spiraling red-and-brown carpet, a feature Runstom hadn't noticed was missing from his own office until he stepped onto it in Horus's. And finally, the desk was a dark, slick wood – or wood-like substance – that was punctuated by a gold-lettered, glowing placard that read, *Victoria "Big Vicky" Horus, Director of Market Strategy Management.*

"It's real wood," Horus said, slipping into the chair behind her desk and looking up at Runstom, who had unconsciously put his hands on the surface. "Imported. Have a seat, Stanford."

Runstom sat in one of the chairs that faced the desk. "I'm glad you have time to talk," he said, trying to build courage. "I just have some questions—"

"Hey," Horus said, leaning forward and pointing. "How's the apartment, huh? Right in downtown Grovenham, I understand. In the Pearl District. Very nice, is it?"

"Well, yes, it's nice." It had been nice. Runstom had only stepped inside it for the first time yesterday. It felt too nice for it to be his own. It felt like a hotel room – albeit a very large one, more like a suite – and he found sleep very difficult.

"Well, don't worry too much about getting hung up in our gravity here," she said. "We'll have you out and about on assignment. It won't be that different from your last position, in that sense."

"Yes, about that," Runstom said, fumbling for words. "I'm still – I uh – I'm sorry. It's an honor to have received the promotion."

"You're welcome," Horus said with a big smile.

"Right, thank you. I just don't understand." Runstom looked at his hands, then back at Horus. "Why me, ma'am?"

"Vicky."

He stared at his new superior for a moment, finding it difficult to be so informal. "It's just that this job, it's not like anything I've done before."

"Let me show you something, Stanford." Horus tapped at her console and a nondescript cabinet against one wall folded away, and a small holovid unit extended from it. When it winked to life, the image quality was unlike anything he'd ever seen before, and the sound was clear and radiated throughout the room.

"And now onto our next story: Corruption within Modern Policing and Peacekeeping, our continuing coverage of the scandal that rocked the known universe. The scandal that

Mark Xavier Phonson, a one-time lieutenant and later high-level administrator for ModPol, and his cronies perpetrated—"

The video sped up as Horus tapped at her console. "Ahem," she grunted with a smile. "Let's just skip to the important part. Ah, here we go."

"Now let's go to Missla Hanchorkif, who is talking to ModPol Officer Stanford Runstom, widely recognized as the hero who blew apart this conspiracy."

"Thank you, Jerry. And thank you, Officer Runstom, for taking the time to answer some questions for us."

"You're welcome, Miss Han— Handkerchief. Thank you for having me."

Runstom remembered the interview, but had never gone back and watched the recording afterward. He'd done several and never watched any of them. He felt a mix of displeasure at hearing his own awkward voice played back to him and pride at having been brave enough to talk to the press. He shamefully admired how much better he looked in holo; the four months of mandatory paid vacation since then had not done his physique any favors.

"Now, Officer – let's start from the beginning. When did you first suspect something was amiss? Was it during the investigation on Barnard-4?"

"Um, well, yes, I suppose I was – concerned – at that time."

"Why was that?"

"Well, the investigation – the crime was on such a massive scale —"

"Thirty-two dead at the scene."
"Right. And yet the investigation was over so quickly."

"Ah, more morbid details," Horus said, once again tapping the controls. "Oh, here we go. This is my favorite bit."

"It's incredible that you, a low-ranking ModPol officer, were able to turn your dedication and loyalty to the job into a full-blown mass murder investigation that took you from Barnard-4 to a Royal Starways Superliner, where you tracked down a corrupt politician who had been blackmailed into transmitting the signal that opened that dome, and from there to the moon Terroneous where you tracked down the cryptographer who encrypted the original deadly code, and from there to Sirius-5 where you found the original programmer of that code.
"I mean, this is a level of commitment that's unheard of, no matter what the job!"

At the last statement, the interviewer turned to face the camera, to show the viewers her sense of awe. Horus paused the recording, and the reporter perpetually stared at them in wonderment.

"I've got dozens of files like this, Stanford," Horus said, leaning over her desk. "Dozens. This whole mess was a media storm. It could have been bad – real bad – for ModPol. Maybe you don't understand how badly it could have spun, maybe you do. But the fact of the matter is, every time your face showed up on a holovid, people stopped seeing a corrupt organization and started seeing a hero."

"Well, I don't," Runstom started, unable to find the

words. Those so-called morbid details she'd skipped over were the most important parts to him. Take away the details, and what else was there?

"A hero that neatly served up all the conspirators on a plate," Horus said, as if mind-reading his question. She stood up and came around the desk to lean against it, her legs crossing at the ankles. "Do you see? Not everyone loves Modern Policing and Peacekeeping, Stanford. There are people out there that do not like us. They would have loved to turn this story the other way, to present ModPol as having a culture of corruption. But you were at the center of it all. The media loved you. You're honest – a straight-talker. And you've always believed in the ModPol mission, haven't you?"

"Yes," Runstom said quietly, again looking at his hands. Then he braced himself, looked Horus in the eyes. "Ma'am. I just believe I would serve ModPol best as a detective."

"Stan, I know that becoming a detective was a lifelong goal for you. But sometimes what we want is just not what we're best at. Sometimes we don't know we're going to be really good at something until it happens. I'm telling you, Stan: this is what you're meant to do."

"I'm just not sure—"

"Now I also know that you've always wanted to follow in your mother's footsteps – maybe even go undercover, like she did. Believe me, I understand, and it's admirable, but we aren't our parents. Hell, my mother was a chemist. Worked in a lab all day long. She wanted me to go into science. Nearly flipped when I moved into the marketing world. And my father was a terraform engineer. Can you imagine how boring that work would be? How long it would take to see the results of your work?"

"I don't know who my father is," Stanford said flatly.

Horus sighed. "You have to trust me, Stanford. This is the right thing for you. This is where you're going to excel. Think of it this way: instead of sitting around waiting for crimes to happen and then investigating them after the fact, you get to be *proactive*."

"It feels like a sales position."

"No, no. It's not sales, not at all. It's furthering the ModPol mission. When the human race started colonizing these systems outside of Sol, we had a chance to start things fresh. We came out here with Utopian ideas, you know? And we deserved that – hell, we'd mastered interstellar flight. It's just unfortunate that there will always be a fringe element. And that's why ModPol is here. We take care of the ugly things that ordinary civilians pretend don't exist. It's not because they're ignorant. It's because they deserve to live worry-free. They're the ones playing by the rules, being civilized. I know you believe that. Tell me you believe in the ModPol vision."

"Of course I do," Runstom replied, louder than he'd expected. He took a breath and controlled his voice. "I just don't know the first thing about public relations."

Horus looked slightly up and away, a thoughtful expression on her face. "Did you know that I started with ModPol just last year?"

"Okay." Runstom knew nothing about his new boss. Didn't know he had one until the transfer order had come in less than a week previously.

"I was with ZebraCorp." She stared at Runstom as though expecting a reply.

"Consumer electronics," Runstom said. "Pads and whatnot."

This caused Horus to lose just a touch of her smile. "Yes,

if by 'pads' you mean the highly successful HandiMate. The WrappiMate was the last launch I worked on." She stuck out her arm to indicate the device wrapped around her left forearm. "Everyone has one. It's the pinnacle of Mate technology. You can operate it like this, but it can also be extended," she said, pulling the flexible screen out of its sheath to form a flag-like handypad that unfurled from the band.

"Yes, I've seen all the advertisements," Runstom said. He had, but hadn't actually paid attention to them enough to know what the damn thing looked like, until now.

"You don't have one? We'll make sure you get one."

"Thanks. But—"

"The point is, Stan," Horus continued, "at ZebraCorp, our products were everywhere. Every market, in every economic class. I worked there for ten years, for the last three as the VP of Marketing. Zebra went from a guy working out of his garage in some suburbs here on Sirius-5 to a multi-stellar operation with factories on three planetoids."

After a pause, Runstom said, "So why did you come to ModPol?"

Horus pointed at him and he knew he'd taken the bait. "Why did I come to ModPol: an excellent question. Stan, I'd done it all. The WrappiMate had the most successful launch of any product in the history of mankind. We made more money in one month than OrbitBurner, Royal Starways, and even ModPol make in a year, combined. There were no more worlds to conquer at ZebraCorp. So why did I come here?"

Runstom scowled. He hated being led along in a conversation, but this was his new boss. "For the challenge?" he guessed.

"For the challenge," Horus repeated, then went silent for a moment. Finally she pointed to the device on her arm again. "It's a marvelous piece of technology. But in the end, it's just a tool. A product. ModPol is not a product. It's a service. What service does ModPol provide?"

He squinted at the Sirius-fiver woman. "Law enforcement and defense."

"Freedom," Horus said with the point of a thick finger. "We handle the ugliness of police-work and defense, and the civilized worlds have the *freedom* to live in peace."

Runstom sighed. He thought he'd better agree or the speechmaking would continue. "Okay, well...you said I'm not going to be selling anything. So what am I doing?"

Horus leaned back and tented her fingers against her lips thoughtfully, her brow creasing. "Listen, Stan. I wasn't entirely truthful before, when we watched that interview clip. There's no denying how much you helped ModPol save face by getting out there and telling the truth of what happened. Regardless, our name has been tarnished. Now I know as an officer, you've been aware of our operational reach. We're solid in the domes on the inner planets, but our other contracts have always been tenuous at best. This whole catastrophe has really hurt those positions."

Horus stood and opened a cabinet. She brought out a pair of tumblers and a bottle of maroon liquid. She filled each halfway and handed one to Runstom. Standing over him, the Sirius-fiver took a sip and sighed lightly. "You did the right thing, Stanford. Through and through." She shook her head and glared and her voice hardened. "But even right things can have consequences."

Runstom wanted to blow up then, to throw the glass at his superior, curse her for what she was suggesting. That this shitstorm was somehow all Runstom's fault. What held him back was the fact that for the past four months, he'd been watching it happen. He'd seen the organization he loved being worn down by the negativity. His old co-workers found creative ways to keep him up to date on the contracts that his actions had fucked up. He never believed ModPol to be corrupt by nature; he was after X and his cronies and that was it. But by doing what he thought was right, he'd hurt the organization he believed in.

"Where is Jack Jackson now?" Horus asked suddenly.

The question sent a spike of adrenaline through Runstom. He stared up at the looming woman. "I don't know."

"He's on the run."

"Yes."

"Because the ModPol Justice Division hasn't absolved him yet."

"No, he hasn't been absolved."

"You brought them the real killers. You brought them the evidence. And they still want to track down and arrest Jackson. For what?"

Runstom grit his teeth. "For being a fugitive."

"Right." Horus laughed once. "For making them look bad. Stanford, you don't have any friends in Justice any more. You and Jackson – you made them look like bumbling, incompetent fools. They'll never let you become a detective. Not after that. But in *this* division – in Defense – you have friends. In this division, we believe what you did was right. In this division, you're a hero."

Runstom stared at his glass, slowly turning it and watching the liquid drip down the sides. The guilt burned him. Jax was out there somewhere. Maybe on Terroneous, maybe not. In hiding, because Runstom had failed to come through. But there was nothing else he could do. Nothing but believe that Jax could take care of himself.

"So what do you need me to do." He didn't have the enthusiasm to lift the words into a proper question.

"Take a drink, Stan." Horus sat back behind the desk. "It's easier than you think. You go out there, and you listen. You listen to our clients, and when they ask questions, you give them straight answers. You do what you can to make them feel safe."

What else was there? Runstom could think of nothing else. She was right; he wasn't going to become a detective, not anytime soon, not until Justice had time to cool off. The whole department was wary of him now. Heads would soon be rolling, and maybe someday after the fallout, after enough turnover, Runstom would be welcomed back. Until then, well, this was something. It would get him out of the domes, get him back to work. Public relations. How hard could it be?

"Listen to them," he muttered. "Give them straight answers."

"Nothin' to it." Horus's too-broad smile betrayed a mixture of victory and relief.

Runstom let the strong wine burn down his throat. "What's my first mission?"

CHAPTER 4

The chamber was dark, except for the bright-orange flicker of fire at the far side. Dava could recognize Moses Down by his shape, even in the darkness. More than his shape, the way he breathed, pulling long breaths into that tall frame. He sat at his desk, his back to her. The candlelight jumped in and out of space with the slow motions of his arms, the shining flash of playing cards appearing momentarily in his right hand.

"You're too trusting," she greeted.

A flicker of reflection from his left side came as he lifted a slender green bottle to his mouth and tipped it back. "Trust," he said when the bottle came back down. "Trust is a release."

"I don't know what that means."

"Of course you don't." He gave her a three-quarter turn so that she could see the bright white of his right eye against the darkness of his skin. It disappeared in a wink. "You don't trust no one."

She came up behind him and watched him draw a card,

consider it, then flip it down into place. "You gonna invite me to play?"

"This is a solitaire."

She put her hands on her hips, but he wasn't facing her to see her impatience. "Well, I guess I'll leave you to it."

"Dava," he said, flipping down another card. "The last mission."

"What about it?"

"Did it go as planned?"

She sighed and folded her arms. "That depends on whose plan."

"There's a chain of command."

"Look, Moses," she said, standing next to the desk so she could see at least the side of his face. "I'm an assassin. If you want someone to torture people and then turn them over to ModPol, get Johnny to do it."

"You can't only be an assassin, Dava. I need you to be more than that."

"What else could I possibly be?"

"The others look up to you, you know."

"They don't look up to me. They're afraid of me."

"Don't take respect for fear, Dava."

"Moses," she started. He was impossible to argue with, but she came in here expecting a fight. Jansen was meticulous with his mission reports, and no doubt painted her in an unfavorable light. She didn't know what he might have said, but she knew he didn't like her, so she prepared for a spat with Moses. Now in his presence, she struggled to find purchase. Where were all the thoughts she'd rehearsed? "Is there a problem?" she finally asked, hoping to get attacked so she could defend herself.

"No, Dava. No problem. I just want you to think beyond assassination."

She swallowed and narrowed her eyes at him. There was nothing to read, just the slow flip of another card. "This is my contribution to Space Waste." She waved a hand at the world outside the room, even though he wasn't looking at her. "Everyone in this outfit is a criminal. We're all thieves and murderers. It's only natural that some of our people are going to cross us – it's in their nature. Let's face it – my job is to show everyone that it's not acceptable to cross us."

"Dava, we love you because you're ruthless."

"Moses..."

"Listen to me, girl." He set down the cards and turned to face her. In the candlelight, the shine of scars ridged up and down his left cheek like tiny mountain ranges alongside the valleys of wrinkles. Three large rings of gold jangled in his earlobe. "I know what your job is. But it can't always be that way. Sooner or later we're going to run out of double-crossers to knock off. Sooner or later, everyone is gonna get the message: if they got a problem, it's better to come to me than to steal from the family or try to handle it on their own. So what happens when that day comes? When everyone is true to Space Waste? When there's no one left to hunt? Then what are you?"

"There will always be someone to hunt."

He laughed, deep and short, picking up the bottle. "Sure, Dava. You'll always be hunting for something," he said, punctuating the comment with another swig.

She felt heat run through her arms, hairs rising. "What the fuck is that supposed to mean?"

"It doesn't matter." He turned back to his cards. "We still have a chain of command here, and I'm at the top of it. And when I send you on a mission with Underboss Jansen, you take orders from him."

"I don't trust Jansen."

He sighed then, a deep, weary sigh. He gave the bottle a shake, but it made no sound. He stood and turned to a cabinet, swapping the empty for another, then pulled a second. He turned to her, and she could feel him looking down on her, a full foot taller, but there was no intimidation there, no threat.

"Who do you trust? Who? Anyone?"

"I don't know."

"Do you trust me?"

"Of course I do…Moses." His name caught in her throat. She didn't know what to do with the way she felt around him. It wasn't lust, she'd figured that out long ago. It was something else she didn't understand.

"I ain't gonna be around forever, you know." He uncapped the bottles one at a time and handed her one.

She took a long drink immediately, letting the fire and spice of the strong warm beer fill her up from the inside out.

"People like RJ have a place here," he said, watching her. "He's smart."

"He's shady."

"We're all shady, girl."

"Well then, what makes him so goddamned special?"

Moses sighed through his nose. "He's connected. He knows things. When we know things, we're better. More efficient. There are more opportunities."

Dava remembered Jansen making a similar claim on the Superliner shuttle. "Did he tell you about the Misters?"

"Yeah, yeah, the Misters." He laughed and took a swig.

"Small-time gang, trying to get a piece of our pie. Them," he said, pointing the mouth of his bottle at her, "you can hunt. But not right now."

"There was one among us. Was that their plan? Get recruited so they could steal from us?"

"Most of the Misters are just out-there folk. Like we were." He nodded. "Like you were."

She didn't need to be reminded that when Moses found her, she was an outcast looking for trouble. It was almost impossible to get arrested in the domes, especially as an adolescent. They were so damned convinced they could fix her. And that by fixing her, they could make her one of them. But they couldn't fix what she looked like, where she'd come from.

"So?"

He nodded at the table. "Same deck, Dava."

Whatever that meant. She was too annoyed at Jansen to sift through Moses's riddles. She drank and stood quiet for a moment, letting the alcohol relax her filters, her inhibitions. She knew she shouldn't say it. Chain of command. But the strongest link in her chain was her instincts. They kept her alive before Space Waste, and they would keep her alive after.

"He tried to stop me from killing Sandiego."

"He did?" Moses cocked his head, but that was the limit to his reaction. She wanted an explosion, and she barely got a pop.

"He wanted to let ModPol arrest him."

"He must have had a reason. Did he tell you?"

"No."

"Did you ask?"

Dava considered the question. She had avoided conversation on the topic, letting Jansen think he was in control. "No."

"So what happened?"

"We left Sandiego there with an unconscious Pollie. There was a patroller inbound as we were leaving."

He waited for her to say more, but she left it at that. Finally, he prompted, "And?"

"And what?"

"You left Sandiego unconscious." Moses turned his hand in an *out-with-it* gesture. "So he's still alive?"

The door comm buzzed from behind them. "Sir? Underboss Jansen is here."

Moses gave a look to warn her the conversation wasn't over. Then he leaned past her and hit the wall comm. "Let him in."

The circular door lock spun and the door creaked open slowly by not much more than a foot, and Jansen leaked into the room through the crack. As the door closed behind him, he straightened up and nodded at Moses, and Dava could see him suppressing a salute, a long-ingrained reaction to the presence of a superior.

"RJ," Moses said. "What's this about Sandiego? He's still alive?"

"Yes, he is." Said with confidence – overconfidence – perhaps covering up for the shame of being caught in a poor decision. Jansen was giving his full attention to Moses, but Dava caught a split second of his eyes in her direction. "I have a man on the inside in Barnard Outpost Delta, where ModPol would have taken him. I want him pumped for more information on the Misters."

"The order was to find out what he knows and kill him."

Dava held her tongue. A minute ago, Moses was lecturing

her for being nothing more than an assassin. Next he'd be tearing Jansen a new one for letting someone live. It was nonsense, made no sense. What the hell did he want from any of them?

"That order still stands," Jansen said, again pushing confidence. "We're not done finding out what he knows. I don't waste a resource until it's completely used. But when it is, I'll make sure he's taken care of."

"Okay." Moses nodded slowly, looked from Jansen to Dava. She could see cards flipping into place in his mind. "Okay, good."

It was now or later, so might as well be now. "Sir."

Jansen didn't realize he was addressing her, not immediately. After a few seconds, he saw her looking at him. "Yes, Capo Dava. What is it?"

She restrained from rolling her eyes at the title. If they wanted to put her in charge of a bunch of grunts, so be it, but everyone could just call her Dava. The name had served her for her entire life, no decoration necessary.

"I don't know that Sandiego will make it to the outpost," she said.

"What do you mean?" Moses asked.

Jansen shook his head. "The leg wound was severe, but not fatal. ModPol would have no trouble stabilizing the bleeding with QuikStiks from a first-aid kit."

Dava shrugged. "I'm an assassin, sir. When my knife goes in, it's for one purpose."

Jansen's mouth hung open, then snapped shut. "What does that mean?"

"What was on the blade, Dava?" Moses asked.

"An anticoagulant. Derived from some kind of big swamp leech native to Terroneous."

"But the QuikStiks—" Jansen started.

"The stuff in QuikStiks is just a synthetic coagulant, mixed with glue. It'll hold the wound together, but internally..." she said, and then spread her fingers apart.

Moses sighed and shook his head. "She's an assassin, RJ."

Jansen swallowed and for a moment, Dava could see a crack in his demeanor. The distress vanished quickly, and she was unable to judge if he were the galaxy's best actor or if he truly didn't care if Sandiego died after all. "Then that's that," he said. "Sir, I came to give you an overview of the next mission."

"Good," Moses said. "Please excuse us, Dava."

A moment later she was in the hallway, feeling like she'd been flushed out of the room by the force of Moses's words. A part of her wanted to be in there, to help plan this mission, to contribute. But there was no point to it. She worked alone. She was just a card in their deck, a weapon for eliminating enemies when they needed it to be quick and quiet.

She went back to her room to recoat her blade.

* * *

After Runstom figured out how to access the terminal in his new office – an affair that involved enough initial failed attempts to cause a tech to make an appearance at his door to make sure he wasn't a hacker, then proceed to go out of her way to help him once she found out who he was – he caught himself up on certain ModPol-related interests, events, people. The comings and goings of those he hadn't talked to in four or more months. Some of his squadmates

– former squadmates – had been assigned to some new security detail for superliners. Information on Jax was a black hole, which he hoped meant that the operator was safe. Mark Xavier Phonson, alias "X", was in custody, but had been transferred to an outpost in the outer Sirius system, and there was very little record on him: an empty visitor log, empty request log, empty everything. Detectives Brutus and Porter had been suspended pending investigation; Brutus went back on the job three months ago, but Porter's investigation was still open.

There were a few more names on his list, but one revealed a need for timely attention.

In addition to A, B, and C-deck, ModPol HQ had sublevels AA, BB, and CC. In the elevator, he ran into the tech who had helped him get into his terminal. She was eager to help him get familiar with the building, so he let her lead him to sublevel-CC, which, according to her, was a simple matter of following the changing colors of the walls. It bothered him that he always missed the changing of the damn colors. A detective would notice a detail like that.

In any case, he wouldn't have found CC without her, but once he got to the entrance to the sublevel, he thanked her and requested solitude. She lingered in her good-bye until he agreed to take her card and seek her out for assistance again if he needed it.

The elevator that descended eight floors into sublevel-CC was not as seamless a ride as the one he'd experienced in B-deck. It accelerated quickly, then decelerated hard when it reached its destination, springing the doors open. They snicked back together as soon as he stepped out.

There were no colors on the walls any more, just a muted gray everywhere he looked, except for the bright shine of camera eyes dotting the ceilings. A guard sat behind a large window with a speaker mounted in the middle of it.

"Identification?" The guard stood and pointed down.

Runstom slid his card under the hole under the window until it beeped. "I was hoping to make a visit."

"We don't get many visits from Market Strategy down here, sir," the guard said through the speaker.

"I used to work in Justice."

"Yes, sir, I know." The guard tapped at a terminal. "It's chow. Want to wait until after?"

"I'd rather not wait. Where's the mess hall?"

"Regulation requires we call it a cafeteria," the guard said. "The cafeteria is down that hall, on the left. I'll buzz down and let them know you're coming."

"Thank you."

"And don't worry. There's no danger."

Runstom stared at the guard. Physical danger wasn't what was on his mind at the moment. The guard shifted uncomfortably and motioned again down the hall, but said nothing. Runstom nodded. "No, I'm sure there's no danger."

The cafeteria was massive compared to the narrow hall that led to it. There was a sea of tables, several dozen at least, each large enough to seat four. Almost all were empty. There was a woman with long, black hair in the back corner of one side and another woman in the opposite corner whose head was shaved to a shine. Both of them had the pale skin of domer life.

Somewhere in the middle, just off-center, was a woman with long, brown hair, tied in a knot behind her head. Her skin was a dull gray-green, not at all the vibrant color it'd been when he first saw her in a bar four months ago. She slouched over a plate of food, chewing slowly, her eyes closed.

After exchanging pleasantries with the guard at the entrance of the cafeteria, he approached her.

"Um, hi."

Jenna Zarconi opened her eyes halfway, but did not lift her head. "Officer Stanford Runstom. Or I suppose I should be calling you Detective Runstom by now."

He sat on the bench opposite her. "No. It's still Officer, only now it's Public Relations Officer."

She raised her eyes and frowned at him. She sat back and shook her head. Strands of her hair loose from the knot waved around her like clouds. "I'm sorry, Stanford. That was an unnecessary thing to say. I already knew that they transferred you to Market Strategy. Word travels, even down here."

They looked at each other in silence. She looked tired. Defeated. Empty. The meal in front of her was nothing more than piles of goop in varying shades of brown. He hunted in her eyes for any flicker of the life that was there, to chase that spark he'd felt the first time he met her. To chase that bold thought that awakened in the back of his mind, the one that said maybe someday he could have a normal life. Maybe he could find love, or at the very least find someone he liked. He looked into her eyes and sought that feeling that came before everything else destroyed it. Before he found out what she really was.

"Of course, there's one word that doesn't travel here," she said, looking back down at her lifeless food. "X."

"No, I figured not."

"So have you heard anything?" Still looking down.

"I suspect I know less than you."

She sighed, long and hard, then cut her breath short, swallowed. “He’s too deep. He’s got too many friends in too many places.”

“Jenna, there’s the recording,” Runstom said gently. “He gave us everything.”

She pushed her tray aside. “So where is he?”

Runstom felt cold. “He’s going down for this—”

“Where is he!” she shouted suddenly, her face coming up and her eyes stabbing at him. He hadn’t noticed the thin gray wire around her neck until her veins bulged against it. “Where the fuck is he?”

Spots of red began to light around the wire. The guard from the back of the room boomed over a loudspeaker. “Prisoner six-gamma-eight. Reduce your heart rate or you will be sedated.”

She closed her eyes and her mouth went tight. He could see her nostrils move as she breathed hard and fast, then forced herself to go in slowly, hold, go out slowly.

“You’re right,” she said finally. “There’s too much evidence. The media has a hold of the story. He’ll get his. I just,” she said, then swallowed again.

“I just hate not knowing,” Runstom said, using the words he knew she wanted to say. “I’m sick of not knowing.”

Her eyes opened and a hint of a smile broke into one corner of her mouth. “I don’t get many visitors. At first there were friends, but they’ve all disappeared over the months. They didn’t want to believe I had a hand in killing those people. I started to tell more truth than they could handle.” Her voice softened. “I should thank you for coming to see me, Runstom.”

“I only just found out you were here. Otherwise I would have come sooner.”

She sighed, letting the small smile dissolve. "I know you would have." She turned her head, staring into nothing. "I don't blame you, you know."

Runstom huffed. "You should. I arrested you."

"But it was my crime. The funny thing about it, Stanford? I never had a plan."

"You seemed to have the whole scheme pretty well planned out to me."

"No, I mean for after," she said. "Even if I had gotten away with it, I had no plan for afterward. The whole plot – the dome malfunction, creating a trail to lead back to X, framing him for mass murder – it was a short-term goal. What was I going to do after?"

"You had a job."

"Yes, but that was temporary. Could I live a normal life after that? I've had months to think about this, and I'm not sure prison life is all that different than my life would be on the outside had I not been caught."

"Except that an innocent man would be here in your place."

She turned to face him again. "Would that have hit me, eventually?"

Runstom looked at her for a long time. She was one of the few people he'd met that had the green-tinted skin like he had. Born on a ship with unnatural light and whatever filters there were for solar radiation and everything else bouncing around space, skin pigmentation not behaving quite the same way that it did on Earth.

"You know, Jenna," he said. "I don't think you're a monster. I think somewhere inside you is a good person. But somewhere else inside there was something bad, something that wouldn't let go. It condemned you a long time ago."

"Maybe so," she said. She sounded unconvinced.

The subject died on the table. "I saw that you're getting transferred," Runstom said after a moment of silence.

"Yes. Back to Barnard. ModPol Outpost Alpha."

"Have they set trial dates?"

"I haven't been informed if they have."

"Well, if you're going to Alpha, it's close," he said. "Anyway, I wanted to see you before you left."

"Oh?" she said, touching the rim of her cup. "What about?"

He shifted, feeling his leg falling asleep in the hard plastic chair. "Oh, I just – you know, it's just weird that we haven't seen each other since – well, since, you know."

"Yeah."

He drummed his fingers on the tabletop and noticed the wood grain. "Imported?"

She laughed then, a genuine out-loud laugh. "Hardly. Looks real, though, doesn't it?"

"Real enough to fool me," he said, allowing himself to smile at his own expense.

"So what do they have you doing now, exactly?"

"Oh," he said, jarred by the change of topic. "Well, I'm going – I'm not sure if I'm supposed to talk about my mission."

"Your *mission*?" she said, raising an eyebrow. "Something tells me they don't call it that."

"No, they call it something else." He couldn't remember all the new terminology that was being thrown at him.

"Come on, Stanford," she said, leaning over the table slightly and showing him her eyes. "You can tell me. What am I going to do? They don't even give me terminal access. My only connection to the rest of the galaxy is a holovid in the rec room that's stuck on one channel, and it's some ModPol-produced 24-hour news network."

Runstom sighed. "Well, okay. It's not that big of a deal I guess. I'm supposed to go to Vulca – that's one of those outer moons here—"

"Yes, I know what Vulca is. The company I work for – worked for – uses some of the test facilities up there."

"Right, sorry. Anyway." He pulled her tray back over to the middle of the table, which caused her to lean back. "So we're here on Sirius-5," he said, gesturing at the tray. He took a small sauce dish from the tray and placed it just off the side of it, then did the same with a couple of spice shakers so that the three outer objects were roughly equidistant from each other. "We have these ModPol stations in orbit. They facilitate communication and monitor everything that happens on the surface of Sirius-5, mostly around the primary dome clusters."

"And Vulca," she said, picking up her cup and placing it farther off on the table. "Is way out here. About 700,000 kilometers, I think."

"Yeah, something like that. Anyway, it rotates around." He dragged the cup a few centimeters across the table. "And is usually in good position to be monitored by the ModPol stations."

"Except for the far side." She took the cup from his hand and drained the rest of the water from it.

"Right," he said. "So with the rotation, which is really slow, facilities on the surface can be on the far side for stretches of months at a time."

"And?" She gave him a look he couldn't quite read. A dare, perhaps.

"Well, they're pretty much unprotected."

"Unprotected by ModPol."

He huffed. "Unprotected period."

"What could happen to them?" She cocked her head in mock ignorance.

He narrowed his eyes. It felt like he was already out there, being grilled by his new clients. He hadn't been through the material yet. He had no idea what could happen to the far side of Vulca. It was just a moon with a handful of research stations on it. "They could be attacked, I suppose."

"By whom?"

"Well, I'm not sure." Would someone tell him? Were the threats properly outlined in the briefs sitting in his office? "I think it's more a matter of identifying vulnerabilities."

"Oh, I can think of a dozen ways to exploit those facilities," she said with a wave of her hand. "I was up there once, managing a stress test on some new life-support hardware. But it seems to me the *who* would be more important than the *how*."

He slid the tray back down the table and leaned forward. "Tell me one."

"One?"

"One way to exploit the facilities on Vulca. Give me the biggest weakness you can think of."

She smiled unnervingly, then purred as if mulling it over. "Hmm. I'd have to say power."

"What do you mean?"

"Well, it's all solar power up there. But parts of the moon can go for months in the dark because of the slow rotation. So they have these massive collectors – four of them, if I'm not mistaken – all around the middle of it."

"The middle? You mean like, along the equator?"

"Yeah, more or less. They're all connected. They have these substations between them, but it's like one power lifeline that runs around the middle of the moon. So even if you're in the dark for a month, you can draw power from down the line."

"So you're saying if the line were severed, it could be bad." Runstom thought it over for a moment. "Wouldn't they have backup power, reserves of some kind?"

"Of course," she said. "But remember, we're talking months of darkness. And these people use a lot of power. A lot. Anyway, it's a ring, so you could lose the connection in one direction and still have one in the other direction."

"Still sounds tenuous to me."

"Well, they've never had a problem up there. But then again, no one has ever attacked them. That's why I think you need to ask *who*."

"Maybe." He shrugged and felt a little ashamed to feel like that didn't matter. "I guess what we have to convince them of is that there could be a threat."

"I see," she said. "Market Strategy. Expanding your available market?"

"Something like that."

"Well, you know you can always come to me," she said, glancing at the wall clock, which was closing in on the end of the lunch hour. "I know I'm never going to see the outside of a prison again. But you can help me do something right once in a while. Just ask for my help, and I'll be here – or in a ModPol prison somewhere. I know you have as few friends as I do."

"I don't think," he started, then stared at his hands. Who was he kidding? "Yeah, you're right."

"Speaking of your very small number friends," she said, "how's Jax?"

"Off the grid."

"Even to you?"

He stared at the fake woodgrain that ran through the top of the table, trying to compare it to the memory of the supposedly real wooden desk in Victoria Horus's office. It all looked the same to him.

"Even to me."

* * *

Jax tugged at his sleeves. The work shirt fit fine, with the cuffs reaching down around his wrists, but he couldn't help feeling too long for it. He tried to bring his attention back to the food in front of him. Even as hungry as he was, it felt like work.

The place he was in – well, he didn't really know what to call it. A market, he supposed. It was named Wei's Wares. The word *ware* made Jax think of hardware and software, but the wares in this place were mostly anything but. They sold everything from prepared food to clothing to tools and equipment. Sure, some of the equipment was hardware running embedded software, but what Jax found more surprising was the number of tools that required no power at all. Human-powered. Is that what the locals would call it?

His fingers were at his sleeves again. It wasn't his clothes that made him feel awkward; they were a set from a work uniform he'd acquired on the superliner. It was the fact that he stood at least a head taller than everyone he met. The fact that the hands in front of him were so pale they practically glowed in comparison to the mélange of skin tones around him. He had hopes he might see at least one other domer on this rock, just one person that looked like him. None so far.

He took a bite, knowing he had to eat something. It was some kind of hand-held food. A square of spongy, flour-based material wrapped around a mix of cooked meat and vegetables. He had to admit, it was quite delightful. The overwhelming flavors reminded him of why he chose this place to come back to.

If he'd gone back to Barnard-4, he could have blended in. Everyone else, tall and pale like him. He could have obscured his identity, found any number of jobs, and found a place to live. Hiding in plain sight – that's what Stanford Runstom would've called it. And things would be back to normal. Not back to normal, but closer to normal.

"What's normal again?" he muttered to his lunch.

He took a large bite to occupy his mouth, in hopes of diverting from the fact that he was talking to himself. He was in public, and Wei's Wares had a number of customers milling about. It'd been a long, isolated journey to get to Terroneous. He was talking to himself more often these days.

But he wasn't afraid. Or he was so afraid, every moment of every day, that fear became normal and no longer affected him. The run used to have purpose. Running toward clues. Now he was just running. Hiding. Trying to stay out of sight, and trying to stay alive. But the latter was growing increasingly more important. He wasn't just on the run from ModPol. He was on the run from hunger and poverty.

Homelessness was difficult to achieve in the domes. Every living human was guaranteed shelter. But out here, outside of the domes, without a direction, without a purpose, without a job or a place to live that's what he was. Homeless.

Maybe that's why he had a hard time feeling the fear. What was there left to lose? Even convicts had a roof and food.

Before he knew it, the last of the delicious wrap had disappeared into his mouth. The fact that he could remember the taste of it was enough to keep him moving. *Stay human.* This time he said the words in his head, and not out loud.

For lack of anything better to do, he decided to wander through the store's offerings. Maybe if he could get a sense of what kind of objects one could find in a bazaar such as this, he'd learn a little more about life on Terroneous. What his life might be like.

He'd come in to Wei's to sell some clothes. With the little cash he had running out, his only valuables were the clothes in his bag. All of them were acquired on the superliner, not just the outfit he was wearing. As he'd combed through them that morning, deciding what he could let go of, he was flooded with the memory of those weeks he spent on that ship. The Royal Starways Interplanetary Cruise Delight Superliner #5. Those were his first days as a fugitive, wearing disguises and tracking down clues. Teaming up with Stanford Runstom, the ModPol officer who put everything on the line to help Jax.

Because they were so often in disguise, and they had gotten a hold of a wad of money by unsavory means, they bought a lot of clothes. Sometimes they were work outfits, made to blend in with the maintenance staff, the kitchen staff, the cleaners, the stockers, whatever. The superliner employed over three hundred people. Other times, the clothes they sought were meant to help them blend in with the passengers. People who individually had more money than entire subdomes had back on Barnard-4. To look the part, Jax and Runstom spent far too much on flashy clothing that had little use anywhere else in the galaxy.

But here at Wei's Wares, all manner of trade was accepted, and Jax was able to unload a particularly fine suit of a silky, deep-red material, dotted with clear gems along the sleeves and pockets. It was garish by anyone's standards, but sometimes the occasion called for garish. For that reason, the manager of the market was giddy to take the suit off Jax's hands. She pressured Jax to consider trade, and so he promised to take a look around. But he knew he'd need to take cash, even if it meant a lower value. What would he do with anything he found here? He had no home. He wasn't even sure he would stay in this town.

"Look, pal. How much you expect for something that's broken?"

As Jax brushed his fingers against some brutish construction tools, he paused to listen to the conversation between the manager and a newcomer.

"It's not broken, I swear." The man was stout and had light-brown skin. He wore a broad-rimmed hat and a loose, dusty-gray suit. "It worked a few days ago. It's mint!"

Jax angled his head to get a look at the object in question. It was a Kitcheny, a combination storage unit and cooker that was common in domer apartments. The dull-white, round device stood about a meter and a half tall and looked as out of place as Jax did. The surface touch panel that would normally report on what food was available in storage and provide an interface into selecting and preparing a meal was unsettlingly dim. Jax realized he'd never seen a Kitcheny without power.

"Well I don't know what to tell ya, pal," the manager said.

The man reached behind it and Jax could hear the click of a reset switch. The Kitcheny made a sort of an odd humming sound, then went quiet.

"Dammit," he said, frowning at the thing.

"What's it plugged into?"

They turned to stare at Jax in silence.

"For power?" Jax prodded, trying to lean close enough to look at the device without imposing.

"Right back here," the manager said. She gave him a wave. "We got a converter we use for domer stuff."

He followed the cable that came out of the back of the Kitcheny into a converter box. Another cable from that ran down under the shop counter.

The two of them seemed to back away as he approached, so he took it as an invitation to get a closer look. They must have known he was a B-fourean, from his appearance. Maybe they had faith that he'd know what to do with it. He bent down to inspect the converter.

"Oh yeah," he said, seeing the problem right away. "This part here – this triangle. It needs to be lined up with the triangle on the box."

"That's supposed to be pointed up," the manager said. "It's an arrow, not a triangle."

"Noooo," Jax said cautiously and detached the cable. "See the matching triangle here on the base of the converter box?"

They stared at him in silence for a moment, then at each other. Jax clicked the cable into place and stood up. He hit the reset button on the back and the Kitcheny came to life with its expected jingle. Its face bloomed with a swirl of colors, and after a moment the animated interface revealed it to be devoid of food and ready to call home for a re-stocking. Home being a dome on B-4 or B-3, and unreachable, of course.

"See, like I told you," the man said, stretching his arms out. "Mint condition!"

"Right." The manager frowned down at the device and Jax caught her glancing at him sideways. It struck him that it was possible she'd connected it wrong as a ruse, a way to buy the unit for a much cheaper price.

"Of course, it can't connect back to the central service," Jax said with a dismissive wave. "Any food you put in there will have to be registered with the device by hand."

"Sounds like a pain in the ass," the manager said with a nod. "I'll give you two hundred for it."

"You kidding me?" the man shot back. "It's worth four hundred at least. You could turn around and sell it to some richie for double that."

"Where did it come from?" Jax wondered aloud. The look he got from both of them made him wish he hadn't asked.

"I traded for it," the man grumbled.

"Two-fifty," the manager said.

Jax ducked away while they continued their negotiations. He tried to look at some of the other items in the store, but he was too distracted. It wasn't the banter, nor was it the guilt that he'd imposed on the deal. It was the damn Kitcheny. How something like that got from the domes to Terroneous was anyone's guess. What did it matter? What bothered him was how glaringly out of place it was. Its presence was nothing short of *wrong*, sitting in a makeshift market in a small backwoods town on the frontier moon of a gas giant millions of kilometers from the domes of Barnard-4.

Where did you *come from?* the voice in his head spat.

He could have gone to Barnard-3 as well. Dropped in on his father and his stepmother. They'd have understood his situation, helped him hide from the authorities. Would he even have to hide from local authorities? It seemed like it was only ModPol that wanted him.

In his pocket he kept his notebook. It was Stanford Runstom who got him into the habit of writing by hand, scratching ink onto paper. At first Jax hated it, how sloppy his words were, how much it hurt his hand. Then after a while, he began to relish it, knowing there was no power involved, no electrons jumping to and fro. No tracking, no ether for data to swim around in. Just the physical presence of a notebook tucked into his pocket.

And in that notebook were letters unsent. Dozens. All to his father. The man had moved from B-4 to B-3 a few years previous, to be with his new wife. To live the high life of the better domes on the better planet. Which Jax hated him for. But he never truly hated the man.

His fingers felt the ridges along the side of the notebook, but he kept it in his pocket. Kept it safe. There were letters he'd send when he could. D-mail from one planet to another was expensive, he reminded himself.

He couldn't yet afford to send them.

"That was impressive."

Jax flinched at the voice from behind, feeling heat flushing his cheeks. He turned to face a man almost as tall as himself, though not nearly as pale. He was well dressed in a high-end, polyester, green-gray jacket and similar pants. His brown hair spilled in waves around his head in a way that should have looked disheveled, and yet was perfectly placed. He held a hand out, expectant.

“Thanks,” Jax said, shaking the man’s hand out of reflex.

“I’m David,” he said. “David Granderson. I hope you don’t mind that I was observing your…interaction, a moment ago.”

“Observing,” Jax said. “Uh.”

“It’s what I do.” He beamed a reassuring smile. “No, I’m not a stalker. I’m an observer. Actually, I’m a documentarian.”

Jax let go of his hand and nodded slowly. “You make documentaries.”

“That’s right. And you,” he said, then paused to turn his hand upward. “You fix things?”

“I do?” Jax cleared his throat and glanced at the counter. The negotiations had ended and the manager was counting out credits to the stout man. “Yes,” he decided. “I fix some things.”

Granderson beamed, not just a smile but his eyes seemed to shine. “Excellent. I am in need of a fixer. I recently acquired some new cameras that – well, they’re just a little off.”

“Oh. And you think I might be able to fix them.”

“You seem to know your way around dome tech.”

The term caught Jax off-guard. He hadn’t really considered technology to be specific to a place, but he supposed it made sense. “You may have noticed,” he said with an ungainly shrug, “that I am from Barnard-4.”

Granderson’s smile widened. “Naturally. And you possess a…technical inclination?”

Jax couldn’t help but to return the smile. “Yes, I suppose so.” He leaned in a little. “But I don’t normally work for the fun of it.”

The documentarian waved and gave a fake-pouty frown. "Never you mind that. I can make sure you're paid well." He paused, mouth half-open, then continued. "Although, I *am* based in Stockton. It's just a little ways from here." He leaned in and lowered his voice. "Begging your pardon, but I've been around a bit. Gotten to know people. You're on the move."

"What if I am?" Jax used what little height advantage he had to attempt to glare down at the man menacingly.

Granderson leaned back with a smile, though there was a sadness to it. A pity. "What's your name?"

"Jack," he said reflexively. *Jack Jackson of Barnard-4.* "Fugere."

"Jack—"

"I prefer Mr. Fugere, please."

"Fair enough." Granderson's stance opened up, as though he might wrap an arm around Jax, but instead giving him a cautious buffer of space. "Come to Stockton. It's a lot bigger than this place, and a lot more diverse. They're a little more used to seeing domers from time to time. And there are people there who could use your services. You could settle for a little while, do some free-lancing."

"Stockton." Jax sighed. He repeated the name in his head. *Stockton.* Could that be a place to call home? Or at the very least, shelter? "How do we get there from here?"

Granderson's smile re-widened. "I have a car."

* * *

Constellations drifted across the black like leaves floating down a slow river. Interstellar flight. She wasn't sure what it was exactly – the God-defying speed, the freedom, the danger – but Dava couldn't get enough of it.

She didn't turn from the window as the others came into the briefing room. She tuned out the jolly shit-talking between Johnny Eyeball and Captain 2-Bit. She tuned out Rando Jansen's awkward attempts to force casual camaraderie. She tuned out their dumb jokes, their bombball talk, the updates on their kill counts. She tuned them out and watched the stars.

Jansen's voice beside her broke through. "If you're looking for Sol, it's on the other side."

She sighed through her nose. "I'm not looking for anything."

"I'm sorry," he said. She didn't want to look at him, but staring at the stars made it hard to tell if he was being genuine or if he was trying to push her buttons. "I guess I assume you must miss it."

Now she turned to face him. He blinked vapidly, and she decided to give his ignorance more credit than his wit. "Of course," she said. "Everything except the end."

"Hey, are we early or something?" Eyeball said, his question cutting across the chamber. "I fucking hate being early."

"No, no," Jansen said. She saw him using the interruption to extricate himself from a dangerous conversation he wished he hadn't started. "I wanted you three in here before I talk to the rest of the squad. I need to go over some… particulars."

Dava turned from the window and looked from Jansen to 2-Bit. "Someone want to tell me why we're getting briefed halfway to the mission? How are we supposed to prep? We're already in transit. All the stores are back at the base."

Jansen smiled his overconfident smile. "We have everything we need, trust me." He motioned to the table. "Have a seat."

The others sat but Dava remained standing near the window. Jansen turned and put up an expectant hand. "Sir," she said, narrowing her eyes. "You don't know everything I need."

Jansen nodded. "Something tells me you are always prepared."

"Are we going to blow anything up, RJ?" Eyeball interrupted, drumming his muscled hands on the table.

"Take it easy, Johnny," Captain 2-Bit said, reaching a steadying hand across the table. "We're here to loot first, destroy second."

"We're where?" Dava asked.

"Thank you, Captain," Jansen said, silencing 2-Bit before he could answer. "We're not destroying anything we don't need to. I want your team focused on the goal."

Dava turned back to the window. "And the goal is what exactly?"

"We're headed to Vulca," 2-Bit said. She could hear him tapping away at the table's viewscreen. "It's a moon of Sirius-5."

"So there will be Pollies." Eyeball's statement wasn't a question, but sounded more like a promise.

"Well," Jansen said, drawing out his words. "Maybe. Not likely. There will be a local security force, of course. But they're not used to much action."

Dava huffed. "But Sirius-5 is under ModPol jurisdiction."

"Yes, that's right. However, the contract that ModPol has with Sirius-5 does not extend to the planet's satellites. According to our intelligence."

"We've got three dozen guns on board, and four personnel

carriers." Dava turned away from the window again and started to walk around the table to get in front of him. She wanted to look into his eyes. "For an inexperienced local security force?"

"We're splitting up," 2-Bit said in his matter-of-fact, don't-worry-about-it voice. "That's how come we brought so many boys."

"What are you talking about, Cappy?"

"There will be a main strike force," Jansen said, motioning to the viewscreen while 2-Bit pulled up a map. "Led by Captain Tubennetal—"

Eyeball stopped drumming and leaned forward. "Who?"

"Uh..."

2-Bit laughed and slapped a hand on Jansen's shoulder. "It's okay, you can call me Cap'n 2-Bit. Don't think of it as an insult."

"Right," Jansen said. "Okay. The main strike force will be led by the captain here. They'll make a push for this observatory. It's about one hundred and twenty kilometers east of the rest of the Vulca research complex. Capo Dava and...ah...Capo Eyeball."

Eyeball smiled and winked as Jansen seemed to wait for approval to continue.

He scrolled through a HandiMate, and for a moment Dava was surprised the posh underboss hadn't upgraded to one of the new WrappiMates. "Uh, you'll take Special Ops Freezer and Squaddie Barndoor, and uh...Squaddie Thompson-Gun...uh..."

"I never knew we had so many damn titles around here," 2-Bit said into his chest. He held out a hand and Jansen reluctantly gave up the HandiMate. 2-Bit squinted at it and nodded. "Okay, so's it's Dava and Johnny, plus

Thompson-Gun, Barndoor, and Freezer." He looked up. "Good unit."

"Thanks," Jansen said, taking the pad back. "Captain," he said, motioning to the viewscreen with the map. 2-Bit panned around for a moment, then stopped when he found the particular group of rectangles he was looking for. Jansen pointed. "Outside of the main city is a research station that just received brand-new radiation detection equipment. It's supposed to be for solar storms and other astronomical anomalies."

"But it also picks up most kinds of ships," 2-Bit said with a proud smile.

"Right," Jansen said. "It's capable of measuring the traffic patterns of almost half a system from one location."

"Really?" Eyeball's one good eye widened and he spoke with hushed intensity. "You guys...we gotta get that thing."

"Good idea, Johnny," Dava said. "That scanning gear should be our goal."

She put on a pensive face, covering her smirk with a gloved hand as 2-Bit and Jansen stared at them incredulously.

"That *is* the goal," 2-Bit said, throwing his hands up.

Dava glanced at Jansen, who furrowed his brow and looked at her suspiciously. She turned away and walked back to the window.

"Anyway," Jansen said. "We're taking the bulk of the force to that research facility. This equipment is of substantial mass, and we're going to have to load it up on the transports."

"They'll see those coming a mile away," Dava said as the stars drifted by.

"You're right," 2-Bit said. "Which is why you and Johnny and the other boys are going after the power. Come take a look, Dava."

She pulled her eyes from the black and back to the table, where 2-Bit was anxiously jabbing at the map. He had zoomed out, so that the cluster of rectangles got smaller and four smaller squares appeared near the edges. "Here and here are the power stations. And here is a relay."

"What's this one?" Eyeball asked, half-squinting and pointing.

"That's the observatory," Jansen said.

"That's where they keep the detection equipment," 2-Bit added.

"So that's where we're going."

"No, that's where *we're* going," 2-Bit said. "You and Dava and your squad are going here. This relay station is the weak point. There's barely any security, and from there Freezer can hack into the whole control system. He flicks off the lights and over here at the observatory, they won't know what the hell is going on. That's when we waltz it, fire a few rounds to scare the crap out of everyone, then we stroll out with the goods."

"Good plan," Eyeball grunted.

"Well, it's RJ's plan," 2-Bit said sheepishly.

Dava came back around the table to get one more look at the map. "So we go in, cut the power, and then you make your move." She looked at Jansen, who wasn't forcing a smile for once. "I suppose it's not the worst plan."

"Thanks." His eyes flicked to hers and then back to the map, then down to his hands. Pre-assault nerves. He knew what he was doing, and he was sharp, but she wondered if he was really cut out for Space Waste.

"Whatever you have on the relay station," she said, waving at the viewscreen, "send it over to my room. And then don't wake me up until we get to Vulca."

CHAPTER 5

The holding room inside the Vulca Research Park's main office building – no one had called it a holding room, but that's the only way Runstom could think to describe it – was a perfect circle. There was only one wall, and it curved around on itself in a way that made him dizzy. The only corners in the room were where the wall met the flat ceiling, several feet above his head.

Vaguely to his left, a doorway appeared when an unseen panel slid upward with a mechanical swish. He was pretty sure it wasn't the same door he and his companion came in through, but having lost his sense of direction in the angle-less room, he couldn't be sure.

A woman in a white lab coat came in. "Hello, Mr. Troyo," she said, the door quickly sliding closed behind her before Runstom could see where it led.

Runstom's companion was an account manager named Peter Troyo. He'd only just met the man a few hours before, when he'd picked Runstom up at the landing pad on the other side of the moon. The train ride from there gave them plenty of time to get to know each other.

"Heya, Johanna, great to see you again," Troyo said, reaching out to take her hand before she could extend it. "How is everything? This is Stanley Runstom."

"It's Stanford—"

"Dr. Leesen. Pleased to meet you, Mr. Runstom."

Troyo released his grip so that Runstom could shake hands with her. "Nice to meet you, Doctor."

She was short and a little stocky and had beige-white skin, like most Sirius-fivers. Her light-brown hair was pulled back into a ponytail and beneath her white lab coat was a pale-gray shirt and matching pants. When Runstom first met Troyo, he was impressed by the man's platinum-colored suit – matching jacket, shirt, tie, and pants – but next to this woman in this circular space, he was another white-and-gray Sirius-fiver. The two of them made Runstom feel like a square peg in the round room.

"Johanna is the head scientist around here," Troyo said, beaming his practiced smile.

"I'm the Director of Research." She produced a small translucent card and handed it to Runstom. He took it gingerly and turned it into the light to read it, but all it said was *Doctor Johanna Leesen, Director of Research, Vulca Research Park*.

"We're very proud of the work we do around here, Mr. Runstom. What we do benefits all mankind."

Troyo nodded knowingly and looked at Runstom. "Sounds like a place worth protecting, doesn't it?"

"Yes," he said, drawing out the word longer than he wanted to as he watched the doctor's eyes narrow ever so slightly at Troyo.

The door opened again and a tall woman with dark skin

and a finely-cut lemon-yellow jacket came through.

"Oh, hi, Rhonda," Troyo said. "Glad you could make it." Runstom had read the prep notes and was pretty sure there was no Rhonda on the list of people he'd meet. That meant she was unexpected, but Troyo played it off like it was planned. "Rhonda, meet Stan Runstom."

"Nice to meet you," Runstom said, offering a hand.

"Rhonda Harrison. Peter can never remember my title. I'm the Facilities Manager."

"Hey Rhonda, don't you have a cousin or something that plays bombball? Hey Stan, aren't you a big bombball fan? You like the Pioneers, right?"

"Ah, yeah, I'm a Poligart fan."

"Tough luck with the Sirius Series, eh?" Troyo yammered. "Bumped in the first round?"

"Right," Runstom said, trying to gauge the woman's interest in pursuing the conversation.

"So Rhonda," Troyo continued. "Your cousin, he's like a backup center or something? Is that what he is?"

"He's the black one."

"Uh—"

"He's a lefter," she said without missing a beat. "But he got injured after the All Star break so they had him playing as the designated bomber."

Runstom couldn't help himself now. "Wait, your cousin is Jojo Harrison?"

"Second cousin, but yeah," she nodded.

"Oh, he's amazing!" Runstom said, allowing himself to slip into a time when the total excitement in his life centered around watching bombball games on the HV back on ModPol Outpost Gamma. "The way he swings the plank – he's not a hacker, he's got a true whip to it."

"Nice of you to say, but the boy couldn't buy a bomb in the Series."

"Right, sorry. I missed most of it. Because of, uh..."

Troyo leaned in and nudged him in the ribs. "Well, don't be modest, Stanley."

"Stanford."

"Stanford here was only tracking down a mass murderer across the galaxy! That's right – this is *the* Stanford Runstom."

"Yeah, I know," Harrison said, looking him up and down. "I recognize him from the HV."

The director looked up from a handheld handypad she'd been occupied with. "So Mr. Runstom: are you another account rep?"

"Oh no," Troyo laughed, planting a hand on Runstom's shoulder. "We wouldn't give someone like Stanford a lowly job like mine. He's a celebrity." Coming from anyone else, it would have sounded like sarcasm, but Troyo put on a face of sheer pride, though oddly placed. As though he wasn't proud of Runstom's efforts as much as he was proud of being the account rep that showed up with a celebrity.

"I'm a consultant."

"Our celebrity consultant," Troyo said, beaming.

"If he's that good, then what is he doing here helping sell security upgrades?" Dr. Leesen asked, turning up the palm of her free hand. "Why isn't he out chasing down criminals?"

"Well, uh, that's because—"

Runstom put a hand out to still the suddenly anxious Troyo. "The ModPol mission is to prevent crime. We'd much rather keep crime from happening than spend effort tracking and punishing criminals."

The three of them stared at him in silence for a moment. Troyo seemed to be holding his breath while the doctor and facilities manager probed his face in search of sincerity. Runstom realized that the circular room had the odd effect of making it obvious whether its occupants were standing near each other or keeping their distance. With no flat walls to block out the space, it seemed that no matter where he was in the room, he felt as though he were favoring one person over another.

"Of course," Dr. Leesen said, breaking the silence. "Prevention is preferable to punishment."

He glanced at Harrison, but she only shrugged and nodded slightly, as if to concede: *good enough*.

The door opened again – though Runstom still wasn't sure if there was a single entrance to the disorienting circular room or if there were several that could appear anywhere in the uniform surface of the wall – and another Sirius-fiver joined them.

"Hey, Petey-boy, how you goin'?" the new arrival said, pointing gun-fingers at Troyo. "You come back up here to pay me that money you owe me?" The man nodded at the facilities manager and the director. "Hey Rhonda. Dr. Leesen."

"Willy, good to see you!" Troyo said, edging the others out of the way not with physical force, but with pure enthusiasm. He wrapped an arm around the man's shoulders. "Hey, you're gonna love this – check it out: Stanford Runstom."

"Well, I'll be – how you goin', sir? Willis Polinsky. It's very nice to meet you."

Runstom shook the man's hand. "Nice to meet you too, Mr. Polinsky."

"Willy is the head of security for the research base," Troyo said.

"I'm a big supporter of ModPol. My daddy was an officer. He was always so proud. Died in the line of duty."

"I'm sorry to hear that," Runstom said.

"He fell into a methane swamp on Sirius-7."

"Methane isn't toxic," Dr. Leesen said, narrowing her eyes at the security head.

"Oh," Polinsky said quietly. "Well, it was deep. He drowned."

"I think we're all here then, aren't we?" Troyo said before Runstom could attempt to offer more condolences. "Yes? Shall we begin the tour?"

"Yeah, let's get on with it," Harrison said. "Follow me."

* * *

The tour ate up most of the day. Runstom had no idea what he was supposed to be doing in his new position, so he did what he always did: he took notes. He jotted down any useless, insignificant details he noticed, not really sure if he was trying to do real work or just stay awake. They went from building to building, compound to compound, even to a marketplace at one point, though briefly – there was no time to shop – and eventually to the living quarters of what Rhonda Harrison bitterly referred to as "the defense contractors", by which she meant the ModPol Onsite Rapid Defense Unit. It was there that the rest of the party clocked out for the evening, leaving Runstom and Troyo to finish the tour on their own.

There was a reception area to the "Guest Defense" quarters that had decor more appropriate for a hotel than barracks, and after they checked in with the clerk at the desk, Troyo led Runstom down a series of hallways that ended at a large set of double doors. The doors swung open as they approached and a short woman with red-brown skin poking out of silver-and-gray patterned fatigues stepped out.

"Captain Oliver," Troyo said, giving the woman a half-hearted salute before turning and gesturing. "Allow me to introduce you to Stanford Runstom."

"Nice to meet you, Captain," Runstom said, offering his hand.

She pulled off her cap to reveal stark red hair. "You can call me LJ, everyone else does," she said, tucking the head-wear under her arm to receive his handshake. Her hands were strong and wiry and she gave him a solid up and down motion, meeting him eye-to-eye. "Very nice to meet you, sir."

"I assume you know about Stanford's exploits," Troyo said with a nonchalant twist of his hand.

"Of course," Oliver said with a smile. "Pretty impressive work. For a Pollie."

"Ah, yes." Troyo looked to Runstom, unsure of how the comment would go over.

Runstom opened his mouth, but the captain raised her hand. "No offense meant, sir. After all, way the story goes, you were the most competent person involved in the whole ordeal."

Troyo sighed, his smile taking only minor damage. "I'm afraid that qualifies as high praise coming from Captain LJ, Stan." He flinched then, reacting to an unseen interruption, and glanced at the device on his arm and frowned. He tapped at it – one of the ubiquitous WrappiMates that

Victoria Horus was so proud of. She'd even given one to Runstom, though he'd forgotten to wear it. "I'm sorry guys, I have to deal with this. I'll be back in a few. Stanley, can you hang out here for a bit?"

"Sure." When the other man didn't wait for his answer before flitting out of the room, Runstom found he didn't mind. He turned back to Captain Oliver. "It's Stanford, by the way."

"He was right, you know," she said. "That was the highest praise you'll get from me. You might be a darling on the HV and around HQ, but not everyone can swallow what you're selling." When his jaw dropped open to respond, she held up a hand. "I'm not calling you a liar, don't get me wrong. It's just that no one really knows what happened, except you, Deputy Inspector Phonson, and that civilian woman. And the only word in the media comes from you."

"So you don't believe my side of it." Runstom felt a tingle of fire in his chest, something he hadn't felt in a long time. "With all the evidence I collected? With the recording we got of Phonson?"

She looked away and flicked her hand. "Oh, the evidence is there, I don't doubt that. But it's not the whole story. It's never the whole story."

"No," Runstom said firmly and waited for her eyes to meet his once again. "It's not."

"Well, I guess you should meet the squad." She flicked her head toward the room behind her.

Before he could respond, she spun around and was on the move. He followed her into what looked like some kind of recreation hall. There were a few long tables, and about half a dozen men and women sat at one pushing colorful playing cards around its surface. A few more were standing around chatting and picking at a spread of food along one side of the room. A third cluster were sitting at the far end of the room in front of a holovid, quietly immersed in some slow-moving drama.

"At attention, Defenders," Oliver belted with alarming volume, causing Runstom to flinch.

The faces in the room all turned at once, frozen for only a few seconds that felt like an eon. Then one woman stood and saluted, and the action took on a contagious quality, causing others nearby to stand and salute and spread the sentiment to their neighbors.

"Stanford Runstom, I present to you Squad TORDU-12. The finest Defenders in all of – in Sirius – on Vulca." Oliver's head wavered from side to side for a moment. "Well, they're fine troops. Damn fine Defenders."

They stared at him and he was suddenly struck by panic, fear that he was expected to give them some kind of speech, or at the very least, a public-relations-sounding greeting. "Uh, hello."

"At ease, Defenders," the captain shouted, releasing him from the public-speaking death-grip. The room resumed where it had left off, into a sigh of quiet conversation.

"This is the whole unit then?" Runstom tried not to sound disappointed.

"Yes, sir," she said, leading him off into a quiet corner. "Twenty-four men and women. All of them from Sirius-5, if you couldn't tell." He hadn't put any thought into it, but her comment made the squad's homogeny suddenly obvious: they all had the pale skin of domers and the short, broad bone structure of the heavy Sirius-5 gravity that had weighed on him for the past four months. She leaned in a little closer. "None of them have ever seen combat. Other than simulated, of course. Most are here just trying to earn housing credits for the subdomes. Some got families planetside, crammed into those little apartments in big cities like Grovenham. The subdomes are a dream for folks like these."

"At least their captain has seen live combat," Runstom said.

She looked at him, her eyes going up and down for a moment. "Yes."

"Sorry, Captain. I read your file on the ride over. There wasn't really any data on the squad, except for a short dossier on you."

He paused then to see if she would offer a comment, though he didn't expect her to. There was only one real skirmish she had been involved in, but it was enough.

"I don't really know why you're here, Runstom."

"I'm a public relations manager."

"I know what your title is. I got a dossier on you too."

"Look," he said, folding his arms. "All I know is I'm here to talk to customers. I'm not a salesperson. I'm just here to answer questions."

"To make us look good, right? Being that you're a celebrity and all."

"Yes," he said sharply, causing her to blink. "We might as well be honest about it. I'm not a very good liar."

A smile escaped her. "Well who am I to say? Me and my unit are armed to the teeth, but we'll never fire a shot."

"I hope that's true," Runstom said quietly.

She lost her smile. "Did they at least give you a tour?"

"Yeah, they did. Administration building, staff quarters, some kind of marketplace, then out to the research park."

"Good. At least you've got a feel for the place."

Runstom thought about his desperate note-taking, and

how disconnected it had felt. He tried to place everything he listed off onto a map but he couldn't. There was no map in the files they gave him, and during his whole tour he never got a chance to look outside; every building was connected to the others by tubes and tunnels. He spent the whole day in mazes of twisting corridors and he had no way to establish any sense of direction – in fact, still didn't.

"To be honest, we could be standing upside-down right now and I wouldn't have the faintest. I haven't seen the surface since I arrived."

She snorted. "Yeah, this place will do that to you. And people are always telling you to go down the 'maroon hall' or through the 'azure door'."

Runstom's face wrinkled. "Right, and when you think you've found the right blue door they go, 'No, you don't want the cerulean door, you want the azure door!'"

She laughed. "Glad I'm not the only one."

"Tomorrow I'm supposed to go out to the observatory."

"Then you'll get to see the surface, cuz it's a drive. No train either, you'll have to go over in a rover." She looked at him a moment, then added, "I'll get a MapPad sent over to you. Something more tactical than anything Peter Troyo might have."

"Thanks, Captain," Runstom said. "I appreciate it."

She shrugged, almost sheepishly, her eyes turning away from him. "Don't worry about it. I've been looking forward to giving you shit ever since I found out you were coming. Turns out you're not a whole lot of fun to fuck with."

Runstom felt himself smile. "Never been happier to disappoint."

She returned his smile, but then the conversation suddenly went flat.

"This crew," Runstom said after a moment's thought, gesturing at the nearby group that was playing cards. "You called them TORDU-12 earlier. Onsite Rapid Defense Unit, that's ORDU. What is the T for?"

She followed his gaze to the card players. "Trial," she said quietly, and looked away.

CHAPTER 6

"Come on, man."

"Nah."

Dava tried to ignore Freezer's pleas and Eyeball's comebacks as she peered through her nightscope across the desolate landscape of Vulca. There was nothing since they'd left the little outpost – what the locals endearingly referred to as a city, what others would barely call an outcropping – and started making their way to their target. It was a trek measured in hours and, at Dava's insistence, made on foot and in the dark. The former was made awkward by the weak gravity and the thin atmosphere, but the latter was made easy by the slow rotation of the moon and the shadow of Sirius-5.

"Come on! Last time there was all kinds of shooting going on. I'm defenseless here!"

"You're not defenseless – you got me."

She was sick of telling them to keep quiet, so she concentrated on getting them into position. She'd have made better time without Eyeball, Barndoor, and Thompson, all three weighed down by unnecessary weaponry and armor, and Freezer, whose idea of a hike was going from his bunk to the canteen and back. But she'd done all her lamenting on the drive from their drop point to the town and finally decided she wasn't going to gripe, even to herself.

"Psh. Uh, I mean –" Freezer changed his tone. "Of course I appreciate that you got my back. But what happens if you have to go...take care of something? Or someone? What if I get jumped when I'm all alone?"

"You ain't gonna be all alone," Eyeball muttered.

"It could happen."

For whatever reason, Moses had been cutting down on Dava's solo missions and forcing her to go with small strike forces. Sure, whatever reason. He'd gotten it into his thick old head that she needed to be around other people more often. She pocketed the nightscope and turned back to them.

"Freezer, you gotta be dense or somethin'," Barndoor said, brushing his long inky hair out of his face. "I ain't been a Waster much longer than you and I know better."

"Yeah, but *you* have a gun. Why can't *I* have one?"

Dava took a moment to glance at Freezer, then at Barndoor. The latter was wearing his favorite leathers and toting a leg-sized spray-n-pray shrapnel gun. She looked at the scrawny, lanky hacker and decided he would buckle if he even tried to pick up Barndoor's gun, let alone fire the monstrosity.

"Ain't what I'm talkin' about," Barndoor said. "I think you should have a gun. Bigger the better. But if you want one of Johnny's – and he's the only one who brought extras – you gotta give him something for it."

"Right. Right." Freezer tapped his head in thought. "Of

course. Of course, Johnny. I didn't mean I wanted you to just *give* me one. I meant, I want to trade."

"For what." Eyeball had a way of turning questions into statements.

"Well, I uh – what do I have..." Freezer seemed to struggle for a moment and Dava was hopeful he might drop the whole thing. She didn't think he needed a gun, but then again, she didn't want Barndoor with his shredder, Thompson with her custom submachinegun retrofitted with a drum magazine, or Eyeball with whatever the hell ballistic, incendiary, or explosive nightmares he'd brought along. But she wasn't going to gripe. And she knew Johnny Eyeball and his guns were not easily parted, so she let the hacker go on with his begging.

"Oh, I know," he said with hope in his voice. "I can fix you up with my old pad-stack. It's sick – I overclocked the proc and jacked up the wireless range."

"Is it a WrappiMate? I been thinkin' about gettin' me one of those," Eyeball said, though Dava knew he was pulling Frank's leg. Johnny wasn't the "personal device" type – it was hard enough to get him to carry his RadMess for communication.

"A WrappiMate?" Freezer said, jolting his hands out incredulously. "What, so you can be some corporate tool? You know Zebra tracks everything you do on one of those? Tracks everywhere you go? Forget that crap, man. I custom-build my gear. This stack's got hardware-level encryption and decryption packages, loaded up with all the fastest crackers – you get within ten blocks of a bank and you can spring the vault doors wide open half an hour before you rob the place."

"Pass. I don't rob banks no more."

"Yeah, but it's really—"

"Pass."

"Okay, okay," Freezer said, going quiet for only a few seconds. "What if I got you access to some funds?"

Eyeball snorted and winked his one good eye. "I don't rob banks because I don't need money."

"Oh come on, Johnny. Everyone wants money."

Eyeball tipped his chin up and expounded, "I've evolved past it." This brought a chuckle from Barndoor and Thompson and even Dava felt herself smile.

Freezer slowed for a moment, looking at each of them as they walked past. He skipped back to Eyeball's side. "What do you mean?"

"He means he doesn't pay for things any more," Thompson said, grinning ear to ear.

Dava slowed and split off to the side, her eyes on the pre-dawn sky. There was a haze in the air that caused the low light to shimmer if she stared at any spot too long. She scanned the horizon with her nightscope. The little bump in the night that she'd had her eyes on for the past twenty minutes solidified into a building in the green-lit view of the scope. She pulled it down and rejoined the group.

"Wasters." Dava got in front of the group and pointed. "Up ahead. No more distractions. You need to keep your eyes on that building. Watch for movement."

Freezer squinted and turned his head, trying to follow her finger. "What building?"

They all looked at him. Dava looked at the bump in the distance. It wasn't a building until someone said it was, then it was as clear as day.

Thompson leaned into him, peering at his face. "How far can you see?"

"Whaddya mean?" Freezer leaned back away from her. "It's fucking dark out here."

"Never mind," Dava said with a hushed voice. "Just keep it down, and keep low. Anyone sees movement, you stop and tell me. I want to know numbers."

Freezer squinted at the horizon and opened his mouth to protest, but caught Dava's glare and huffed it shut. She thought about giving him her nightscope, but then decided maybe he was less of a liability if he was kept in the dark.

"Here." Thompson pulled out her own nightscope, which was twice the size of Dava's. It hummed when she flicked a switch. She peered through it at the building in the distance for second, then handed it to Freezer. "Take a look through this."

The hacker took the scope greedily and brought it to his face. A smile quickly appeared. "Oh, yeah. Now I see it. Man, this is nice. I gotta get me one of these."

"Not nice enough to save the guy I took it off," Thompson said, pulling it back out of his hands.

"I heard you traded for it," Barndoor quipped.

"Squaddie, shut the fuck up."

They crept in silence for at least a full minute and Dava thought maybe it was going to be all-mission from there on out, but Barndoor's last comment must have wormed its way through Freezer's head, getting him thinking about possible trades again.

"Oh, I got it," he said, too loudly. He flinched when Dava and Thompson both shushed him.

"You ain't got it," Eyeball rumbled.

Freezer got close to him and whispered, "I heard you were getting The Diet."

Johnny stopped and it was as if someone dropped anchor;

the whole group stopped and looked at him. "You heard," he said.

"Y-yeah." Freezer had the look of a man whose body wanted to peel itself away from the idiot brain that should have known when to keep its mouth shut.

"From who."

"Um, well, no one."

"From who." Eyeball didn't raise his voice, but its force seemed to hit Freezer in the chest.

"I was just poking around through the system back at base," he said, glancing around at all of them. "You know, just a little...security assessment."

Eyeball began to wink angrily. "And."

"Uh, so I saw it there – in the inventory control. I saw that – that you're on limited...rations."

"Damn," Barndoor whispered.

Dava felt like she should put a stop to the whole conversation. She was leading this mission, and their banter had gone way off track. But what should she say? She had no idea how to deal with these idiots. This was human resource-level nonsense. She hadn't known Johnny was getting The Diet, but it didn't surprise her either. It was so far outside her realm of responsibility, she didn't have an opinion on whether it was right or wrong. Or what the consequences should be if he broke it.

"It's goddamn bullshit is what it is," Eyeball growled. He took a step toward Freezer and coated him in even darker shadow than the night offered. "So what, you gonna hack my canteen file? They'll just put it back how it was."

"No, Johnny," Freezer squeaked, then cleared his throat. He nodded at Eyeball's chest and drew in a breath. "You – you give me one of those pistols. I give you my weekly bottle."

"One bottle?"

Freezer swallowed. "For a whole month. That's four big bottles, of whatever you want. Rum, vodka, whisk—"

"Whiskey." Johnny stepped back, releasing Freezer from his shadow. "Four whiskeys."

"Four whiskeys."

"Son," Eyeball said, a grin growing from ear to ear. "You may have just saved my life." With one motion and a sound no more than a snip, he pulled a ham-sized pistol from out of a strap and slapped it into the hacker's shaking hands.

"Great," Barndoor said. "The nerd is armed."

"I hope you know how to use that thing," Thompson said, distancing herself with a nonchalant step back.

Dava leaned close to Freezer's face and made sure she captured his eyes. "You don't fire that unless you absolutely have to."

"Of course," he said quietly, eyes going cross at her proximity.

"I mean it, Frank. You do *not* want me on your bad side."

He jumped when Eyeball smacked him hard on the arm. "You don't."

"Round 'em up, Johnny," she said, then turned to the lonely silhouette in the distance. "And keep 'em quiet. We want to be right on top of the targets when we make our introductions."

* * *

When Troyo showed up at Runstom's room in the morning, he seemed disappointed at how quickly the door was answered. "Well, you're an early one, aren't ya, Stanford?"

"I'm just on a different cycle is all." Truth was, Runstom hadn't slept much to begin with. He was anxious, still uncertain about what the hell he was doing on Vulca.

"Oh sure, of course," Troyo said, shedding his disappointment with a sly grin. "But I bet you're an early one no matter the cycle."

"I suppose."

"Knew it." Troyo waved him into the hallway. "Come on, let's get some breakfast, shall we? LJ and Dr. Leesen will meet us in the cafeteria."

Runstom glanced at the wall clock. According to the day's schedule, they were supposed to head out to the observatory in an hour. Did they have time for breakfast now? He stared at Troyo's expectant grin and decided it wasn't worth arguing over.

He followed Troyo down a series of gradient-colored hallways. The mess hall he was referring to turned out to be two buildings away, and again, they made the journey solely underground.

"Is the sun up?" Runstom asked, realizing his room had no windows, much like the rest of what he'd seen of the complex so far.

"Uh. I don't know. Probably not. I don't think they get much of it here."

"It's not tidally locked."

"What's that now?"

"Vulca. It's not a tidally locked satellite."

Troyo stopped walking. The hallway was a deep shade of red.

"What does that mean?"

Runstom frowned. Astrophysics definitely wasn't his area of expertise, and although he'd been around enough to have picked up a thing or two, he didn't want to have to explain it. "When a moon is tidally locked to the planet it orbits, it always has the same side facing in toward that planet. It rotates at the same rate that it orbits."

"Really?" Troyo cocked his head. "That doesn't sound right."

"Tactically, it's useful to know."

"How do you know Vulca isn't – what'd you call it? Totally locked?"

"Tidally. Like the tides of an ocean."

"Well," Troyo said with a shrug and what seemed like a relieved sigh. "We don't have any oceans on Sirius-5."

Runstom slid his notebook out of his pocket and flipped through a few pages. "Vulca rotates on a...three-to-two ratio. Three rotations for every two trips around Sirius-5." He looked up. "Of course, they get sun sometimes. But I bet that kind of cycle makes it feel erratic. But there's still a pattern."

"Hmm." Troyo frowned slightly. "I can't say as I've noticed. Let's get to the cafeteria. It's just down this corridor. I'm starving."

Runstom closed his notebook but didn't tuck it back into his pocket. He felt some level of reassurance, having its small presence there between his fingers. This was the kind of thing they'd brought him in for, wasn't it? To make observations, anything that might be of tactical interest? He wished that at least Troyo believed that, and he tried to shake away Captain Oliver's implication that he was just there for his celebrity status.

He thumbed the pages at his side as they went down the hall. He was never terribly great at astrophysics, but he knew the basics. He'd been on just about every type of rock a human could set foot on in the Sirius and Barnard systems, and he knew how to land a few standard ModPol ships, all on the small side. Troyo's indifference soured his mood. He didn't *want* to know this shit, he *had* to.

They found Dr. Leesen sitting at a table at the back of the cafeteria, already finishing up her breakfast with one hand while scrolling through a HandiMate with the other.

"Hey, Johanna!" Troyo said, his ear-to-ear smile back. "Looks like you got a head start on us. I hope we're not too late. Stan here still doesn't know the place all that well and it takes him a while to find everything."

He looked at her and opened his mouth to protest, but she rolled her eyes and scrunched up her mouth. "You're not late. It's good to see you again, Mr. Runstom."

"Good morning. It's good to see you too, Doctor."

"I'm going to grab some grub," Troyo said. "It's all self-serve, right over there along that wall. Make sure to get enough, Stan. We'll be out all day and won't have time for a proper lunch."

"Don't rush yourself," Leesen said as Troyo bounded off toward the dispensers. "Nothing moves very quickly around here. Peter is always in a hurry, but that doesn't change procedure."

"Thanks." He glanced at her HandiMate, but she brushed it with one hand and the screen went dark.

She dabbed at her mouth with a cloth napkin and turned her head slightly, nodding. "Here comes Captain Oliver."

"Captain," Runstom said as Oliver approached. "Good morning."

She was in dark-gray fatigues and kept her cap on her head. Four others from the Onsite Rapid Defense Unit followed her. She nodded shortly. "Mr. Runstom. Dr. Leesen."

Troyo came back brandishing a tray of pastries. "Hey, LJ. Better get some breakfast so we can take Stan out to the observatory." He leaned forward and squinted at the name tag on one of the other soldiers. "You too, uh, Lieutenant..."

"Anderson, Beckass, Cato, and Yurikov," Runstom said.

"Well," Troyo beamed. "Someone did his homework! How'd you know all their names? You know all the names in the unit?"

"No," Runstom said, meeting Oliver eye to eye. "Just the names of the officers. And this is all of them." She frowned at him and waited for him to finish. "Which means something is up."

"We aren't going."

Troyo smiled. "Sorry to hear that."

"Yeah, I'm sure you'll miss me." Oliver looked at the three of them and nodded. "Okay then. See ya."

"Wait," Runstom said, holding out a hand. "Why aren't you able to go? I uh – I was hoping I'd be able to ask you some more questions about the ORDU on the drive out."

"I'm sorry, Mr. Runstom. A report came in this morning and I've got orders. Maybe we can talk tomorrow."

"What kind of report?" he asked, putting a hand on her arm as she turned to go. He decided to test his authority. "I wasn't notified of anything."

"I'm sorry, Mr. Runstom," she said again. "I've got orders."

"Well, then, off you go," Troyo said with a wave. "Stan, you have to try this sweet biscuit they do here. The low gravity makes it—"

"If it's related to the defense of the facility, I think I should know," Runstom said.

She stopped and stared him down. "It's my understanding, Mr. Runstom, that your role is to *consult* on the defense of this facility. Plan. Strategize. But not participate." She put her hand on her hip and he noticed a laser pistol on her belt. "We each have our own jobs to do."

"A fair point, Captain," Troyo said. "Stanford, let's let them get to their job. We've got a full schedule today. The folks at the observatory are very excited to meet you. Some of the top researchers are going to be there to greet us, isn't that right, Doctor?"

Leesen occupied her mouth with a cup of coffee, so Runstom kept talking. "If anything comes up, I want to know about it." He watched Oliver's face harden and lowered his voice, choosing his words more carefully. "Captain. If, during the course of your duties, you gain any information that could help me…fill in the gaps of my knowledge of operations at this facility…I would be very grateful for it."

He watched her jaw slide slightly from one side to the other. "Of course, Mr. Runstom."

"And I'd prefer it if you called me Stanford." He was going to have to get used to not being addressed with a title, but he couldn't stand being called *Mister*.

She paused and that tiny turn in the corner of her mouth appeared. "As you wish."

Troyo and Leesen both stared at him awkwardly as the Defenders left. Runstom put on a stern face to ward off any embarrassment at having to practically beg for information. He flipped open his notebook, but he had nothing to go on, so he just noted the time and the fact that Captain Oliver was not joining the party at the observatory.

"Pen and paper," Troyo muttered with a chuckle. "You are unique, Stanford."

"Yes, well." He tucked the notepad back into his pocket.

"Why don't you use a HandiMate, or a WrappiMate like Peter?" Leesen asked. Her tone wasn't challenging, but of genuine curiosity. It made him feel like a specimen.

"I do," he said, but then realized he'd forgotten to wear it again. "When necessary. These are just notes to myself. It's better for me to write them."

"My second husband was an engineer," Leesen said. "He was fond of making a point via anecdote. One he told on more than one occasion was a story about the Global Space Alliance – no, I'm wrong. It was the American one – back when governments were funding space exploration. NASA. Very early in its life. 20th century. They were just getting started in those days and they had realized that ink pens relied on gravity to work. You see, they knew that their astronauts would be floating around in a craft outside the pull of Earth's gravity and they would be taking readings and making notes, and they would need to do this with pen and paper. Have you heard this story?"

"No," Runstom said. Troyo said nothing, but seemed to feign patience while picking deliberately at a pastry. "So what did they do?"

"Well, they did what they always did back then; they threw exorbitant amounts of money at the problem. Industrial and astronomical engineers, spending countless hours developing the world's first gravity-free pen. They did it and were very proud of their achievement. Some saw it as a sign that space travel was nothing to be feared, that human ingenuity would overcome any obstacles."

"That's the story?" Troyo said, pointing at her with a powdery finger.

"The story is not the Americans. It's in their rivals, which at the time was the Soviet Union. The USSR was neck and neck with NASA when it came to pushing the limits of space exploration. They also had the problems with ink pens without gravity."

"So lemme guess," Troyo said. "They had to bargain with the Americans. Beg for their help?"

"No," she said. "They used pencils."

Runstom watched as Troyo furrowed his brow and muttered, "I see." He pointed at her again. "Not all problems are about solutions. Sometimes problems are opportunities. Stanford, you still haven't eaten. I'm going to get you some breakfast." He stood up and strode off to the dispensers.

Runstom watched him, then turned to Leesen. "I think you struck a nerve."

"He knows I don't approve of your presence."

Runstom thought about it for a moment, then nodded. "We're the over-engineered pen to your problems."

"Peter's smarter than I thought. I didn't think he'd put that together."

"Well, this is just a trial, Doctor. If there's not a reason for us to be here..." Runstom trailed off, unsure of how to finish.

"We already have local security. We're not completely helpless." She glanced at Troyo who was still filling up a tray, then leaned in to Runstom. "Why did you think something was up with Captain Oliver?"

"Uh." Runstom fidgeted with his hands, wishing for the security of the notebook he'd just tucked away. "Well, she had all four lieutenants with her. And they weren't wearing dress uniforms, they were wearing combat fatigues."

"All four?"

"Four of four. Which means whatever they were about to go do, they're taking the whole unit with them. Or close to it."

She leaned back. "That's either quality deduction or mild paranoia. Reminds me of my third husband."

"Was he a detective?" Runstom hoped aloud.

"No," she said. "He was paranoid."

* * *

Dava introduced herself not with a blade, but with a slapstick that she had relieved from an insistent security guard while poking around the underground quarters of Barnard-4. She had been saving the flimsy weapon for an occasion when she needed to let her targets keep a heartbeat.

For twenty minutes, she'd forced the others wait with her in the shadows a few dozen meters away from the perimeter of the building so she could track the movements of the guards. As it turned out, the two stout Sirius-5 souls at the front gate did little moving other than yawning and scratching.

She didn't want to give them a chance to alert anyone else, so she'd decided to slink along the low fence and then show herself when she was close enough to smell their bad breath.

The guards flinched in synchronicity. "Whoa there," one of them said. "Where'd you come from, ma'am?"

She watched their eyes, moving slowly. They stood rigid and watched her, unable to work out her unbidden presence.

"This uh – this is a restricted area," the other one said. When her silence extended, he looked at his partner and whispered, "She looks like she's all painted up."

"Dude," the first one spat back in a hush. "She's not painted, she's...like Mrs. Harrison." He turned to face her and raised his voice. "Do you have any ID, ma'am?" He put a hand on his hip so that he could surreptitiously flick the strap of his holster open.

She held out her right hand and their eyes went to it. The weapon extended from a palm-sized rod into a meter-long stick with a twitch of her wrist. They wore helmets, but the coverage was poor. With a flick, she slapped the first one across the temple with a sharp diagonal stroke. The contact flashed blue as the burning-plastic smell of electricity bloomed forth and the guard's legs twisted, then buckled.

The other had his pistol out already. "You're the fast one." She twirled the stick around and brought it close to her body.

"Lady, drop that fuckin' weapon." He put on a stern voice and leveled his gun at her. "Drop it or I'm gonna drop you."

"I'd advise you of the same," she said, meeting his eyes. "But it won't be as fun if you give up that easily."

"Hey, you done yet?"

The voice from Dava's right caused her to flinch, but she held her sight on the guard. His head whipped toward the sound and his gun shook as if it didn't know which way to point.

"I really gotta take a piss, Dava. Did you kill those guys or what?"

The guard's eyes widened and his gun made its decision to point at the new target. She sighed, but she understood. Based on appearances, Eyeball always took the Most Threatening title.

She spun the slap-stick and caught the guard on the underside of his outstretched forearm. The insulation of his uniform protected him from the zap, but the whip was nasty enough for him to lose his grip on the pistol. She reversed the spin to catch him on the top of the arm, sending the gun clattering to the ground.

He clutched his arm and took a few steps back, eyes darting from Dava to Johnny. She stalked closer as he inched toward the wall where there was no doubt an alarm. Without taking her eyes off him, she slowly bent down to retrieve the gun with her left hand, keeping her stick-wielding arm outstretched.

"Is this a stun gun?" she asked.

"Uh…"

"Answer me."

"Y-yeah. It's a stunnerrrRRAAAHH!"

"Man, I hate those things," Eyeball said as he stepped to Dava's side and they watched the man twitch violently before coming to a clenched fetal position.

"You were supposed to hang back until I gave the signal."

"I know, but I told you – I really gotta take a piss."

"Johnny—"

"Hey, wait, how come you didn't kill those guys?"

She sighed and looked around. The others must have had enough sense to wait, so she turned her head back to the darkness and blew out a low whistle.

She stepped up to the first guard and bent down to take a closer look. One side of his face was marked black and his eyes were squeezed tight, but he was breathing shallow, spasming breaths. She rolled him over and lifted his jacket from behind to reveal the monitor strapped to the small of his back. It was a black rectangle smaller than a hand and there were a couple of tiny lights, all blinking green, as well as a little LCD panel that read, *STATUS: OK*.

"We don't kill anyone until we have to," she said, looking up at Eyeball. The others were approaching, so she stood up to address all of them. "This is what I was talking about. See the monitor on his back? His heart stops or his breathing stops, and this damn thing will have the whole moon on alert."

Johnny shifted his massive laser rifle from one shoulder to another. "Whole moon's gonna be on alert anyway."

"Exactly," Dava said. "Which is why we need to get this place shut down, quickly, without hiccups."

She looked at Barndoor, Thompson, and Freezer. "Tommy, you take this stunner." She kicked at the guard at her feet. "Barney, you get the one off this guy. Frank – you keep that blaster in your pants."

"Yeah-yeah, of course." She watched him look over each shoulder several times, unable to find a place to put his hands, kneading them nervously across his stomach.

"Alright," she said. "Let's go. We don't know how many more are inside, so nice and slow."

"Wait," Freezer said suddenly. Just inside the gate there was a side door that he had his eyes on. "Is that the guard-house?"

They all looked at it and the brazen red lettering that proclaimed NO ENTRY. Dava could feel the energy level tick upward as her companions itched to cross a portal they were told was off limits.

Johnny took a step forward and wrapped his meaty hand around the door handle and gave it a good yank, but it didn't budge. He yanked again, then took a step back and pulled his gun off his shoulder.

"Hold on, hold on," Freezer said, jogging up to the big man and putting a hand on his arm. In the other hand, he dangled a keycard on a chain. "Got it from that one. You're going to have to pick him up. His thumb needs to be on this side of the card when it goes into the lock."

Eyeball frowned, winked, and grunted at Barndoor, who took it as an order to help him hoist up the limp guard and drag him toward the door.

"Shit, these Sirius-5 motherfuckers are *dense*," Barndoor said, trying desperately to keep his half of the unconscious man moving at the speed of Johnny's half. "Can't imagine trying to move a body planetside if they're this heavy on a moon."

"Good thing you didn't kill him," Freezer said as they got the man's hand close enough for him to pin the thumb to the keycard. He slid it into the slot and they heard a click. "Wouldn't work otherwise."

"Stunners," Dava said, directing Thompson and Barndoor to cover the door as Eyeball yanked it open, a lot less carefully than she would have preferred.

The small room was empty except for a couple of desks and a cabinet. She flicked her slap-stick open, stepped inside, and checked the corners. She retracted the stick and Freezer came in behind her.

There were screens and indicators set into the surface of the desks, but they weren't active. She turned her interest to the cabinet, which was tall and looked sturdy, like the kind of cabinet that weapons were stored in.

"I wouldn't do that," Freezer said. "That thing will definitely set alarms off. I can smell the hot wires running through it. Probably only opens at shift change."

"Right," Dava said. Maybe bringing the kid along was

worth the extra babysitting effort. "Well, anything else? Can you get these monitors on?"

"No. But." He slid open a few drawers until he found a handypad of some kind. He toyed with it for a moment, mumbling to himself. "Ah, yes. Yes! Still logged in."

She leaned over his shoulder to see the screen winking with activity. He tapped around for a moment and then a map came up. "Is that this building?" she asked.

"Sure is. And check it out – see those red dots?"

She looked at the small blips that wavered in various parts of the map, some inside hallways, others bobbing around in rooms. There were about ten altogether. "What are those? Wait – are those – you're kidding me."

"Yep. That's our security."

Dava grinned. All mapped out. This was too easy. "What about other personnel?"

Freezer tapped around the screen. "Nope. This is just tracking those vita-stat monitors. Including those two," he said, pointing a thumb over his shoulder.

She took the pad from him. He was useful, she had to admit, even if knowing where all the guards were took the fun out of infiltrating a building. Given that her stealth was hampered by the team that had been forced on her, she would take any advantage she could get.

CHAPTER 7

The map made it trivial for Dava to weave her way to the main control center of the building, her team following close behind. They didn't have to deal with a single guard, which was both good and bad: it maximized their chances of getting Freezer where he needed to be in order to disable the power relay, but it also meant they would have to face the lot of them when the alarms inevitably went off and it was time to make an exit. But this mission was all about timing, and as much as she would enjoy it if Rando Jansen's plan failed, she was in it for the duration and was going to do her job the best that she could. And that meant giving the other team the time they needed to get to the observatory in force.

She looked at the map. "No security inside," she whispered. "But there will be a couple of operators."

"We'll take care of them," Thompson said, reaching back for her submachinegun.

Dava put out a hand. "Too noisy. If the alarms go off, then you bring out the big guns – we'll want them to think there's an army in here. Until then, we're nothing but shadows."

"Yeah," Freezer said, coming close to the door. He wiped sweat from his brow, then wiped his hands on his pants. That big, stupid pistol jutting from his waistband. "Besides, these guys are just operators. You don't need to hurt them."

"Well," Barndoor said, shrugging. "We probably *are* going to need to hurt them."

"Whatever, but you don't need to kill them," Freezer said, his eyes almost pleading. Dava saw his finger absently tapping the butt of his handgun.

Thompson sighed. "Soft spot for the geeks, huh? Fine, fine. They can live."

They nodded to each other and then all turned to Eyeball, who held the rear. He seemed oddly calm. Dava wondered if he was dreaming of whiskey.

"Frank wants them to live, then they live," he grunted with a wink.

"Thompson, if I give the signal, get their attention." Dava flicked the stun-stick and put a hand on the door.

She went in first, making her way across the back of the room quickly and quietly. It was dark except for a myriad of tall screens, about a dozen in all, across one side of the broad room. Two women sat at consoles in the center, half-heartedly tapping at keys and flipping between views of the system while engaged in conversation.

"So how much longer you got?" one said. She was a Sirius-fiver with straight blond hair, combed back and cut off just below her ears.

"Oh I still have eighteen months," the other said. "Gonna take forever." She was also a Sirius-fiver, slightly heavier with hair that must have been dyed black and curled. Dava could smell the goop that held it in place as she crept through the shadows along the back of the room.

The blond sighed. "I just started. Signed up for a four-year."

"I'd tell you it goes quick, but I'd be lying."

"Hey, what does this mean?"

The two of them bent forward to inspect a monitor up close. Dava slunk forward, coming up behind them. She glanced at the door. Thompson and Barndoor slid into the room, splitting up to hug the wall on either side of the doorway. They moved into position and Dava took a steady, deep breath, then let it out. She stuck a finger upward, and Thompson whistled. The heads of the operators snapped to the sound.

"Hey," the senior operator said. "Who the hell are you? Do you have a paaAAAA!"

She practically flipped out of her ergonomic chair as Dava slipped the slap-stick up under one of her arms. The blond spun around to watch her co-worker spasm to the floor, then followed the long weapon to Dava's hand.

She looked Dava in the eyes and her hands shot up. "I give up!"

Dava sighed. "Fine. Thompson, get over here and tie her up. Make sure to gag her. Johnny, you stay at the door. Barndoor, check the other exits. And Frank – are we happy?"

Freezer was already perusing the monitors and controls. "Yeah. We're definitely happy." He kept looking over his shoulder, flinching at every unheard sound.

"Then get to work."

"Who the hell are you people?"

There was a door in the back of the room that hadn't been on Dava's map; probably a restroom. A heavyset figure stood silhouetted against the yellow light that winked out as the door swung closed, revealing a man in the same uniform as the other operators.

He was practically on top of Barndoor, who reached back for his scattergun.

"No!" Freezer shouted. "Get down, man!"

The big, stupid pistol came out. The ceiling above the new operator exploded with fire. He threw himself to the floor, covering his head.

Then the whole room turned red.

The ceiling rained white, like frenzied snow. As the tiny blobs of anti-inflamant touched anything with heat, they expanded and coated. Within seconds, they were all sticky with the stuff.

Klaxons bellowed, mixed with a vocal recording that repeated, "Warning: fire in the building. Please evacuate." The blond began to scream and cry and rock back and forth, half-tied to her chair. Freezer and Thompson dove for cover under the console. Barndoor flailed his long hair wildly, trying to keep it from being glued to his face by the goop.

Johnny Eyeball stood silently at the door. His whole head was white, his shoulders were white, his arms were white, shading red with each flash of the alarm lights.

He winked his angriest wink.

Then roared. A pulse rifle appeared in his hands and began chewing up the corridor. The sound faded to a distant high-pitched snapping as he disappeared down the hallway.

Dava hit the floor under the console next to Thompson and Freezer. "Frank, can you shut that shit off?"

"Yeah, maybe." He was shaking, the pistol gripped tightly in both hands.

She covered his hands gently with hers. "Okay, Frank. Take a breath. We have a job to do, and now we have to think fast. I hear you're good at that. Is that right?"

"Wh-what?"

She tugged lightly on the gun and he released it. "You're good at thinking fast."

"Y-yeah." He swallowed and looked at her. "Yeah."

The raining goop sputtered out. "Did it stop?" Thompson said. "Why did it stop?"

"Room temperature," Freezer said. With the gun out of his hands, he loosened noticeably and his words began to speed up to their normal run-on pace. "It must have a shut-off if the room temperature is below a certain value. That crap is expensive, they wouldn't want to waste it."

"Okay, good," Dava said. She stood up and looked around. It might have looked like fresh snowfall if everything wasn't glistening and the warning lights weren't making everything glow crimson. The cold floor was the only part of the room not covered in the stuff. Barndoor shambled around like the bloody ghost of a snowman. The blond operator sat whimpering in her chair next to her still-unconscious companion. The third who'd come from the restroom was nowhere to be seen.

Any moment, guards would be headed to the control center to see what caused the alarm. Eyeball would definitely slow them down, but he might need backup. Dava gestured for Thompson and Freezer to come out and yelled over the alarms, "Thompson, you and Barney go find Johnny and keep the heat away from us. Frank: can you still operate any of this stuff?"

Freezer came out and looked at the whitewashed console. He walked to the middle section and began feeling around, picking at it with his fingernails. "Yeah, here we go," he said, pulling a stretch of the stuff away from a control panel. "It's already solidified. It'll peel off like plastic. You wanna give me a hand? We just need this section here."

Together they worked quickly to clean away the flame retardant and expose a handful of controls and a couple of screens. Freezer gave the console some experimental tapping and images and read-outs began to flicker. To Dava, it looked like a jumble of blueprints, gauges, and statistics.

"Okay, okay, okay," Freezer whispered as he navigated the system. "Okay. We ready?"

"How is this going to work?" Dava asked.

"I'm locking out the intake of power here, on this side," he said, pointing at some kind of map on the screen. "From the power station. So that means, no more relaying power from there to the observatory over here. However, there is another power line directly on the opposite side of town. That one goes straight to the observatory. See? It makes a big ring."

Dava didn't really see it, but ventured a guess. "So we're breaking the ring?"

"Right, that's what we do first. But the reason it's built like a ring is so if there is a break, power can still flow around the other way."

She sighed. "I don't get it. Why are we here if the observatory is still going to get power from the other station?"

"That's where we get crafty." Freezer smiled and cracked his knuckles. "See, this whole redundancy ring has a priority system built in. And Vulca City gets priority over everything. So all we have to do is convince this far power station that there's a problem, and then it will stop sending power to the observatory because the town has priority."

"So how do we do that?"

"From here, I can start an emergency drain. This will suck power from the observatory like air out of a hull breach." He curled his hands into a tube and put them to his mouth, making a sucking sound. "Like that, right? The drain will pull power from the other side, right through the observatory. The other side will detect the massive spike in load and go into an emergency cut-off so as not to deprive the town."

She slapped him on the shoulder. "You know, Frank, you're a lot more useful when you don't have a gun in your hands."

Freezer sighed. "Yeah, I know. I know. Alright." He tapped at the keys. "Let's kill the lights in this motherfucker."

* * *

Once the doors of the transport opened into the garage in Vulca City, Runstom was so wound up he practically sprinted out. Troyo bobbed along behind him, trying to keep up while warning him not to get involved. He found the exit and looked up and down one of the short, wide corridors that he saw everywhere in this place.

Re-routed, with no explanation. The damn bus had just turned around halfway to the observatory. He knew something was up, and no one was telling him. Not Captain Oliver, who was not answering any of the messages he sent to her. Not anyone on the transport. His traveling companions, Dr. Leesen and Peter Troyo, we just as clueless. He needed to find someone who knew what was happening.

He grabbed the arm of a woman in gray coveralls who

was passing by with her face in a large handypad. "Where's the security office?"

"What?" she said, looking up and blinking.

"Stan, just leave it be," Troyo tried to say, but Runstom waved him away.

He pulled out his notepad and flipped back a few pages. "Willis Polinsky. Head of Security. Where would I find him?"

"Oh. Um, Willy's office is just down the auburn side of the hall."

He looked up and down the corridor. The walls in either direction were painted a kind of reddish brown. "Can you just point, please?"

She leaned back and cocked her head slightly. "Yeah, that way." Her eyes went to Runstom's notepad. "Hey…is that paper?"

He ignored her and stalked off down the hall. Behind him, Troyo was saying, "Stan, slow down. Sheesh, I coulda told you where Willy's office was."

Runstom was moving so fast down the rust-colored tube, he went by a door and didn't register the words *HEAD OF SECURITY* until he'd passed it. He turned around to see Troyo standing there waiting for him. He pointed at the door, then held out a hand. "Willy's office. I'll do the talking."

Troyo opened the door and Runstom was forced to bring up the rear. Willis Polinsky was pacing around the back of the small office, talking on a headset. There were no details in this side of the conversation, just a few yeahs and nos. He nodded to them as they came in and held up a single finger.

"Yeah, okay. Fine." He tapped the headset and put on a wary smile. "Petey. Stanford. What brings y'all to my office this morning?"

"Willy," Troyo said, taking a step forward as if to block Runstom slightly. "What's going on? We were on a transport out to the observatory and it stopped and turned around."

"Ah, that." Polinsky looked down at his hands. "Had to come back in."

"But why?"

"Protocol." He'd shaven since Runstom last saw him, and it made the man look young. Too young for the job.

"What protocol?" Runstom asked, sidestepping Troyo.

"Well, I can't really say."

"Willy, come on, man." Troyo put on his broad smile. "It's me. You can fill us in a little, can't you?"

He looked from Troyo to Runstom and back. "It's just – well, for security reasons, I can't really say."

"For security reasons," Runstom said.

"Yeah," he replied, drawing the word out.

"Who else knows?" Runstom prodded.

"Uh. What, uh, what do you mean?"

"Who has clearance? Who could we request clearance from?"

"Well, I'm not sure. I – I don't know."

"Aren't you head of security?"

"Okay, Stan," Troyo said, making his way around the room and putting a hand on Polinsky's shoulder. "I think that's enough. Willy would tell us if he could."

"You're right." Runstom blinked in revelation. "He doesn't know what's going on."

Polinsky frowned and looked at his hands. Troyo took a step back and looked at him. "Really? Willy, you really don't know?"

"Dammit," he said, slapping his hands down on his desk. "No, I don't know. It's an alarm. It's just a damn alarm from the guys over at the south power relay station. I don't know why it went off or who tripped it." He looked up, his eyes beginning to water. "No one will answer the damn radio!"

"An alarm," Troyo said.

"From the guys?" Runstom asked. He took out his notepad. "You mean the guards stationed there? At the south power relay station? What time did it go off?"

"A little after nine."

Runstom took a step forward. "What time, Willy?"

Polinsky sighed and shuffled to his desk, picking up a handypad. "Oh nine oh seven in the A.M. It went off at 9:07."

"Okay." Runstom jotted down a note and then spun toward the door. "Thank you, Willy."

He hit the hallway and kept marching, not knowing where he was going next, only knowing that he was being kept in the dark. His whole career he'd been kept in the dark, and this new position hadn't changed anything in the slightest. He needed to talk to Captain Oliver.

"Look, man." Troyo came up behind him, then came around in front of him to stop him in his tracks. "Look, just stop a second."

"Get out of my way."

"No one is more pissed about this than me, okay?" Troyo's face turned dark, rare creases forming in his forehead and around his eyes. He stuck an arm out to gesture at something in the distance. "I had a whole fucking day planned out there. You know, it's not easy to get all these assholes to come see us. None of them fucking want us here, and I have to put on a smile and practically beg them to show up for these little shindigs. All so we can show

how fucking nice and shiny ModPol is and what great chums they are to have around. So I don't even know what the hell you're so mad about. You didn't really want to go out there – hell, you don't even want to be here. You know it and I know it. So what's your problem right now?"

Runstom glared at him for a moment, then decided he wasn't the enemy, not for the moment, anyway. "My problem is Oliver. Something was going on this morning and she deliberately kept it from us. She kept us out of the loop. I hate being left out of the loop. We're supposed to be part of the same team."

"Yeah." They were walking again, Runstom swept up in Troyo's sudden determination. "I mean, now you're getting the other side of it. You're getting what we have to deal with. We're supposed to be the face of this company, but it's like the muscles aren't connected to the skin. The muscles go off and do whatever the fuck they need to do, and we have to bend and flex and make it look like everything's as it's supposed to be."

They'd gone around a corner and Troyo stopped at a door, waving a keycard in front of it. Once the door was opened, Runstom recognized the account manager's office. He hadn't realized this was that hallway; that their march had taken them to that one color of maroon.

"I'm going to check my messages," Troyo said. "See if I can get any idea of what's happening."

Runstom pulled out his on-loan handypad and checked to see if Oliver had written him back, but there was nothing. He poked at the thing pointedly, trying to get it to refresh, retry, resync, whatever it needed to do to make a message show up.

"Here we go." Troyo was behind his desk but was still

standing, bending over to read from his terminal. "From one of Oliver's Lieutenants. Lt. Beckas. He says they went out on perimeter watch this morning. Out to west power station, then down to the south power relay."

"Beckas? You mean *she*. Why did she tell you? Why didn't I get a message?"

Troyo looked up at Runstom. "Did you check your mail?"

He looked at the handypad. Lt. Cato had only set it up for guest access into the MPORDU intel and address book. Runstom couldn't check his own mail on it. "This is a loaner from Cato." His face felt hot and he swallowed. "I left my WrappiMate in my quarters this morning."

"Well. Shit." Troyo bent down to his screen again. "Anyway, it says they received the distress call from the south power relay station. It says they believed the station was..."

"What?"

"Under attack."

"Under attack? Who attacked them?"

"Doesn't say. That's the end of it."

Runstom stood silent in thought for a second, then popped his notebook out. "What time did that message come in?"

"Uh, let's see...9:13."

As he wrote it down, he tried to decide if he wanted to go back to his room to get his WrappiMate. He turned to the door, then stopped and looked back at Troyo. "Come on, Peter. Let's go."

Troyo came around his desk. "Where are we going?"

"You know the quickest way to the barracks?"

"Barracks?"

"I mean the Defense Unit's quarters."

"Oh, right." Troyo stepped past him into the hallway

and gestured. "Yeah, it's just down this way, around the corner and into the magenta hall."

They headed straight down the corridor for a few minutes and then Runstom heard familiar voices. It sounded like a heated discussion.

"Hold up a minute," he said and backtracked to a large double-door. The sign above read *FACILITY MANAGEMENT*. He caught the word *observatory* coming from the other side.

"That sounds like Dr. Leesen," he said.

"Come on, let's see what's up," Troyo said, pushing his way through the doors.

They entered a large room some fifteen meters deep and twice that across. There were four sets of long, multi-screened consoles situated in the middle, each occupied by a pair of operators. Rhonda Harrison stood on a slightly elevated platform in the center of the room, in between all four consoles. Dr. Johanna Leesen was trying to talk to her, but the facilities manager kept spinning around to ask for status updates from the operators.

"I mean, I just got a flood of messages from my researchers," Leesen was saying as they approached. "Some of them were seeing power fluctuations, others were losing power altogether. Then everything just stopped."

"Power fluctuations?" Runstom asked. He had a feeling of *déjà vu*, then realized he was remembering the conversation he'd had with Jenna Zarconi in the prison mess hall back at ModPol HQ.

Lessen turned to face them. "Oh, you two. Did you find out why our transport was turned around? Was it because something is happening at the observatory?"

"Well, not really," Runstom said. "Mr. Polinsky said it

was protocol. An alarm went off at the south power relay and they were under orders to pull all transports back to the city."

"What sort of alarm?"

Runstom looked at Troyo, who pursed his lips. "We don't know, exactly." He took out his notebook. "Why don't you tell me what you know. What time did the messages start coming in from your researchers? And what time did they stop?"

Her eyes went to the notebook in his hands for a brief moment, then she lifted her handypad and poked at it. "Let's see. The first one that mentioned power issues came in about 9:30."

"At 9:30 exactly?"

She frowned. "At 9:34."

"And the last message you got from anyone at the observatory?"

Leesen scrolled down with a finger. "9:46."

They both looked up at the clock. "That was only twelve minutes ago," Runstom said.

"I know," she said, then showed him her handypad. "But look. It was a steady stream – every single team was mailing me – and then it just stopped."

"They're cut off." They turned to face Harrison who was stepping down from the podium. She walked to one of the large console banks and the three of them trailed her. She pointed at a crude map on one of the screens. "Power grid. Or what would be a grid if we were anything bigger than a spread-out research facility."

It looked like a trapezoid, with a rectangular block overlaying the middle of the longest side and smaller rectangles positioned at each corner. "This is the city?" Runstom asked, pointing at the largest block. It was flipped around, but now he could see the resemblance to the map on the handypad that Lt. Cato had given him.

"Right," Harrison said. She pointed around the map as she spoke. "See how we're all blue lines here? Over here, the observatory is red."

"So they have no power?" Leesen's usual calm demeanor was starting to waver. "Why? Rhonda, what's happening?"

Harrison sighed. "All I can tell you is that the south power relay, over here? It stopped accepting power from the west power station. Normally, that wouldn't be a total cut-off to the observatory, because they'd still get it from the east station over here. But something else is wrong. There was a heavy drain detected at the east station. Way beyond normal. The safety switches tripped, in order to preserve power to us here in town in an emergency."

"What's going to happen to them?" Leesen gripped Harrison's arm. "Are they going to…?"

She shook her head. "They should be okay for a while, running on emergency power. But I need to get a team out there, and soon. I'm going to go request transport."

She started to walk toward the door, but Troyo's words stopped her. "But Willy said that—"

She looked at him. "Said what?"

Troyo looked at Runstom, who frowned and nodded. "Willy said something is going on. Security-related. No transport is allowed."

"What the hell are you talking about?" Harrison said, planting her hands on her hips.

"Security-related?" Leesen said.

Runstom put out his hands. "Look, just calm down. We're still piecing everything together."

"Are you going to go out there?" Leesen pulled up close to Runstom. "Please tell me you're going out there."

"Well, I—"

"Mr. Runstom. My – my people are out there. I handpicked the research personnel in this facility. I can't – I need them to be..."

"Johanna," Troyo said, touching her arm. "It'll be okay."

"Fuck you, Peter," she said, yanking her arm away. "This is what you are supposed to be here for, isn't it? Isn't this the whole point of this defense contracting bullshit?" She stabbed a finger into his chest. "How about you go out there and fucking defend us?"

"Alright," Runstom said, pulling Troyo away. "You're right. You're right, Dr. Leesen. We'll get out there."

When they hit the hallway, Troyo leaned into Runstom. "Stan, for all we know, LJ and her troops are already out there."

"We don't know anything yet."

* * *

They went around a bend and then another and another and a few minutes later Troyo was pulling Runstom's swift stride to a halt to point him to the quarters of the ModPol Onsite Rapid Defense Unit. The door was locked but Troyo's keycard opened it.

Inside, they found three men and one woman sitting around a small round table playing cards. The four privates looked up as they came through the door. One of them, a dough-faced young man with short, wiry, blond hair stood and saluted Runstom. "Sir," he said, then looked at his companions, who remained seated.

"He ain't Defense," one of the others said, scratching at his poorly-shaved cheek.

The standing one held his salute and looked sideways at the other. "Royi, I think he outranks us," he said under his breath.

"At ease, Defender," Runstom said. The private flinched, then dropped his hand, still standing. "Where is everyone?"

The privates looked at each other, then the poorly-shaven one spoke up. "On patrol."

"We know they went out to do perimeter watch," Troyo said. "Where are they now?"

"Uh." The private looked at the others for help, but they all suddenly seemed interested in their cards. "Well, one squad went east, and one went west."

"Squad?" Runstom said. "How many?"

"Ten. In each."

"Do you know about the attack at the south relay?" Troyo asked.

"No. Well, just that there was one."

"We're still waiting for an update," the female private said.

They collectively spasmed, everyone except Runstom. The four privates reflexively reached for their military-issue handypads and Troyo checked his WrappiMate.

"What is it?" Runstom asked. "Is it Captain Oliver?"

"They're moving inside the building," the standing private said. "Inside the power relay station. In pursuit of..." He seemed to lose his voice.

"What is this?" the woman said. "Is this real?"

"Shit." Troyo extended the screen on his WrappiMate and angled it at Runstom as Harrison, Leesen, and Polinsky appeared in the doorway.

"What, what is it?" Leesen said.

"You were right," Harrison said. "Willy won't let me go out there, the sonovabitch."

"Rhonda, I told you," Polinsky said. "It's protocol."

"What is it?" Leesen repeated, touching Troyo, then Runstom.

Runstom looked at the screen. He pulled out his notebook and noted the time.

The poorly-shaven private looked up from his handypad. "What's Space Waste?"

CHAPTER 8

Dava looked down the hall. The klaxons had finally ceased their bellowing, but the lights continued to tint everything red. The hallway looked like a war zone, with the scorch marks of Johnny Eyeball's pulse rifle running up and down both sides, the color of the lights making it look like the walls themselves were bleeding.

She listened to the gunfire in the distance. It was short. Bursty. Steady in volume. Not moving. Probably not hitting anything, but not wild or desperate. Someone was holding position. She pulled out the handypad with the map on it. Either it was broken, or all the guards were dead; no red blips appeared on the screen.

So then who was shooting, and who were they shooting at?

She ducked back into the control room. "Frank, we almost ready? It's time to go."

"Yeah, yes. Almost locked up."

Freezer had spent more time covering his tracks than he had on disabling the system to begin with. He kept going on about how he was going to make it impossible for anyone to reverse what he'd done. It seemed critical to him that his sabotage stuck. She wondered if he was just busy leaving his mark.

Eyeball came trotting down the corridor. "Where's Frank?"

He was coated in shreds of flame-retardant and his armor smoked where laser fire had scorched it. "Frank's here, we're almost ready. Where are Thompson and Barney?"

"Covering the front."

"Guards?"

"Drying on the wall. But we got other problems." He strode to the console. "Get up, Frank. We're leaving and I'm not letting you out of my sight until we're back at camp and I have my whiskey."

"Okay, okay," Freezer said as he tapped. "Okay. Done! By the way, you can have that gun back. Dava took it."

Eyeball hauled the hacker to his feet and yanked him toward the door. "Don't want the gun. Want the whiskey."

Dava let them take the rear. She went ahead with her own pistol drawn, a compact piece that she didn't bother with unless she really couldn't get close to her targets. She wove her way through the corridors, passing the occasional crumpled uniform, vita-stat monitors faintly glowing red. When she reached the front hall, Barndoor and Thompson were on either side of the main door. Thompson had her Tommy-Gun and leaned out every few seconds to fire a burst. There was the limp, broad body of a guard lying between the open doors.

Dava slid up behind Barndoor. "What's the situation? Who is she shooting at?"

"Fuckin' ModPol." He spat and then winced. His right

arm was soaked wet with dark plasma and he held his scattergun weakly in his left hand.

She watched Thompson and when the burst came, Dava used the cover to lean around the door and take a look. She pulled back as a retort sprayed at them, peppering the doorway. She'd seen a few vehicles, armored rovers of some kind. The Pollies were using them as shields. She guessed they had a lot more ammo than her Wasters did.

"They got a sniper," Barndoor said. "Hit me in the fuckin' arm."

"Maybe it'll improve your aim," Thompson yelled over between shots.

"Fuck you, Thompson! Fuck your stupid skinny ass!" He looked at Dava. "First I get stunned by one of those dumb-ass guards. And when I come to, we come back here to check the perimeter and freakin' ModPol shows up. And not the cop edition either. These fucks are military. Not Pollies. Fenders." He grunted as he inspected his wound, then looked up at her again. "What are we going to do? We can't take 'em. There's too many."

"No, I don't think we can," she said. She looked back to see Eyeball holding Freezer around the corner, well out of line of anything that might come through the open doorway.

"Wish I had a sniper rifle," Barndoor muttered, then leaned his head back to yell. "If I had a sniper rifle I'd kill every last one of you fuckers!"

"Are you kidding me?" Thompson stopped shooting to pop the ammo drum out of her gun and replace it. "Barney, even if you had a sniper rifle, you'd be lucky to hit a barn door. That's why we call you Barndoor!"

"Fuck you, Thompson!"

"Sit back," Dava said, pushing down on Barndoor's shoulder. "Let me get a QuikStik out of your pack so you don't bleed out and slow us down."

He sat back and closed his eyes while she dug out the medkit and pulled his sleeve back. The shot had gone clean through his forearm. She couldn't tell if it hit any bones, but it was bleeding excessively. She applied the QuikStik to both sides and it gelled up and set almost instantly. The stuff doubled as a painkiller, so she hoped it would help Barndoor hold it together.

"Okay, stand up." As he did, she stood up with him and pulled the strap of his scattergun over his shoulder. "I know you can't use that right arm, but just hold the gun like this and do the best you can with it. It's good for short range, at least."

"Okay," he said quietly.

"Thompson, cover fire!" she called. "Come on, Barney – fall back to where Johnny and Frank are."

They quickly got back to the corner and she shoved the handypad into Freezer's hands. "What are our options? We need another way out. Is there anything underground?"

He tapped at the pad. "No, nothing underground out here. Hmm. I think this might be a garage, back here. Which would mean a door, and maybe even a vehicle."

"Atta boy," Eyeball said, slapping Freezer so hard on the back that he almost dropped the handypad.

Dava took it so she could see the map and plot a route. "Okay, I'm going to lead us to the garage," she said, tracing her finger along the path so that Freezer could see it. "The four of us need to move to that side while Thompson covers. When we get there, Johnny: I want you to cover so she can get back here to us. Ready?"

Freezer nodded, Barndoor grunted, and Eyeball winked. "I can almost taste that whiskey now," he mumbled dreamily, then leaned around the corner and shouted. "Thompson, cover fire! Give us four bursts, then come back!"

She slapped a new drum into the submachinegun and let rip, and Dava sprinted across the space and into the far corridor. Freezer and Barndoor were right behind her, with Eyeball trotting behind them. He leaned out and the pulse rifle chirped its high-pitched report. Seconds later, Thompson was diving behind him and sliding into the hallway on her belly.

"Try to keep up," Dava said. She rehearsed the route in her head and took off.

She had not chosen the most direct path to the garage, but instead created one that included short sprints and corners. They made it through the first few turns before they could hear the ModPol bullhorn echoing through the building, demanding their surrender.

Eyeball whooped as he blasted away from the rear. "Gettin' hot back here, Dava!"

"Keep moving," she yelled. "We're close."

She came around another corner and almost barreled into a man in a long, white coat. He was gray-haired and tall for a Sirius-fiver. While she twisted to keep her balance, he spread his arms wide and wrapped them around her.

"You bastards attacked us!" he yelled, lifting her up from behind. He was strong, and her arms were pinned and her legs came off the floor. "You won't get away with this!"

"Dava!" Thompson shouted. She leveled her gun at him. "Put her down, you old ass!"

"You're not going to shoot me," he said, slowly backing into a side room. "You'll hit your friend, here."

Barndoor shoved Thompson aside and aimed his scattergun by laying the barrel across his bad arm. "Oh, I'll shoot you, you sonovabitch."

Dava lifted her legs, bringing her knees to her chest. When the man's legs came into view, the scattergun erupted. She crashed to the floor as the man howled.

"Goddamn, Barney," Thompson said. "You shredded his foot! Not a bad shot from three meters away."

"Alright, dammit," Barndoor said over the wounded man's frantic screams. "Let's just get the hell outta here."

Dava picked herself up, cursing herself for being careless. Trying to keep track of the team and keep track of herself, it was too much.

Johnny's gun burst once from the last corner they'd come around, then she could hear it clicking dryly. She sprinted back to lean around and look, Thompson and Barndoor following close behind.

"Let him go!" Eyeball roared, clubbing a Fender with the empty rifle, then pulling back to crack another in the helmet with the butt of it. There were six or seven of them, a tangle of arms and guns, Freezer and Eyeball wrapped up in the melee.

"Sonova." Barndoor leveled his shotgun.

"No!" Thompson pulled him back. "You'll hit Johnny and Frank!"

A couple of the Fenders shot looks at the sound of her voice. Barrels raised and lit up the corridor. The three of them ducked back around the corner.

"Dammit, what are we going to do now?" Barndoor said.

Dava looked the other way. "The garage is just down there."

"So what, we're just gonna leave them?"

"No," she said. "Yes. No. We have to get out of here. If we can get to the observatory we can get everyone else. There's a lot of them but we've got more. We can come back and overrun them."

"ModPol's not even supposed to be here." Thompson looked like she was trying to control her breathing. "Boss Jansen said they didn't have jurisdiction on Vulca."

"It doesn't matter," Dava said, swallowing down any thoughts she wanted to spew about Jansen. "They're here. Now we need to get back to the rest of the crew if we want any chance of getting Frank and Johnny back. Let's go."

* * *

Runstom stared half at his notebook, half at the floor of the barracks, trying to think. The others hovering in the corners of his vision – Leesen, Polinsky, Harrison, Troyo, and four privates in the Trial ModPol Rapid Onsite Defense Unit – had all gone silent at the last words spoken: *Space Waste*. It wasn't even that they all knew what that meant; it was that they could see on his face that he knew what it meant, and it was bad. He just had to think it through. What were they doing on Vulca? How did they get as far as they did without putting the whole moon on alert?

"Willis," he said, raising his head to meet the security head's eyes. "Is there any way to find out if there were any landings?"

"You mean, like ships?"

"Yes. Any kind of vessels landing on the surface."

Polinsky scratched his head. "Well, ships land at the dock every day."

"What about elsewhere?" Runstom asked. "Somewhere

outside of a dock. Would any landings like that be tracked?"

"Traffic Control might know. I guess."

Runstom took a step toward the security officer. "How do we contact Traffic Control?"

"I guess we can send a message…" he said, looking away.

"Then do it." Runstom turned to Leesen. "Doctor. Nothing in the messages you got from your people said anything about an attack?"

"No," she said quietly. She had her handypad in her hand, lifted to her chest as if she might re-read the messages, but she just stared ahead. "No, nothing like that."

"Wait," Polinsky said. He cocked his head at his pad. "I just got something. There's a radio call coming in."

"Radio?" Leesen said. "You actually use radio?"

"Only for emergency communication." He tapped at the pad and then tapped at a small earpiece. "Hello? Can you read me?"

"Can you put it on speaker?" Runstom asked.

"Yeah," Polinsky nodded. He padded around his waist until he found a small rectangular device, matte gray with mesh on one end. Speaking into it, he said, "Gorman, start over. Can you hear us?"

"Yeah," the speaker crackled. It sounded miles distant, weak. "Yeah, I'm here."

"What's the situation?" Runstom said, leaning close to the device.

"I just got out of there. It's – there's a whole army down here." There was a pause. Runstom thought he heard some noise, almost like the clearing of a throat. Then the speaker blurted back to life. "I know I'm not supposed to leave my post, but all our comms are down. I made a break for it on an ATV so I could get on the radio."

"Gorman," Polinsky said, enunciating into the device. "How many are there? How many?"

"I have no idea." There was almost a laugh, but it was hard to tell through the static. "I saw half a dozen vehicles coming when I first took cover. When they overwhelmed the front and came in, I started to make my way to the back where the garages are. Every room I passed, there were these guys in black jackets swarming over everything."

Runstom took a breath. "They're after something."

"What?" Troyo looked from Runstom to Polinsky. "What are they after?"

"Gorman," Polinsky said into the communicator. "You still there? Gorman?"

"What would they want out there?" Troyo turned to face Leesen. "What would they want from the observatory?"

"Maybe they want to do some research," the scruffy private chimed in before he was shushed by his squadmates.

"Well, looks like we lost Gorman," Polinsky said, angling the comm device to look at some lights on the side. "Not a scrap of signal now."

"Stanford, what are we going to do?" Troyo leaned in close to Runstom. "Maybe it's time we thought about getting out of here."

"No, we're not leaving."

"But these guys are – I mean, do you know what they're capable of? This is Space Waste."

Images of the prisoner barge being torn apart flashed in Runstom's head. George Halsey's face, blood running from both nostrils and from his mouth as he lay helpless in a bullet-stormed corridor. The last of his strength used to clutch a live grenade. Swarms of leather-clad psychopaths loosing hell from jagged weaponry. The narrow escape before

Halsey blew up himself and Runstom's pursuers. The desperate, cowardly flight Runstom took on the stolen personnel transport. Pulling away from the barge and watching it slowly bleed air and any chance of anyone else making it out alive.

Runstom found himself pinning Troyo against the wall with a forearm. He released the man and swallowed. "Yes."

"Space what-now?" Polinsky said. "What are you fellas talking about?"

"Space Waste," Harrison said. "Figures you've never heard of them."

"What's that supposed to mean, Rhonda?"

"It means you Sirius-5 domers are goddamn sheltered—"

"Stop," Leesen said, cutting her off. "Mr. Runstom. What does this mean?"

Runstom sighed, looking at them each in turn. The four privates looked confused; he guessed that some of them had probably heard of Space Waste, but nothing more than scary stories told by more experienced Defenders. Harrison might have heard enough to know they were to be feared, but had she ever encountered them? She was not afraid enough for him to believe that she had. Polinsky looked skeptical, but Leesen was getting paler. Troyo looked as though he wanted to find a nice solid bomb shelter to lock himself into for the next week or so.

"It means Vulca is under attack," he said.

"We should prepare to defend the city," Troyo said. "Willy, how many security personnel do you have on staff here?" Runstom looked at the man, trying to determine if he'd had a change of heart about facing Space Waste. Then he realized Troyo was just playing the odds: the city would be easier to defend than any other part of the facility.

"Well, I have about – uh, sixteen on duty right now. In town anyway."

"Altogether?" Troyo said. "On and off duty?"

"Oh, uh, forty-seven. Some of them will be sleeping right about now."

"For fuck's sake, Willy," Troyo said. "Didn't you hear Stanford? We're under attack!"

"Wake them up and get them on alert," Runstom said. He looked at his notebook again, and with renewed focus started reading what little he had. One event at a time. What did it mean?

"What about the observatory?" Leesen said, coming between the three of them.

"Maybe they're okay," Polinsky said. "The alarm was at the power relay."

"Yeah, that's where Captain Oliver said she was engaging them," one of the privates said. "At the power relay."

"Why would they go after the power relay?" Troyo said. "There's nothing there."

"The power relay is attacked," Runstom said, reading from his notebook. "Then the observatory loses power."

"That's the target?" Troyo said. "The observatory?"

Runstom looked at Leesen. "What's at the observatory, Doctor? Anything worth taking?"

"Equipment?" she said, her breath halting. "Hardware? I don't know. The people are worth more."

"Yes, yes," Troyo said moving in on her. "Who or what, then? What's there they would want?"

"I don't know," she breathed. She looked Runstom in the eyes. "What will they do to the people there? My – my researchers?"

Runstom looked at Troyo. "Maybe nothing. If they stand

aside, the Wasters – the attackers – might leave them alone. Come on, Mr. Polinsky," he said, heading into the hallway. "We need to secure the city."

"Mr. Runstom!" Leesen came swiftly into the hallway and spun in front of him, stopping him with her hands, then brought them together in a clasp. "There's something else."

"What?"

"My – my first husband," she said. "He's a researcher at the observatory. We don't even really speak any more, but I don't want him to – I don't want..."

Runstom pinched his temples with one hand and tried to drive away the visions of the prisoner barge. There was no guarantee that Space Waste wouldn't harm anyone out there, whether there was cooperation or not. People were going to die. People were probably already dead.

He looked around at them. Leesen, Harrison, Polinsky; their wide eyes on him, just grasping that their formerly banal research compound was under attack. Troyo, glancing over each shoulder, the drive of a sale eclipsed by the drive for survival. The four privates, heads cocking and eyes narrowing, a cross of curiosity and caution, trained for this moment, but probably never expecting to need such training.

They should defend the city, that was the obvious choice. It was the sane choice, the safe choice. But Runstom knew the Wasters weren't coming that far. Why would they? The power outages, the panic. It was all so they could home in on their target. He didn't know what they wanted at the observatory, but he knew they would find it fast and then be gone. And they wouldn't spare any lives.

"Willis," Runstom said. "We need vehicles."

"Hey, man, I wish I could." Polinsky's voice was distant, frail. "But it's protocol."

"Surely you can override it," Leesen said. She sidled up to Runstom and he could feel her pushing her hopes onto his shoulders.

"It's VCP," he said helplessly.

"What's VCP?" Runstom asked.

"Guess our high-ranking consultant didn't do his homework," Scruffy muttered.

Runstom swallowed the urge to punch the kid. There hadn't been anything in the briefing documents about VCP. Had there? Had he missed something? So much of it had been irrelevant, he could barely stay awake reading it.

"Vulca City Protocol," the female private answered. "They got all their ground transports wired to it. Freakin' ridiculous, if you ask me. When it kicks in, like for an emergency, the cars come home but they can't go anywhere else."

"What about Captain Oliver and the others?" Runstom asked. "Are they stuck out there? Or will they be forced to drive back?"

Scruffy laughed. "Nah, man. Defense don't deal with that. We got our own rides."

"Are there any here?"

The privates frowned at each other, and the one standing said, "They're all out on patrol."

"So this protocol," Runstom said to the woman. "Private...?"

"Private Mikas, sir."

"Private Mikas. This VCP – how is it wired to the transports?"

"I think they do it at the garages whenever new vehicles

are brought in. It's an add-on to the standard navigation computers on all Sirius-5 built models."

"Alright," he said, thinking. "Alright. An add-on."

"Yeah, if they get it in there, it's pretty impossible to remove."

"If they get it in there." Runstom paced and then came upon the privates and faced them head on. "Defenders, I want you to go to your armory and get as many weapons as you can carry. Especially anything long-range. The louder and flashier the better. You got anything like that?"

"Well, not really," the standing private said.

"There's Billy," the unshaven one said, smiling.

"Oh right, Billy," the first said. "Ballistic Incendiary Long-range Explosive."

"Kinda heavy though," Scruffy said. "Especially without wheels."

Runstom leaned over him. "We're at point two five Gs on this moon, Defender. Is the weapon too heavy to get from your armory to the center of town?"

"Uh, I guess not..."

"Then bring it. And anything else you can carry. We'll find wheels there."

"This is crazy, Stanford," Troyo said. "What do you think you're going to do? Willy already said all the transports are locked down. And Private Whatserface said it's a city-wide protocol."

"Transports that have the add-on installed."

"Yeah, so? Where are you going to find any that don't have it? She said they all get it."

"It's not that hard, Peter," Runstom said. "We just need to find someone who doesn't obey the rules."

CHAPTER 9

The whole of Vulca City had plenty of space to stretch out under the low rows of hexagonal dome ceiling tiles. Most of the buildings were wide and short, and The Rambling Whistle was no exception. When Runstom had received his initial tour of the moon's facilities, the fairly good-sized tavern had stuck out in his mind as a possible escape from the drudgery of public relations, mainly because it had so many people coming and going, he knew no one would bother him if he found himself a corner to hide in. That and the Whistle had been the only place he'd seen on the tour that looked like it served a decent drink of any kind.

Inside, it looked much different than he expected. The rest of the town was so stark; all the buildings were a shade of gray, the lights were bright, there was always a dampened quiet, and everything was so sparse, and so clean. But here inside the Whistle, it was anything but those things. There were colorful paintings adorning the walls, so many of them they almost touched frame to frame, varying from abstract to photo-realistic. Music that seemed to sway between dreamy waves and punchy rock pulsed through the air like a heartbeat. It smelled real, a mix of cheap alcohol, cheap wooden furniture, and cheap clothing. And it was well attended, the chatter of a few dozen conversations mixing with the music like background percussion. It wasn't so packed that Runstom and Troyo couldn't move, but there were enough people to bump shoulders a few times on their way through the crowd. Among the majority, which were stout, light-skinned Sirius-fivers, Runstom noticed significant diversity in stature and skin color.

Not that he saw any green hues. Not that he ever did, even if he always caught himself looking. When he was a cop, scanning a crowd was taking stock: it helped to know where folks came from. Betelgeuse-3 dome. Barnard-3 dome. Barnard-4 dome. Sirius-5 dome. Terroneous. Poligart. A mining colony. An outpost. Even Earth. They all grew up somewhere. Unless their mother raised them on a ship. Always on the move. Never breathing an atmosphere. Never knowing sunrises or moon cycles. Artificial gravity exercise routines. Food from a tube.

When he was young, she wouldn't stay put. Couldn't stay put. Shadows on the horizon, ever closing. When he was old enough to fend for himself, she disappeared. Contact after that was on her schedule. Her prerogative.

He wasn't a cop any more. So scanning the crowd, taking stock, what purpose did it serve? What was he doing? Not a cop, but still trying to get to the bottom of a situation. Not a cop, but still butting heads with criminals. Not a cop, but still trying to protect people.

"Now what?" Troyo said, relieving Runstom of his swimming thoughts.

"We need to start talking to people."

"Okay." Troyo looked around. "Where do we start?"

"Just—" Runstom didn't know where to start. He needed people with vehicles. People who would have found a way around the Vulca City Protocol. The place had the feel of people who didn't fit the rest of the complex, that was certain. "Let me just think for a minute."

"Well, if we're going to stand around in a pub, I'm getting a drink."

Runstom followed Troyo up to the bar, where they found a pair of squat stools unoccupied. Troyo sat down in one and whistled over the din. For lack of any other direction for the moment, Runstom sat next to him.

The bartender was a broad, heavyset Sirius-fiver with only scraps of black hair lining the crown of his head. He waddled over to them and leaned across the bar. "Fellas. You two are new to town."

"Yeah, but not new to alcohol," Troyo said. "I'll have a gin and tonic."

"Gin, tonic. You?"

Runstom frowned and chased away the thought of how good a drink might taste. "Nothing for me."

"Fella, we're busy this morning. If you're not here to drink, get off the stool."

"Come on, have a drink, Stanford." Troyo flashed a card. "ModPol's buying."

He sighed. "Beer, please. Something light."

The bartender signaled to a woman behind the bar to pull the beer from a nearby tap while he went off to make Troyo's drink.

"Excuse me," Runstom said, leaning over the bar to address the woman. She was another Sirius-fiver – squat, but lean and muscular, dark hair drooping in curls around her face. “Is it usually this busy in here? It’s ten o’clock in the morning.”

“It’s the protocol,” she said, sliding his beer across the bar.

“The protocol? The VCP?”

“Yep, that’s the one. Half these people should be out working. The other half showed up because the lockdown seemed like a good excuse to drink.”

She walked away and he turned to Troyo. “I need to get everyone’s attention. There’s got to be a bunch of drivers here who have unlocked transports.”

“Then why aren’t they out driving them?”

“Well, then they would get caught.” Runstom sipped his beer and thought. “Right? They wouldn’t drive them unless they had to. No point in getting fined for violating the protocol for nothing.”

“More than fined,” the bartender said as he traded a drink for Troyo’s card. “Arrested.”

“Wait, that’s an expense account?” Runstom asked as the bartender took the card and waved it at the register behind the bar.

“Yeah, of course,” Troyo said. “You have a card, don’t you? You haven’t used it yet?”

He had been given a card, but no one really told him what constituted an expense. “They said I could buy clothes.”

Troyo leaned back in his stool to look Runstom up and down. “You haven’t even done that yet?”

“What, no – these are some of the clothes I bought.”

“Stanford,” Troyo said between sips of his cocktail, “you need to learn how to spend the company money.”

Runstom looked around the room briefly. He didn’t have

time to think about shopping and they didn't have time to sit around and drink. He needed to start talking, and he needed people to listen.

"Yeah, you're right, Peter." The bartender handed the ModPol expense card back to Troyo, and Runstom snapped it away and pointed it back out. "I'm going to start right now. Bartender – a round of drinks for everyone in here."

"Fella, you know how many people are in here?"

"Is there a limit on this thing?" Runstom asked Troyo.

He shrugged. "I haven't hit one yet. But I don't think this is going to help your cause."

"Do it," Runstom said to the bartender. "One condition, though. I need you to turn off the music."

"I don't know about that."

Runstom stood up and leaned over the bar. "Look. I just need a few minutes. A few minutes and everyone in the house gets a drink on me. And I'll put something extra on the card for the service."

The bartender studied him for a moment and then took the card. "Have it your way, fella."

"This isn't going to work, Stanley. You can't bribe these people with booze."

Still standing, Runstom looked down at Troyo. "It's Stanford."

The music stopped abruptly and after a moment, there was a collective groan of disapproval that continued to grow in volume.

"Listen up, folks." The bartender had a small microphone and his voice projected from the speaker system. "We've got a newcomer to The Rambling Whistle, and this fella claims he needs a few minutes of your time." The rumblings of the room amplified and Runstom looked around to see disapproval everywhere. "Now to make up for the interruption," the bartender continued, "this fella is buying everyone in the house a round."

The reaction was mixed, from muted celebration to sullen distrust. Whatever the case, he seemed to have their attention. The bartender handed him the microphone and Runstom looked out at the crowd. He was a bit taller than most Sirius-fivers, but not by enough. He took a deep breath, then stepped up onto his stool.

As he looked out over the sea of faces, now all turned on him, he decided to get quickly to the point. "Who here has heard of Space Waste?"

There were some low murmurs, and then someone called out, "Space Waste ain't real, ya dummy."

From the other side of the room an answer came: "They hell they aren't! My cousin's trawler was blinked by Space Waste."

Shouts and jeers popped up around the bar. "I wish they weren't real," Runstom said, overpowering the discourse with the speaker system. "I wish that I'd never seen what they can do. I wish I'd never seen them murder two dozen of my colleagues, along with as many passengers. But I have." He went quiet for a few seconds to make sure he had the pub's attention. "I wish I thought they were a story. But they're not. And I wish I didn't have to stand here right now and tell you that they're on Vulca."

At this, the crowd erupted into a mélange of fearful questions and distrusting dissent. He could hear the words *not real* bouncing around the room, balanced by the words *kill us*, the latter delivered in an anxious, higher pitch.

"Listen to me," he said, then had to repeat himself to regain the stage. "Listen to me. These Wasters, they're bloodthirsty, savage bastards. But they're just people. They act like animals. They think like animals. They only pick a fight when they know they can win. And like animals, they'll run from a fight they might lose."

A large man pushed his way to the front of the crowd. "What are you gonna do, huh?" His voice was rough, and his once-black hair was showing streaks of gray. He was too tall to be from Sirius-5. "You gonna buy them rounds of drinks until they run away?"

"No." Runstom looked at the man, then back out at the crowd. "They attacked the observatory. They aren't coming here. Understand? If they were coming here, they would have come here first. But they went there. They want something in that observatory, and when they get what they want, they're going to kill everyone there."

Another man pushed his way to the front, though with greater difficulty. He was thin and tall and he had the stark-white skin of a B-fourean. "My wife Linzi is out there," he said, looking from Runstom to the big man and back. "She does research at the observatory. You're saying they're going to kill her?"

Runstom wanted to answer in the affirmative, but looking the man in the eyes, the words stuck in his throat. "I can't promise they won't."

The big man looked at the B-fourean. "What does he know?" he said, waving a dismissive hand at Runstom.

"Hey, you're Officer Stanford Runstom." A small, red woman with a wire-laden, bowl-shaped device strapped to one side of her head appeared at the edge of the crowd. "I recognize you from HV. You're him, right?"

Runstom pursed his lips, then nodded slowly. "Yes. I'm Stanford Runstom."

More noise rippled through the pub, though this time it was little more than murmurs and whispers.

"Officer Runstom," the B-fourean said, raising his hand hesitantly. "My wife is out there. I – if there's the slightest chance of danger – well, I don't know what to say. I don't know what you plan to do, but I – I'm in."

"Poppin, don't be stupid—" the big man started.

"No, Koin, I'm going."

"What are you going to do?" the woman said, aiming her helmeted head at the B-fourean called Poppin. "Walk to the observatory? We all know VCP kicked in about an hour ago."

"Not every vehicle is locked down," Runstom said. The room mumbled and nearly all of its occupants began to glance left and right, expressions ranging from sheepish to paranoia-fueled nervousness. He put up a hand "It's okay. We aren't going to—"

"No," Troyo said suddenly. He was up, standing on his own stool, jabbing a finger out at the crowd. "It's not okay. It's against the law. We got a few protocols of our own." He turned to Runstom. "I say we go to every garage in this two-bit town and do an inspection."

Runstom put a hand up to the subsequent grumblings. "We don't have to do that."

"Come on, Koin," Poppin said. "You want them to impound that sweet rig of yours? I know you don't have the add-on."

"Damn it, Poppin. What the hell is wrong with you? Why would you tell them that?"

"Koin, we can save my wife's life." Poppin put a hand on the big man's shoulder and pleaded into his eyes. "And you get to keep your truck."

"We'll get ourselves all killed is what we'll do," the short woman said.

"I promise you, you won't have to engage them directly," Runstom said. "We just need vehicles. As many as we can get."

"Hey, do you think the Wasters knew about the protocol?" Troyo asked after slurping the last of his gin.

Runstom flinched and looked at him. He lowered the mic. "What?"

"Do you think—"

"Shit," he said. He closed his eyes. He needed to stay in the moment, but he also needed to reason it out. "If they knew…then they knew no one would come out if the power was cut."

From somewhere near the door, a voice floated over the crowd. "Hey Koin, Poppin. You guys. There's a couple dudes outside in camouflage, and I think they have…"

"What?" Koin shouted.

"I think they have a hovercart. Full of guns."

There was a surge toward the front windows, and it swept up Poppin but not Koin.

The short woman whistled. She was standing on a table looking out. "That is a lot of guns."

Runstom felt Koin staring up at him. "You said we're not going to engage."

"We're not," Runstom said. He stepped down off the stool to meet the other man face to face. "I figure, we ride out there at top speed, discharging our loudest, brightest weapons."

The big man's lips tightened and he gave a short nod. "You aim to scare 'em off."

Runstom felt his face go hot. Suddenly, his plan sounded

less heroic than he'd hoped. "Trust me, this is the best way out of this."

"I agree," Koin said, scratching at the stubble of his chin. "Tactically, it's a good move. Minimize losses on both sides, including civilians."

"Tactically," Troyo said with a short laugh as he slipped off his stool to join them.

Runstom looked at Troyo and then at Koin. "Have you served?"

He sighed deeply. "Yes. I was stationed at the outpost on Sirius-8 for twelve years. We fought off Waster raids on more than one occasion. And I agree with you: they know when to gun, and when to run."

"We'll be outnumbered and under-experienced," Runstom said. "But they don't know that. ModPol Defenders routed some Wasters from a power relay station only hours ago. Right now they're wondering how many more Defenders are on Vulca. So we really need to sell it. We need to be loud, and we need to kick up a lot of dust."

"Puff yourself up like an animal."

Runstom leaned in close. "I need your help."

Koin grunted and frowned. "I'm supposed to be retired."

"I'm supposed to be in Public Relations."

The big man's chest bounced with a short laugh. "Show me your armament."

Outside there was a growing crowd, and not just from the patrons of The Rambling Whistle; small packs of people were drifting down the street from three directions. The four privates seemed to drink in the attention from the civilians ogling their cart of destruction.

"Officer Runstom," one of the Defenders called when she saw him. "Just got a message from B Team."

"B Team?"

"The patrol that went east this morning. They're on their way here. ETA twelve minutes."

"They're coming here?" Troyo said. "Why?"

"When they got the message from Captain Oliver, they had orders to come back to town to secure the area."

"Good," Runstom said. "They're coming with us."

"Roger that," the private said.

He looked around at the milling crowd. "Where did all these people come from?" Runstom asked, not directing his question at anyone in particular.

"I got the word out." The short, red woman with the half-helmet device on her head appeared next to them. "Name's DAI, by the way."

"Die?" Troyo said.

"Not like die as in dead. It's D, A, I. My initials."

"What do they stand for?" Troyo pressed.

"Doesn't matter," she said, then tapped her helmet. "In my network, I'm DAI."

"These people," Runstom said. "Are in your network?"

"Yep. Most were just sitting around wondering what's up with the VCP lockdown."

"Are they going to help us? They have transports?"

"Yeah, some of them, I imagine." She shook her head lightly. "I still think you're going to get everyone killed."

"Then why'd you bring all these people?" Troyo asked.

She smiled broadly, closed her eyes, lifted her head, and sighed. "Only thing that beats the rush of being on the scene first when something big goes down? Being the one to make it big by inviting everyone else."

She spun around and dove into the crowd to do some of

the highest-speed mingling Runstom had ever seen. Troyo leaned into him. "She's a weird one."

Runstom nodded. "Grassroots media junkie. I've run into her kind before. When I was an officer. All they care about is their social reach. The bigger the story, the bigger the reach."

"Sounds like a pain in the ass."

"They are," Runstom said. "When you're an officer, they get in the way."

Troyo slapped him on the back. "And when you're a public relations officer, they're on your side."

* * *

The all-terrain vehicle tore across the bleak surface of the moon, the throttle cranked. They only managed to secure two of them, so Thompson and Barndoor had to share, and they were drifting farther behind, according to the crude radar screen. Dava couldn't verify this by sight because of the amount of cold dust that was kicking up behind her.

The naked atmosphere on Vulca wasn't bad enough to kill a person outright, but too much exposure and the toxicity would start to worm its way into the system. She and the others had already crossed the landscape on foot in the middle of the night, and now the thin air was stinging her eyes and nose. Through the blur of tears, she could see the observatory dead ahead.

And something else to the left. Some kind of storm on the northern horizon. She'd done a little research on the weather systems on Vulca while planning for her team's approach to the power relay station, and what she'd learned was that the moon was extremely mild weather-wise. Minimal winds, and due to a lack of major bodies of water, no precipitation. There was nothing about dust storms or anything of the like.

Whatever it was, it was on the move. She gritted her teeth, leaned forward, and pushed the throttle to its maximum.

She saw a couple of grunts standing watch outside the matte-gray walls of the observatory when she finally eased off on the ATV and let her stinging eyes clear. They raised their rifles in her direction for a moment, but quickly recognized her and lowered them. Even at a distance, her dark skin guaranteed little chance of mistaken identity.

When she got off the ATV, the grunts weren't even looking at her. Their attentions were focused on the northern horizon. One of them had binoculars and was lifting them, pulling them down, readjusting them, lifting them again.

"Some kind of dust storm?" she asked as she walked up.

"I don't think so, Capo Dava," the one without the binoculars said. She felt an internal twist at the formal use of rank. Jansen's influence was spreading through Space Waste like an infection. "Listen," the grunt said.

She listened and heard nothing. She stopped breathing. Then she heard it. A distant grumble. "Thunder?"

The grunt with the binoculars said, "Engines."

She pulled them away from his face and took a look. They were right. Vehicles in the distance, moving fast enough to kick up a serious amount of dust. She counted from left to right and could make out eight. She couldn't tell what they were, how big they were, or who they belonged to.

"Where's 2-Bit?" she asked, shoving the binoculars into the grunt's abdomen.

"Captain 2-Bit's somewhere inside. Probably up in the top where the target is."

"Raise him and tell him to get his ass down here."

"Capo Dava, we're supposed to be radio-silent—"

Dava took the grunt by the scruff and pulled him close. "Raise him. Now."

"Y-yes, sir." She released him and he pulled out his comm. "Captain 2-Bit. Come in, Captain."

The reply crackled through after a few seconds. "Who the hell is this? I ordered radio silence."

"Give me that," Dava said. The comm was on a short wire to the grunt's suit, so when she yanked it out of his hands, he was forced to lean into her as she put the device to her ear. "Captain 2-Bit. It's Dava. We need you out front."

"Dava? What's going on? The power went out, so I thought we were a go."

"Just get out here, Captain." She released the comm and when the grunt regained his composure, she asked him, "How long have they been inside?"

"About thirty minutes?"

"Have they loaded anything out?"

"Not yet, but someone came out just a few minutes ago to tell us they'd be loading soon."

2-Bit came out of the building just as Thompson rolled up on the other ATV, Barndoor sitting behind her.

"We ready to roll?" Thompson said. "To go back for Johnny and Frank?"

"What's this about Johnny and Frank?" 2-Bit said.

"Captain." Dava took him by the shoulder and pointed him to the north. "Look."

2-Bit squinted. "Some kinda storm?" She took the binoculars from the grunt and gave them to the captain. He looked at her and cocked his head, then used them to look to the horizon. "What the hell is this?"

"Trouble."

"Local defense force?"

"I don't know," she said. "But ModPol showed up at the power relay station."

2-Bit dropped the binoculars. "What? Are you sure?"

"They took Johnny Eyeball and Freezer," Thompson said.

"And I got shot," Barndoor added, holding his bad arm up with his good arm. The sticky bandage oozed a blend of red and white. He swung a leg around to dismount the ATV and almost lost his balance.

2-Bit looked back out at the approaching storm. "More ModPol?"

Dava shook her head. "I'm not sure. It's hard to tell."

"They aren't supposed to be here," Thompson said. "Boss Jansen said—"

"Forget about what *under*boss Jansen said," Dava spat. "They're here. ModPol is here. In force."

"How many were at the relay station?" 2-Bit asked.

"Had to be a dozen," Barndoor said.

"We took a few out," Thompson said, pulling the ammo drum out of her gun to check it. "And Johnny is probably giving them all kinds of hell right now."

"I think those are civilian transports." One of the grunts had retrieved the binoculars. "Hard to tell, but they all look different colored."

"The ModPol vehicles at the relay station were armored and camoed," Thompson said. "Those military types. Fenders."

"Oh, yeah," the grunt said, still looking through the lens. "I think there might be one or two camoed trucks in the pack."

"I don't like this, Captain," Dava said. "We need to pack up and get out of here."

"What? Retreat?"

"Captain, we've been ambushed. And we're about to get ambushed again."

"This is the best score we've had in ages," 2-Bit said. "RJ said—"

"Fuck RJ," Dava said. The reaction from the rest of the group was restrained, as though everyone knew it was wrong for a squad leader to disrespect an underboss, but it wasn't like Space Waste was a real military outfit. And very few dared cross her, regardless of rank. "He was wrong about everything. Did you even find the equipment that was supposed to be here?"

"Yeah," 2-Bit said quietly. "We think so."

"You think so." She sighed through gritted teeth. "Well, ModPol is on Vulca. We *know* so. And we came here expecting *local security*. So does that make us prepared for this fight?"

"Prepared?" 2-Bit's face began to redden and his voice took on a rare acidity. "Listen to me, Capo. We don't run from fucking Pollies. We shoot fucking Pollies."

"Fenders," Thompson grunted. When 2-Bit looked at her, she said, "Told ya, ain't Pollies. Fenders. That's how come Barndoor got shot through the arm instead of just stunned."

"We shoot Fenders too," 2-Bit said, but with much less gusto.

Dava waved at the growing clouds in the distance. "We don't have a lot of time here. Who or whatever that is out there is about to ruin our party. If we got what we came for, we need to move."

"What about Johnny?" Thompson said. "And Frank?"

There was an audible crack then from the distance, and they all stopped to look. A thin trail of white smoke drew its way up the pale morning sky, then began to fatten in reverse.

"Is that – a missile?" one of the grunts whispered.

They all dove for cover. The closest solid object to Dava was an ATV, and she found herself behind it, moving on instinct, but regretting in her conscious mind the fragility of her chosen shield. She peeked up over the front fender to see the projectile in the distance. Coming head on, it was hard to tell how far it was, but then it hit the ground suddenly, a good hundred meters distant. The resulting fireball was massive, a pure white sun exploding in her eyes before she ducked back behind the ATV.

"What the fuck was that?" Barndoor yelled as the rumble died down.

"It's a Billy," 2-Bit shouted from the side of the observatory. "Nasty bastard."

"It didn't come anywhere near us," Thompson said as they all tentatively poked their heads from their hiding places. "Hey, Barndoor, someone out there is a worse shot than you!"

"Fuck you, Thompson!"

"Captain," Dava said. "It's time to pull back and regroup."

2-Bit was talking into his comm, then he finally called back out. "The shuttle is due south. I just checked with them and they aren't seeing anything down there. We can hold this ground until we know what we're up against."

"Wait, you guys, shut up," Barndoor shouted. "Listen!"

The rumbling of distant engines was augmented by higher-pitched popping. Dava squinted into the horizon. The vehicles were close enough to make out with the naked eye. All around them, tiny pops of white appeared. Muzzle flashes.

"Well, the vehicles might not be military, but the weapons are," Thompson said.

"Fuck this," Barndoor said. "I'm with Dava – let's get the hell out of here. I don't want to get shot again for at least a week."

Dava flitted across the open air and slid into a space next to Captain 2-Bit by the observatory wall. "With all due respect," she said, "Jansen's intel was wrong. But that doesn't mean he would want us to get killed out here. He would want us to cut our losses and pull out. I mean, you can always get the shuttle to relay a message to him, if you want to wait around for him to respond."

She knew he wouldn't, not because of the time it would take, but because that would mean letting the absent under-boss make a decision about an operation in progress. Captain 2-Bit was old school. If he was in charge of a mission, he had to make the choice of when to gun and when to run.

2-Bit sighed. He lifted his comm. "Alpha Team: get as much of that gear as you can carry into the trucks and be prepared to leave. We're evacing in five minutes. Anyone not on a truck in five minutes is getting left on this dustball." He frowned and looked at Dava. "Satisfied?"

She looked out at the growing storm of dust, the sparkle of gunfire glittering across it, then her gaze drifted to the west, where the relay station lay.

"Sorry, Johnny," she whispered.

CHAPTER 10

The first thing Lealina noticed when she came through the door was the flashing number four on the screen just to the left of the TEOB sign that spread across the top of the opposite wall. Below the flashing number were three status screens lined up vertically, and each of those was marred red by some warning she couldn't make out from a distance. Instead, she looked at the map under the TEOB sign. The map – the largest feature of the room, displaying a flattened projection of all of Terroneous, largest moon of gas giant Barnard-5 – had become nothing but wallpaper to her over the last four years. Occasionally, it presented a blip here or there – a spike in weather or an equipment malfunction – but she'd never seen it complain about more than a single event at any given time. As the door closed behind her and took the glare of the morning sun with it, she watched four small circles pulse steadily at various locations around the map.

"Riky, what's going on?"

The young operator on duty spun his chair halfway to

face her. "Oh, Lealina. Good, you're here." He spun back to face the smaller monitors that curved around the half-circle console.

"Four alarms?" She stepped closer to lean over his shoulder, trying to take in all the panels at once and failing to assimilate anything useful. "Another gas pocket?"

They both looked up at the flicker of movement when the looming number four was replaced by a five.

"Damn," Riky breathed. He scratched at both of his dark arms, one followed by the other. "No, not a gas pocket. Magnetic."

"What, really? We've never had one of those. Have we?"

"I've never seen one." The comm on the side wall lit up, flashing white and jangling its jingle. "Can you get that, Lea?"

She crossed the room and tapped at the comm and the small image of a gray-haired woman appeared. She was too short for the unit on her side and the top of her head ballooned as she angled it up.

"Terroneous Environment Observation Bureau," Lealina said, but the woman started talking over her halfway through.

"Hello? Hello! This is Kay Klosky at the Stockton Public Library. One of those...thingies...is making all kinds of racket."

"Yes, ma'am," Lealina said, glancing back at Riky. He pointed to a screen at his console but she couldn't see it from her angle. He stuck up a thumb, then went back to his keyboard. "We can see that one of your sensors is in an alarm state. Rest assured, we're looking..."

She trailed off as the librarian cocked her head and turned away from her. She disappeared from the window, and Lealina could hear muffled conversation.

"What...where?...cross the...bank? Oh my."

"Six," Riky called from behind her. She turned and stared at the counter as if she didn't believe it could go that high.

"What's happening?" The librarian's panicked voice brought Lealina's attention back to the comm.

"We're looking into it ma'am," she said. "I have to go now. We have your contact information and we'll let you know as soon as we know more."

"But—"

Lealina flicked off the comm and went back to the console. "Are the others..." she started, then leaned over again to try to make sense of the middle-right panel.

"All magnetic," Riky said, pointing at what she could already see. Six lines stacking up, all of them alarms on magnetic sensors.

Colonizing strange moons was never a sure bet, even after decades of surveying and preparation. Although Terroneous was as close to Earth as anyone might hope, there were always dangers to be on alert for, and having been born and raised on this moon, Lealina was as indoctrinated as any local on the perils of such threats. The Terroneous Environment Observation Bureau kept an eye on the most deadly possibilities: rising solar radiation, seismic activity, volcanic fissure vents, pockets of gas appearing just below the surface, and changes in the atmospheric mix, to name a few.

They also tracked fluctuations in the geomagnetic field.

"It's got to be a localized disturbance of some kind," Lealina said, shaking her head. She looked up at the map, the blips refusing to congeal into a pattern. "But they're not localized."

"They're not even all in the same city," Riky said, tapping

sharply and then pointing at the center screen. The circles on the map grew larger as he zoomed in and panned around it. "Three in Stockton. Two over here in Nuzwick. One all the way up at the d-mail station. One here in the Low Desert."

"That's seven."

They looked at the counter. It was already at seven, and they hadn't noticed. It changed to eight before Lealina's eyes. Riky silently tapped at the keyboard, and the map expanded to reveal the newest pulsing red dot, far to the east.

"They're all over the place." The operator pushed his chair away from the console and stood, still staring at the screens. "What does that mean, Lealina? We never get magnetics."

"It means we need data. We need to know how strong the flux is."

The comm rang again but she ignored it. "I'll get it," Riky said after it went unanswered for several tense seconds. He got up and went to the wall while she stared at the map. Three more red circles appeared. She felt transfixed, hypnotized by the patternless events, surprised at herself for not being able to panic. All of the events were magnetics. There was only one explanation.

Riky came back. "That was the research outpost in Low Desert. I told them we're looking into it." He paused, then added, "What are we looking into here?"

"Shit, Riky," she said. "I think this is bad."

"What could it be?"

The comm rang again and this time they both ignored it.

She swallowed, tried to make sense of the numbers. They were bottoming out. "It looks like we're losing it."

"Losing it? What's *it*?"

"The magnetic field."

"What?" Riky took her arm to pull her eyes away from the screens. "What does that mean, Lea?"

She stared at him for a moment before registering his face. "One of the things that makes Terroneous such a perfect moon to live on: the magnetic field. It protects us from solar radiation. Makes it so we don't have to live in domes."

"How could we be losing it?"

She shook her head. "Back on Earth, they knew that throughout the planet's history the magnetic field had flipped. North became south. It was extremely rare, but...devastating. We've always known that the magnetic field here on Terroneous was a little on the unstable side; one of the reasons we monitor it so closely."

Riky's voice squeaked. "Are we going to die?"

She closed her eyes and tried to breathe slowly. The comm continued to ring. "No. We don't know anything yet. We need more data."

"How much time do we have?"

"We have time. These systems are designed for early warning. We just have to be sure. Worst case, we'll have to evacuate the planet."

"God damn," Riky breathed.

"Let's hope it doesn't come to that," she said. "It probably won't. Just keep watching the monitors. I'm going to set an auto-reply on that comm. Everyone on the moon is going to be calling."

* * *

"Greetings. You have reached the Terroneous Environment Observation Bureau. We are aware that many people are reporting alarms on some of their local sensors. We are very sorry for the inconvenience. We are investigating the root cause of the problem and we will be dispatching technicians as soon as we are able...You don't need to contact us, we will contact you. Thank you."

The screen on the comm phone was only a few inches in size, but the picture was clear. The woman's skin was a reddish pink, her hair was light brown and cropped short, and her eyes were a bright blue, with a warmth that he'd never seen before, though they shined with wetness. Her smile was nice, but it wavered. Even through a recording playback on a tiny screen, he could sense her unease.

"She's very pretty," Librarian Kay said. "Don't you think, Mr. Fugere?"

Jax felt his face warm and he pulled away from the image, which had frozen at the end of the message.

"Oh, don't tease him," Librarian Elle said. "The Bureau is practically on the other side of the moon."

"Hush, Elle. Love can find its way around a tiny moon."

"Love? It's a bloody recording!" Elle shook her head, then added, "In any case, you heard the girl. Nothing to worry about."

"Nothing to worry about," Kay muttered. "What about the blasted noise the thing is making? This is a library!"

The sensor located behind the counter continued the relentless series of beeps that had started up twenty minutes ago and refused to quit. Jax didn't recognize the model and the librarians didn't seem to know anything about what it was there for, only that the TEOB had installed it about a year ago and told them it was important.

"Librarians," Jax interrupted. "Do you mind if I have a look?"

They looked at each other. "Oh, I don't know," Kay said. "We're not supposed to let anyone back here. And the Bureau put that thing in and said not to touch it."

"Kay – Mr. Fugere has been coming here almost every day for weeks now. He's our best patron and probably the smartest person in Stockton."

"Thank you." Jax would have blushed at her flattery, but there was already plenty of heat in his cheeks from their comments about the girl in the recording. "But I'm not really – look, how about I just take a quick look. I won't touch anything."

They looked at each other again, Elle nodding. Kay sighed. "Okay, Mr. Fugere," she said, then smiled mischievously. "Maybe you'll find an excuse to talk to that lovely girl at the Bureau."

"Oh, Kay," Elle said, shaking her head and opening the gate to let Jax behind the counter.

It was true, he had been coming to the library every day since he discovered it. David Granderson had brought him into town, and Jax had helped him calibrate a pair of new camera-hoverbots that "fell off the back of a truck" somewhere and he needed to "put to good use", or so the story went. The hoverbots were slightly used, but with a trip to the library for some old manuals and a couple of resets, Jax was able to get them to sync up with the source camera system. He had to admit, the resulting film was much better at capturing all three dimensions as the bots rotated around objects in response to the source system's tracking. It felt good to fix something, and he felt an immediate attachment to the library.

After he'd gotten Granderson's camera-bots working, the documentarian had paid him just enough to cover a month's rent in the cheapest building in town: something between a short-term apartment and a long-term hotel. It was a roof and four walls and nothing more. Jax had no idea he could be so content with so little. But it was shelter. It wasn't what he wanted to call *home*, but it was the closest he'd had in – how long had it been? He'd lost track. Stopped counting the months. Stopped counting the days between meals. Knowing where he was going to sleep at night did something to him, something inside that he had a hard time understanding. It gave him a piece of his humanity back, something he hadn't known he'd lost all that time on the move.

Obviously he had no extra money for enjoying himself around town in any true sense of the word *entertainment*; no holofilms, no pubs, no game halls, not even any art galleries or museums. The library, however, was open to the public and didn't charge unless he checked something out and took it home. To save money, he usually did his reading on the premises.

More than the free entertainment (such as it was), Jax liked coming to the library for a sense of order. He didn't allow himself to regret coming to Terroneous, but the moon's townships were, well, *settled*, as opposed to *engineered*. Growing up in the domes, everything made so much sense to him; everything was somewhere it was supposed to be, because someone deliberately put it there. In a town like Stockton, the buildings and streets grew like plants; they wound around themselves, going where they needed to go, when they needed to go there. The library was the one place Jax could go and unwind whenever the chaos got to be too much. It was a grid, it was organized, hell it was even catalogued. It was worth putting up with the paper books to enjoy the architecture and the systematic filing.

The librarians stood behind him – looking over their own shoulders more than his – as he took a closer look at the device mounted on the wall. It was a console of some kind, not much larger than the comm unit. It was flat and white, and there were a handful of lights along the top, one a steady green and one blinking red. Below them there was a panel that his fingers itched to pry open, but he kept himself in check. He promised the librarians he'd only look, not touch, and he really didn't want to get on their bad side.

There were two cables coming out of the top of the device. One, black and thin, ran off to the side and he suspected it was for power. The other, blue and thicker, ran up and disappeared into the ceiling.

"Any idea where that goes?" he asked.

"Oh, right," Elle said. "There's a bit that went up on the roof. Like an antenna or something."

"And a dish," Kay added. "An antenna and a little satellite dish."

"I see," Jax said. At the top of the device's front panel was the logo for Pulson Integrated Sensor Systems, Inc., and there was an alphanumeric code running along the bottom. He pulled out his notepad and jotted it down. "I'll see what I can find out."

He left them and found a nearby terminal to look up manuals for Pulson Integrated Sensor Systems equipment, realizing with sudden dismay the manufacturer's unfortunate acronym. He shook his head and pawed through search results until he found a section that looked useful. The manuals all started with three letters, and the model number he'd written started with MFS. He made a note of which section he wanted and got up.

"Mr. Fugere, Mr. Fixer!"

He flinched and saw Lonny Chen, one of the local livestock raisers. "Hey, Lonny."

"Man, I was hoping to find you here," Chen said. "You know that stat-monitor you helped me get set up a few weeks ago?"

"Yeah, of course." It was a LyfStat brand monitor, originally designed for short-term (nursery) or long-term (elderly) care; at least, that's what it would have been used for on Barnard-3 or Barnard-4. Somehow Chen had gotten a hold of one and was told it would be good for monitoring his livestock, which were some kind of small herd animal that produced edible eggs as well as milk. Jax couldn't remember what they were called.

"It was working great for a while. It even helped me spot a sick kibu before she infected the others."

"Kibu," Jax said, mostly to himself so that he would remember the name of the animal. "Glad to hear it."

"Yeah, so, uh, anyway," Chen said, bowing his head sheepishly. "I was showing off the monitor to my buddy Gary, and I guess I got too excited and hit the wrong button. Now it doesn't work. It's all locked up or something."

Jax frowned. "Probably just needs a reset." He looked around briefly. "Did you really come here to find me?"

Chen looked up hopefully. "Of course. You're always here, and if you're not, the librarians usually know where you went off to. So you can take a look at it?"

Jax allowed himself to turn his mouth back up into a grin: he was officially a regular. "Yeah, I can look at it. Do you still have the manual we checked out?"

He shook his head. "No, I brought it back here after you set everything up."

"Okay." All kinds of equipment like Chen's LyfStat monitor showed up on Terroneous. No one questioned where it came from, and it was usually last-gen, but it was obvious that none of the locals really knew how to use the stuff. It was as strange to them as the kibu were to Jax. The upside was that it gave him some value around this place. He was pretty useless when it came to laboring of any kind – gardening, building, even cleaning – but he could figure out just about any piece of equipment originally meant for B-3 or B-4, especially with access to a well-stocked library. He waved his notebook. "I still have the info written down, I can grab the manual and bring it by a little later."

Chen smiled widely. "Thank you so much, Fugere-the-Fixer! Hey, I'll get you some credit at Bonnie's store. She just got in a batch of that dark ale. I know you love that stuff."

Bonnie was Chen's second cousin and she owned a very non-specialized store that carried everything from food to tools to clothes. "That sounds great, Lonny," Jax said. His background as an operator was more than just useful; it was a way to make a living. He didn't know how much he should be charging people, but they were always grateful and he often got cash or trade that was enough to keep him going from day to day. There were a few things he needed from Bonnie's store, and he almost thought he should go with Chen right then and earn his credit. But something about the oddity of this sensor alarm tugged at him. That and a vision of the brightest blue—

"Great, great. So when do you think you'll come by?"

Jax blinked and looked at him. The faint beeping of the

sensor alarm was beginning to blend in with the atmosphere. It was probably no big deal, and the woman in the message *had* said they would send someone out. He thought it might be better to take the paying job and leave the interesting job alone. "You know what? I was just about to pick up another manual, so let's grab that and the one for your LyfStat and then we'll head over to your place and get that monitor reset."

CHAPTER 11

Runstom followed Troyo down a series of greenish-blue hallways until they arrived at a conference room, where they stopped just outside the door.

"Hold on," Troyo said in a low voice, putting a hand on Runstom's chest. "This is almost there. We just need to give it a nudge to nail this deal."

"Seems pretty straightforward to me," Runstom said. "They came under attack. They have no defense."

The events of the previous day flooded into his mind. He'd been so spiked on adrenaline, unable to process them fully, even later in the evening when he calmed down with a few celebratory drinks. In the cold gray of morning, he couldn't believe it had even worked. They'd only gathered a handful of vehicles, and their arsenal was sparse. But somehow they'd managed to kick up enough dust and noise and flash to send Space Waste running for their dropship. Runstom had driven the lead rover, and somehow found a balance – they'd gone fast enough to appear as a threat, but not so fast as to actually engage the gangbangers. If his enemy had gotten a good look at the hodgepodge force, they would have hunkered down in the observatory and turned it into a real, bloody fight. But his gambit paid off. They ran.

"Yeah, it does seem that way," Troyo said. "But we still need a little finesse here. Not everyone is sold."

"No? Like who?"

Troyo leaned in. "Willy, for one. His security team looks like the failure here. He's going to look for ways to redirect the blame. Rhonda, I'm not so sure about. She's always distrusted ModPol. And Dr. Leesen – well, she's always been skeptical."

"You don't think an attack on her research team will change her mind?"

Troyo nodded. "If it did, that helps our case big time. We need her on our side."

Runstom looked at the door and caught himself adjusting his jacket. Troyo had insisted on treating him to a shopping trip that morning, and he was wearing what the account rep would consider classy clothing, but to Runstom it was uncomfortable and too bright. "Let's get this over with," he said.

"One more thing," Troyo said. "I know you have this bad habit of telling the truth. I need you to follow my lead, and anytime something needs uh – a little spin – you leave it to me."

"What, why? What part of what happened needs a spin?"

Troyo gave him a stern look. "Stanford, you armed a bunch of civilians. And it worked. I mean, thankfully none of them got shot, but it's not great for us."

"Oh." He hadn't felt good at all about the danger he'd put the civilians in. But he wondered if that was what Troyo was getting at. "Why not?"

"Stan," Troyo said, again leaning close. "We don't want them to get any ideas about defending themselves." He paused, and as Runstom's own mind birthed the question that maybe they should defend themselves, Troyo seemed to read it on his face and answered. "They'd end up getting killed. We're the specialists. We handle this shit. That's what we're selling."

Runstom sighed and nodded. It was the ModPol mission: protect people so that those people could live their lives without violence and warfare. "Okay," he said.

Troyo's trademark smile sprang to life. "Let's close this baby."

The conference room was another one of those completely circular spaces, with walls so white and no place for shadows to lurk. It was like standing in empty space, and it made Runstom's stomach lurch. The drinking he'd engaged in the previous night along with half the city of Vulca didn't help his state. He was determined not punish himself over it; it'd been a long time since he had a reason to celebrate.

Already present were Willis Polinsky and Rhonda Harrison, sitting next to each other at the large round table in the middle. Troyo pulled a chair opposite them and gestured for Runstom to sit, then sat next to him.

"Good afternoon, Willy, Rhonda," he said. "How are we all doing?"

"Okay, Pete," Polinsky said.

"Fine," Harrison said. They both wore wary expressions. "Dr. Leesen will be here any minute."

"Great," Troyo said with a smile. "I believe Captain LJ will be joining us as well."

Fortunately, they didn't have to sit in the uncomfortable silence for long. Leesen came in with a stocky Sirius-fiver man with black-specked white hair and a large bandage under one eye. They were both wearing white lab coats, as if the debriefing of the attack on their research station was just another meeting interrupting their otherwise normal workday.

"Hello, everyone," Leesen said. "This is Dr. Contrellis."

She led him around the circle to exchange pleasantries with Polinsky and Harrison, and when she was on the opposite side of the table from Runstom, Troyo leaned in and said through his smile, *Ex-husband.*

As the researchers took their seats, Captain Oliver came in, with Lt. Cato following her. "Sorry we're late," she said. She glanced sideways at Runstom, then looked quickly away when he met her eyes. She and Cato sat down, and he noticed her arm was in a sling. "Let's get started."

"Great, let's," Troyo said. "Now I think we can all agree what happened here yesterday was a near-tragedy. Fortunately, losses were mitigated—"

"Hold on a minute, Peter," Rhonda said, a hand in the air. "I want some questions answered before we start talking about how great ModPol is."

Troyo's smile shrank, but did not disappear. "Of course. Ask away."

"Our power grid is designed very specifically for redundancy," she said, making slow chopping motions as though she were measuring something out. "Power flows two ways, in a circle. Break the ring, and power still flows the other way."

"But that's not what happened," Leesen said. "The observatory lost power."

"Exactly," Harrison said. "There was a specific failsafe that protected the town from losing power in the event of catastrophic failure. But the scenario that triggers that fail-safe is very obscure. I didn't even know it would do that."

"But it did," Leesen said, her eyes cold on Harrison. "Whether you knew it could or not."

Harrison frowned. "What I mean is that we've never seen the system do that. We've dealt with all kinds of power issues here. There's not a true grid like you get back plan-etside. The ring is more delicate. And yet we've never had it do this."

"Well, that's certainly interesting," Troyo said. "Is there a question?"

"Yeah, there's a goddamn question." The chopping hand slapped the table. "How the hell did Space Waste know how to trip that failsafe?"

"What makes you think they knew?" Runstom asked. When she shot him a glare, he coughed politely. "If you don't mind sharing, it sounds like you've got more than a hunch about it."

Her narrowed eyes softened slightly. "We're running an audit on the system at the power relay station right now. We don't have all the data, but it looks very bizarre. Like it's been tampered with."

"The data?"

"The system."

Runstom got out his notepad. "Tampered with – you mean, as of yesterday morning."

"That's right. Like I said, we're still collating, but at a first pass, it looks like everything started to go funny some-time after 9:00AM."

"The alarm came in from the relay station at 9:07AM," Runstom read, then looked up at Polinsky. "According to Willis."

"So Space Waste caused the power issues," Troyo said. "Let's just assume."

"I don't like to assume," Leesen said.

"Okay," Troyo said. "Let's say that hypothetically, they did." Leesen's facial reaction indicated she didn't care much for hypotheticals either, but she let Troyo continue. "It just goes to show what kind of threat this facility was facing yesterday. These are organized, lethal criminals. And if it weren't for—"

"I want numbers," Leesen said.

"Uh," Troyo fumbled. "I beg your pardon?"

"I want to know how many people died. How many were injured. What the damage was, and what equipment was stolen."

"I've got some people working on the damage assessment," Harrison said quietly. "I can give you an estimate later today."

"How many died?" Leesen's question silenced the room.

"At the relay station," Polinsky started timidly, his face suddenly buried in his handypad, "there was seven guards killed and three wounded. Plus three non-combat personnel were injured."

"And at the observatory?"

Polinsky looked up briefly and swallowed, then back to his handypad. "Five guards were killed. There were six more on duty, and they got pretty banged up but nothing more. One non-combat personnel has a concussion from getting hit in the head and two others are suffering from substantial cuts and contusions after trying to engage. Several minor scrapes and bruises for the others, but nothing else serious."

"We lost two Defenders at the relay station," Oliver said coldly, her voice loud in comparison to Polinsky. She leaned back and her slinged arm rested against her chest. "And six wounded."

The room went quiet for a moment, and Runstom dipped his head and stared at his hands. The thought of those people dying, that they never expected to have to deal with monsters like Space Waste – even the guards were unprepared for the slaughter. It wasn't fair.

"Dr. Contrellis works at the observatory," Leesen said, cutting through the silence. "Can you please tell us what was taken, Doctor?"

Contrellis cleared his throat. "Yes, of course. They – the attackers – they kept asking us for this detection equipment. Scanning equipment. I didn't know exactly what they wanted. All of our equipment does detection of some kind. They said they wanted to be able to scan for ships. We don't have anything like that."

At this point, Contrellis seemed to struggle for a moment, trying to find his voice. "It's okay, Jordan," Leesen said. "Take your time."

"I'm sorry," he said. "I've never dealt with anything like this. They – they roughed some of us up. We just didn't know what they wanted. Finally one of them said that we had radiation scanners – something that could scan warp-drive exhaust. None of us know anything about spaceships. We're astronomers and astrophysicists."

"But they took something?" Leesen prodded.

"Yes. We – I just got so scared. Afraid they were going to hurt someone, really hurt someone. We just got this new equipment that measures radiation. We use it to study background radiation and search for anomalies, and it helps us detect solar activity from Sirius A and B. Traffic control uses that data."

"Wait, they took the new modules?" Leesen said, suddenly stiffening. "Do you know how much those things cost us?"

"No, no," he said. "We had the old modules still there. We'd just removed them to install the new ones last week. We had put the old ones in the new packaging so we could send it back planetside to be recycled. So..."

"So you gave them the old equipment and told them it was new," Runstom said.

"Yes." Contrellis looked worried, like he'd done something wrong.

"Oh, Jordan," Leesen said, her hands to her mouth. "That's brilliant!"

"Bravo!" Troyo added with a clap.

"Could they actually use that equipment to scan for drive exhaust?" Runstom asked. "Since it can detect radiation?"

"Yes," Leesen said. "But it's outdated. The precision and range is no better than any scanners that come stock on most spacecraft. Plus you'd need the system to run it. The software is half the cost."

"They didn't go anywhere near the system itself," Contrellis said. "I figured they had their own software."

"That seems unlikely," Leesen said. "But I won't pretend to know anything about these criminals or their resources."

"Something else." Contrellis closed his eyes and swallowed a few times. "They were loading the equipment up and they forced us to gather in the garage. They made us kneel."

The room grew quiet. "Why would they do that?" Leesen asked tentatively.

"They were going to execute them," Oliver said firmly.

The others gasped and Contrellis opened his eyes, a single tear escaping. He pointed at Runstom. "He ran them off.

He saved us." He stood and looked at Runstom, clasping his hands together. "I've heard of you before, Officer Runstom. From the HV, about how you solved that murder case. You are a hero. I owe you my life, sir."

"Well, I don't—" Runstom tried to say.

"Yes!" Troyo exclaimed. "That's precisely why we brought Stanford to Vulca. He is a hero, and ModPol is in the business of creating heroes. And even though this facility suffered a terrible, tragic attack, I think we can all agree that it would have been much worse without the trial ModPol Rapid Onsite Defense Unit."

The room didn't erupt into agreement, but the reserved silence that followed indicated that at the very least, there would be no disagreement. Contrellis composed himself and found his seat. Polinsky and Harrison glanced at each other, as if to gauge whether a pre-agreed stance of obstinacy was still in effect, but neither said a word.

Leesen put her hands together. "Okay. Mr. Runstom. Captain Oliver. We are in your debt. Mr. Troyo, send me your quote and I will present a budget to the finance committee."

Troyo's smile went from ear to ear. "Absolutely, Dr. Leesen."

* * *

When they got up to leave, Runstom caught Oliver by the arm. "Can you spare a moment?" he said in a low voice.

She nodded shortly and they hung back as the others filtered out of the round room. Lt. Cato stood there smiling and waiting, and Oliver dismissed him.

"Yes, sir," he said, then turned to Runstom. "I just wanted

to say that it was an honor to work with you yesterday, Mr. Runstom."

"You as well, Lieutenant."

Cato left and Runstom shut the door. "He talked about you all night," Oliver said, pulling off her cap and moving an inch closer. "I got a first-hand account of everything that happened once his patrol returned to Vulca City and caught up with your...posse."

Runstom nodded slowly. "He's a good Defender."

"What would you have done if Space Waste fought back?" Her question was phrased as a challenge, but her tone carried a level of curiosity.

"It was a gamble," he admitted. "I honestly don't know. We probably would have retreated at the first sign of return fire."

She huffed in amusement. "I can't believe you wasted our only Billy."

"You only had one?"

"This is – was – a trial unit."

"Right," Runstom said. He walked to the table and leaned against it. He wanted answers, but he knew aggression would only close her down. "You were out on patrol that morning. Was that part of the trial?"

She looked at him warily. "We only have twenty-four Defenders here. The trial is just a show. Get dressed up, strut around the facility, get introduced to as many people as possible. We did a small patrol a few weeks ago, but that was really just so we could get a sense of the layout."

"So yesterday was...unusual."

She frowned and looked away. "I had orders."

He wanted to curse at her, to shake her, to demand to know why her orders were not also his orders, because they were both ModPol, they were all ModPol. He took a breath and said, "I wish you had shared them."

"They were very specific, Stanford. They were not to be shared."

"You were ordered not to share them."

"I wanted to, if you want to know the truth." He looked up at her and she shrugged. "I mean, I almost just told you anyway. But we'd just gotten them that morning, and my lieutenants were with me. They knew the orders were Defender-eyes-only, and I didn't want to disobey them in front of everyone."

He tried to read her eyes. He was never great at spotting a lie, especially when it came to women, but he decided to believe her. "It's okay, I guess."

"Now I wish I had just told you."

"The orders only came in that morning?" He resisted pulling out his notebook. "And all they said was to do a patrol?"

"That was it, pretty much. Normally our patrols are smaller, but they said to take as many as possible."

"And by coincidence your patrol came upon Space Waste at the relay station."

She stared at him in silence for a moment. "I'm sorry, Stanford. I don't ask these kinds of questions. That's why I'm good at what I do."

He sighed and nodded. "I saw in the report that you took two prisoners. They weren't identified."

She frowned. "Yes, but now they're not prisoners, they're criminals."

He thought about her words for a moment. "Justice?"

She nodded. "Your old friends are going to pick them up and ship them off to Barnard for a quick trial."

"I'm surprised Defense doesn't want to try to get some information out of them."

"Like I said, Stanford: I don't ask those kinds of questions."

"Right." Which left him alone to ponder why Defense would kick prisoners of war over to Justice for criminal proceedings. Maybe it was a sign of the dual halves of ModPol attempting to get along. He put it at the back of his mind and pointed at her arm. "How bad is it?"

She looked down at it. "Caught a round in the forearm. Cracked a bone. They got me all patched up, local anesthetic and all that, so it's not so bad." She looked up at him. "No patrols for me for a few weeks, anyway."

"You didn't expect to get stuck here on Vulca, did you?"

She laughed then, out loud. "Yeah, I guess this place is going to be home for a while. Honestly, I didn't think you and that idiot Troyo were going to pull this off." Her smile dipped slightly. "No offense."

Her image drifted from his vision as the words wound around his mind. "No, of course not," he said, his own voice sounding distant in his ears. "How much longer would the trial have lasted?"

"There was only another month. I mean, if Space Waste hadn't shown up…" Her voice trailed off but he didn't notice until she touched his arm. "Stanford. I'm sorry I was an ass to you before. And I'm sorry for the secrecy yesterday. And even though I'm stuck here now, I still owe you a thank you."

He hadn't known how much he wanted to hear that until he did. "You're welcome."

"So," she said, taking a step back and gesturing, turning her good hand up, creating distance between them. "Where are you off to next? Headed back home?"

"Home," he said, the word sounding strange in his mouth. Captain Oliver might be one of the few people who would understand his inability to connect to the concept of *home*, but he couldn't bring himself to open up to her. He shook his head. "No. I mean, I'm heading back down to HQ on-planet, but it won't be for long. Director Horus already has another assignment lined up." That much he'd seen in a message when he woke up, but she hadn't said exactly where he'd be going – just that he should pack for a long-distance trip.

"Well, next time you're on Vulca – I mean, if you ever make it back here," Oliver said and trailed off. She dipped her head only slightly, but it caused a lock of her hair to shield her eyes. She flipped it back and donned her cap in one motion. She saluted and walked away.

"Yeah," Runstom said to himself. "If I ever make it back here."

An alarm on the WrappiMate he'd finally remembered to wear caused the device to buzz lightly and he tapped at it to see that it was just reminding him he had a shuttle to catch. He wiped away the alert and headed to his room to gather his single bag.

CHAPTER 12

In the morning, Jax wandered back over to the library. The previous day, he'd fixed Chen's LyfStat monitor and then made use of his new credit at Bonnie's to stock up on some food and some beer. He spent the evening with four glass-bottle pints of a rich, dark porter and the sensor manual he'd picked up for a bit of light reading.

He'd learned that MFS stood for Magnetic Field Sensor, and once he found that out, its function was obvious, though he had to admit he didn't have a clue as to the particular application of the sensor in the library. There was a remote data relay, typical in these kinds of sensors, and that explained why the librarians said there was a dish on the roof. Terroneous had a few satellites used for communication, though they were restricted to government agencies and collectives; no commercial or for-profit transmissions could be afforded on the limited bandwidth.

It was at the bottom of his third pint that he'd caught himself humming a catchy tune, only it wasn't really a tune, just a rhythm. *Doot doot doooooo doot doot, Doot doot doooooo doot doot.* He couldn't remember where he'd heard it until halfway into his fourth pint, when he realized it was the alarm at the library. It wasn't a rhythm, it was a series. It was a code.

He'd flipped through the manual, almost spilling his beer but then realizing he'd only knocked over an empty bottle, and eventually found the section detailing the audible fault codes. Two short, one long, two short: *device data storage minimum availability fault.* Jax's best guess was that it was an obtuse, engineery way of saying the thing was out of memory, or disk space.

At the library, the alarm was still singing its fault song. He headed straight for the desk. "Librarian Elle, good morning."

"Oh, hello, Mr. Fugere. Any luck with Lonny's kibu thingy?"

"Yeah, he's all sorted out. I came by because I think I might be able to make that alarm stop."

Her face twisted and the normal smile she gave him broke. "Well, goddamn. I don't mind telling you, that fucking thing is driving me crazy." She popped the gate open. "Have at it. I don't care if you break the thing. Just do it quick before Kay gets in. She'll have a conniption if she catches you messing with a Bureau device."

"Right, I'll be as quick as I can."

Jax slid past the librarian to the back wall. He tugged a nearby bookcart over and situated it underneath the sensor console. Then he got his portable terminal and the Pulson Integrated Sensor Systems Incorporated Magnetic Field Sensor manual out of his pack and set them on the cart. He popped the panel off the wall console and poked around at the switches as the manual suggested to prep it for local maintenance. Then he pulled a few cables out of his pack and identified the one with the right connector and hooked his terminal into the console's access port.

Next to the manual, he placed his notebook. The information was all right there in the manual, but ever since his days with Officer Stanford Runstom, he found himself with an uncontrollable desire to write everything down with pen and paper. More than once, his notes had been handy enough to save him time, but never useful to the extent they were when he and Runstom were trying to solve the murder that Jax had been accused of. The flipside of using a paper notebook was that every time he opened it, he thought of his friend, whom he hadn't seen since fleeing Sirius-5. Was the officer his friend? Or just an ally? He hated thoughts like that. It would be so much easier if he could just talk to Runstom.

He also hated that he was still on the run. Despite all the work they'd done, all the evidence, everything.

He shook the thoughts away. He had plenty of time to dwell on that situation, and there was no sense in wasting a good distraction. On his terminal, he flipped to the window with the connection display.

MAINTENANCE MODE INITIATED. AUTHENTICATION ENABLED. ENTER PASSWORD TO CONTINUE.

"Password," he mumbled. What would they have made it? He tried *TEOB*.

INCORRECT PASSWORD. 1 OF 3 TRIES BEFORE SYSTEM LOCKOUT.

As much as it pained him to do it, he tried *PASSWORD.*

INCORRECT PASSWORD. 2 OF 3 TRIES BEFORE SYSTEM LOCKOUT.

He sighed. One more shot and then he'd have to give up. He had an epiphany and flipped through the manual's early chapter on device initialization. "Default password," he mumbled to himself after scanning the pages. "Well, here goes. Glad they didn't use the company initials."

PULSON SYSTEMS
PASSWORD ACCEPTED. MAINTENANCE MODE ACTIVE. ENTER COMMAND.

"Yes!" Jax cried, then flinched, remembering he was in a library.

Using the manual as a guide, he spent a good twenty minutes poking around configuration settings, looking at the system stats, and analyzing logs. As best he could tell, the thing was mostly using default settings, and by default, it never purged any data. It had been collecting data for almost a full year and had finally just run out of space and thrown up its hands in alarm. He thought about the software engineers who designed the system and probably never tested it for more than a week; to them, the device had infinite space on it, so of course they assumed it was safest to keep all data by default. If he had an Alley for every time he found a difference between the world of an engineer and the real world, well, he probably wouldn't be in the library trying to fix an alarm and hoping for pity charity for his work.

He was packing up his terminal when the librarians came

over. "All set," he said. "It was all full up with data, so I reconfigured it to do a nightly purge of any data that's older than six months." He paused as he saw their pale faces.

"Mr. Fugere," Kay said. "Haven't you heard?"

"Heard what?"

"It's not for certain," Elle said.

"Certain or not, everyone has to get ready, Elle."

"Ready for what?" Jax asked.

"Evacuation."

"What?" Jax blinked, the thrill of the fix draining away in an instant. "You mean, of the city?"

"No, Mr. Fugere," Kay said. "All of Terroneous."

He stood up. "What the hell for?"

They looked at each other and Kay handed him a handypad. There was a kind of news story on it, part journalism and part Bureau emergency warning. It described in brief some of the early-warning systems that the Terroneous Environment Observation Bureau employed: radiation levels, seismic activity, gravitational anomalies, and so forth. And magnetic field fluctuation. For this last one, there were sensors installed at various townships and outposts that took magnetic readings and transmitted them via satellite to the TEOB station in Fort Krylon.

A statement was issued by Lealina Warpshire, bright-blue-eyed (there was a distracting photo) acting director of the Bureau, that sensors all over the moon were in an alarm state. She warned all residents of Terroneous to prepare for possible evacuation. Jax scanned past the details of where residents would be evacuated to: some townships had emergency domes, others had underground facilities, and some would have nowhere to go but up. At the bottom of the article, he found links to related information, and he followed the one to an older article that reported on the original installation of the new magnetic field sensors.

Evidently, Pulson Integrated Sensor Systems had donated several dozen of the MFS-19 models, with comm dishes and wall consoles included. It was noted that the MFS-25 had recently been released and was being heralded as the galaxy's foremost leader in magnetic field measurement technology. Whatever the case, the TEOB had been extremely grateful for the donation, as the moon had no other means of measuring field activity on a global scale. The article was a little over a year old.

Jax looked up, the handypad going slack in his hands. The details of the data were left out of the article. Would it have meant anything to him if they included the data? Probably not, nor to anyone else who wasn't a geophysicist. Still, it was a conspicuous omission. "I have to check something," he said, handing off the pad and turning back to the wall console.

He unpacked his terminal and repeated the steps to get connected to the console's maintenance port. After a few minutes of digging, he turned to the librarians and announced, "I have to talk to the Bureau."

* * *

The headquarters of the Terroneous Environment Observation Bureau was a building much smaller than Jax had expected. It was a long, thin structure, with only one floor – at least, above ground – with a chest-high chainlink fence around the perimeter. As Jax and his companions approached, they could see that behind the building, the fenced-in yard extended a few dozen meters to accommodate an array of satellite dishes of all sizes.

A man sat on a wicker chair (a kind of fibrous, thin wood that wound around upon itself, something Jax had not encountered until he came to Terroneous) in front of the building. He was positioned in a spot that suggested he was a guard, but was not armed and certainly not alarmed at the arrival of newcomers to the remote facility. He barely looked up from his paperback.

"Personnel only, fellas," he said as they approached.

"I was hoping to talk to—" Jax started, and stopped when the door opened.

Lealina Warpshire, acting director of the Bureau, came halfway through the doorway in mid-conversation with another woman – older, with long black hair fraying its way out of a ponytail – who was fussing with a handypad.

"Make sure that—" she started, then stopped and looked at the new arrivals. "Charlie, who the hell are these guys?"

Charlie the guard looked up from his book, glared at Jax, rolled his eyes up to the director, then rolled them back down to his book. He seemed to be the sort that didn't bother answering a question he didn't know the answer to.

"Uh, hi," Jax said, lifting his hand to wave sheepishly.

"David Granderson," one of his companions said, thrusting out a hand for someone to shake. "Creator of holofilms *The Real Streets of Stockton* and *A Tune for Terroneous*, just to name a few."

Jax cringed. Granderson was an entertainment mogul; well, a mogul in the small township of Stockton anyway, which meant he'd done a bunch of semi-documentary, semi-reality holovid films and broadcasts. He was used to being well known around town, so he fancied himself a celebrity.

After Jax had looked through the logs in the magnetic sensor console at the library one more time, he verified what he hoped was true. He couldn't make any sense of the data, but based on the size of the data and the timestamps, it was as steady as clockwork. This was good news, as it meant there wasn't anything out of the ordinary: the disk hadn't filled up suddenly from an onslaught of data, it had filled up one drop at a time until there was nowhere to put the next drop. As he originally suspected, the problem was nothing more than a misconfiguration.

When he got the librarians to try calling TEOB again, they got another recording, this one different than the first. It wasn't the acting director, but another employee who emphasized the need for everyone to prepare for evacuation and gave very little information other than that. Jax had left a message, but had little hope of getting a reply.

With no way to contact anyone at the Bureau to warn them their alarms might be false positives, Jax started looking for ways to get out to the TEOB headquarters. No mag-trains were running as a precautionary measure, and all sub-orbital flights were suspended as the flight centers prepped for full orbital launches on a mass scale. His only option was to find a self-powered land vehicle; fortunately, he knew someone who'd given him a ride once before.

When Granderson heard Jax's story, he was immensely interested in helping. It wasn't only that he didn't want to evacuate, which he really didn't (he'd have to leave all his possessions, and he was really attached to his possessions), but he also decided that the whole situation would make for great reality HV.

Jax hadn't given Granderson much in the way of his background, but since the day they first met, the man had clearly known Jax was hiding something. Granderson seemed to respect Jax's need for privacy; nonetheless, the presence of cameras made him nervous. But he felt in debt to the documentarian, and realized he was digging that debt deeper. If Granderson got something out of it, then it felt less like begging a favor. So they came to an agreement: Granderson's cameras could roll, but they'd use the facial detection software to blur any images of Jax and hide his identity.

It had taken two days of solid driving for them to get to the headquarters.

"Hey," Charlie said, suddenly losing interest in his paperback. "Do you do that one show, *Over the Moon*? Where all the people can't handle living on Terroneous and just wish they could go back to the domes?"

Jax frowned. He didn't own a holovid, so he didn't know, but he really wished that wasn't a real show.

"That's right," Granderson said with a smile. "That's me."

"Oh, man, I *love* that show!"

"Look, I don't know what you two want here," Lealina broke in, "but you need to leave. This facility is personnel-only. No public access allowed."

"Well, except for tours," Charlie said. The look she gave him indicated his comment had not helped the point she was driving for.

"Ms. Warpshire," Jax said, putting out his hands. "Please, I need to talk to you. It's about the MFS units."

She stiffened at the last sentence. "What do you know about them? Who are you?"

"My name is Fugere. I used to live on B-4." This caused all four of them to glance at each other. Jax knew his pale, white skin and tall, gaunt build pegged him as an obvious B-fourean, but sometimes it felt necessary to say it out loud. He cleared his throat. "Anyway, I used to be a life-support operator. I've had a lot of experience with Pulson sensor equipment."

The last part wasn't really true, since Pulson mainly manufactured geological and geophysical sensors, but he figured he knew as much as anyone, given the state of the configuration he found in the console at the Stockton library.

"Mr. Fugere, we don't really have time for this." She turned and tilted her head to look at something on her companion's handypad.

"It's a false positive," Jax blurted.

"What?" Now she gave him full attention again.

"The alarm on the MFS-19. It's not really an alarm, it's a device fault."

"What the hell are you talking about?"

"The disk drives that the data is stored on – the internal memory banks – in the consoles. They're filling up."

She shook her head. "That doesn't make any sense. The remote units send the data back to us via satellite."

"Right," Jax said. "But first it collects locally. I looked at the configuration of the sensor console at the Stockton library and it had the default settings. It never purged any data."

She frowned at him, eyebrows pinching together. "That's just one unit. We're getting alarms from units all over Terroneous."

"All the sensors were installed at the same time." Jax tried not to let himself smile as realization crossed her face. He continued with as little gloat as possible. "If they're all collecting data at the same rate, and they all have the same size storage because they're the same model, they'd all fill up at about the same time, give or take. At least within a few days of one another."

Her jaw slowly dropped and those bright-blue eyes lasered in on him. He swallowed and looked around. "Oh my god," she whispered. "You better come inside."

"Ah, Director?" Granderson said, raising a finger.

"Yes?"

"Do you mind if I bring a camera in? For the sake of historical documentation, it would be useful to capture this crisis on film as it unfolds."

She looked at him warily. "Yeah, whatever. If you think it's any more exciting inside than it is out in this wasteland, you're in for disappointment."

CHAPTER 13

"You mean we flew all the way out here and now I gotta sit around and babysit Lucky Jerk?" Thompson said. "While you two go off and have all the fun?"

Out here was the edge of some desert on Terroneous, largest moon around Barnard-5. Dava was cranky enough from the Xarp travel back from Sirius, especially following the Xarp trip out there with little recovery time in between. Everyone had slapped each other on the backs about the score at Vulca, even though Johnny and Frank had been arrested and several others had been wounded. No one died and they got the equipment they'd gone after, so it was an apparent success. Rando Jansen, the so-called underboss, capitalized on the momentum by slinging Dava and a few others back into Barnard space to chase some new rival gang that might or might not have a presence on Terroneous. Dava woke up from the FTL nap realizing she might or might not give a shit either way.

Thompson had also made the back-to-back trips and was possibly more cranky than Dava. "This is bullshit. I have to stay here but *he* gets to go? I'm the only one here who's seen the Misters before!"

She had a bad habit of pointing during conversation, with the barrel of her loaded submachinegun. She also lacked anything that resembled subtlety in the wardrobe department. There was no way Dava was taking her into town in a bright-red nylon jacket that was covered in Space Waste patches.

"Please don't point that at me," Bashful Dan said, shrinking from her gun. The tracker was much more appropriately dressed, although he always preferred muted colors and avoided anything that might shine or flash in the lowest of light.

The lanky Lucky Jerk struck a pose, flight helmet under one arm, twirling an invisible baton in the other hand. "Tommy, you know I used to run with the Misters. If anyone can spot them, it's me."

"Shut up, all of you," Dava said in a low voice. They were miles from anywhere so there was little need for restraint, but she wanted their full attention, so she spoke quietly but firmly. "What we need on this mission is discretion. What we don't need is you and your goddamn Tommy-Gun shooting up the city. We need someone to guard the dropship."

Thompson lowered her gun and frowned. "You're the capo, Dava. But if you kill any of them without me." She seemed unable to finish her thought, shaking her head and looking away.

Dava had just learned during the mission briefing that Thompson and Barndoor had a run-in with the Misters on Poligart a few months back. Lost a couple of mates in a shoot-out. "I'll try my best to wait," she said. "But we need to scout it out first. And that means discretion."

"I want a shot too," Lucky chimed in. "Those bastards had me over a barrel."

Lucky Jerk was one of the few of the Misters to survive the shoot-out on Poligart. He'd surrendered, and Thompson had nearly killed him anyway. But he was a pilot and she'd been in need of one. And he was eager to betray the crew he'd been press-ganged into to pay back some gambling debt. Space Waste never passed up a recruit with talent, and Lucky proved his value quickly. Even if he did have a bit of a mouth on him.

"Not gonna happen," Dava said. "You'd definitely get recognized."

She signaled to Dan to get the ATV out of the ship. She started to check her belt and the attachments affixed to it.

"Hey Dava," Thompson said. "Can I at least come to town to get laid?"

"We can worry about that after the job is done," Dava said. Satisfied with the belt's occupants, she concealed it by wrapping her duster around her body. "Listen, Thompson. I brought you along because I don't know what we're up against. I might need backup. So no slacking off. Be alert. And you, Lucky," she said, pointing at the dropship pilot, "stay close to the radio."

"Aye, Capo Dava," he said with a sigh.

Dava watched Dan roll the ATV down the ramp and start digging through a bag on the back of it. "You almost ready, Dan?"

He paused, bag open, marking inventory in his head, then nodded. "Ready."

The four of them pushed the ATV through uneven sand for about a hundred meters, until they reached a trail where the ground was a little more packed. She flicked a hand at

Thompson and Lucky, and they turned to head back to the ship. She could hear their conversation trailing off into the hot wind.

"Hey, Tommy," Lucky said, "if you want to get laid—"

"Lucky, I will break your tiny little prick off and use it for target practice if you don't shut the fuck up."

"Eh. I've had worse."

"I believe it."

Dava looked at Bashful Dan, who just shrugged and made for the back seat of the ATV. Then he stopped. She could see him chewing on a question.

"What, Dan?"

He frowned and moved his jaw around for a few seconds before saying anything. He looked at his armband. "The shuttle from the Royal #3 is due to arrive in ten days, fourteen hours."

"Good."

He fidgeted. "Doesn't that make us a little early for the hand-off?"

She nodded. "Yes. But I suspect Mr. Hill is already here. He's either a resident on Terroneous, or he's coming in from somewhere else, and moving that kind of cash, he'd want to check the place out first."

This seemed to ease the tracker slightly, and he slackened his stance. "Good call. So what's our move?"

Dava smiled. "You do what you do and I do what I do. Let's see if we can sniff him out."

"Sunderville is a pretty good-sized town, and we don't know what he looks like."

"Because I killed Sandiego," she said. Dan was always beating around the bush, but she could usually tell what he was driving at. One of Jansen's mysterious informants reported that Mr. Sandiego perished in ModPol custody due to excessive internal bleeding.

"Yes, that's true," he said quietly. "It would have been... useful...if Sandiego had survived."

"Well, he didn't," Dava said, hopping into the driver seat. "The Misters are still new to the organized crime gig. I'm counting on them being flashy with their cash. So we're going to hit the most expensive places we can find and keep our ears open and our mouths shut."

* * *

By the second night, they'd caught a whiff of Mr. Hill. He wasn't alone. There was a Mr. Guy and a Mr. Pellinarri also in Sunderville. The three of them were not shy with their money, and not shy with their affiliation: they were more or less advertising that the Misters had arrived.

"Well, so much for tracking," Dan said with a sigh.

They were sitting in a dark corner of Angry Candy watching the table of Misters boisterously order drinks and rank female patrons. Not that the garish pink and purple-lit bar had much in the way of dark corners, but that didn't hinder their stealth. The way these idiots were partying, they clearly had no idea that Space Waste was hunting them.

"I thought they would at least try," Dava admitted.

"So what's next? There's three of them. Maybe we should get Thompson."

She rolled her glare from the Misters to Bashful Dan.

He coughed. "On the other hand, there's only *three*."

Several bottles made their way to the table and Dava sighed, thinking it was going to be a long night. But then it appeared that they weren't opening the bottles, they just wanted something to take with them. They were ungracefully getting out of their chairs and rounding up their goods.

"Come with me to the street," she said. "We'll tail them. Once we find out where they're staying, I want you to hang back."

Dan nodded wordlessly. She figured he was grateful to be left out of the action.

The three drunk men wound their way through the streets of Sunderville, occasionally stopping to hoot at someone on the street, or to spat with each other about whatever bullshit one of them was trying to pass off as "a true story". Eventually they came to the Hotel Vitis, which would be expensive for Terroneous, but was probably not all that much in reality. The doorman nodded as though he recognized them, and gave them a wide berth when they stumbled past.

She motioned a sign to Dan, pointing to her ear and mouth with her thumb and pinky and then pointing to the hotel. He nodded and drifted back the way they came. She went down the side of a nearby shop, all closed up for the night, and found a back alley that led to the rear of the hotel.

Her arm buzzed with Dan's coded message. He'd called the front desk and found they were in room 405, top floor. Dava looked up. She would get to scale a building. She hadn't done that in a while. She almost felt good, then noticed that there was an old-school drainpipe leading up the brick-surface walls. So much for a challenge.

She tapped at the armband to let Dan know she was going in. After a moment of hesitation, she added, *Update Thompson.*

Minutes later she was clinging to the side of the building

and peeking into an unlit room. Music thumped from somewhere nearby. The Misters were still partying. She took out her light and dialed it down to a soft red. She pointed it into the dark room and saw a made bed in a very large room. No one had booked this suite tonight, and if she had to guess, probably none of the other suites on the top floor were booked. None but 405.

She popped her multitool from her belt and scanned for a sensor. Nothing. Well, it was Terroneous. There was a metal-latch lock on the window, and that was probably all that was needed in a place like this. She flicked the tool until she got the hook she wanted, then used the microvibration mode to slide it into the space between the window panes. The lock gave way without complaint, but the window didn't glide open. The elements had been harsh to the hotel and the wood had swollen. She had to force it open, which took a few minutes and caused a bit of a ruckus, at least by her standards. But the music was still pulsing through the walls and soon she was floating into the darkness of the empty hotel room.

She went to the door, then stopped, putting her ear to the surface to listen. Her nose twitched as she smelled something that raised the hairs on her neck, but she couldn't place it. Breathing deeper only brought her musty smells of mold and the sharp, chemical citrus of cleaning supplies.

Through the peephole, the hallway was empty. As best she could tell, there were six rooms on the floor. It was obvious where 405 was now: the end of the hall, the source of the music.

Slowly she opened the door. The hallway was dimly lit by yellow ceiling lights. She found the switch and turned them off. Froze and counted to one hundred to ensure her eyes were adjusted. She risked blindness if they had bright lights in the room, but her plan was to get the door open and then get to the side and wait for them to come out.

From her belt, she took the jackpop, a small, sticky, directional explosive, perfect for blowing the locks off of doors; or the whole knob assembly, in most cases. She affixed it just below the doorknob of 405 and tapped the timer and stepped back to position herself.

Thirty seconds.

She held a stunner in her left hand and a knife in her right.

Fifteen seconds.

She closed her eyes and counted.

Pop.

The volume of the music doubled as the door swung open. The light coming through was bright, which was good for her because it meant they wouldn't be able to see once they came into the dark hall. She aimed the gun and gripped the knife.

"Now!"

She heard the sound of multiple doors opening at once. Down the hall, figures sprang out of the other rooms. She swallowed, realizing someone came out of the unoccupied room she was just in. That smell she had smelled. The faint whiff of cologne.

"Fucking Misters," she whispered and got down low. The hallway was still dark, but so were all the other rooms.

"Don't move!" The voice came from 405. "We'll cook you right here in this hallway!"

She fired her stunner at the figure closest to her and while it broke into spasms, she spun around it and through the open door. Shots rang out but she felt nothing, no one had hit her – yet. She slammed the door shut, but it stopped inches short. The convulsing body had an arm draped through. She ducked behind the wall as more shots were fired, then realized she didn't trust the walls of the wooden hotel to be bulletproof, and she hit the floor.

If she had a real gun, she might be able to shoot them right through the walls. But no, she had her stungun and her blade. Had intended on sending a message, one that was slow and painful, not quick and loud. She cursed her carelessness, wanted to reason out how they had managed to ambush her, but pushed the thoughts aside. Survival was all that counted at the moment.

"Get the fucking lights on. All of them. She loves the dark."

The hallway lights sprang dimly to life. A hand appeared above her, finding the switch next to the door. Instinctively, she plunged her blade through it before the owner had a chance to flick the switch.

He screamed. She yanked the knife out, and he screamed louder.

"Get the hell out of the way, Mr. Guy!"

Someone behind the wounded man shoved him off to the side and fired wildly into the room. She sprung along the floor, rolling to a position behind a heavy couch. Heavy or not, bullets would make short work of the furniture. She needed out of the room.

She glanced at the window. Four stories up. The gravity on Terroneous was almost a full G.

The room. Furniture, desk, a chair, a bed, a lamp – a floor lamp. She swung out to grab it by the base, flipped it around. The base was heavy. She launched it like a javelin at the window. The old glass smashed to pieces, and she caught the top of the lamp before it passed all the way through. Raked the makeshift pole around the edges of the frame once to clear as much glass as she could in those few seconds.

The light came on. She spun and fired the stunner repeatedly. The man in the doorway jittered but the gun was drained. She dropped it and went out the window.

This room wasn't close to the drainpipe. She considered the drop. Too far. Turned her head up.

"Don't let her get away!"

Without thinking, her hands were on the top of the trim along the outside of the window. Her feet were each reaching for the sides, gripping along the brick. She was pushing upward, a small leap, her hand finding the half-pipe that ran along the side of the roof. Her legs swinging up and over as gunfire erupted below.

She lay flat on the roof. Ventured a glance over the side. The window below. A head poked out. Mr. Hill.

"She's on the roof!"

He disappeared.

She went for the corner at the other end where the pipe she came up was. Started to swing a leg over then jumped back when it lit up with sparks from gunshot.

On her back on the roof, she controlled her breathing. She looked at her armband to send a message to Dan, but one was already waiting. *Heard gunshots. T-Gun ETA 5 min.*

How could she have been five minutes away? She was supposed to be out at the dropship. She must have been in town. Maybe she came as soon as Dan checked in. Maybe she came even earlier.

Dava didn't like it, the thought of them hovering so close,

encroaching on her work. But there she was, outgunned and outmanned. She needed them.

She needed to find a way off the hotel roof.

She was creeping up to each side to cautiously look over to see if there was anything she could grab onto when she smelled the smoke. Before long, she could see the orange light emanating from all around her. They weren't just going to smoke her out, they were going to burn her alive, even if it meant burning down the whole damn hotel.

Trying to control her breathing, she circled the roof with a deliberate, measured pace. She could hear them inside now, the heavy thump of running feet, growing distant. Going down the stairs to head out the door. She went to the front, unable to get too close as the flames began to spill out and upward, forming a dancing fence of heat along the edge of the roof.

They shouted down below. Whooped congratulations of victory.

Then came a raucous sound. It was unmistakable, the steady rat-a-tat-tat pulse of Thompson's submachinegun. Dava never thought she'd be glad to hear that obnoxious racket.

The joyous whooping turned to panicked shouts. The Misters were returning fire, but they had not expected their ambush to be ambushed. She could hear the chaos in their efforts. They had no plan. The electric zap of Dan's stungun making them jump, the cutting punch of Thompson's gun breaking their bones.

She felt useless, and the flames were getting higher. Temperature rising. She felt sweat trickling down her face. Then the shooting stopped, only minutes after it started.

"Dava!"

They were shouting to her from the far side of the hotel. She went there, but couldn't see them down below, not without sticking her face into the flames.

"Dava!" Dan's voice was odd at that volume. It had a projection and an authority she'd never heard before. "Dava! You have to jump!"

"He's right, Dava." Thompson's voice, higher in pitch, cut through the night. "Just take a running leap! You can make it!"

They continued to shout, but she couldn't make out the words. The fire was growing to the point where the rush of air being chewed away into smoke muted the world around her.

It was Bashful Dan and Thompson. They weren't stupid. When it came down to it, they were some of the brighter ones. But take a running leap? From four stories up?

She looked up at the sky. The tunnel of smoke billowing upward revealed a cluster of stars through the opening at the end of it.

"Fuck it," she sighed.

She walked to the opposite end of the roof, turned around, and sprinted.

And leapt.

CHAPTER 14

"Okay, so my friend Stanford and I are on this cruise ship."

"Wait, you were on a cruise?" Lealina said. "You mean like a Royal Starways thing? Together?"

"Yeah, well," Jax said. "I mean, we weren't *on* a cruise, we were on a cruise *ship*." He paused, carefully thinking about how to phrase his time on the Royal Superliner #5. He cleared his throat. "It was a work thing."

"Oh, okay."

They'd been out all night, starting before dinner when she took him on a tour to see some of the sights around Stockton. Places he'd already known about, but hadn't known what they'd meant to *her*. They went to dinner and he was able to treat, thanks to a generous discount the owner gave him because of a filtration system bug he'd sorted out a few weeks prior. After that they'd planned to go to a holofilm, but the planet, Barnard-5, was almost full and she knew a secret spot for viewing it above the mountain tops just outside of town. They took her car and parked and watched the crimson gas giant drift slowly through the sky.

It seemed like it should have been romantic. They'd gotten to know each other in the couple of weeks that followed their first meeting at the TOEB headquarters, when they trekked around the moon with a small team and reconfigured countless sensor systems. But in that moment, in the quiet of the night with the magnificent roiling presence dominating the horizon, they both got very uncomfortable very suddenly. Jax hadn't felt anything for a woman in quite some time, and he didn't know what to do with that feeling. He suspected she had a similar issue.

So they had decided to get drunk.

"We were mostly down in the worker quarters of the superliner for those couple of months." He leaned against the bar at one of his favorite public houses in town, *The Wretched Sunrise*, gesturing with his ale. "Once in a while we'd make it up to check out the fancy spots, but you know, not to socialize. But one day we decided to borrow some clothes so we could go to a party."

"You mean, rich-people clothes?"

"Yeah, kind of. But it was a party, with like a period theme. So no one really had expensive clothes, they all just had whatever clothes they could get their hands on that looked the period."

"What period?"

"Earth, New Year's Eve, 1999."

"Wow, really?" Her eyes lit up with her open-mouth smile, then turned upward in thought. "End of the twentieth century, hmm. So like, lots of denim, right? That's all I can think of."

"Oh yeah, a lot of that, but some people with shirts that had short sleeves but with the collar that folds over. Or some people just wore T-shirts and black leather jackets.

Not animal leather of course, but you know. And there were a lot of those old-timey sports hats where the brim only sticks out of the front. What else...? Lots of fake beards – some with, some without fake mustaches. Anyway, you get the picture."

"That must have been a riot, seeing all those rich people dressed up."

"Well it would have been, but seriously, more than half of them didn't dress up!" Jax had to rein himself in after an arm gesture almost spilled his beer. "It was like some unspoken rich-people code of irony to go to a costume party and not wear a costume."

"What the hell?"

"Yeah, I think they see it as ascending to some upper-upper class, where they can watch the middle-upper class act like fools and entertain them or something."

"But you and your friend were dressed up."

"Of course. And we made up these stories – like these personas, right? So Stanford – well, Stanford's mom was in ModPol. She was a detective. So Stanford decides his 1999 persona is going to be this undercover cop, which doesn't really make sense, because he's telling everyone he's an undercover cop."

He lost himself for a split second, thinking back to that night. They were working through their passenger list, trying to get in as many conversations as possible, but needing to fit in at the same time. Given Runstom's inability to lie effectively, Jax hit on the brilliant idea that he *dress up* to be an undercover detective.

She laughed. "That's great! What were you?"

"Oh," he said with a laugh. "Well, it wasn't easy finding a costume for someone tall like me. One of the guys in maintenance said I should dress up like a ball player. There was some sport back in the twentieth century where tall guys would wear short pants and shirts with no sleeves, and so that's what they cobbled together for me."

She leaned back – which Jax found perilous given her increasing inebriation and the lack of back support on the bar stool – to look him up and down. One of her eyebrows went up. "That must have been a sight."

"Not pretty. Not pretty at all. Needless to say, Stanford got most of the attention."

"Oh, you poor thing." This sounded like sarcasm, but she included a brief hand on his knee, so he accepted it whether she was teasing him or not.

"Trust me, it was great. He's really getting into the role, see. I mean, we were uh – we were both stressed about... work." Yeah right, *work*. Work being that Jax had been wrongly accused of murder and the real killer was still out there somewhere, and they were on that stupid cruise ship trying to track down whoever had transmitted a virus long distance from the ship's deck to a subdome on Barnard-4. He saw her looking at him, waiting for his story to continue, so he took a drink and went on. "And it's an open bar, so we're both drinking pretty heavily. By about his fourth cocktail, you'd think Stanford had been in law enforcement himself, the way he's cutting loose with the lingo. And by the sixth cocktail, he's revealing to everyone that he's really, *really* undercover and he's trying to solve a murder. And he's telling people that I – the half-naked B-fourean who is supposed to be an old-timey ballplayer – that I've been wrongly accused of this murder he's trying to solve."

"You've got to be kidding. Your friend must be quite the actor."

"Yeah, Stanford." Jax's eyes rolled up to the ceiling for a moment. "What an actor."

"So they were just eating it up?"

"Yes, exactly. Now – here comes the best part. He's divulging all his secret theories on this undercover case to this woman. She's a gorgeous B-threer with long flowing blond hair and a long blue-and-green dress – I mean, it's just super long and flowy. She's obviously not dressing the period, which means she's in that upper-upper who's there to be entertained by someone like Stanford."

"That's kind of sad."

Jax shook his head. "Anyway, Stanford really has her locked down. He's really getting into it, and it's like she's trapped, she can't get away from the intensity of his story. I mean, there's dead bodies, there's gunfights, there's clues that lead to *this very cruise ship*. It's amazing. But – but I'm the only one who notices that she can't pull away from him because *he's standing on her dress*."

She laughed out loud, "What?"

"Oh, it's glorious. Her friends are calling to her from across the room, and she can only gesture to them, because she can't interrupt Stanford's flow to get him off her dress. It's impossible, he's on such a roll."

"Oh my god, that's hilarious. Serves a poor rich girl right."

"Finally, I take pity on her, and I know I have to do something. So I go and get Stanford a new drink. He takes it and in the two seconds that he's distracted by it, I lean over to the woman and whisper to her, to tell her that she should tell him she overheard someone on the other side of the room talking about a *murder*.

"Now, this woman definitely does not want to stoop to

the level of fantasy that we're engaged in, even though it's a freaking period costume party, but she's desperate enough to take my advice. Stanford is so anxious to home in on his next target, that he spins around real fast, twisting his feet up in this super-long dress…" With this, Jax took a paper napkin from the bar and planted two fingers down on it to demonstrate the twisting of legs into extravagant cocktail dress.

"Oh no…" Lealina whispered, putting her hands to her mouth.

"Well, he goes down to the floor—"

"And she goes down with him?"

Jax shook his head. "This woman does not fall. She is the type of fancy that just does *not* fall to the ground. So instead…" Jax pulled the paper napkin in half.

"What?" she laughed. "Really?"

"Yep," Jax said with a tight smile and a shake of his head. "The whole dress just *rips* in half. I think she nearly died of embarrassment."

"Oh, that is too funny," she laughed. "I wish I had some adventures like that."

"You live on Terroneous," Jax said. "I would think there are plenty of adventures living in the wilderness."

She laughed again and angled her head to give him a glare. "Give me a break. Wilderness. Just because it's not under a dome?"

"Hey, no offense. It's all pretty wild to me. Have you ever been off-planet?"

"Actually, yeah, I have. I went to school on B-4."

Jax stiffened. "Get out, really? Where did you go?"

"South Haven Institute of Technology," she said.

He nearly choked on his drink. "That's where I went! Back in '93, to '97."

"Super weird. I was there in '94, '95."

"We could have crossed paths there – gone to the same classes even."

"Yeah, I suppose," she said with a shrug. "Not that I would remember. I was in a sea of tall, white-skinned people."

"Oh, I definitely would have remembered you," he said, nodding deeply before taking a pull from his beer.

She flinched and frowned. "Yeah, I guess I didn't really belong there," she said quietly.

"No, uh – no, I uh," Jax stuttered. "I'm sorry. That's not what I meant." He wanted to tell her it wasn't because she would have been an outcast among the B-foureans, that it was her bright-blue eyes, that if he'd seen them he would have jumped at a chance to meet her. But his tongue swelled up in his mouth and all he could do was sigh and take another pull of beer.

They looked at each other in silence. "So," she said uncomfortably.

Jax nodded, then blurted, "You know what? They renamed it the Blue Haven Technical Institute a few years ago."

She grinned. "It'll always be SHIT to us, won't it?"

"It will," he said, returning her smile. "I really didn't mean—"

"It's okay, Jack," she said. "I guess we both know what it's like to be a fish out of water, don't we."

"Yeah," he nodded, pulling from his beer again, which was becoming gravely light. He wanted her to call him *Jax*, but it didn't work with his alias, Jack Fugere. He turned the phrase she just used around in his mind. "So, fish don't like to run out of water?"

She laughed fully then. "What – wait, do you really not know what that expression means?"

"I'm really bad with those animal metaphors," he said sheepishly. "We didn't have any live animals on B-4."

"Wow, you really *are* a fish out of water then."

"What does that mean? By not understanding the expression, I'm somehow strengthening it?"

She laughed again. "Yep, I'm afraid so."

He grinned happily. "This is so unfair."

Her laughter settled and she smiled at him with those bright-blue eyes. She put a hand on the bar, close to his, and touched his finger with hers. "I'm having a good time."

"Me too," he said. "I'm glad you got over the intense hatred you had for me when we first met."

She pursed her lips. "Yeah, me too. You know I was under a lot of stress—"

"Oh, I know," he said. "It was fun, really. Trying to win you over."

She dipped her head shyly. "You really saved our butts." She brought her head up to take a drink, then chuckled. "I still can't believe I almost had the whole moon evacuated because of a stupid misconfiguration."

"That shit happens more often than you think. Engineering mistakes keep people like me employed." He raised his glass. "To engineers and all their fuckups."

She laughed and clinked her glass to his. "I'll drink to that."

They tipped their glasses back, swallowed, and smiled at each other. "Tell me how you ended up at the Bureau," he said.

Her eyes went upward for a moment in thought. "Hmm, okay. So my mom is a custodian, and my aunt is an assistant nurse. They both wanted me to have a better opportunity, and they have this Terroneous pride about the kids being the future and all that, so they spent their combined life savings to get me to B-4 to go to SHIT school."

He stifled a chuckle at the name, not wanting to laugh at the sacrifice her family made. "So you did a two-year program?"

"Yes. I got accepted into the four-year, but when it came down to it, two was all we could afford. I took lots of general operations classes. Out here, we need people who can do a little of everything."

"Who can adapt," he added. "Improvise."

"Pretty much. When I got back after two years, there were openings at the Bureau for operators, and it was a perfect first job. I mean, it's mostly watching numbers come in all day long, but I was good at it. I'm kind of an organization freak."

"Not a bad thing."

"Not bad when it's needed. And TEOB needed it badly. So after my first year, I was promoted to senior operator, and then a few years after that, there was an opening for operations manager at the headquarters, and I landed that position."

"And now you're director?"

"Well, no, not really. I'm still technically the operations manager. The director, Esan – Esan Pholoulous – took a leave of absence about six months ago. I took over as acting director." She frowned a little, her nose twitching. "It seems like a big deal, but there are only twelve full-time employees at the Bureau."

"Still seems like a big responsibility to me," Jax said.

"Yeah, I suppose it is."

"Do you like it?"

"I," she started, then shrugged. "Yes and no. I don't know."

He nodded slowly. "I know the feeling."

"You don't even have a job," she said with a mischievous smile.

He couldn't help but grin back. "Hey, I work! I'm a freelancer."

"Yeah, but why *don't* you have a job?" she said. "You're obviously qualified for *something*."

He hid behind his mug for a moment. He was getting a reputation around Stockton as a go-to fixer for anything that came with a manual (no one read manuals) and made enough in cash and in trade to feel comfortable financially. Or at least, more comfortable than he was when he was on the move and homeless. But the truth was, he wanted something real; he wanted a solid job, because a job was a *place*, a belonging. Responsibility. But he couldn't. He couldn't put his name on any piece of paper, he couldn't be traceable, he couldn't do anything that might get back to ModPol. Even as untouched by ModPol as Terroneous was, it was too much risk. No one there even knew his real name was Jackson, and he needed to keep it that way.

"I'm still looking," he said weakly.

She frowned and leaned close. "Please tell me you're not leaving the planet anytime soon. You're one of a kind, Jack, and I'd be very sad to see you go."

As those bright blues gleamed moist at him, he felt a hole tear open in his stomach. He swallowed to find his voice. "I want to make Terroneous my home."

She stared into his eyes. "You *want* to?"

He nodded shortly and she leaned back. They both turned

to the bar and ordered another round. It came quickly, and they stared into their glasses.

"Lealina, listen," Jax started, still looking down.

"Hey!" She grabbed his arm. "Look – that's HQ on the holo."

He looked up and followed her pointing finger to the end of the bar where a holovid was playing. There was TEOB headquarters, just like he remembered it on the day he met her. Three-dimensional words danced into view:

David Granderson presents...
... a docuvid you can't afford to miss...
TERROR ON TERRONEOUS
the Disaster that Almost Was
... starts this Friday at a holo-theater near you!

Cuts of various shots faded in and out and Jax felt his stomach begin to turn. His guts dropped completely when Lealina's face appeared.

Lealina Warpshire, Acting Director of TEOB

"Hey, that's me!" she exclaimed. "We're going to be on holovid! Did you know we were going to be on this?"

The understanding he had with Granderson...if his face came on screen, it would be blurred. And how would he explain that to Lealina?

He'd used that arrangement with Granderson to let his guard down. To forget about his fear, so he could focus on magnetic field sensors. So he could focus his energies on stopping the evacuation. All he was thinking about was helping others. All he was thinking about was helping her. All he was thinking about was fixing the problem that was right in front of him at that moment.

Now that the problem was solved, he felt a cold rock in the center of his chest. What had he done? Even with his face blurred, would he be exposed?

"Look, there's you!"

Fugere, The Fixer

The holovid went blurry and he turned to face her, but she was blurry too. The whole world had gone blurry.

"Jack?"

He'd gotten too comfortable, entertaining the notion of finding home on this moon. Made too many friends. Attracted too much attention. Lost his invisibility. Now he was going to lose it all because all he wanted to do was fix someone else's problem.

"I am so fucking stupid."

* * *

With the action over, Dava had Lucky Jerk hop them over to the other side of Terroneous to a little township called Nuzwick. Since they weren't planning on causing any more trouble than a few rambunctious nights of drinking, they parked the dropship at the local port.

"What did RJ say?"

She knew Thompson was only asking the question because they hadn't stuck around Sunderville very long.

"I told him we killed three, wounded one, two got away," Dava said. When Thompson had shown up, she managed to scatter the Misters pretty quickly. Two of them made a break for it while the rest dove back into the burning hotel for cover. Dan had zapped one of the runners – Pellinarri, from the bar – but at a distance the stungun lost some of its charge and though the target went down, he'd gotten back up soon enough. Once Dava made it off the roof, Thompson gave her a pistol and together they peppered the four Misters who were smoked out of the hotel and into a storm of bullets. That included Hill, the apparent ringleader, who caught a bullet in the neck, as well as Guy, who survived the barrage. "He said we should let the others live, send a message."

"That guy loves to send a message," Thompson said with a short laugh and shake of her head.

"Tell me about it," Dava said in a low voice. She couldn't shake the feeling that Jansen was chaining her missions together without a break to keep her busy. Out of the way. "Anyways, he told us to get out of Sunderville, just in case we stirred up the local law enforcement."

Thompson laughed again. "Yeah, you bet your ass we did. 'Course, we did them a favor by cleaning out their Mister problem."

Dava nodded. "S'true. We move on and they can call it a wash."

The bartender came around and set down a massive pitcher of amber beer and four mugs. The place was some kind of brewery, and the smell was somehow bad and good at the same time. Bad because it was wet, funky, and sweetly bitter, but good because it was like beer. Aside from that, it was dark and had a kitchen, so it suited their needs just fine.

Dava took a pull at her beer and finished her thought as the bartender left with instructions to bring back a few plates of whatever their specialty was. "So I told RJ, that's fine about the two that got away, but the one we wounded is locked in the hold of the dropship. I said, what do you want me to do with him?"

Thompson frowned. "Probably wants to let him go too."

"Actually, he thought about it for a minute, then said we might turn him into the authorities for causing the fire. I was about to tell him he's crazy, but then he just sighs." Long-range communications that took several minutes to go from the Space Waste base in deep Barnard down to Terroneous, and the man actually sighed into the transmission. "Says, 'You know what, Dava? I leave it to your *discretion*.'"

"No shit."

"S'what I said." She drained her mug and motioned for Dan to refill it. Something about talking to Jansen always made her want to drink.

"So," Lucky said carefully, testing the waters. "What are we going to do with him?"

She chewed on this thought for a moment, and it was sour. Why did she have to decide? Her plan was to kill him, but that was before. Somehow it was simpler before. Mr. Sandiego and the Misters stole from Space Waste. So she came here to enact justice. But they were ready for her. Why were they ready for her?

Maybe the Misters had been trying to a send a message of their own.

The ale swirled around sweetly through the spaces between her ears and eyes. It wasn't the time to solve that little mystery. It was the time to be glad she wasn't burned alive.

"I'm just going to hold onto him for a while," she said.

Instantly, the rest of them relaxed. "Good," Thompson said. "One less thing to think about. Let's drink!"

"We *are* drinking," Lucky said, then laughed at his own joke as he tipped back in his chair, flinching and grabbing the table when he almost went all the way over.

"You tell RJ about your little spill?" Thompson said, then hid her shit-eating grin behind her glass.

Dava tried to glare and found herself unable keep a straight face. "No, I didn't tell him." The pool at the other side of the hotel. She hadn't known it was there, which was her fault for not getting a full perimeter before moving in. She shook her head as she thought about that fact: she had no idea why they were telling her to jump. Were they going to catch her? What was their plan? She hadn't known. And yet she jumped. She took a long pull of her beer. Why had she jumped?

"Yeah, I wouldn't have told him either," Thompson said. "Pretty embarrassing dive if you ask me. Looked like a cork popping out of a bottle. You landed ass-first into that shit."

"Fuck you, Thompson," she said with a grin and the others laughed, even Dan.

"I think she was on fire too," Lucky added.

"I know, right? Smoke comin' off her as she cannonballs through the air—"

"Son of a bitch."

They all went quiet and looked at Bashful Dan.

Dava huffed, still grinning, then quickly frowned as she read his face. "What is it?"

He pointed and they looked. There was a holovid in the corner of the bar. It was showing some advertisement for a film. There, in the three-dimensional image that swirled with the smoke of a nearby cigar, was a face she did not expect to see.

"No fucking way." Dava slapped her hands on the table and stood up. "We *have* to see that movie."

* * *

There was a showing that night, so they went. Thompson and Lucky didn't know who Jax was and didn't seem much to care, but the theater served beer, so they managed to entertain themselves. In terms of content, it was a little on the boring side. There weren't any real villains, only the looming threat of magnetic field flux, which the film went through great lengths to explain would result in the whole population of Terroneous getting cooked alive.

Most of it was a mix of actors re-enacting the scenes that led up to the almost-evacuation and real people being interviewed documentary-style about the geological science and the technology involved. Occasionally, there were clips of "real life" footage. These were actually fairly tense, with people arguing and frantically wrestling with the systems, but would have gotten mundane if they hadn't been such short edits. It was during these sequences that Psycho Jack made his appearance. Interestingly, whenever his name appeared on-screen it was just "Fugere", or sometimes "Fugere, The Fixer", but never Jack or Jackson.

Was he hiding out on Terroneous? Why else would a B-fourean be on a rock like this? And if he was hiding, why did he let himself get filmed for everyone to see? Not that Dava thought this trash would make it far off-world, but it was bound to get back to ModPol somehow.

"So who is this guy?" Thompson said, leaning over her armrest to talk into Dava's ear, but not exactly whispering.

Dava tilted her head away from the sweet-and-sour buffet of alcohol that came with the question. "That's Psycho Jack. Was Johnny Eyeball's cellmate once. Supposed to be a mass murderer. Did a whole block in a dome, like thirty, forty people."

Thompson attempted a whistle but failed to make more than a puff of air. "Damn."

"But turns out he didn't do it. He was framed by these corrupt Pollies."

"Fuckin' ModPol."

"He figured it all out though. He and this cop – I guess one that's not corrupt – they tracked down this lady who hacked the dome or something. I can't remember what the whole deal was."

"So he's not a psycho."

"No," Dava said wistfully. "Too bad too. He's smart."

Thompson seemed to consider this. She cocked her head at the holoprojection. "Kind of cute."

"Unbelievable," Lucky moaned from the seat in front of them. He turned to face them. "Really, Tommy? This guy?"

"I swear, Lucky, if you don't turn around I'm going to cut your face off and wipe my ass with it." Thompson waved at the screen, where Psycho Jack and a woman from some environmental agency were working at a console. "Seriously, you think I'm checking out this lanky pale-ass domer? I'm talkin' 'bout the girl, you ass."

Dava choked back a laugh, not wanting to encourage their banter, but not exactly sober enough to put a stop to it.

Dan turned around as well. "Dava, you think he's still here? On Terroneous?"

She gave him a look. "Maybe. Why?"

He hesitated, which meant he was going to say something that was probably a good idea but was going to involve pissing her off in some way. She motioned with her hand. "Out with it."

"Well," he said. "We lost Freezer at Vulca."

"*I* lost Freezer at Vulca," she muttered. There was the bit that pissed her off. The memory of the fight at the relay station drifted in, swirling and bubbling, questions surfacing in the haze of her alcohol-addled mind. Questions like, weren't Johnny and Frank worth more than some stupid equipment? Was the point of the mission the equipment, or had there been another reason for such an attack?

"And? What—" She stood up, spilling popcorn onto the floor. "We get Psycho Jack to sub for Frank?"

Dan nodded and even smiled a little. "That's what I was thinking."

It was a good idea, for sure, because they needed another hacker. And Psycho Jack clearly had the knowhow, being that he tracked down a murderous programmer, plus they just watched a holofilm about how his skills saved the whole moon from – what, exactly? Something about a magnetic field, and Jack hacking into the system to make it all better. And he was already an enemy of ModPol, which made him as good as an ally.

But what made it a *very* good idea was that Jansen had been talking about bringing in his own man to replace Frank. If Dava could get Psycho Jack, then they wouldn't need another hacker and Jansen would have to cool his heels.

Not that she wanted to play games with Jansen, but there was just something about him she still didn't trust. Jack, she could trust. He was a fugitive. He was one of them.

"You're a genius, Dan! Can you find him?"

Dan lifted a handypad. "I've been taking notes."

CHAPTER 15

Jax flung the suitcase from its place in the bottom of the closet up onto the bed. He flipped it around to open it, realized he'd flipped it backwards, righted it and tried again. Whipped it open so hard that it tipped backward and slid off the bed.

"Jack."

He bent down to get the case and then with determined focus pushed it down onto the bed and opened it to face the closet.

"Jack." Lealina's voice was soft but firm.

"I don't know what I'm going to do," was all he could manage in response. He started pawing through clothes, selecting them more or less at random and shoving them into the case.

"It looks like you do."

He paused for a moment, staring at the closet. "Like I do what?"

"Know what you're going to do."

He looked at her. "Well I don't."

She scowled, her hair coming down in front of her eyes. "Then why are you packing?"

He turned back to the closet and reached for a shirt. "I have to."

She put a hand on his arm, pulling hard. Her unexpected strength almost broke the spell, almost brought him into focus. But when he looked into her eyes, all he saw were storms in the distance.

"You need to tell me what's going on." Her anger scared him. He didn't like seeing her eyes like that.

He forced his arms down to his sides. Forced air into his lungs, slowly. Forced himself to sit on the edge of the bed. Forced the words out of his mouth. "I'm innocent."

She stared at him for years. "Innocent," she said, handling the word like a freshly sharpened knife. She bent slightly to meet his eye-line. "Of what?"

He felt disconnected from his own body. Like he was watching the conversation play out from a distance. He watched himself as he motioned to the desk on the other end of the room and spoke. "The top drawer."

She glanced at it, gave him a look, then walked over and opened it. She pulled out the folder and flipped through the pages. "What is all this? Why do you have these print-outs?"

"I made them at the library."

"Don't you have any handypads?"

"No." He abstained from explaining that he needed to stay offline, hoping she would pick it up soon enough.

She didn't press. Instead, her attention went to the pages. "The Dome Killer," she read. "I remember this. Back on B-4?"

"Yes."

"Jenna Zarconi," she read, then began to paraphrase as

she flipped pages. "ModPol tracked her down, all the way to Sirius-5. Scary stuff."

"You have no idea."

She looked up. "What does this have to do with you?"

Jax had spent months combing through every news article from every outlet in the known galaxy looking to see if there were any references to a B-fourean fugitive. Some outlets played up the success of ModPol, others highlighted the possible corruption that had opened the door to the murders, or covered them up after the fact. Some even mentioned Officer Stanford Runstom, whether to note his sheer luck or his perseverance and dedication to justice in cracking the case. There were interviews, and Jax read them, watched them. The name Jackson was never mentioned, for which he knew he had to be thankful.

In one interview, Stanford had turned to the camera at the end and nodded curtly. Not in response to anything the interviewer was saying. Not to acknowledge the audience, nor anyone off-camera. Just one short nod. His eyes looked through time and space and digital recording, looked right at Jax and nodded.

Jax had to hide in the restroom of the library for an hour after that.

He felt Lealina's eyes on him and cleared his throat. "There's more to it. Something that's not in those articles."

She stared at him and closed the folder.

"The murders – you know how they happened?"

She nodded slowly. "Something about the airlock vents opening up at the top of a block. Both at the same time. Some kind of system hack."

"On B-4, we have Life Support operators that monitor those blocks every hour of the day. Do maintenance things like change out the air, turn on the rain, fluctuate the temperature—"

"Turn on the rain?"

A small corner of his mouth curled reflexively. "For purification purposes. Everyone gets a warning ahead of time so they don't get wet."

"Weird."

"Lealina," he said. "I was a block operator."

"Oh," she said quietly. She cocked her head. "Did—"

"It was my block. 23-D, in Gretel."

They both grew quiet. Her eyes scanned him, searching for answers. Instead of peppering him with questions, she just said, "I'm sorry, Jack. That must have been…horrible."

"There's more," he said, even though he knew she knew that.

And he proceeded to tell her. Once it started, he just couldn't stop. He told her about his arrest, about being grilled by ModPol, about his useless lawyer, about their decision to haul him off to prison at the outpost at the edge of the system. That he got off the transport barge before it was destroyed.

"What happened there?" she interrupted. "The official story was that it was a horrible accident. But I heard it was an attack. Some people even said it was Space Waste, but that's just kind of ridiculous, isn't it?"

He grew quiet. It must have been hard for ModPol to swallow that. But to save face, they had to go with the accident story. They couldn't admit to the known galaxy that a misfit outfit like Space Waste planned such a coordinated and deadly effort against them.

"Stanford," he started finally, "Officer Runstom, I mean—"

"The one who they say tracked down the killer?"

"Yes, that one. He was with me on that barge. He got me off in one piece."

"I don't understand, Jack. What does this all mean? Why are you hiding? They found the real killer, right?"

"Yes," he said. "But the corruption part – that's real too. And even if I didn't commit those murders, I'm still a criminal. I escaped their custody."

She scowled again, this time not at him, but at the folder twisting in her hands. "I knew there was something not right about you."

He straightened up at that, frowning. "What the hell does that mean?"

"Because I fucking like you!" She slapped the folder back down on the desk. Her head bent down, away from him. Quieter, she said, "I really like you."

He sighed, and an unexpected roughness in his throat caused him to cough. "Believe me, Lea. I wish it wasn't true. I don't want to run. I don't want to run for the rest of my life. I don't want to run from here. From…" he trailed off, looked at her, then looked away.

He heard her release air, a deflating sound. "I'm sorry. I don't know what you're going through."

He still couldn't face her, but he had to ask. "Do you believe me when I say I'm innocent?"

She was quiet for another eternity. Then she sat next to him on the bed. "I believe you."

A tear came loose then, followed by another, and another. He wiped his face ungracefully with his shirt sleeve. "Thank you," he managed.

She put her hand on his leg. "Just breathe for a minute."

"I'm scared," he whispered. A secret he'd kept in all the months he'd been living there.

"It's okay. It will be okay."

"What am I going to do?"

"Jack, believe me," she said, a small upward swing in her voice. "You're not the first person who came to Terroneous to hide. From ModPol, or anything else."

He sniffed. "I suppose not."

"Seriously. We've got lots of hiding places on this moon. We just need to talk to some people." She lifted his head with her fingertips. "Okay?"

He looked at those eyes, blinked away the storm and tried to see them as the bright blue that he was first enchanted by. "Okay." He swallowed then straightened up. "I want you to call me Jax."

"Jax? Not Jack?"

"My name isn't Jack Fugere. It's Jack Jackson."

Her head tilted slightly. "You're telling me your real name is Jack Jackson?"

"My dad," he started then shook his head with a soft laugh. "It's ridiculous, I know. Something in my dad's engineer brain latched onto a name that lined up." He looked into her eyes. "I kind of hate it, which is why I prefer Jax."

The corner of her mouth turned up and her eyes crinkled with the grin. "Okay. I like Jax."

"Good." The smile he felt growing across his face lifted him up, and he rose from the bed.

"We'll get through this," she said, standing with him and gripping his arm. "Jax. We'll find a place for you, Jax."

He nodded, the lightness giving way to a sudden anger. "Before we do anything, we need to find David Granderson."

* * *

Granderson was difficult to track down. He seemed to be hopping all over Stockton, on some kind of movie-promotion mission. They'd gone to his studio, only to be told by one of the other artists that rented space in the same building that he'd gone off to a gallery. They went to the gallery to find fliers for the film, Jax's face part of the montage that adorned each and every one. According to the security guard, Granderson had left for a restaurant just a few hours previously. They went to The Golden Krogg and found that the dinner party had wound down to nothing but dirty plates, drained glasses, and handwritten invites to an after-party at The Sundown Lodge on the edge of town. The staff were reluctant to give these up, as the growing entourage that Granderson was acquiring was having a blast and they wanted to ensure they could get into the after-party themselves.

So Jax and Lealina showed up at Sundown uninvited.

"Sorry, folks. Private event tonight." The broad doorman didn't give them much of a look, seemingly distracted by the evident fun just beyond his post. He thrust out a hand. "Unless you have an invite. Or, you know." The fingers wiggled. "Whatever."

"Can you at least tell Granderson we're here?" Jax said.

"Who're you?" A choral whoop caused him to turn his head fully away from them, and he peered down the hall into the darkness.

"I'm Jack Fugere."

Finally he looked Jax full in the face. "No shit – you're the bloke from the film!" He looked at Lealina. "And you're the bird!"

"Can we go in?" Lealina asked.

"Yeah, of course, of course." He stepped aside. "Hey, if

you see Muri in there, tell him it's his shift. I want to go in."

"We'll be sure to do that," she said and pushed past, pulling Jax by the arm.

Inside, the small bar was packed. The lights were low, but not so low they couldn't see. And there was music, but it wasn't loud. In fact, it seemed to be just the right volume to be present, but not loud enough to dampen an enthusiastic and experienced storyteller, should one embark on a tale or two.

In fact, one just happened to be so embarked.

Though members of the crowd whispered among themselves, as a whole they were fixated on the voice at the back of the room.

"So then I said, Maximus, listen pal..."

Lealina wasted no time. She began pushing through the crowd, Jax still attached by her grip. People invariably gave them a look of protest that quickly turned to recognition, followed by a step back to let them through.

"The only way that thing is coming out of there is if you've got something for it to eat..."

The front row was particularly dense. With his height, Jax could see Granderson perched on a stool, gesturing grandly in between pulls of a bright-green conical cocktail.

"And this thing only eats *live* food!"

Gasps and laughter and even a few claps broke out across the listeners, but it was short lived. Everyone went silent as Lealina pulled Jax past them all.

"Jack! Lealina!" Granderson's face went from shock to mild anguish to a wide grin. "Welcome, so glad you could make it!"

"What the hell, David?" Jax said. He glared at the man with the angriest face he was capable of making.

"What? Oh sorry." He leaned in close. "I know I didn't invite you out tonight, but you know. It's reality HV. You're not actors, you know what I mean? It's just kind of – it takes the *reality* out of it if I invite the subjects to the premiere party."

"We need to talk," Lealina said. "Now."

Granderson leaned back away from them and tilted his head up. "Everyone, this next round of drinks is on me, so you better make your way up to the bar while you can."

The crowd began to mill and small conversations were born all around them. Jax felt his face redden as he heard his name in snippets from various parts of the room.

Granderson leaned in again. "Is this about the cut? It says right there in the contract you signed that your percentage is paid out after expenses are cleared, not before. I was very up front about that, in the wording."

"David," Jax growled. "I thought you were going to use actors."

He blinked. "We did, Jack. Lots of actors. I told you I was going to have to re-enact most of it because we got filming so late in the storyline."

"But there are parts of it with me in it! When you were shooting at TEOB, you said you were just gathering – source something."

"Source material? Well yeah, I was." He blinked and looked at his glass, but didn't dare to drink under the heat of their angry glares. "It was just that…it turned out better than I thought it would. I mean, I had to edit the hell out of it, let me tell you—"

"Dammit, David," Jax said. "I didn't want to be in it at all! You were supposed to blur my face! You weren't even supposed to use my name!"

He blinked, then tilted his head. "Really? Why not?"

Jax breathed through his nose. "Don't you remember when we met? Don't you remember the state I was in?"

Granderson's look of innocence melted as his mouth drooped and his eyes widened. "Jack. I remember – I remember a lost man. A man trying to escape an old life, trying to find a new one. But...I just...what is it? Jack... Jack, why don't you want your face to be seen?"

The question caused Jax to huff, to wring his hands, but he could give no answer except through clenched teeth, "Because."

Lealina got between them. "David, someone is after Jack. He's in hiding."

Granderson's jaw slackened. "What, really? Who?" He looked at her, then over her shoulder at Jax, then he frowned and his mouth tightened. "No. You shouldn't tell me who. It's better not to know."

"We need you to pull the ads," Lealina said. "We need to get Jack's face off the airways."

"Of course. Of course. I'll do a recut and a re-release. No Jack, none at all."

"Wait," Jax said. "Did you say the premiere was tonight? Has it already played?"

"Yeah, tonight it has. But I can do an all-stop right now, get it pulled from the theaters—"

"How many?" Lealina asked. "How many theaters?"

"Well just two here in Stockton," he said, then pursed his lips. "And one in Nuzwick and one in Sunderville."

Jax tried to control his breathing. "Why the hell didn't you tell us you were going to do this? Why didn't we even get to see it?"

Granderson stood and put a hand on Jax's shoulder. He

was almost as tall as Jax and tried to meet his eyes. "I'm really sorry, Jack. It's just how it's done. You two are subjects of the film. You're not stars. You're not even actors." He swallowed and looked away. "And you're not partners."

Jax brushed away the hand. "Fuck you, David."

Lealina stepped between them again. "Look, what's done is done. Do what you can to clean it up, David."

"I'm not contractually obligated to," he said. When they shot him a pair of glares, he raised a hand. "I'm just reminding you. I'll clean this up, I promise. As your friend."

While Jax's vision began to haze, he felt Lealina's hand on his chest. "Okay, David," she said. "Thank you."

"What are you going to do?" Granderson asked.

She was quiet for a moment, then said, "There's a TEOB facility in the Low Desert. It's hidden away, not for any reason other than being remote and underground – to measure magma flow under the crust. Only problem is my car won't get there. I need an all-terrain, and I don't want to use one of the TEOB vehicles if I can help it."

"I know how you can get there," Grandson said quickly. "It's the least I can do."

Forty-five minutes later they were on a private gyrocopter heading for the middle of the Low Desert.

CHAPTER 16

"I was just passing through," Runstom said. "I thought I would come by and see how – to see what – well, to see…"

"To see if I'm still locked up?"

"To see you're being treated fairly."

"I appreciate that, Stanford."

Jenna Zarconi rose from the cot and went to the sink where she filled a small plastic cup with water and sipped at it. The cell was small, but it was another temporary hold. Before coming in, he'd checked on her transfer status. Outpost Gamma was the last stop before she would arrive at her permanent residence at the zero-G prison facility at the edge of the Barnard system. Runstom was only in the outpost momentarily, a stop on the trip to his next mission. This was place that housed his old precinct. Perhaps that was why he avoided contact with anyone in Justice – all his old co-workers – other than to gain access to the holding cells.

"I heard about your success on Vulca," she said, turning from the sink.

"Oh?"

"Well, news of the attack was all over the media. Some mention of the heroics of the ModPol Defenders stationed there. A trial unit that was upgraded to a full contract."

"The media said all that?" He wondered if his name had been mentioned. He'd hated all that media attention after the arrests on Sirius-5.

She smirked at him and shook her head lightly. "Only if you have the time to dig past the headlines. And time is all I have."

His hands turned over themselves involuntarily. "Did they uh..." he started, trailing off.

"Mention you? Not by name. But some of the details, the stories." Her smile grew wide. "I couldn't help but to recognize your trademark bullheadedness."

"Yes, well..."

"I don't expect you to tell me what happened."

"I can't."

"I know." She paused, turning away to pace the short distance back to the cot. "But obviously you got to the bottom of the attack." As if an afterthought.

"Yeah. I..."

"Yes?"

He wanted to stare her down, challenge her with his eyes, but then he remembered who she was. He couldn't intimidate her. He could barely hide from her. "I wish I could have looked a little harder at the details," he admitted. "That's what you want to hear, isn't it?"

"But you were unable to."

"No. As you said, a new contract was signed. They didn't need me there anymore so I got whisked off to the next assignment."

"Which brings you back to Barnard," she said. "That's quite the trip."

"You would know," he said, unable to resist the shot laid out for him. But her shot had already landed: he wanted to dig, and instead they'd sent him to an entirely different star system.

She gave him a short laugh. "I'd ask you how the flight was, but you're right, I just took it myself. One good thing about a life sentence is that I'll never have to do cryosleep again."

He smirked, and tried to hide it, disgusted with himself for finding humor in her misfortune. But it wasn't misfortune. It was her own actions that brought her here.

"Yeah, hate that cryosleep," he muttered for lack of anything better to say.

She nodded quietly, then said, "Back in Barnard. Who in this system needs your public relations magic?" She stood with her cup in hand and turned her head to the upper corner of the wall, looking through a non-existent window. "B-3 and B-4 are locked in. Terroneous is too independent. Too large a land mass with minimal, siloed governments spread across it."

Runstom grunted. "Peter – I mean, the account manager for Vulca – he told me Terroneous is the keystone. Seems impossible to get them under ModPol, but if it happened, all the indies would follow suit."

"That's probably true," she said, still looking into the distance. "The other independent settlements see Terroneous as proof of the prosperity that's possible. If they don't need ModPol, then no one does. But you're not going to Terroneous."

"No," Runstom agreed. "Not Terroneous. In a few days

I'm going to Ipo. It's a smaller moon of B-5, where there's an ore refinery."

"Really." She turned her head slightly, still not looking at him. "ModPol Defense services for miners?"

"It's grown large enough in population to become an incorporated district." He suspected she already knew this. She had nothing to do but sit around and read up on current events.

"Which means a handful of public services to manage," she said softly, nodding. "And taxes to collect."

"I suppose."

"Some say Ipo is just another Terroneous settlement. It just happens to be on a different moon orbiting the same planet." Again, she looked into the solid wall. "Makes sense that ModPol would seek a foothold there. Strike while the opportunity is fresh. How long will you be there?"

"Two months, give or take." He was feeling dangerously close to the border of what he should be sharing with an inmate. "I guess I better study up a little on asteroid mining."

He gave an awkward chuckle at this last statement, but she turned to face him fully, her expression stone. "I wish I could say I was surprised to learn that Jack was on Terroneous, but I wasn't really."

"What did you say?"

"No one told you. That also does not surprise me."

"Jenna, what the hell are you talking about?"

"Had you heard about the magnetic field disruptions on Terroneous a few weeks ago? It would have been just before your interstellar trip."

"Yes." He'd caught the news story while back at ModPol HQ on Sirius-5. Hundreds of thousands of lives were in danger, so of course he was concerned, but he couldn't help the selfish concern for Jax most of all. Because of the scale of the problem, it was easy to gossip with others about what might happen without revealing he knew anyone on the moon. Sadly, the general opinion around Sirius-5 was that those endangered people should have been living in domes anyway. "What does that have to do with Jax?" he asked. How could she know he was there?

"Turns out there were no magnetic field disruptions," she said with a turn of her hand. "Turns out it was all a bunch of misconfigured equipment. See, on Terroneous, they get all this hand-me-down equipment. Take whatever they can get. But most of the time they don't know how to use it, or only half know. So here's this planet-wide crisis – well, moon-wide I suppose – and a B-fourean with technical operation experience pops his head out of the ground and saves their bacon."

"Oh, that stupid sonofabitch."

"They think he's a hero."

"Yeah, well. Sure. I'm sure they do." He suddenly wondered if there were any mics or cameras in her cell. He realized he should assume there were, but he needed to know what she knew. He leaned in close to her. "How do you know it was Jax?"

"Watch an HV sometime, Stanford."

"Jenna!" he whispered.

She rolled her eyes and stepped back, projecting her voice. "Some holographer made a film about the whole incident." She too must have suspected recorders in the cell, and was letting him know she was only sharing widely-known information. "Got Jax on camera a couple of times, under the name Jack Fugere. They call him 'Fugere The Fixer'. The original film never made it off Terroneous, but the previews did. Some of the fringe networks picked it up and pieced together the story. Asking the question, 'Who is this *Jack Fugere*?'"

Runstom clutched his temples with one hand. What could he do? It was a matter of time before Jax would be tracked down – he'd always known that. But now, the B-fourean was daring ModPol to come get him.

Except he was on Terroneous. "ModPol has no jurisdiction there," he said aloud as he thought it.

"No," she agreed. "Not as such."

"What does that mean?"

She looked away, as if distracted, then turned to face him, her voice dropping to a whisper. "I don't have to explain it to you, Stanford. ModPol may not have jurisdiction, but deals have been struck. The governments on Terroneous are weak and sometimes desperate. You know he's not safe there."

He frowned. "He's not safe anywhere," he mumbled.

He had to turn from her then, before he started tracing everything back to the start, before he started thinking too much about how it was all because of her, this woman, this psychopath.

Instead he focused on what he could. Was there anything he could do for Jax? He'd truly hoped that the case would have moved along by now, that they would have exonerated Jax. Any inquiries he initiated were met with stone-faced replies. He was Defense now, and Justice felt like they owed him no explanations.

"I know you think I feel no remorse," Zarconi said, breaking his thoughts. "And in many ways I don't. But I am sorry, Stanford. I'm sorry that your friend's life has been destroyed."

He glanced at her over his shoulder, then looked down. Took a step toward the door. "I don't know why I came here."

"I'm sure the mines will wait, if you take a detour," she said, freezing him before he reached the door. "If you happen to swing by Terroneous, take a moment to say hello to your old squadmate, McManus."

He spun to face her. "McManus?"

She finished her water and set the cup down on the edge of the sink. Looked around the room, as though she had more important matters to attend to, then finally answered him with disinterest. "This whole outpost is like a sewing circle. No rules against loose lips."

So McManus was the one they would send after Jax. Runstom figured the other officer still held a grudge against both of them. He was a useless and petty man. He no doubt volunteered for the mission as soon as word got around. Not that there would be much in the way of word; not many would even know who Jax was. But McManus did.

Still, he couldn't go down to Terroneous and flat out arrest Jax. No, it would have to be an undercover operation. Runstom didn't like that thought at all: McManus hunting Jax down on that independent moon without any oversight.

"I have to go," he said.

"I'm sure it will be a grand reunion." She placed a hand on his hand and gripped his fingers tightly. Looked directly into his eyes. "The old gang, getting back together."

There was a flick of her eyes, darting upward then back to him in a micro motion. She knew more that she couldn't tell him. More that wasn't getting through his thick skull.

He pulled his hands away. "I have to go," he repeated.

"Good luck winning the mines," she said idly.

CHAPTER 17

"Nice studio."

The man at the controls spasmed and twisted around in his chair. "Who the hell are you? You scared the crap out of me!"

It was a long, narrow, dark room with shelving units trailing down the sides three-quarters of the way, cleared away at the end to make room for a broad, makeshift control center, patched together with mismatched speakers and monitors, a mix of flat and holo. The room's original purpose must have been storage, possibility even food storage, being below ground. Instead the shelves were sporadically occupied by strange hunks of electronic equipment, presumably for filming.

Dava motioned the others into position without taking her eyes off their subject. "Are you David Granderson?"

"Yes." His head bobbed from side to side, his eyes trying to adjust to the darkness of the rest of the room, probably having spent hours staring at the brightly lit screens and holovids that glowed behind him. "I mean, who wants to know?"

"We're looking for Jack," Dava said. She moved slowly toward him, so slowly he squinted, as if unsure whether she was drawing close or if it was just his imagination. "He was in your holofilm."

"I make lots of holofilms."

"Mmm," she purred. "Only one has Jack Fugere."

"Yes, w-well," he stammered. His body language shouted that he wanted to spring to his feet, but he was restraining himself, trying to appear calm in the face of intrusion. "I suppose that is true. But that was some kind of mix-up. That footage didn't belong."

"A mix-up?" Thompson said with a laugh. "Get a load of this guy – a mix-up? How do you accidentally put footage into a holovid? And was it a mix-up when it was in all the previews too?"

Granderson lost his restraint and stood up. He turned to face them fully and his voice grew loud. "Yes, that's right. It was a mix-up. Just what business of—"

"You're going to want to sit back down there, Mr. Granderson."

Thompson's voice cut through the air like a bullet. Granderson flinched, then took a long hard look at the menacing submachinegun that she casually aimed in his direction. He risked a glance behind himself, as if some part of his brain was more concerned with damage to his equipment than to his own body, then he sat back down. He took a look at each of them in turn: Thompson in front of him, Lucky Jerk by the door, Bashful Dan lurking in the back, and Dava twirling a blade and drifting slowly toward him.

"Man, that guy wasn't kidding when he said someone was after him," he sighed. "Look, I don't know what you want from me. I already told your friend everything I know."

"Someone from ModPol?" Dava asked.

"What? ModPol, no. Never see ModPol on Terroneous. Was just another jerk like – uh, I mean, was just some jerk."

"Describe him."

Granderson frowned. "I don't know. I thought you were with him."

Dava looked at Thompson. "Destroy something."

She flipped the submachinegun over to single-shot mode and with a crack put a bullet through a small speaker mounted on the wall behind Granderson.

"Fuck!" he yelled and waved his hands high. "Those are expensive!"

"Something else," Dava said.

"No, wait, wait." He stood, lowering his hands down to chest level, palms still facing out. When Thompson's gun swung back to him, he sat back down quickly. "It was a pink-skinned guy. Like from B-3. And he was big, you know, built. Hair was a buzz cut. No uniform or colors even, just wore a lot of grays."

"Was he alone?" Dava said.

"Yeah. No. I mean, he spoke to me alone, but I saw him meet up with some other guys. Two other guys. Also in just grays and browns."

"Did you see a ship or a vehicle?"

"No."

"Not much use," Thompson said with a sigh.

"Wait, there's something," he said, putting his hands up high again, but careful not to stand. "You know, the clothes – they weren't from around here. They weren't cloth or hide or anything. They were hybrid mesh fabric."

"The kind that makes you look big and flashy?"

Thompson said. "Like you got more muscles than you really got?"

"No, well, yeah," he stammered. "Same kind of stuff – I use it all the time in my films. But instead of being flashy, it was doing the opposite. Like, like a muting effect. Not quite camouflage, but enough to make it so most people would never notice these guys walking around."

"Interesting." Dan's quiet voice was so unexpected, it almost made Dava turn to look at him, but she kept her eyes on Granderson.

"What did you tell him?" she said.

"I want to be clear," he said slowly and deliberately. "I don't know Mr. Fugere all that well. I don't even know his real name. I don't know exactly where he went—"

"But you have an idea," Thompson prodded.

Granderson stared at them in silence for a moment, looking from Thompson to Dava and back. He hung his head. "Yeah. He said he was going to the Low Desert."

"Why?" Dava said. "What's there?"

"Some hidden facility." He lifted his head and crossed his arms, his lips pulling tight across his face. "That's all I know."

"So like an underground building in the desert?" Lucky Jerk asked from the other end of the room, suddenly interrupting the conversation.

"I don't know," Granderson said through clenched teeth, glaring at the flyboy.

"Yeah, I bet I know right where that is."

"How the hell would you know that, shit-for-brains?" Thompson said, the barrel of her gun straying in his direction.

"Because, Tommy-girl," he said with the taunting voice

of a younger brother, "when we were looking for a solid place to put the dropship out in the desert, I was doing a density scan. We flew right over a spot that looked like a perfect rectangle somewhere under the sand."

"What the hell, Lucky," Thompson said. "There was an underground building out there and you had us parked next to it?"

"No, dammit," he said, practically stamping a foot. "Listen to me. I saw it and put us on the other side of the desert just to *avoid* it."

"Perfect," Dava said. "Mr. Granderson, thank you for your cooperation."

"Are you," he started, and she heard his voice crack a little. "Are you going to hurt him?"

She took a step toward him. With the slow drifting, she was now practically on top of him. "No, don't worry about your friend." She looked him in the eyes and cocked her head slightly. "We're going to rescue him. And then we're going to recruit him."

"R-really?"

"If he gives us any trouble after that," she said with a twirl of her blade, "then we're going to hurt him."

* * *

The personnel at the TEOB Magma Center were anxious to give Jax an in-depth tour of their facility. He wasn't in a hurry, knowing he could be stuck there for an indeterminate length of time, but they acted like he might evaporate before their eyes and they needed to show him as much as possible before that happened. Maybe it was just that they never got any visitors.

Lealina was off on some administrative errand. In order to get him past the visitors' area of the structure – which was no more than a five-meter-square room with half a dozen plastic chairs on a floor specked with sand tracked in from the desert – she had to file some kind of contractor-evaluation paperwork. She explained that was just the beginning, that in order to let Jax stay in the facility, she'd have to have someone complete the evaluation and then he could be hired as a consultant. Hired but not paid, simply because there was no budget for it. However, room and board would be provided.

So he'd left Lealina on the first sublevel and followed a trio of technicians around the second sublevel as they pointed out the living facilities: bed-chambers, a small kitchen, showers, a tiny game room, and so on. The halls were narrow and short, and Jax had to duck just a few centimeters any time he passed through a doorway. Every time he did so, he thought about the tons upon tons of desert sand bearing down on the walls and then had to think of something else.

Before long they took him in an elevator down to the third sublevel, which they explained was where most of the observation work was done. There was a fourth sublevel, but none of the technicians were keen on making the trip down. Evidently it wasn't much but darkness and heat and noise, as the fourth sublevel was where holes had been drilled deep below the surface and various sensor equipment went down. A handful of people worked below to keep the systems running with the aid of some maintenance bots, and neither group was what the technicians considered hospitable company.

They pulled him into an observation room that was full

of monitoring and recording equipment. It seemed they could carry on three simultaneous conversations independently from one another with no lack of enthusiasm or momentum, and he desperately tried to pay attention to their overlapping exposition. He was going to have to earn his keep, and he wanted to contribute eventually, but he was too distracted in that moment to follow half of what they told him about their operation.

What was he going to do? He couldn't keep running and hiding forever. All the news he'd been following, all the crap he'd accumulated in his folder of fugitivity, none of it was pointing to his freedom.

He should have been thankful. Lealina was looking out for him in a way that no one ever had, with the exception of Stanford Runstom. Hell, even Granderson did his best to make his wrongs right, got an associate to fly them out to the middle of the desert in a gyrocopter. And Jax was thankful. It was just the not knowing that was killing him. What kind of future did he have, what kind of life could he make, always looking over his shoulder?

The trio of techs prattled on and he thought of Runstom. He knew the officer's reach was very limited, and he knew it was in his best interest that Runstom not seek him out. But he desperately wished he could hear from him – something, anything. And even though it was a dangerous idea, he briefly entertained the fantasy of Runstom swooping down to Terroneous to rescue his ass one more time.

"Hey guys." Jax turned at the sound of Lealina's voice and found immediate solace in those bright blues. "Mind if I steal Mr. Fugere for a few minutes? I've got some forms for him to fill out."

The techs happily shook his hand and went about their

business and he followed Lealina back down the hall and into the elevator. While they rode she gave him an overview of the virtual paperwork he would have to deal with back on the first floor.

"But first, I want to show you to your room," she said, getting off the elevator on sublevel two. "They aren't the best accommodations, but they're private. I had someone bring your stuff down already."

She handed him a keycard and led him to the section of corridor where the living quarters were. They found his room and went inside. It was definitely small and sparse, but it was livable. A bed, a desk with a terminal, a closet, a dresser, and even a small holovid in the corner. His bags were piled in the middle of the floor.

"Not bad," he said, then looked at the light-gray walls. "Could use some color."

"I'll get you something," she said, quietly closing the door behind her. "Some art."

"That would be nice." He looked at her and looked away. To get him something meant she would be leaving. He bent down to shuffle through his bags. "Guess I'll make myself at home."

"I'm going to stay for a couple of days," she said.

"That's good."

"Then I have to get back."

"I understand."

"I'm still acting director and all."

"I know."

"Of course, I'll be back. I come here a couple of times a month for work."

He stood up and tried to smile at her. "Lealina, everything you've done for me—"

"I know." She took his hand. She looked at him for a moment and they were quiet. He wanted to be angry at the universe for giving him something only to take it away, but those eyes would not let him be anything but at peace.

"Jax?"

"Yes?"

"I know this is a *moment* and all, but like I said, I can only stay a couple of days."

He released her hand. "Right."

"So we're going to have to fast-track this," she said and unbuttoned her shirt.

* * *

Two days at the facility and Jax had gotten enough orientation to begin work assisting the techs in one of the observation rooms. It was a lot of watching for anomalies that never appeared, and there was an odd familiarity that nagged at the back of his mind until he finally cornered it and realized it was very similar to the work he did as a life-support operator back on B-4. The thought paralyzed him momentarily: had he really traveled so far, experienced so much, only to end up doing the same thing he was doing less than a year ago?

He shook it off. He reminded himself that this was survival mode, reminded himself that he would do what needed to be done, day by day. Every day he woke up free was a victory. It didn't matter what he was doing to earn his keep. Did it?

Kuri, a mousy, yellow-skinned tech in his mid-forties, interrupted Jax's pontifications. "Mr. Fugere," he said, pointing at the ceiling. "Director Warpshire is requesting your presence up top. Something about paperwork finalizations."

"What?" He followed the finger up, then looked back down instead of staring uselessly at the ceiling. What paperwork was there left to do? None, of course. "Oh. Right. Guess I'll see you after lunch," he said, already having learned the technicians' strict adherence to the break timetables.

"Yes, of course."

Jax went up the elevator to the top. He asked for Lealina at one of the front desks and a clerk told him that she went outside to take some readings. He gave the man a curious look. What readings would she be taking in the middle of the desert? None, of course. He smiled and nodded and headed for the stairwell that led to the small opening above.

Lealina was about twenty meters out, just at the top of a nearby dune. He frowned at his improper clothing; not only was it not fit for walking through the desert, it would collect sand, and the techs would no doubt give him a lengthy lecture about the dangers of bringing the stuff into the observation chambers. He watched her for a moment. She was turned away from him, a scarf wrapped around her face, hands in her pockets. She looked peaceful.

He trudged up the dune, acquiring several kilos of sand in his low-top shoes in the process. He took a place next to her and looked into the distance, where she looked. The dunes were like frozen waves. Views like this always hit him particularly hard, both with a sense of beauty and a sense of vertigo. Just being able to see into such distance was still a shock to him at times, having grown up in domes which themselves were divided into subdomes and blocks and chambers and corridors.

"My mom," he caught himself saying unexpectedly. "Uh…"

She turned only slightly, still mostly facing the landscape. "Yes?"

He cleared his throat. "My mother, she was a terraformer. Sorry, I just remembered her now. You never see the surface on B-4. Well, you were there, you remember."

"Yeah. Claustrophobic."

"Yeah," he said, trying out a few different meanings for the word before coming up blank. "What's that one?"

She laughed from behind the scarf and her beautiful eyes rolled at him. "Fear of being closed in."

He considered that. "It seems like a valuable fear to have," he said, mostly to himself.

"You were talking about your mother?"

"Right. My mom. Once in a while when I was young – like seven, eight years old – she would bring me to work. I never got to go out onto the surface of course, but she let me see it."

"Out here, Jax?" she said, turning to look him directly in the eyes and taking his hand. "This is how we know that not everything is made by the human race. That – in fact – most of the universe is not under our control."

He grinned at her. "I like that. But I'm not sure everyone would agree."

"That's because most people are fucking stupid," she said, pulling the scarf down and grinning right back at him.

He kissed her then, for a length of time he could not possibly estimate, while the warm air lightly danced around them, specking his skin harmlessly with sand. When the movement of time began again, it was due to the interruption of a sound that could only be made by the human race.

They pulled apart reluctantly. Her face turned from warm bliss to cold terror. He followed her eyes to the distant sky. A black form, heavy and unnatural in its defiance of gravity, cut through the sky in a zagging pattern. Searching. Seeking.

"Jax." She tugged at his arm. "You have to get inside."

* * *

Though his technician hosts had avoided giving him the tour of the bowels of the station, he was forced to visit them anyway. It wasn't as dirty as he thought it would be, but the air was very stale and the noise was incessant. A combination of clamor from drills and fans and other machinery that gelled into an irregular white noise that was peppered with odd pangs and thunks. He found himself shaking slightly, but was unable to decide if he was afraid of ModPol or afraid of the walls coming down around him.

He recognized some of the faces down below, having passed them in the halls or seen them in the cafeteria. The workers there paced slowly around the equipment, in and out of boring rooms and processing chambers and filtration closets. There couldn't have been more than six or seven, but their unceasing movement made it seem like they were an entire colony.

One of them returned from a comm, which had to be entirely enclosed in a soundproof circle. She was a young woman and Jax could see the lines of her muscles through the tightness of the uniforms the workers wore out of necessity.

"Mr. Fugere," she said, coming close enough to be heard over the din. "I'm not going to ask you any questions. We don't need to know."

He nodded at her, and had nothing else to say, other than, "Thank you."

She shook her head once to discard his gratitude. "Warpshire says we need to find a spot for you."

Lealina had left him at the elevator up above. She insisted he go down while she stayed to get rid of the interlopers. He wasn't sure of her strategy; it seemed to be a combination of denial of any knowledge of Jax and an insistence that ModPol had no jurisdiction on Terroneous. If they were already there, he didn't imagine they would give up their search easily, but she insisted that he hide so that she could deal with it.

The worker who spoke to Lealina took him through a labyrinth of carved-out tunnels that led away from the safety of walls and structure. The paths were lit by strings of lights and there was some kind of reinforced mesh that held the sides and ceilings of the tunnels together. She explained that it was sprayed on and when it touched the dirt, formed a molecular lattice that was almost as strong as steel. He didn't care for the *almost*. The floor was less reinforced, and at such a depth the dirt was wet. Between ducking under the low ceiling and sliding around in the mud, Jax felt like he was making no progress. Every step forward was a step backward in such muck.

Finally they arrived in a larger space the size of a small room. There was a desk and a couple of chairs and some equipment stacked in a corner.

"This is as comfortable as it gets down here," she said, then gave him a handypad. "Go ahead and do some reading or something, I guess."

He took the device, which was heavy and encased in extra layers of hard plastic. "Thanks."

She approached the desk. "There's a comm box here. It'll broadcast announcements once in a while, if you're down here long enough. Otherwise, if you need something you can hit this all-call button here and use this headset. Someone will pick up eventually, just keep hitting the button if you don't get a response right away." She looked at him for a long hard moment. Even though she had promised not to ask questions, he could feel her examination of him, her judgment. "I have to get back to work. We'll come get you when the director says so."

And then he was alone. He looked at the blank handypad but couldn't bring himself to wake the screen. The irregular walls of the room curved around him and up into a low ceiling that made him feel like he was trapped inside his own skull.

"Claustrophobic," he mumbled, trying out Lealina's description of the domes.

He sat at the desk and put his head down. It could not go on. How could it?

And what would happen if they did take him in? His fear was that he should not have run in the first place. That every day he spent on the run was another sign of guilt. That even if they found him innocent of those terrible murders, they would lock him up for hiding from the law.

Why couldn't they just leave him alone?

Time passed as he stared at the emptiness of the room and fought back the thoughts of what his life would be like in prison. The sounds of the work were lessened in this space, and he was thankful for that. From where he was, they sounded like distant scratchings and scrabblings. He tried not to think of it as the work of insects, which no doubt lived in the walls of dirt all around him. He was still not used to insects.

The comm box buzzed to life and he nearly jumped out of his chair. He had no idea how much time had passed, as he still found himself unable to activate the handypad. Half an hour? An hour?

"Attention, everyone." There was a great deal of static, hissing and warping the voice that came out of the comm speaker. "Attention. This is Sergeant Jared McManus of Modern Policing and Peacekeeping. We are looking for a fugitive named Jack Jackson, also known as Jack Fugere. We have reason to believe Jackson is here in this facility. We require your cooperation."

He stared at the box as if it were a bomb, freezing him in terror, as if to move even a centimeter would cause it to blow him up.

"We will search this entire facility," McManus continued. The name sounded familiar, but the voice did not. One of the officers who arrested him on B-4? "So if you are aware of Jackson's whereabouts, you can make this easier for everyone by letting us know now."

"Easier for everyone," Jax mumbled. Everyone but himself.

He continued to stare at the box, but nothing else came out. Had the search begun? Or was someone outing him at that moment, talking to ModPol about where he might be? If they really did search the whole place, would they come down this far? Would they crawl through tunnels to get to him? They'd already come farther than they should have by coming to Terroneous, so there was no reason to expect them to leave empty-handed.

It was quiet for a few more minutes, then the speaker barked back to life. "This is Sergeant McManus again, folks." Through the distortion Jax could make out a taunting, matter-of-fact quality to the tone. "I just thought you should all know that we've arrested Director Warpshire for obstructing justice."

There was a brief pause and Jax's head felt light. "Warpshire was seen with Jackson in a holofilm that was shot here on Terroneous. Additionally, she has tried to prevent us from entering the facility. We had no choice but to assume she is aiding and abetting the fugitive."

Jax tried to stand and found he had to grip the desk for support. They were arresting Lealina. How could they arrest Lealina?

He swallowed, his throat felt dry. He put on the headset and pushed the all-call button.

The line was answered quickly. "Hello?"

"It's Jax. Tell them I'm ready to give myself up."

"Oh...okay. Are you sure?"

He didn't even know who he was talking to. It didn't matter now. "Yes. But only if they agree to release Lealina."

* * *

"What is that thing?" Thompson asked.

"ModPol," Dava said.

They lay in the sand at the top of a dune in the middle of the hot wasteland, Bashful Dan's shimmering invisi-screen wavering in front of them. The device allowed them to see through in one direction, cloaking them from the opposite line of sight. What they could see was a black mar on the white desert sand, a jarring hole of titanium. It was hexagonally shaped and a few dozen meters long.

"It's a Black Maria." Dava glanced back at Lucky Jerk. He shrugged. "You know, like a prisoner transport kind of deal."

Thompson huffed. “It looks like a damn tank.”

“It’s built like one,” he said.

“Stay behind the shield, jackass!” Thompson swatted Lucky as he edged around closer to the top of the dune.

“Okay, sheesh,” he said, slinking back.

Dava shushed them with the closing of her fist and turned her attention back to the ModPol ship, scanning the area with a pair of binoculars. The entrance to some underground facility was barely visible as a gray bump coming up out of the sand. The rear of the Black Maria folded down and a figure stepped out, a rifle held crosswise against his chest with one hand, the other hand on his earpiece. He came down halfway and then stood sideways. The door to the facility opened and three figures came out. One was bound, hands behind his back.

“Here they come,” Thompson whispered. “That our man?”

“Tall, skinny, white as snow,” Dava said, watching the prisoner through the optics. “Gotta be Psycho Jack.”

“How many Pollies?”

“Three that I can see,” Dava said as they walked Jackson up the ramp, his head down, his gait a defeated shuffle.

“Probably a pilot inside,” Lucky said.

“Let’s assume there are a couple inside,” Thompson said. “What do you think, Dava? Should we move on ’em?”

“No fuckin’ way,” Lucky said, too loudly. He lowered his voice to an intense whisper after a look from Dava. “You see the turret on that baby?” he said, pointing at the top of the Maria. Four large barrels mounted on a cone, two to a side. “You go running across the wide-open desert spraying that Tommy-Gun, they’re just going to get inside and lock ’er up. Then they warm up those cannons and turn you into dust.”

Dava sighed. "He's right. It's too wide open here." There was nothing they could do other than a dead run at them, and there was no cover whatsoever.

"I suppose you got a better idea, flyboy?" Thompson said.

Lucky sat up and crossed his arms, then looked down at the Maria and resumed his prone position behind the screen. "Yeah, I do. We go back to the dropship. Up to the star-hopper. Tail the Maria out past the gravity field of B-5. They can't go into subwarp until they clear gravity. Then I pop out in the dogfighter."

"We only have two dogfighters on the starhopper," Dava said. She thought back to the argument she had before leaving the secondary Space Waste outpost in Sirius. 2-Bit had been preoccupied with some special cross-system training program that Jansen had cooked up. The captain had refused her request for pilots and ships to bring to Terroneous. Not that she felt she needed them, not for the Misters. But she needed at least one pilot and one interstellar ship to get from Sirius to Barnard, so 2-Bit allowed her that. "And we only have one pilot."

Lucky huffed. "I can fly circles around that Maria." He leaned in closer to them and smiled. "And I know its weak-ness."

"What the hell are you talking about?" Thompson said.

"It looks like a tank but it's not a war machine," he said. "It's a transport. Made to keep its occupants alive above all else."

"Well, that's good," Dava said as she began to slide back down the dune. "Because we mostly want Psycho Jack alive."

* * *

Even having come out of a cramped, airtight, underground facility, where the air was anything but fresh, the smell in this place was worse. It wasn't just that it was lived in, that it too was airtight. There was another foulness that Lealina could detect, and it made her want to quit breathing altogether.

She absentmindedly reached for her face to scratch and itch, forgetting she was bound at the wrists momentarily and yanking her own hand painfully. "Dammit," she whispered. She wanted to cry, but she narrowed her eyes and tightened her face. Her hands flopped back down into her lap.

She was seated on a crate in the middle of a small storage room. All the walls were cabinets, and she briefly entertained the idea of rooting through them, but from the looks of the small slots on each of their doors, she guessed they were locked anyway. It was convincing enough to keep her stuck to her crate. What if she found something in those cabinets? What would she do? No matter what she found, there was no good answer. At best, she might find a weapon. No; that would be at worst. She could get them both killed.

The only door to the room lay tauntingly wide open in front of her. She could see the shoulder of the man on guard in the corridor beyond.

She stared at her hands in the dim light.

What would they do with him?

The ModPol cop who called himself Sergeant McManus came through the open door and she looked up. The man's frame was large, blotting out the narrow exit. She refused to let him intimidate her. He had the pink skin of a pampered B-threer.

"Seems my hunch was spot on," McManus said with half

a grin. "Jackson likes you. He gave himself up once he found out we'd arrested you."

"You have no right." She tried to make her voice firm, but it wavered. A mix of fear and anger. "ModPol has no jurisdiction here."

He took a step forward, looking down at her. "And who does have jurisdiction here, huh? Who? We're out in the middle of fucking nowhere."

"We have a government—"

"You've got shit." He shook his head and turned away from her, as though looking into the distance. "A bunch of councils. Loose treaties. Local constables."

"But no ModPol." She was feeling her determination slip away, and her voice got quieter. "ModPol has no authority here."

He turned to face her again. "ModPol has authority to go wherever the fuck it needs to go." He jabbed a finger in her direction. "You were harboring a wanted criminal. Wanted by ModPol." His hands turned up. "And when we're chasing a *fugitive*, we go where we damn well want."

She took a deep breath, returning her gaze down to her bound hands. "Sergeant McManus," she said without looking at him. "Is he guilty?"

She heard him huff a few times, then laugh, but it sounded less than genuine. He grew so quiet, she looked up to see if he was still there. His face bunched up and he spoke in a low voice. "Lady, we're all guilty of *something*."

She sensed a small opening. "Why can't you let him go? The real murderer was arrested. Just go back and...and report that you searched Terroneous. Report that you searched, but you never found him."

He stared at her for a long time then, his eyes seeing

something else, something distant. Then he reached for her hands. She flinched and leaned back, and then realized he was deactivating the restraints on her wrists.

"Come on," he said. "You should say goodbye to him."

He turned and went to the door. She blinked, unbelieving that he was going to let her go at first. He started down the corridor and she broke the mental locks on her legs and stood and followed him.

They reached another door that opened into a wider space, some kind of cargo bay. Jax stood at the far side, his back to her, facing a row of stasis chambers. A young woman crouched next to him, pressing buttons on a panel. Lealina took a step and McManus put out an arm as she came through the door.

"That's as close as you get," he said quietly. Then he raised his voice. "Jackson, turn around."

Jax's head lifted slightly, then turned. His eyes locked with hers and he turned fully to her. His fallen face read defeat, but even across the room, she could see the smallest change when his eyes met hers.

"I'm sorry, Jax," she said. The bay grew quiet. The young woman at the stasis controls carefully stood and stepped away from him. McManus lowered his arm, but put out a flat palm, ordering Lealina to stay where she was.

"Lealina," said Jax. His throat was dry, breaking his voice. "Are you okay?"

"I'm okay," she said quickly. "They're going to let me go."

"Good." On this, his voice sounded firmer.

"I'm sorry," she said again. "I don't – I don't know what to do."

"Don't do anything," Jax said. "You did everything you could. I just want you to be safe."

And she just wanted him to be safe. She just wanted him to be in her arms. She wanted to kick and fight and scream and make them let him go, but she could not. She felt weak. Useless.

She shut it all down. What he needed was not her pain, what he needed was her support. He'd given himself up to save her; he needed to know he didn't make his sacrifice in vain. "It's going to be okay, Jax. I'm going to be okay. I have contacts with the Terroneous government. I'll find a way to get you released. Back to us. Back to Terroneous."

Back to me.

His mouth opened slightly, forming the barest hint of a smile. "Thank you," he said, though she knew it was not to thank her for her promises. Those were futile and they both knew it. He was thanking her for their short time together. He was thanking her for saying goodbye.

The air on her cheeks turned cold, and she realized they were wet. McManus gestured at the door. "Okay, that's enough. Time to go."

She felt so weak she couldn't walk, but soon she was stumbling into the hall. McManus hit the door latch and the cargo bay slid from view.

"Damn you," she managed.

"Listen, lady," he said. "I've got orders. So spare me the waterworks."

He had one of his men escort her out of the ship in a blur. Then she was standing in the sand, staring at the massive black cube that obstructed the view of the desert. She couldn't even see any ModPol designations on it. It was just a box. An inexplicable structure that had materialized out of nothing to imprison him.

Within minutes, she heard machinations emanating from

the thing. Outer doors sealing, exhaust doors opening, engines powering up. The stupid black cube, blurred through her tears, whining and shuddering to life. Stirring the desert sand into clouds of yellow around it.

She never felt so useless, so helpless. Terroneous was a force of nature; life on the moon was a constant struggle against odds. Everything was a fight for survival. But every struggle could be overcome, every fight could be won. This time there was no way to win, because there was no way to fight.

Or maybe there was a way to fight, and she just didn't know how. But someone out there did.

When the billowing sands became too much, she finally heeded the shouts from the co-workers behind her and sought shelter back inside the TEOB outpost.

CHAPTER 18

McManus sealed the hatch on the prisoner transport module. Jackson was sedated and wouldn't be coming out of his box until he reached the ingest bay at Outpost Gamma, where he'd be unwrapped like a present.

He sighed. All that running, only to give up so easily at the end. He expected more of a fight, maybe a chase. It just solidified that the whole ordeal was all Stanford Runstom. Without Runstom, Jackson rolled over like a dog.

The room shifted and he buffered himself against the wall with a grunt. The paddy-wagon had no artificial gravity, which was hard enough to deal with, but Katsumi's erratic piloting made it worse. He secured himself with the handholds on the wall and picked his way to the bridge.

"What the hell, Cadet?" he blurted as he came through the hatch. "Your driving is going to make me lose my lunch."

"Just getting into position, Sergeant," she said, head down, hands busy jumping between controls. "We'll be ready for sub-warp in twenty-eight minutes."

"Good." He picked his way to one of the rear chairs.

"The sooner the better. Any contacts?"

"No, sir." She turned momentarily. "Is the prisoner secure?"

McManus huffed as he strapped in. "How about me? Ask me if I'm secure?"

"Sergeant, we're going to go from sub-warp to full warp. Prisoner transport regulations—"

"I know the damn regulations, Katsumi. The prisoner is secured in his module and fully sedated." He lowered his voice and muttered, "Unlike me who has to sit here awake and have my brain fried while we cheat God."

"You didn't tell me the target was going to be Jack Jackson." Her head was down again but her voice was loud and clear.

He grunted. "Why should I have to tell you who the target is, Cadet? And how do you know it's Jackson?"

She laughed mirthlessly. "A B-fourean on the run? Who else would it be?"

"Don't worry about it."

"Plus his girlfriend called him 'Jax'."

"I said don't worry about it." He could've done without the blubbering girlfriend. Not that he cared whether poor Jackson's heart was broken or not. It wasn't his job to care. And it wasn't Katsumi's either. He decided to focus his energies on berating his pilot. "I brought you on this mission because I needed someone I could trust."

"Trust, sir?" She turned to look at him. "Then why withhold information from me?"

"Trust to keep to the mission parameters," he growled. "Which includes keeping your goddamn mouth shut. *Cadet.*"

She shook her head and went back to her work. "I don't

understand why we're arresting Jackson. Seems like Officer Runstom proved that Jackson isn't guilty."

He considered ignoring her, but heard himself answer anyway. "Innocent men don't run from the law."

"They might if they're chased," she said, barely loud enough for him to hear.

He scowled at the back of her head. He didn't give a shit about Jackson. The man was a fugitive, plain and simple. It didn't matter if he was innocent of the murders, he was guilty of plenty else. And so was Runstom as far as McManus was concerned, but since Runstom was being paraded around like a hero and getting promotions, he would have to settle for the next best thing: arresting Jackson.

He scratched his thigh and tried to tighten his strap, damning the grav-free chairs. It was true that everything about the mission was tight-lipped. His orders had come through on a secure message. He hadn't spoken to anyone in person. But he was promised a bonus for completing it. An instant promotion to sergeant just for accepting it. And he was given orders to choose his own crew. The paddy-wagon had already been checked out for him, not under his name, but under a code. Finding a few grunt-officers who wouldn't ask questions was no trouble, but finding a pilot was more of a hassle. In the end he settled on Katsumi only because of her low rank and obligation to subservience. Plus he had to admit, even if she was a bit hard on the controls, she was a damn good pilot.

None of that mattered, he decided. The job went without a hitch. In less than thirty minutes, they'd hit sub-warp, and then warp, and before he could scoop his brains up off the floor they'd be at Gamma and he'd be counting the Alleys all the way to the bar.

"Umm." Katsumi cocked her head and tapped at her controls. "Sergeant McManus. Contact."

Probably a ship inbound for Terroneous. "Is it in the database?"

"Yeah," she said, drawing the word out. "Actually it is. Interstellar-capable ship, Klondike Sailor Mark Three-B. Registered to Nadia Gravitas, a shipping merchant headquartered on B-3."

"Must be making a delivery," he said with a yawn.

"This Klondike was reported stolen about sixteen months ago."

"Uh-huh," he said, still fiddling with his strap. Then he looked up. "What the – what?"

"Stolen—"

"Prep for evasive action," he interrupted. "How soon are we going to hit sub-warp?"

She tapped. "About twenty-two minutes, sir."

"What's the trajectory—"

"Sir, another contact."

"Is it hostile, Cadet?" McManus leaned forward against his strap, trying to decide whether or not to relocate.

"It's a Drake Quadwing 4505. A single-pilot fighter." She whistled. "Man, look at the specs on that thing. She's a mover."

"Yeah, no kidding." McManus had seen a demonstration of the Drake 4000 series about a year ago when his precinct was considering upgrading the patrol fighters around Outpost Gamma. They'd gone with a cheaper manufacturer, but the Drakes flew circles around everything else.

"Trajectory of the Drake suggests intercept course," Katsumi said. Despite how much she always talked about wanting some action, her voice was beginning to waver in the face of it.

"Go to yellow alert and make sure our guys aren't in their tubes yet," McManus said. If they were, they were going to have to take shots to wake back up. He didn't envy the hangover they'd have. As he unstrapped, he added, "And warm up the turret."

As the yellow lights flashed, he picked his way out of the bridge and up through the narrow hole of a passageway that led to the turret capsule. He could have sent one of the boys up there, but he only brought brutes, in case he ran into resistance on that damn independent moon. Of the crew, McManus was the best to operate a turret-gun; and he was pretty damn good. As he strapped in, he shook his head to chase away the knowledge that he'd never shot at anything other than drones.

Katsumi's voice came over the comm. "Drake contact incoming. Definitely on an intercept course."

"Range?"

"Four K and closing fast."

"Shit," he cursed under his breath. "Go to red alert."

He stabbed at the console to get the turret extended. Katsumi had activated the core systems, but thanks to all the damn safety features, the functional components needed assurance that the turret operator was properly authorized and qualified and also comfortable to some unnecessary specification, to ensure accuracy and optimal decision-making. He'd never heard of anyone being *comfortable* while firing plasma blasts at an incoming fighter travelling thousands of kilometers per hour, but the damn thing wouldn't let him take one shot until it was convinced he was in the right state of mind.

He leaned against the back of the chair and looked between the contact map and the small, blank viewport before him. He took a deep breath, held it, then released slowly. He could feel the heat rising up inside him, coloring his skin red, but he held it together enough for the machine to let him do his job. The turret extended and the viewport revealed the black of space.

The Drake was coming in fast. He plotted a solution through the computer and then nudged some of the shots a few degrees this way and that, purely based on instinct. His preferred strategy wasn't about trying land every shot, but like a good bombball pitcher, he wanted a few misses to get the target moving in the right direction before hitting it with a blast straight down the strike zone.

The target came into range and he let it rip. Through the viewport he could see the balls of orange light flashing as they sang forth from the pair of barrels at the top of the turret. The Drake dipped and wavered predictably and he waited for the series to play out. By the time the fifth blast was away, the target was right in its path.

"Now I gotcha—"

There was an explosion a second too soon and the Drake kept on going. In its wake was a cloud of dust. He anxiously scanned the monitors for any sign of a hit, but there seemed to be no damage done to the target. He tapped through the scanners and got a quick light-refraction analysis on the cloud to see if anything worthwhile had been hit, but it turned out to be ice and rock.

"An asteroid?" McManus sputtered. "I hit a goddamn asteroid? That lucky jerk! The nearest asteroid field has to be a million K from here!"

Then his world lurched.

"Incoming fire!" Katsumi shouted through the comm. "Taking evasive action!"

The icons on the contact map spun on all three dimensional axes. He wrestled with the firing controls but the damn thing had lost its target.

There was a shudder then and all the lights turned red. The damage monitor showed small hits all across the bottom.

"Katsumi! He's below us," he spat into the comm. "You have to get turned over so I can get a shot at him."

"Aye, Sarge!"

The world lurched again and the targeting computer bleeped happily. He whipped up the quickest solution he could, mostly random shots in the vague direction of the Drake. Once again, orange flashes lit up the viewport.

He watched the Drake's icon zip around the contact map. He was good, whoever he was, but McManus only needed one hit to do major damage to such a small ship.

"Come on…come on…"

Pulse after pulse rang out and the damn Drake eluded them all. It started to make its way back down.

"Katsumi! Keep him above us!"

Again the sporadic shuddering and again the damage monitor lit up, showing hits along their bottom.

The ship continued to lurch, dip, and roll. The comm came back to life. "Sarge, he's too fast and this goddamn Black Maria flies like a tank!"

"You're lucky it's built like one or we'd be dead by now!"

The universe spun and black clouds gathered at the edges of his vision. He heard the target computer chirp and he laid on the guns, minimizing power in favor of maximum spread and rate of fire. The guns screeched above him with terrifying anxiety.

The targeting computer bleeped a new tone. He blinked away the blackness as much as he could and squinted at the monitor.

"I got him! I clipped him!"

Then the ship shuddered hard and lurched. The red lights dimmed so suddenly that McManus thought he was blacking out, but then they came back up just as quickly.

"Sarge, he got us in the tail!"

"What?" he blurted, mostly to himself. He looked at the damage monitor. "Oh fuck. Primary thrusters? Katsumi, what's our status?"

"I've got stabilizers and buffers but no thrust. We can spin and push but we can't maneuver."

"Dammit. Well, at least turn us so I can take another shot at him."

"Aye, Sarge."

The ship started to spin more slowly that it had before, and just as the targeting computer beeped, there was another shuddering hit. This time the damage monitor showed a red rectangle somewhere in the rear of the ship.

He took aim and released everything they had left, squinting in anticipation of the bright orange flashes that would light up the viewport.

But nothing happened.

The targeting screen read, *SAFETY LOCKOUT: POWER LIMITATION.*

"Katsumi, I can't fire!" he bellowed into the comm. "What the hell happened?"

The response was slow in coming. "He punched through to the main power plant, sir."

"We have reserve power…"

"I know, sir, but the safety overrides have kicked in. In the event of any damage to the power plant, all high-drain systems are deactivated so that there is guaranteed power for life-support systems."

"So we can't move and we can't shoot? What good is life support going to do when they blow us to smithereens?"

"Sarge, the other ship is on the move. Intercept course."

He punched at the useless controls, cursing them to come back to life. "What is the fighter doing? It's not firing on us anymore?"

"No, sir. Just seems to be taking position behind us."

Ready to blow them away if they tried anything funny. "Katsumi," he said, hearing the resignation in his own voice. "Secure the bridge for full lockout. I think they intend to board us."

"Oh," the cadet said over the comm. "Crap."

CHAPTER 19

Jax awoke in a coffin.

The top slid away with a musical series of beeps when he spasmed and flailed at the sides, hitting an unseen button, some kind of release mechanism. He immediately put his head out and vomited over the side.

It took several minutes of panting and heaving before Jax's vision would cooperate. His memory only went back as far as opening the lid. To make up for the lack of other faculties, his sense of smell seemed to be in overdrive, and he gagged at the stench coming from his own mouth. It wasn't just bitter bile, there was a chemical taste that was like chlorine mixed with the tart flavor of medicine.

The floor was only a foot away, so he ventured an attempt at climbing out of his tomb. After a moment of blurred struggling, he was once again staring straight up at the ceiling, but at least he was out of the coffin. He looked at the side of it, squinting until the shapes became letters and numbers. *Sensible Securitube – 595*. Below that, smaller, requiring harder squinting, *Sensibly serving your secure organic transportation needs.*

When he was able to stand, he took a look at the rest of the room. It was cold and dark, lit by a single dull bulb poking out of the ceiling a meter or so above his head. There wasn't much room for anything other than the desk and chair in one corner, the sizable puddle of vomit, and the tube he rode in on.

There was a note on the desk. He ignored it.

Aside from the metallic walls, there was a windowless door and with a numerical security pad next to it. The door had no handle, so his fuzzy mind presumed a code would unlock it. He typed in 12432, which he thought was random. The panel beeped sourly and blinked red. He frowned and remembered that 12432 was part of his address. His house on Terroneous. His home.

The note flashed impatiently yellow.

He sighed and stepped over his sick to the desk. The note was a small rectangle of epaper, and seemed to be affixed to the desk. Next to it was the inexplicably anachronistic presence of a wooden pencil and a paper notepad.

The top of the epaper note read, *ESCAPE*. Below that was a series of letters and numbers. There was no pattern to them, but after a moment of staring dumbly, Jax realized that they used all ten numbers but only the letters "A" through "F".

"Hexadecimal," he muttered. He was tempted to smile at this small mental victory his mud-filled brain had accomplished, but he quickly lamented. "What the fuck am I supposed to do with this?"

ESCAPE, the stupid note said.

He tipped his head back and sighed, then on a hunch

looked around at the corners of the ceiling, hunting for cameras. Maybe this was another chance for Jax to be on reality HV. But no. No cameras. Nothing.

Then it all came back, like a drowning flood. Granderson and his stupid holofilm. Flying to the desert. Hiding in the depths of an underground facility. Lealina in trouble.

Lealina…

He looked at the tube. Remembered getting in it. They had released Lealina – he'd seen them let her go when they brought him out of the TEOB facility. Fucking ModPol. Why couldn't they just leave him alone?

The note continued its slow pulse, the patternless code awaiting his attention.

"What the fuck," he quietly said aloud. Then he raised his voice. "What the fuck? Where's my lawyer?"

He walked over to the door and barked at it. "Hey. Hey! I want my lawyer." He pounded with a fist. "Come on, you assholes. I want my lawyer. I want my call."

Silence rang in response. He raised his hand again to hit the door, then closed his eyes and took a deep breath. There was no point to it. He opened his eyes. Had he heard laughter? He shook his head. "Fucking assholes," he whispered.

He paced the room, coming again to the desk. "Yeah, yeah, escape, escape. What am I supposed to do with this? Hexadecimal. Do they think I'm an android or something?" He sat in the chair and stared at it for several minutes. Trying to distract himself with the puzzle before him. Bright-blue eyes appeared in between byte pairs and he sat back.

He wanted to cry. He didn't want to be here, he wanted to go home. Why were they doing this to him? Why would ModPol stick him in this room with this note—

"Why would ModPol do this?" he asked himself out loud. "ModPol?"

Maybe it wasn't ModPol. Maybe it was some of X's people that came and took him. How could he be so stupid? Of course, that had to be it!

If it was X, then maybe he'd better listen to the note: *ESCAPE*. But he wasn't about to stare at those letters and numbers. He took inventory of the room one more time. No ventilation, which he confirmed by the staleness of the air. No drain in the cold metallic floor, which he confirmed by the unrelenting presence of his breakfast drying at his feet. No bed and no toilet, so it wasn't a cell. Whatever it was he was meant to be doing in here, it wasn't expected to take days. That gave him a little bit of hope – maybe if he just sat there for a few hours, eventually someone would let him out. He let that hope go as the thought of that someone being X came to mind.

"Hello, door panel," he said, getting up close to the keypad. It had only numbers zero through nine, no other keys. "Let's see how you work. Beep boop beep," he echoed while prodding keys at random. "Bzzzt. Well, looks like you take five numbers. That's only 100,000 combinations. I could brute force you."

Was that true? He tried 00001. When the tiny screen turned red, it stopped accepting input for about five seconds. That meant up to 500,000 seconds of waiting. He decided not to do the math because it reminded him too much of programming COMPLEX in the subdomes. He knew an hour was 3,600 seconds, that much was burned into his brain. What a useless piece of knowledge.

It occurred to him that there was a lack of biometrics on the lock. It reminded him of Terroneous. Back on B-4, in the domes, every lock was biometric – fingerprints or retinal scans – but on Terroneous, most people didn't like them. Numbers were just as easy to remember, they said, plus convenient when you needed to share them, like when you needed a neighbor to water your plants. And the most paranoid of them were afraid of determined thieves that might resort to digit severing or ocular extraction. In terms of administration though, biometrics made the most sense because an individual could be granted or denied access to any lock in the system from central management. All of this was a train of thought that led Jax to think he was definitely *not* in a ModPol facility.

On one edge of the panel he noticed a small bump in the plastic: a triangle. He felt the side next to it, and indeed, there was a small divot. "If I had a screwdriver…"

He didn't have a screwdriver, but all he needed was a small wedge. The tube was no use, as it was probably made of indestructible material. The desk was a thin metal and looked sturdy. The chair on the other hand was cheap, molded plastic.

He took it by the legs and slammed it into the top of the Sensible Securitube.

One shot was enough to splinter several small pieces of plastic from the rails that formed the backrest. He chose one that was narrow enough to fit into the side of the panel. After a few seconds of wiggling and leveraging and cursing, the panel cover swung open with a pop.

The keypad remained where it was, but it was as though the clothes had come off around it. Just below there were three unlabeled buttons. On a sticker on the back of the panel cover he saw some instructions. He scanned through them, skipping the setting of timers and configuring for multiple codes and read straight to:

To reset door code: Hold button #1 and button #2 together for five seconds. When screen blinks green, enter administrator password. Enter new door code. Hold buttons #1 and #2 for five seconds to confirm. Screen will go solid green to confirm.

On the sticker, someone had scrawled *11111* next to the word "password".

He held the buttons and when the screen blinked, he tapped in 11111, then typed in 12432. He held the buttons again and the screen went solid green, just as the instructions predicted. He closed the panel cover and snapped it shut. He took a deep breath and punched in 12432.

The panel chirped and the door slid open with a shush.

"Psycho Jack!" On the other side of the door was a man decked head to toe in brown leather, jet-black hair spilling at length around his shoulders, and one arm in a sling. He stuck the other hand out. "Congrats, brother! I'm Barndoor."

"You're what now?"

"Barndoor," he said firmly, twitching his unshaken hand.

"Did you just call me 'Psycho Jack'?"

"Yeah, she said—"

"Who said?"

He cocked his head and narrowed his eyes, letting the hand drop. "Dava." He took a step forward and got close enough for Jax to smell his breath. "You know who Dava is, doncha Jack?"

"Y-yes." Jax swallowed and tried to be assertive even though he felt a desperate urge to back away from the other man. "Where am I?"

"In our secret base."

"Uh, okay. So you mean, in Space Waste's secret base?"

The man called Barndoor blinked. "Man, I thought you were some kind of genius. Yes, Space Waste. Did you decode the message on the table?"

Jax stared at him. Was it a trick question? Should he lie? He felt paralyzed. "What?"

"I mean, you must have, cuz you got the door open. That was a special test that our other hacker designed."

Dava. Space Waste. Jax's brain tried to correlate the unexpected flurry of data it was receiving. He tried to look past the other man. "Is – is Dava here?"

"Yeah, she's around. She said to make you an offer if you passed the test."

"And I passed?"

"You got out, didn't ya?" Barndoor revived his attempt at a handshake. "Congrats, man!"

This time Jax took the offered hand and gave it a short shake before pulling back. "Thanks. Um. Barn. Barndoor," he said. "Wait – what offer?"

"To join Space Waste. We need a hacker because our other one got arrested."

Jax pinched his nose with his fingers, the headache returning. "Barndoor, please," he said. "Can you tell me how I got here?"

"Oh right," he said. "Shit man, I'm sorry. I forgot about that part. We rescued you from the ModPol Black Maria."

"Black Maria?"

"Yeah, you know. The paddy-wagon." He looked at Jax, perhaps scanning for registration, then added, "The prisoner transport ship."

"You...*rescued* me?" Jax felt a sudden lightness as it dawned on him that he wasn't in ModPol custody. His mind allowed him thoughts of Lealina. "Can I go back to Terroneous?"

Barndoor's face fell ever so slightly. "Well, I wouldn't say right now. See, we *do* need a hacker."

Jax bit his lip. "I'm sorry, man. I really appreciate the rescue and all. I just don't think I'm – uh – Space Waste material."

The other man sighed heavily and turned in a way that made Jax realize for the first time that there was a massive firearm of some kind strapped to his back. "Dava was really hoping you'd help us out." He drew the words out carefully.

There was a sudden dull pounding that caused Jax to flinch and look around the hallway. The source seemed to be a nearby door, similar to the one he just came through.

"Mister Guy," Barndoor said, rolling his eyes. "Don't worry, we're going to rename him after initiation."

The pounding faded and Jax was sure he could hear soft crying. "You mean…is he a prisoner?"

"No, he's another recruit," he said with a nod. "He'll come around. They always do."

Jax tried not to stare at the sobbing door. "Did Dava say I could go if I didn't want to take the job?" he asked quietly.

Barndoor's face scrunched up and his eyes rolled around as he made a humming sound. "Kind of. She said if you said no to put you out the airlock."

Jax blew his cheeks out in a sigh. "Does this job at least pay?"

"Of course," he said with a broad smile.

"Good." Jax nodded over his shoulder at the tiny room and the stain on the floor. "I need to replace my breakfast and then have several dozen drinks."

CHAPTER 20

When they came out of subwarp, Runstom made the cadet take the stick so he could talk to McManus. The ModPol sergeant had barely said a sentence since Runstom had come to the rescue of the incapacitated prisoner transport vessel. When he'd shown up outside of Barnard-5, the gas giant around which Terroneous orbited, he wasn't expecting to find anything but the tracks of McManus and his crew. If he were lucky, he thought he'd find them still on the moon, eluded by Jax, but he had not really expected to be lucky.

Instead, he'd picked up their encrypted distress signal. No thrusters, no weapons systems, not much of anything other than life support, which seemed to be normal. As per protocol, they hadn't contacted any civilians to ask for help, since it hadn't yet been a completely life-threatening situation. He didn't imagine they expected another ModPol vessel to happen along where the only life nearby was an independent moon. It seemed to Runstom that they were only going by protocol because McManus had wanted to sit around and stew about his misfortune.

"Now this baby," Cadet Katsumi said a few minutes after taking the pilot seat. "This baby is a mover."

"I can't believe you're letting her fly," McManus grumbled. "She almost got us killed. Supposed to be some hotshot pilot and she couldn't take on one fighter."

"It's not my fault, Sarge!" She turned to protest. "That transport thing has no pickup, no maneuver. It's like flying through mud."

"Turn around and keep your eyes on the road."

She gave him a look that was part challenge, part like she was trying to work out exactly what a *road* was. Her mouth pinched up and then she turned back to the stick. "But this baby, wow. What a rocket!"

McManus cursed under his breath and gave Runstom a sideways glance.

McManus had aged greatly in the several months that had passed since they'd last seen each other. The gray streaks that ran along the sides of his head had gone whiter and more prominent as the rest of his hair had thinned. And the title – sergeant. Runstom found it hard to believe McManus deserved a promotion.

"So what is this," McManus said, as though he could feel Runstom inspecting him. "Is it like the company car or something?"

"Something like that," Runstom said. "It's a little too flashy for me."

The new ride had been waiting for him at Outpost Gamma, fresh in from a shipyard. His boss, Victoria Horus, had ordered it and had it sent to be there when Runstom arrived. She played it up like she was rewarding Runstom, or maybe spoiling him, or maybe trying to put Runstom in her debt. But there was a practical angle too, and that's what her explanation was: that some potential customers were impressed by style and extravagance. Runstom thought that customers would see it as an unnecessary expense, a waste of resources, but Horus waved it off, saying that there were customers who would think, *If they spend this kind of money on their image, imagine how much they spend on their guns.*

So there it was. An OrbitBurner 4200 LX. Top of the line AI-assisted coordination systems, flyable by a single pilot with no other crew, yet large enough to comfortably entertain two dozen guests. Runstom had to admit, it did seem to move like a dream, though at the compromise of having absolutely zero defensive capabilities.

"Well, at least my guys are comfortable, I guess." McManus's crew had found the entertainment chamber and were watching HV. He glanced at the door of the bridge as though he wanted to join them, but was unable to. Trapped by Runstom's invitation that he come up and chat. His eyes swung back around and glared at Runstom. "What the hell were you doing out there at Terroneous?"

"I wasn't on Terroneous."

"You were in the vicinity," he snarled. "And there ain't nothin' else around there."

Runstom was quiet for a second, then said, "First you tell me what happened."

"Why should I tell you?"

"I rescued you, Jared. You can at least do me the courtesy of telling me *why* you needed rescue."

McManus's mouth bunched up. "Fuck off."

"I saw the damage," Runstom said. It was obvious there had been a fight. The thrusters were mangled. Scorch marks all along the bottom of the ship. "Even the airlock. You had to suit up and depressurize the rear cabin just to get out of the ship."

"Those bastards yanked the outer airlock door right off on their way out."

Runstom considered this. "To prevent you from spacewalking out and repairing any damage?"

McManus huffed. "Like I got a crew of engineers here," he mumbled.

He hadn't, Runstom had noticed. They were all bruisers, a collection of security guards and low-ranking officers, plus Cadet Katsumi. Remembering her presence, he glanced over. She was preoccupied but he drew McManus to the corner of the bridge and lowered his voice. "Still, who does that kind of thing?"

"Goddamn Space Waste, that's who."

"Really?" Runstom blinked and almost took a step back. Space Waste used to be nothing more than a fringe problem, but in the past year he'd encountered them far too often. "What did they want?"

Now McManus gave him a long hard look. "Take a guess."

"I don't know. Why were you there?"

"Come on, *Stanley*," he sneered. "I know you know why we were there, Mr. Detective. I'm sure you got it all figured out."

Runstom sighed. "I heard a rumor that Jax – Jackson – had resurfaced."

"You heard we were going to pick him up."

"Unsubstantiated," Runstom said, to mean he may have heard so but had not treated it as fact.

McManus laughed. "You never change, Stanley."

"It's Stanford."

"Whatever. You want to grill me? I want to know what you were doing so close to Terroneous. Why you just happened to come along."

Runstom frowned, not wanting to have to explain himself to McManus, but knowing he needed to provide something. "I was working," he said. "On mission to Ipo. You know, the mining colony there is incorporating. We're trying to sell them ModPol services."

"Right, right."

"So," Runstom said while McManus sat cross-armed and silent. "What happened?"

He threw up his hands. "I don't know, I really don't. It was a cakewalk. We went down there, tracked Jackson to this underground facility out in the desert. And he came without a fight. I mean, he tried to wait us out, but he don't know us. All we do is wait. So after a few hours, he gave himself up."

"And Space Waste?"

"Well that's the kicker, ain't it?" McManus said with an unnecessary grin. "Those bastards come at us, shoot up our tail, then board us. I figure they want the ship. But nope, they just cart off Jackson. Didn't even wake him up or take him out of his Securitube, they just carried the whole thing out."

Runstom chewed that over for a moment but couldn't make any sense of it. "Who put you on that job?"

"Oh, piss off."

"Jared, listen to me – Jackson is innocent, you know that."

"Innocent of some things."

"Of the things that matter." Runstom's voice had gotten louder and now he forcibly lowered it. "Help me out here."

"Look, Stan." McManus's hands went palms up. "I don't know. It was an encrypted order. The key checked out. I don't know who it was or why they picked me."

Runstom sighed, then shook his head. "Because you would jump at a chance to bring him in."

"You got that right."

"Jared, he's an innocent man. He doesn't deserve any of this shit, and never has."

"Yeah, well. Even if he is. We have a process. Or did you forget that already? After you left Justice for Defense?"

"They're both equally important," Runstom said, feeling his temperature rise. "ModPol is Modern Policing *and* Peacekeeping."

"Boy, you sure are the first to drink the company punch when it comes around."

"Now you're going to mock me for my loyalty."

"Come on, Stanford. Defense? What kind of runaround is that? You worked in Justice for over ten years. That's where the work gets done. Defense is nothing but a racket."

"Justice is reactionary. Defense is preventative." Even as he said it, he wondered if he was trying to convince McManus or himself.

McManus laughed, genuinely amused. "You really believe that?"

"I've already seen it," Runstom shot back. "On Vulca, off Sirius-5. Defense fought off an attack."

"Yeah, I heard about that," McManus said with eyes like a trap. "And who did they fight off exactly?"

"Space Waste," Runstom replied quietly.

McManus shook his head. "Stan, Space Waste is not an army. In fact, what they are is organized crime. *Crime.* Justice should be dealing with them."

"Well you're doing—" Runstom started and cut himself off. Was it worth cutting down all of Justice, worth highlighting their failures just to win an argument? Something about McManus always made Runstom's blood boil. He closed his eyes and took a breath, forcing the anger to flush away as best he could. Then he let out a small laugh. "I don't know, Jared. You know I'd rather be in Justice."

"Right," he said, still trying to needle. "Still dreaming of becoming a detective? Just because your mother did it? And how's that working for her? Do you even know where she is?"

"No."

"Why not? She's your mother."

"It's for her protection."

"Sure, of course. What a great detective, can't even find his own mother," McManus laughed. Then he paused and his face flattened. "Wait a minute – you really didn't know that Jackson was on Terroneous this whole time, did you?"

"No," he said firmly. Though in his heart, he'd known it. Jax didn't have many places to go, and had taken a shine to the independent moon. Had talked about it in the last conversation they'd had, now almost half a year past.

McManus laughed again, but this time the amusement was gone and his face turned down. "Well. Whatever. Guess it don't matter now."

Runstom looked past him to the great oval viewport at the front of the bridge. It was something to behold – impractical, for sure, but a naked view unlike any he'd seen in other craft. A few thousand kilometers distant a gleaming speck had formed, and began to grow.

McManus turned to follow his eyes. "Outpost Delta. I'm sure we'll be real welcome there."

"It's still ModPol," Runstom said, but the fight had gone out of him. He could have taken McManus back to Gamma where the Justice precinct was, but had decided it was too short a trip.

"Defense," McManus muttered. "Defenders. Righteous twats."

"This is probably a good time to gather your crew."

McManus grunted and threw out a hand. "Well, as always, it was a pleasure chatting with you, Stan*ford*. Best of luck selling insurance."

Runstom gritted his teeth but withheld any reply, despite McManus standing there for a moment waiting for it. Finally the sergeant stalked off, the bridge door swishing closed behind him.

"Don't mind him, sir," the cadet said from her post at the stick. "He's the biggest kind of asshole."

Runstom felt a smile crack his face. "Thanks, Cadet." He stepped to that massive viewport. "This OrbitBurner sure is quite the sail, isn't she?"

"Oh hell, yes," Katsumi said, her hands flexing on the wheel. She gave a quick look at him. "Sir."

"I thought someone else should have a chance driving," he said. "Feels unfair for me to have her all to myself, to be honest."

There was a silence, as the cadet wasn't sure how to respond. Then she said, "Where are you taking her next?"

It was a fair question. After he'd gotten the message back to Defense that he had to detour from Ipo to rescue some Justice officers on the drift, they canceled the original mission. Told him to report to Delta, with new orders.

He stared at the outpost as it grew larger. "There," he said. "See that interstellar transport docked at the station?"

"Of course, sir," she said. "It's a Colossus 9K. One of the biggest ships that'll do Xarp."

He grinned, her enthusiasm contagious. "She's the *MPP Garathol.* I'm taking this OrbitBurner aboard her and heading to Epsilon Eridani."

She sighed wistfully. "Epsilon. Nothing but wide-open space. You can really open her up there."

The outpost grew closer and Katsumi adjusted their approach speed. He wouldn't be going to the Epsilon Eridani system to play with his hotrod toy ship. He would be heading to Epsilon-3, where a new colony was still under construction. State of the art domes, buoyed by state of the art terraforming and agricultural systems. Victoria Horus saw it as an easy sale: why wouldn't they want to protect their investment? They were spending so much on a new civilization, it only made sense to spend a significant chunk on defense.

The hitch was that it was new space. No one went to Epsilon, because there wasn't yet a reason to go there. There was nothing worth plundering, ergo there was nothing worth protecting. Which was why they were sending Runstom. Someone who could *consult* the new colony's leadership on the dangers of the known galaxy.

And there was already a ModPol Defense outpost established in Epsilon Eridani, ModPol being the proactive organization that it was. Conveniently, a shipment destined from Barnard to Epsilon was prepping for the trip within the week. Horus had made sure there would be room for Runstom's brand-new OrbitBurner aboard that gargantuan interstellar transport. He'd hitch a ride and then be off to EE-3 in a wink.

Just Stanford Runstom, his ship, and all that open space.

He took a deep breath as he watched the cadet ease the ship toward the dock. She had no trouble with it at all. He was impressed with both pilot and vessel. And yet, a part of him resented that modern technology had produced a ship like this that could be flown by a crew of one.

CHAPTER 21

The Space Waste base wasn't much different than any other off-world station, by Jax's initial impression once he'd had a chance to walk around a little. He wasn't sure what he'd expected – maybe more security, or more terrifying decor. Apparently security wasn't necessary because there wasn't anything to steal. Sure, there was plenty of equipment and goods, but the Wasters had a "what's mine is yours" attitude which applied to just about everything except the most personal of artifacts.

After Jax had escaped his cell (if that's what it could be called), the gangbanger who introduced himself as Barndoor took him to trade up the tight-fitting, gray jumpsuit McManus had made him wear for something a little more comfortable. The community clothing selection was divided between leather and high-flexing polymer, the latter being more practical in most cases, of course. Jax opted for fashion over practicality and was glad he did, because he and his leather drew little notice from the rest of the gangbangers he passed. He felt different wearing it, perhaps less vulnerable. No, it was more that he felt more primal in the imperfect but strong material, and thus less concerned with vulnerability. He supposed that this inward-changing attitude was projected outward, making him *belong*, if only to a small degree. A very small degree.

Where the Space Waste outpost differed from anywhere else he'd been was in its abrupt transitions. In heading from the storage vaults to the living quarters, Barndoor had led him down a long, narrow tube of a shaft. This dropped into a larger perpendicular passage that curved downward in both directions. They followed it for a while, more ladders appearing over the horizon at intervals. The effect was disorienting, like walking down a steep hill that had no bottom, until Barndoor indicated a hand-painted sign that simply read *R&R* next to the ladder they needed to climb.

Once they emerged through a floor hatch and into an octagonal hub, Jax noticed right away how different the materials and structural choices were from the storage vaults. When they took another tubular passage to the mess hall and again the style and everything changed, then he understood: the station was cobbled together from a collection of other stations, vessels, and whatever modules and materials the Wasters got their hands on. The center with all the ladders must have been the artificial gravity core which kept the whole place turning at a steady half-G. He wished he could see the base in its entirety from the outside.

"Psycho Jack." The tall, athletic black woman broke his reverie. She gave him an up-and-down look. "Nice digs."

"Dava. I haven't seen you since you tried to blow me up."

Barndoor chuckled heartily. "Tried, eh? Usually there ain't no *try* when it comes to Dava offing people."

"Right," Jax said with a cautious nod. "She was being generous."

"Even less likely," Barndoor laughed, then shrugged. "But it's been known to happen. I'm gonna get some grub."

With that, he wandered off toward some dispensers along the side wall, leaving Jax alone with Dava.

"Hey," he said. "I guess I owe you gratitude. Thanks for breaking me out."

"Yes, well. You owe me more than gratitude."

"I was afraid of that." He leaned in a little closer, as much as he dared anyway. "Look, Dava. You know I'm not really psycho. You know I'm not a killer."

"Your secret is safe with me." A small and sharp predatory grin poked into her cheek.

"Great, I appreciate that. But you know I don't belong here."

"Nonsense," she said, the grin vanishing. "You're a hacker. You're wanted by ModPol. Here is exactly where you belong."

He drooped, then tried to make his voice firm, but quiet. "I want to go back to Terroneous."

"Ain't gonna happen."

"Never?"

She stared at him in silence for a moment, hands on her hips. "Look, Jack. I won't say never. But it's best you don't think about it right now. You got a debt to pay. And we need you for a few jobs. So get comfortable."

He sighed. Was this debt smaller than the one he owed to ModPol? He had to hope it was. "What do I have to do?"

Her eyes rolled around in thought. "There's some equipment we have. Real fancy, brand-spanking new, research-level shit. Except we can't operate it."

"Oh." If Space Waste just wanted him for his technical abilities, maybe it wouldn't be so bad. It sounded like the kind of work he'd been doing on Terroneous. A little less chance the equipment was *found*, and more likely *stolen*, but that was a difference he could get past if he had to. Though, the *research-level* bit worried him.

"Beyond that, well, you passed the door test," she said. "So we'll need you for stuff like that."

"You mean like opening locked doors?" He physically shuddered. Working on stolen gear was one thing – helping to steal gear was something else. "Dava, I'm not cut out for this kind—"

She put a hand on his shoulder. "We'll try to keep you alive, Jack. I can't promise, but I can try. So go get some breakfast."

Of all the emptinesses inside him, hunger was beginning to win out. "Breakfast," he grunted. "At least there's that."

"I meant what I said," she called after him as he headed for the dispensers. He paused and glanced back. "About the digs. That leather is workin'."

As he tried to shake off the comment, he caught a glimpse of his reflection in the window of a beverage machine. The dark brown of the leather was almost liquid in its texture, like landscape eroded by running water, then frozen into form. The Space Waste logo was burned into the right breast, a muted scarring of three black arrows that followed each other in a circle, each turning outward. It reminded him of the first time he'd seen it: on the arm of Johnny Eyeball, his cellmate when he'd first been arrested. *Order into Chaos.* Johnny Eyeball's words. Nearly a year since that day, and as he looked into that reflection, the man who stared back had aged that several times over. He decided it wasn't necessarily a bad thing. Sure, there were the lines cutting through his fleeting youth, but there was a maturity that came with them. More than a maturity though, he realized. A hardness. The tarnish of his skin reflected the corruption of his world. The dome ceiling peeling back to reveal the real sky.

Order into Chaos.

Considering how badly Order had screwed him, Chaos was a temptation.

He loaded up a tray and looked around the room. There were a few gangbangers around, some muscle-bound and leather-clad, some that looked a little more like regular people. Why was he surprised? It would take more than muscle to keep a patchwork station like this running.

He didn't see Barndoor anywhere, so his escort must have eaten and split, his duty limited to getting Jax a set of clothes and a meal. Since the hall wasn't even close to full, Jax opted to take an empty table.

The food wasn't terrible, it was merely bad. He'd never felt so hungry in his life, so he didn't complain. It reminded him of the food in the domes on Barnard-4. The fresh food of Terroneous had spoiled his standards. All in all, the sensation of starving and the act of eating reminded him that he was alive. Being with Space Waste was probably slightly better than being in a ModPol prison. He wasn't sure which would be harder to get out of. In this place, he'd have to convince Dava – or someone else – that his debt was paid and he could go. In the hands of ModPol, he'd be waiting out the justice system. McManus had said that even if Jax was innocent of the murders on B-4, he was still guilty of fleeing the law. Whether or not the court would have mercy on him was a giant question mark. It made him seriously weigh that he had a better chance of getting out from under Space Waste than he had of escaping a prison sentence.

With half his food gone in a rush, he slowed down and paced himself. There was no sense in hurrying now, there was nowhere for him to go. He watched others coming and going. No brawls broke out, no gunshots, no marking of territory. It was just another dining hall.

A man approached Jax's table with a tray of food. "Mind if I sit?"

The manners jarred him. He wanted to return kindness, but he let the leather speak. "Do whatever the fuck you want."

The man stared him down with a frown, but sat anyway. He was the polymer class, not the leather class. "You're new."

Jax poked at his tray with a spoon. "Did I get the wrong slop?"

"That's not what I mean." He seemed uninterested in his own tray, and instead of picking up a utensil, he put his hands together in front of him. "It said in your dossier that your handle is Psycho Jack."

Jax set his spoon down. "You know Johnny Eyeball?"

An eyebrow arched. "Yes."

"I have him to thank for that nickname. What else does it say in my dossier?" He tried to restrain his surprise that Space Waste kept dossiers.

"Not much, I'm afraid. You're from Barnard-4. You're skilled with computers. You're...wanted."

"So what are you, like HR?"

"No, Jack," he said grimly. "We don't have a Human Resources department here. I'm Underboss Rando Jansen."

"Underboss?" Jax rolled this over in his head. He had

no idea Space Waste had titles, and he didn't know what to do with this information. "That's some kind of rank, right? Am I supposed to call you 'sir' or something?"

Jansen smiled. "Call me RJ." He picked up a fork and began twirling a mass of pasta. "I just wanted to get to know you, Jack. Do you prefer Psycho Jack?"

"Jax," he said without thinking.

Jansen shoveled a bite into his mouth, chewed, swallowed. "You know, Jax, all of us here, we never thought we'd end up in a place like this. Once you get to know Space Waste, you come to understand it's not the worst place to be. We're all used to running, and so we look out for each other."

"So, what are you running from?" Jax said, going back to his slop. "RJ."

"A fair question," Jansen said with a smile. "My family got into money trouble when I was young. Got into it and stayed there. My father was a fighter – professional. Zero-G martial arts. And my mother, she was a physical therapist. His physical therapist, actually. That's how they met."

"Are they still around?" Jax wondered aloud. The past tense description made him guess not.

Jansen's mouth turned down slightly and he cocked his head. "They're not dead, as far as I know. We're no longer in touch." He chewed through another mouthful of pasta. "Sport wasn't the only thing they had in common. They were both terrible gamblers. Severely addicted. I think my mother had it the worst."

Jax huffed. "Wouldn't surprise me to find a few gamblers around here."

He nodded. "Of course, you're right. We do what we can to mitigate the effects of all addictions here." He leaned forward. "That's what I mean. This place – this organization. Yes, we're criminals. But we are also a community. If my parents – my mother – had this kind of support, it wouldn't have gotten so bad."

Jax wondered if his dossier had anything about his parents in there. He felt compelled to explain that he'd lost his mother, that he'd been a constant disappointment to his father, just to talk to someone for once. But one part of his mind was still on guard and he refrained from exposing anything more about himself.

"I see what you mean," he said.

Jansen nodded and leaned back. "So Dava brought you in."

"I don't really know her." Jax didn't know why he felt the need to say that. Something about Dava frightened him to his core and he guessed he wasn't the only one.

"Well. It was a good move on her part. We need skills like yours."

"She mentioned something about some new equipment. Can you tell me what that is?"

Jansen's head bobbed from side to side. "Well, we actually have another man on that job. But don't worry, we'll have plenty of other things for you to do." He smiled warmly, then looked at his armband. "You'll have to excuse me, Jax. I have a meeting I have to run to. I'm glad we had a chance to talk."

Jax took the underboss's offered hand and shook it. "Sure."

Then the other man looked up, and Jax heard a deep voice behind him. "Ready, RJ?"

Jansen stood. "Yes, of course, Moses. I was just saying hello to one of the new recruits."

The man behind the voice came around to Jax's right and

looked down at him. He was black – with skin darker than anyone Jax had ever seen – and tall, even taller than many B-foureans. There were scars on his face, but they weren't fresh, and gave him a look that Jax couldn't quite place. Wisdom, he supposed, though also terrifying. But there was something else about him.

"You look very familiar to me," Jax said without thinking. "Have we met?"

His rough face broke into a mischievous grin and he glanced at Jansen. "I'm pretty sure you'd remember me if you'd met me." He offered a large hand, exposing a gray palm. "Moses Down."

"Oh." Jax stood and shook the hand, which had the feel of the leather clothes he'd recently acquired. He recalled the name coming out of Barndoor's mouth, something about the leader of all of Space Waste. His brain was ruminating over smart-ass comments about this being the "Boss Man", but looking up at that face and feeling the grip of that hand, he felt an unexpected respect. "Good to meet you, sir."

"This is Jack," Jansen said.

"Jack," Moses's low voice rumbled. "Ah, Psycho Jack. Welcome to the family."

"Thank you, sir," Jax said, then was at a loss for any other words. This was the big boss, the one man who might grant Jax his freedom if he could be convinced. And yet, somehow the thoughts of escape were fuzzier than they were a few moments ago.

"You survived Dava long enough to make it here," Moses said. "We honor survivors."

Jax opened his mouth and nothing came out. Jansen turned to Moses and said, "Moses, we should be going."

"Of course. See you around, Jack."

Then he was alone again. His hunger abated, the rest of the tray looked like shit. He took it to the bins where he'd seen others dispose of their leftovers. Then out of sheer desperation, he spoke to someone he didn't know: an older man with dark-red skin and plastic clothes. He asked if there was a bar around, and the man gave him a half-grin and directions.

It was just back to the octagon and through another passage. The place was just what Jax was hoping for: it was dark and the tables were small and isolated. There was a sign that read, "Order at Bar", and so he did and then took a very tall beer back to a table off to the side.

The word *family* bounced around his head, having been thrust into it by a terrifying, bloodthirsty gangbanger, who hadn't been as terrifying as he should have been. Moses Down had been familiar and – oddly – made Jax feel safe. Was it that he was the kind of terrifying that felt good to have on your side? That sense that he was a protector? That he would protect his family, and it was better to be in it than outside it?

His mother had made him feel that way. Dad, sometimes, but not in many years. And what difference did that make? She was gone. And he was – well, Jax hadn't spoken to the man since before the arrest. He'd planned to send d-mail. His thoughts turned to his old notebook. A number of letters, unsent, inside. He had to believe Lealina would keep it safe for him.

He thought the beer would make him feel better, but instead it just reminded him of Terroneous. It wasn't as good as the brew he'd had there, that was for sure, but its shortcomings only served to remind him of what he was missing. Good drink, good food.

Bright blues.

He closed his eyes and tightened his throat. For months he'd been on that moon, always careful not to get too comfortable, not to get too close, always reminding himself that he was in hiding. And then she came along. And he wanted it to be normal, he wanted it to be just life, just plain, boring life.

And ModPol had to come along and take it away. To chase grudges against a wrongfully arrested innocent man, for the sake of their process. And their reputation, likely. As he sat there in the corner of a bar tucked deep inside the deep-space headquarters of a criminal organization, he sighed at the realization that he was the safest he'd been in a long time.

He opened his eyes and scowled. Took another swallow of the bitter ale. In that moment, he couldn't feel anything for ModPol but hate. Still, he was no criminal. He shouldn't have to join Space Waste just to escape injustice. He deserved freedom. He deserved happiness. Didn't he?

A slow, rhythmic thumping floated around the bar, coming from unseen speakers, and he took another drink, allowing himself to taste the beer, his tongue to identify the elements of sweetness mixed with sourness, to feel the roughness of bubbles. He'd been through worse shit, he would get through this. He just had to stay calm, do as he was told, and he would stay alive.

And somehow, he'd find a way to get back to Terroneous.

* * *

"So this transport," Captain 2-Bit said. "What kind of ship is it?"

"A Colossus 9K." Jansen paced anxiously around the oval table. "Designation is *MPP Garathol.*"

"And what exactly is on it?"

"Weapons."

Other than the captain and the underboss, there was Moses and another man that Dava didn't know in the war room. She sat next to Moses and fidgeted. She usually avoided this level of planning, but he'd insisted she be there. More of his attempt to press her into leadership.

"What else?" she said.

Jansen looked at her. "Supplies. Probably some other equipment."

"The weapons are the real value," Moses said, his deep voice threatening to lull her into agreement.

If she was going to be forced to attend the planning meeting, she wasn't going to just nod along. "We already have weapons. What's so special about these?"

"Good question," Moses said with a broad smile. "RJ, tell us about them."

"Very well," he said with a clearing of his throat. "They're straight out of the lab. All experimental. Highly destructive while at the same time very highly precise. Designed to strike fast and accurately, reducing collateral damage."

"Since when do we care about collateral damage?" she said.

"Well." He gestured, as though unsure of himself. "There have been incidents where the very goods we are trying to acquire accumulate damage, uh, from—"

"He means sometimes we shoot holes in the stuff we're trying to steal," 2-Bit said, sitting back and nodding with an air of wisdom.

"Yes, thank you, Captain." Jansen continued his pacing.

"These weapons are also a chance for us to take the lead in the arms race against ModPol."

"Exactly," Moses said, pointing a long, dark finger at the underboss. "This is their latest and greatest. If we can get it, not only do we get state of the art weapons for our armory, we set ModPol back several years of development."

Dava didn't like the gleam in his eyes. She wasn't sure if that statement was true; even if they managed to steal some ModPol prototypes, they must have the means to replace them. "So these weapons are so new, they don't even know if they work. Why would they be taking them to Epsilon Eridani?"

"Testing, right?" 2-Bit raised his hand as though he were in school. "Nothing really out there yet, so there's no traffic to get in the way, no civilians to accidentally injure."

They all thought about it silently for a moment. 2-Bit was making sense for once. The first Xarp route to Epsilon had only been established about twelve years ago, from what little Dava knew about the system. There was supposedly one planet being groomed for domes, and that was it. No one else had any reason to go there, at least not yet.

"So ModPol must have a base in Epsilon," she said, thinking out loud. "They're not just going to point their guns out of the windows of that transport."

"Right, of course," Jansen said. He walked to the screen at the front of the room and with a swipe pulled in a system map. "Here's Epsilon Eridani, the star itself, in the middle. There are three planets here – the third is where terraforming work has begun to support domes. Then there is this inner asteroid belt. A fourth planet, a gas giant, orbits outside the belt. Between that and this outer asteroid belt is a gap of roughly ten astronomical units. We believe that somewhere in that gap there is a ModPol outpost. There's enough room there for plenty of weapon and flight testing, with pockets of debris for target shooting."

"Ten AU," 2-Bit said. "That's a big gap."

"There's a good chance it will be close to Epsilon-4," Jansen said, pointing at the planet at the edge of the inner belt. "The gas giant's gravity would clear out most debris, and it gives them a gravity well to orbit around."

"So how are we supposed to find this transport?" Dava said. "Assuming we don't want to go anywhere near a ModPol outpost, especially one we know nothing about."

"Great question," Moses said. "The *Garathol* will be coming from an outpost here in Barnard. It will Xarp into Epsilon space."

"We can't track it through Xarp," she said.

"And it's too big a gap," 2-Bit added. "What chance do we have of getting to it before it gets home?"

Jansen smiled. "I should introduce Basil," he said, approaching the Sirius-fiver who'd been sitting silent so far. "Moses Down, Captain 2-Bit, Capo Dava, this is Basil Roy."

"At your service," the man said, partially standing and giving them a slight bow before sitting back down. He was short and stout, with blank white skin and the tight, defined muscles of an athlete.

"Basil is a systems architect," Jansen said.

"What the hell is that?" 2-Bit blurted.

"I specialize in all manner of technological systems," Roy said. "My skills range from network architecture to programming to general troubleshooting."

"I already found us a new hacker," Dava said, willing herself to remain calm. She wanted to jump out of her chair and slap both Jensen and his tagalong. "Psycho Jack.

Someone we know already, and we know we can trust because we know him to be a fugitive of ModPol. Who the hell is *this* guy?" she asked, looking at Moses.

Jansen leaned over the table. "I can assure you that Basil is trustworthy—"

"Moses," Dava said, ignoring the underboss. "We should be using Jack on this job."

"Alright," Moses said, quieting them both with his low but strong voice. "We've got room for two hackers. Probably more." He turned to her. "It was quick thinking to grab Psycho Jack on Terroneous. We know he's resourceful, and to rescue him from ModPol is a nice guarantee of loyalty. I can assure you we're going to need him on this job. This is an all-hands job. Understood?"

His question was for all, but Dava felt his eyes bearing down on her. "Yes."

"RJ, I understand you want to explain how your hacker, Roy, comes into play."

"Actually, sir," Roy interjected. "I don't really like that term. I'm an architect."

The room stared at him in silence for a moment, broken finally by Jansen. "Yes. Right. So…you all remember the detection equipment we acquired at Vulca."

"I remember finding out it didn't work," Dava muttered.

"Correct," Jansen said, then bobbed his head side to side. "In a manner of speaking. It does in fact work, however no software was installed on it. Evidently, the engineers at the research facility had not had a chance to do much with it before we showed up. Basil?"

"I acquired the necessary detection software," Roy said. "It needed heavy modifications, of course, to work with the new equipment. But now we're confident that we can find the ModPol outpost at a safe distance. We can also pinpoint the location of the *Garathol* as soon as it comes out of Xarp, based on its metallurgical structure and emitted radiation."

"So you're saying, we go to Epsilon," 2-Bit said, "hang out and wait, and as soon as it pops in, we can chase it down before it gets home?"

"Precisely," Jansen said. He swiped the screen a few times until a schematic of a ship appeared. "This is the transport itself. It has several large holds for general storage and about six bays for carrying smaller vessels."

"What about escorts?" Dava said.

"My intelligence suggests they won't use any. Xarp is impossible to track, and no one really knows much about Epsilon. An observer would assume any transport leaving Barnard would be heading for Sirius, not Epsilon."

She cringed at that phrase, *my intelligence*, but she decided to keep comments to herself. "So the assault plan?"

He waved at the schematic. "There's the data. I'll leave the assault plan to Captain Tubennetal."

"Well, let's see—" 2-Bit started.

"We're taking the *Longhorn*," Moses interrupted. He stood and walked to the screen.

"Well, sure," 2-Bit said haltingly. "The *Longhorn* can carry two dozen fighters. But she's our biggest warship. We'd be stretching thin—"

"That's right," Moses said, causing 2-Bit to lean back in his chair and hear the boss out. "We're going all in on this. We load the *Longhorn* with a dozen dogfighters, six raiders, and four loot-mules. The *Longhorn's* missiles take out these guns here and here," he said, pointing to sections of the transport's schematic. "The dogfighters engage any aircraft the transport might launch and clean up any short-range turrets. The raiders move in for breach and board at these corners of the hull. We get boots in the corridors and take out anyone inside who puts up a fight. Once the bridge of the *Garathol* is secure, the loot-mules move in and carve open these holds in the back."

He stared at the diagram in silence, his lines and marks showing red where he'd drawn them. Dava didn't like how he looked at it. There was a pride there that he normally kept in check. "Who's where?" she said.

He continued to admire his work for another moment before turning to answer. "RJ and 2-Bit are on the *Longhorn*, in the command center."

"Along with Basil," Jansen added quickly. "To run the detectors."

"Yes," Moses said.

"So you want me to lead the raiders force to breach and board," Dava said.

"You're second in command of the B-n-B."

Her breath caught in her throat, not understanding what he'd meant. Johnny Eyeball wasn't there, so who else would lead an assault on foot? Then it hit her: he was going. The damned fool was going to lead the charge. She stood, willed herself not to quiver, or even make fists. She looked at each of them, but 2-Bit, Jansen, Roy, none would return her gaze.

"Moses," she said quietly.

"Go prep the raiders, Dava," he said coolly. "2-Bit, get your flyboys ready. Jansen, do what needs to be done to get the detector installed into the *Longhorn*. Dismissed!"

* * *

She caught Moses ducking into the lounge that evening. She followed him in, watched him from a distance. He was making rounds, getting in more face time with the gang than was usual, shaking hands, patting backs, raising glasses. She drifted through his wake of brightened faces, men and women invigorated, recharged for battle.

For a moment she lost him, distracted for only a second when someone greeted her and offered her a drink. When she turned back, he was gone, vanishing into the cigar smoke and darkness.

Then she sensed him again, not by his presence exactly but by the energy in the room, the way it pointed, swirled and vectored like air currents. She saw him sitting at one of the booths along the side of the lounge that had a curtain. He looked right at her, waved her over.

"I'm sorry, Moses," she said as she slid into the seat across from him. She would later punish herself for starting the conversation with an apology, for such weakness. But she couldn't help it; she always showed him her weakest side.

"For coming to my table without a drink?" He had a bottle to himself and a pair of glasses, one empty, one full. He filled the other and slid it to her.

She cracked a grin at his unrelenting, full-faced smile and took a sip. It was bourbon, and it made her think of Johnny Eyeball and Freezer, locked in some cell somewhere, and immediately she lost her mood. "What I meant was, for disagreeing with you in the war room."

"Shit," he said with a wave of his hand. "That's why I brought you in there, Dava."

"Well then," she said with a deep breath. "I left something out."

"More disagreement."

"Yes."

"You want to lead the breach and board."

She took another swallow of the sweet, burning amber. "Yes."

"Why?" He was quick with his words and yet the deepness of his voice seemed to draw them into a timeless space.

"Why?" She turned away from him, then back to face those giant eyes. "Because I don't want you to go," she blurted.

He sighed and refilled his glass. "Wrong answer."

"Moses, it's too dangerous. We need you, what if something..." Her voice trailed off as she searched his face for understanding.

"Now if you had come here and said to me, 'Dammit, Moses, I'm ready. Let me lead them,' then I would consider it."

"For fuck's sake," she breathed. "Forget about me. We *need* you."

He reached out and slid the curtain across, enclosing them in candlelit darkness. "Dava, they don't need me. They need leadership."

"But that's what you are—"

"You gotta get it out of your head that I'm irreplaceable." He leaned back in his seat. "I'm not going to be around forever."

She hung her head. "Moses, not this again." She looked up. "I'm ready. I want to lead them."

He laughed, jarring her. "Dava, come on girl. You got to do better than that."

"Johnny should be going," she said, grasping for threads. "We should be busting Johnny and Frank out. We got Jansen's intel on where they're at."

"We also got intel that it's an impossible job."

According to Jansen, Eyeball and Freezer had been taken to a new zero-G facility in the outskirts of Barnard. The place was supposedly loaded up with state of the art defense systems. "We need them," she said, trying to make her voice firm and failing.

"And after we hit this *Garathol*, we'll have the strength to go get them." He took another sip of his whiskey and leaned back. "In the meantime, you're going to have to settle for an old coot like me to lead the attack."

"Moses—"

"Just stop worrying about me, okay?" he said, his voice turning from amused to forceful. "I'm going and that's all there is to it. I can handle myself. I know I'm getting on in years, but you know I can still bang like the best of 'em. And we're going to work together, you and I. I'm taking command of the B-n-B and you're my second." He took another swallow and pointed his empty glass at her. "And you pay attention and maybe you'll learn something."

So this was his game. Put his fucking life on the line to force her to learn to lead. It was stupid, careless. What frustrated her most was that part of her *did* want to lead. She was trying. She just didn't get it. She was trying to trust her team, but it wasn't in her nature, it felt uncomfortable, made her anxious. When she got anxious, she made mistakes.

She stared at his eyes in the flicker of the candle's flame. Everything she had, she owed to this man. "I know you think they don't need you. But I do."

"I know you don't want to hear this, but someday you won't."

She closed her eyes and took a breath, trying not to let her imagination show her what that day would look like.

What choice did she have but go along with his plan? At least she could be there to protect him. "Jansen's info better be good," she muttered and finished her drink.

The curtain slid back then, Jansen appearing as if at the speaking of his name. He flinched when he saw her. "Oh, hello, Capo Dava. Moses."

"I was just having a chat with Dava here about the raider prep for the B-n-B," Moses said.

"Oh," Jansen said. He weakly waved a handypad. "I uh, I have the personnel data you wanted to go over..."

She got out of the booth, ceding the seat to him. "We're finished. I was just leaving."

"Uh, thank you. Oh, Dava," he said, stopping her with a hand before she could walk away. "I noticed that this Psycho Jack fellow managed to beat Reezer's door test. I mean Freezer. Whatever his name is."

"Yeah," she said. "Jack made pretty good time, and did it after coming out of secure tube sedation."

"Excellent," Jansen said. He looked from Dava to Moses and back. "Well, you should definitely take him along. On one of the raiders, I mean. He'll be very useful once you board the transport."

"Sure."

"As long as you're sure you can trust him."

She stared at him, feeling a burn behind her eyes. She looked at Moses. "He'll follow my lead."

CHAPTER 22

Jax stumbled through the corridors of the massive carrier ship, desperately trying to keep up with his escort. Xarp-sickness didn't seem to affect the rest of Space Waste. Maybe they'd gotten used to it, but this was Jax's third trip between systems and he decided he would never get used to it.

He ducked as the walls bobbed in his direction when he rounded another corner. The damn ship had to be the size of a small city. A wall shoved into his shoulder and he rebounded in the opposite direction with a tilt.

"Come on, Psycho Jack," Barndoor said, turning around and grabbing him by the arm. "Dava's waitin', and you don't keep Dava waitin'."

Barndoor tugged him along, which didn't really help Jax's balance, but it did seem to improve their speed. He thought if he closed his eyes it might be easier going. Then the labyrinth of corridors came to an end and he was hit with the overstimulation of a large room with about a dozen people talking, a few hundred terminals blinking with data, and a massive viewport that showed more stars and space than he'd ever seen. Or at least that's how it felt. He thought he might vomit, but then he got distracted by the smell of coffee.

"She's right over here," Barndoor said with a yank of his arm.

"Barney," Jax said. It came out like a gasp. "Where's the coffee?"

"On the wall dispenser over there." He pointed and then pointed in a different direction. "After you grab some head over there to the starboard side. That's where Dava's prep station is."

"Right, right."

Barndoor and everyone else melted away as he stumbled toward the dispenser. After a few desperate stabs at the machine, he had a hot cup of liquid in his hands. He drank greedily.

After a moment, he was blinking. His vision had sharpened and the tilt was gone. He looked into the cup. Although it was hot and not cold like he preferred, it looked and smelled like coffee, and nothing else. Still, it was intensely effective.

"What the hell's in this stuff?" he wondered aloud.

"Don't ask," three people answered in passing.

When he found Dava, she was flipping through a touch screen that displayed diagnostics on various ships, which he presumed to be the raiders that were going to be used to board the transport. What he knew of their mission so far wasn't much. He knew it involved a Xarp jump to Epsilon Eridani (which he could have done without) and some kind of ModPol Defense transport (which he'd really rather not go near) and several boarding parties (which he'd be a part of and really wished he could find a nice cold airlock to pop out of instead). They were supposed to be stealing something that was kept a secret from most of the gang, but rumors had been circulating that it was experimental weaponry.

"Jack," Dava said without turning away from her screen. "Glad you could join us."

"Yeah, of course," he stammered. "Sorry about the lateness. It's just the Xarp jump—"

"Forget about that." She turned to him and leaned close. "Something you need to look at for me."

"Um, okay."

She looked over her shoulders and pulled him closer to the wall. "You remember how I told you about how we had this new long-range sensor stuff? Brand-new detection equipment we got from a research complex?"

"Right, yeah," he said, lowering his voice to match hers. He thought back to the conversation he'd had with Underboss Rando Jansen the first day they'd met. "You said as your resident programming expert, you'd need me to take a look at it. But I don't think that's going to—"

"That was my plan," she said quickly. "But we got someone else."

"Ah. Basil Roy?" He'd met the other new technical recruit in the secret headquarters of Space Waste a few days earlier. A domer by his unpigmented skin, like Jax, but short and stout like those on Sirius-5. He'd been introduced as another hacker, which he'd been quick to clarify as a *solutions architect*. Beyond that, he was unwilling to share his background or experience. "Not a real friendly guy."

She smirked. "Yeah, well, anyway. He's already re-programmed the equipment."

Jax breathed a little too easy, then coughed to cover up

his relief. He'd still had a fear they would expect him to get some crazy cutting-edge research equipment to work. There was a bit of a gap between *operator* and *engineer*. Or *solutions architect* for that matter. "Well, that's that then, eh?"

"I want you to check it out," she said. "We're not going to be using it for about six hours, if Jansen's information is real."

"Check it out?"

She nodded back to the room and he glanced to see Roy at a console near the center, with Jansen standing nearby. "He's got it loaded up on that console. I just want to know if you can see how it works."

"I can ask him."

She looked at Jax and seemed to consider that. "Yeah, ask him. Get him to tell you as much as he will. Then I'll find a way to pull him away for a few minutes."

Jax took a deep breath. She was asking him to get in there and poke around in someone else's console. He thought about asking her for a guarantee that he wouldn't somehow end up falsely accused of murder, but swallowed those words and instead gave her a conspiratorial nod.

A minute later he was standing over the programmer. "Hey, Basil. I heard you got the detection equipment all set up."

The Sirius-fiver looked over his shoulder at Jansen, but the underboss was engaged in conversation, so he looked back at Jax warily. "Yes. It just needed an interface layer installed and some simple scanning parameters."

"Cool," Jax said. "Does it uh, use, like, COMPLEX or something?"

Roy huffed in amusement. "COMPLEX is a toy language for operators. This equipment is far too sophisticated for that. It uses Qubidense."

"Oh right, of course. Qubidense." Jax tried not to think about a class he'd failed that used Qubidense back in his college years. "That's great. Really cool. Can you show me how it works?"

"Well, okay." Roy glanced at Jansen again, but the underboss's conversation had taken him off to another console. "It's pretty simple really. This is the UI."

He showed Jax a few screens on his console. Not much of anything was happening, but he pointed at various scanners and sensors and their readouts. To Jax it all looked like inert graphs devoid of data. He started to understand that was partly the nature of Epsilon Eridani: there were no ships to detect. Then Roy explained that somehow they'd tuned the equipment to specifically detect the large transport that they were expecting to appear out of Xarp in the next six to twelve hours.

"Heya, there, Basil," Barndoor said, interrupting them from behind. "Did you get a scan before you came in here?"

"A scan?" Roy's face twisted. "What sort of scan?"

"Security."

Roy frowned. "So what, metal detector? X-ray? Ionization test? What *sort* of scan?"

Barndoor tilted his head. "Well…there's one box that does all of it, I think."

"I can assure you—"

"Look, Basil." Barndoor's good arm came down heavy on the other man's shoulder. "It'll be over real quick. If I don't do it now, I'm just going to get in trouble later."

Though his words seemed friendly, his voice was uncomfortably stern. Roy seemed to take the hint. He huffed, then gave a short nod, stood up, and excused himself.

Once they were out of the way, Jax slid into Roy's chair

in what he hoped was a nonchalant motion, though he managed to hook his sleeve on the arm and had to take a moment to untangle himself. He tapped at the screen, but it seemed to have no effect: the same maps, readouts, and graphs hung there as if near-dead, barely twitching once every few seconds. He hadn't seen Roy touch the screen, only use the keys below. There was no terminal prompt or on-screen help, so he must have had the control scheme in his head. Jax wished he had paid more attention to the keys Roy had been hitting instead of staring so intently at the screen that hardly changed.

He sighed. He didn't know how long Barndoor would keep Roy occupied, so he figured he'd better start experimenting. He tried "H" for "Help", then went on to other keys at random, but nothing had any effect. Then suddenly the screen froze; the periodic twitching had stopped. What had he just hit? One of the number keys? He tried "1", and the twitching resumed. There was something off about it, though. It was faster – much faster – and he could swear it was...what? He thought it might be going backwards.

He tried "3" and the movement slowed some. At "5" it stopped completely again. At "6" it was very slow. He focused on one of the data points, a radiation counter or something or other. He watched the number combinations climb tick by tick. Then he hit "4". The same numbers sank. It was going backwards.

"Sonovabitch," he whispered. The damn thing wasn't an interface – it was a recording. The number keys controlled how fast it played. He confirmed it with some experimentation: "5" was the stopping point, "9" was the fastest forward speed, and "1" was the fastest backward speed.

He sat back and frowned. What the hell was he looking

at? If Roy hadn't created a real interface, he'd deliberately created something that was meant to look like one. Which meant the data wasn't real, but it was made to appear to be working. It didn't make any sense to Jax.

Unless Roy was no engineer. Jax had been sweating the possible assignment only a few days earlier. He knew he'd never be able to program that equipment. Maybe Roy had the same problem. If this was his solution, Jax had to admit, it was pretty crafty. But what was he going to do when it came time to look for the target ship?

Maybe there would be no raid after all.

He glanced over his shoulder, but no one was paying him any mind. Dava had sent him over to find out if anything was suspicious, and this definitely fit the bill. Could he tell her though? What would be the point? What if they decided to fry Roy, push him out an airlock for deceiving them? Jax didn't want that on his hands. Plus, then Jax would be the sole "hacker" and they'd probably expect him to come up with something on the spot to make the detection work, and then he'd be in the same situation.

Lying to Dava was not something he felt all that comfortable with; in fact, he felt the opposite of comfortable when thinking about it. But the truth remained: he was no gang-banger. He had no place in Space Waste. He was only trying to appear useful because it seemed like the best way to stay alive. He didn't want to be responsible for hurting anyone, he knew that. He didn't mind stealing; there were worse things in the universe than stealing. But this was Space Waste. They never stopped at stealing.

A rush of air came out his lungs and he hung his head, but only for a second. He'd have to move, keep playing the game. Bright blue eyes waited for him on Terroneous. He just needed to stay alive long enough to figure out how to get back there.

"Jack." Dava had a terrifying ability to appear as though from thin air.

"Oh, uh—"

"Come on," she said, pulling him by the arm. "What did you find out?" she whispered as they marched back to her station.

"Well, it seems to work," he said.

"Seems to?"

"There's nothing out here right now, so it's hard to verify." He paused, then sensed she needed more. "He told me how it works though, and it fits together."

She stared, then nodded softly. "Okay. Let me ask you this," she said. "Could you operate it?"

"You mean using his interface?"

"Yeah, whatever."

He didn't understand the question, and it led him to the worst of conclusions. Was she suggesting that she might take Roy out? And expect Jax to finish the job? Still, it would do him no good to appear incompetent. He thought of the number-keys controlling the playback. "Sure, not much to it."

Her eyes probed his face, and for a moment he had a thought that she could read his mind, or at least tell if he were lying. He wondered: had he lied? He *could* control it as Roy intended to, but not as they wanted him to. Her lips pursed and she looked away. "Good," she said, her voice relaxing somewhat. "You probably won't get a chance to, but I wanted to make sure that it wasn't some power play on Jansen's part."

"Power play?"

"I mean, if no one else could control it but Roy."

If he'd had any doubt that the woman had trust issues before, it was gone. He thought about asking her what it was she didn't trust about Roy, or maybe it was Jansen. But he caught himself. It wasn't his place. He just needed to stay alive.

Just stay alive and get back to Terroneous.

* * *

A frustrating, pulsing alert icon replaced the bombball highlights with a shudder. Runstom sat up in his cot. It was the only furniture in his meager guest chamber, aside from the holovid player.

"Come on, dammit." He swung his feet off the side of the bed to reach for the HV and muttered to himself, "I saved up those recordings so I would have something to do out here in the middle of nowhere."

The HV ignored his prodding, insistent on the ship-wide message it was delivering. Some kind of alert; Defense jargon that he wasn't used to. It was like trying to understand the same language but with a heavy dialect. A yellow alert, it warned passengers to take precautionary measures. It said nothing about the nature of the concern or exactly what measures one should take.

He sighed and stood. They had Xarped into Epsilon Eridani, the least populated of the populated solar systems, only thirty minutes earlier. He'd had one plan for dealing with the Xarp sickness: grab coffee and catch up on bombball. He looked at his empty cup and then at the pulsing yellow icon.

At the least, he could go hunt down more coffee.

As he stepped into the hall, he thought that maybe they were approaching the outpost already. Outpost Epsilon was the only ModPol facility in the whole system. From there they would let him launch his OrbitBurner 4200 LX luxury ship so he could head over to Epsilon-3, where the new domes were being constructed.

If they were almost to the outpost, he definitely needed more coffee.

The hallway flashed an annoying yellow every few meters from ceiling-mounted lights. The occasional staff blurted at him to make a hole before jogging past. With each one, his anxiety notched upward, their urgency being transmitted to him like a disease.

The only real contact he'd had with anyone in charge was when Lieutenant Commander Ploughy gave him a tour of the *Garathol* a few hours before launch. The man was a B-fourean, but other than his height and slight build was nothing like Jax. He was twitchy with a face like a rodent, and he'd given Runstom an unsettling feeling by asking a lot of inane questions and then pointedly ignoring the answers.

Still, the man had been cordial enough. He'd told Runstom that if he needed anything, he shouldn't hesitate to ask. Runstom decided to head to the bridge to see if he could find the lieutenant commander.

After ten minutes of dizzy wandering, he finally found the command center of the ship, which turned out to be much smaller than he'd expected. Though he wasn't sure why he'd expected more; even though the *Garathol* was a Colossus 9K – a massive vessel – there wasn't much to it besides interstellar transportation.

The bridge was flashing yellow, but less so than the halls.

He spotted a coffee pot in the corner and realized he was still holding his empty cup, so he gave himself a refill before seeking out the lieutenant commander.

Ploughy was fidgeting with a narrow console at one side of the room. He twitched when Runstom approached, but quickly turned back to his screens, tapping away at the interface.

"Runstom." He paused and looked at nothing for a moment. "I didn't catch your title."

Runstom coughed. "Public relations officer," he mumbled before covering his mouth with the cup of coffee.

"Public Relations Officer Runstom." Ploughy's focus returned to the console. "I'm afraid non-essential personnel are not permitted on the bridge during any alert condition."

Runstom blinked and looked around the small room. There were six others, most in front of consoles, except for the woman he'd been briefly introduced to as Captain Yakimoto. She was standing at a podium in the center reviewing a handypad one of the others had handed her. Everyone was remarkably calm.

"I'm sorry," he said. "It's just that you said, if I needed—"

"Of course." Ploughy turned and folded his narrow hands in front of himself. "What can I help you with, Public Relations Officer Runstom?"

"Please, just Stanford," Runstom said, feeling his own hand on the back of his neck. "I just – well, I guess I don't know what I'm supposed to be doing. With the yellow alert and all."

"Right." The lieutenant commander looked as though he were holding an insect between his hands, one he didn't want to be caught with but didn't want to continue to hold onto as it crawled around his palms. "Well, it's probably nothing, to be honest. You can just return to your chamber and await further instructions."

Runstom nodded slowly and tried to steal a glance at the console. "Another ship?" he blurted when he noticed the blip on the contact map.

Ploughy sighed through his nose and kept himself from following Runstom's eyes to the console. "Yes, that's right. There's a contact."

"An unknown contact," Runstom said. "Otherwise it wouldn't be a yellow alert."

A twitch. "Yes. Of course. I can assure you, we have everything under control."

"Could it be hostile? All the way out here?"

"Whatever it is, we're prepared for anything."

"I suppose," Runstom said, then glanced around the room. "Of course, there aren't many weapons on the *Garathol*."

Ploughy's mouth opened, closed, and then opened again. "I beg your pardon?"

"Just something I heard from someone who knows ships better than I do." Cadet Katsumi had grown quite chatty back on their approach to Outpost Delta, once McManus had left anyway. She'd gone on and on about the *Garathol*, which was visible as soon as the outpost was. "It's the largest ship capable of Xarp. It's all drives and cargo holds, not much room – or power – for weapons."

Ploughy's whiskery mouth curled and he gave a short nod. "This is true. Nonetheless, Defense is always prepared."

"Lieutenant Commander?" the captain called. "Contact update?"

The man flinched and his eyes scanned the console. He tapped sharply at it. "Contact is still unidentified," he said.

"But the computer found several matches with a non-zero potential."

"Any of them hostile?" she asked.

"Yes," he said evenly. "One possible hostile. A carrier, once belonging to the Defensive Space Brigade of Triton, on Barnard-3. It was...acquired. Approximately two years ago. By—"

"Space Waste." She turned to someone on her other side. "Lieutenant Kilson. Go to red alert."

The room went bright orange and faint klaxons immediately began sounding.

Ploughy turned to Runstom. "Apologies, Public Relations Officer Runstom." He took a step forward. "Now you really must leave the bridge."

* * *

They must be after the cargo, Runstom thought as he was herded out the door. He'd asked about the cargo when he got his tour of the ship, but Ploughy had told him that was restricted information. Evidently Runstom didn't rank very high in his present company.

Still, he was an officer of ModPol Defense. Even if it was public relations officer. Shouldn't he be privy to what they were transporting?

The alarms grew louder as he made his way down the hall and the abrasive sound combined forces with the lingering Xarp sickness to clog his mind with mud.

He began to look for the simple explanations. Space Waste knew the transport had something of value on board. Or maybe they didn't. Maybe they just intended to commandeer the ship itself. It was a skeleton crew, easy to outnumber. But then Space Waste would have to know that, and how could they?

The gangbangers had shown up at Vulca, then at Terroneous when they kidnapped Jax. And now here.

He had a sudden pang of guilt. What had happened to Jax? He missed the B-fourean. He was actually a little concerned. Somehow he convinced himself that Space Waste wouldn't hurt him. If they'd wanted him dead, they could have easily killed him back on Sirius-5. Or they could have simply blown up McManus's ship. But instead, they boarded and kidnapped him.

Runstom blinked. He'd managed to wander far enough through the maze of corridors to see a map with the ship's layout on the wall. Some of the cargo holds were off to his left, the rest off to his right. He considered looking for the kitchen. Would it be open during a red alert?

"Dammit," he cursed aloud. He'd left his cup, full of coffee, back on the bridge.

He went right and approached the door of the first hold he came to. It had a biometric lock, with a retina scan.

"Worth a shot," he mumbled and stuck his face into the receptacle.

To his surprise, the machine bleeped happily and turned green. His name and position flashed on the screen.

Inside, it was cold. His teeth began to chatter almost immediately, and he hugged himself. The chill began to clear away the mud, at least. He inspected the containers that were stacked in rows all the way up the tall ceiling.

It was all food. He'd read an infosheet that said Outpost Epsilon was currently occupied by forty Defenders and thirty non-military personnel. It looked like the precious cargo the transport was hauling was just a restock of the outpost's food supply.

The cold finally drove him out of the hold and he wandered along the hallway rubbing life back into his limbs. The alarms were louder again, and only then he realized they'd been muffled in the hold. A trio of airmen jogged past him. When they rounded the corner, he spotted another cargo door.

It'd worked before, so he shrugged at the thing and stuck his face into the scanner. Again, the door opened. And again, stacks and stacks of food in cold storage.

After a few minutes he'd inspected all six cargo holds on that side of the ship, and they were all food. Enough to feed seventy people for years, he thought. What did he know about it, though? He shook his head at the thought that it made any difference. It only bothered him because he couldn't imagine Space Waste coming clear out to Epsilon Eridani just to steal food. They could steal that anywhere.

Right about then, he wanted to ask Jax what he thought. It wasn't so much that Runstom relied on Jax to know any more than he did, but it was good to have someone to bounce ideas off of, to talk things out. He really hoped Space Waste wasn't torturing the poor man. He wished he had the resources to go after him, but there was nothing he could do. Or so he told himself. But the fact was, Jax was a wanted fugitive, and when a ModPol patrol tried to pick him up—

He stopped back at the junction between the cargo sections and stood staring into space. He'd been working off the fact that Jax had been kidnapped by Space Waste. But Jax had just been arrested. Anyone who wasn't ModPol would have seen it for what it was: they'd rescued him from going to prison.

He laughed then for a moment, then clammed up and looked around to make sure no one saw him standing around laughing to himself. Now he knew Jax was going to be fine. At least physically. What they intended to do with the B-fourean, he wasn't so sure about.

Since he had nothing better to do at the moment, he decided to check the cargo holds off to the left. The first one he came to, he tried the retina scan. It buzzed nastily at him and flashed red, *ACCESS DENIED*. He tried again and got the same result.

Then the door opened, and his jaw dropped.

And the floor shook.

CHAPTER 23

The raider bobbed and swayed, but it was nothing too jarring with the lack of gravity. Dava floated down the line of her assault team as each man and woman showed their weapons and ammo and she ticked them off the list on her handypad. All sixteen were required to have an operational long gun, sidearm, and blade. She knew the blades wouldn't get much use, but she'd have felt unprepared if they didn't have them. Their armor wasn't much to look at, being patchwork leather, but it was reinforced with an alloy lining. For her own blade, she didn't bother with the anticoagulant she'd been using. For this mission, she'd loaded it with a paralyzing poison that came from the first of four stomachs in a large-mouthed lizard-like creature that lived in some particularly nasty swamps on Terroneous. The poacher who sold it to her wove a story about how the beast swallows prey whole, coats them in the paralyzing venom, then digests the immobile victim over the course of a few days. Injecting it into the bloodstream with a needle – or a blade designed to distribute cartridges of poison – was supposed to result in immobility within seconds. She only wished she'd had a chance to test it before the mission.

She snapped each one of them into their wall restraints as she checked them off her list. She flipped the handypad over to the external cameras. It wasn't much to look at, a battle like this. Two behemoths in the distance, streaks of white rocket flare streaming between them, the almost harmless blinking red of laser targeting systems. Swarming, swirling fightercraft like angry insects. From this view it was an organic chaos. She knew in a few days they'd be reviewing the footage from the Battle-Capture probes, which would provide a much better view. Moses never let them go into an operation without his BatCaps. Always something to learn, he would say.

The intercom squawked to life. "Capo Dava." Sandpiper, the raider's co-pilot.

She floated to the comm, bracing herself on a hand-hold when the ship took an unexpected dip. She hit the button. "What's up, Sandy?"

"Moses just radioed in," she said. "All the transport's fighters are engaged and the main guns have been disabled. We're clear to breach."

"Good. Prepping for breach."

They had only waited a few hours post-Xarp before Basil Roy's detection software picked up the ModPol transport. It was near enough that they could close the gap quickly, and far enough from the ModPol outpost to give them the time to do it. Once they'd gotten in range, the Waster fighters launched and slowed the transport down. The Pollies had their own fighters, but it was clear they didn't have many, so the raiders had launched soon after.

For the past twenty minutes she and her team had sat

near the edges of the skirmish, waiting for the superior *Longhorn* carrier to take out the handful of anti-spacecraft guns on the *Garathol*.

Dava flipped the handypad back to the checklist one last time, then hit the comm. "We're ready, Sandpiper. Bring us in."

"Aye, Capo."

Dava made her way to her own restraint and strapped in just before the throttling pull of max-speed thrust accompanied by the terrible screech of the engines.

* * *

Breach. Something else she couldn't see from their drop-capsule, but she could imagine it: the spider-like raider sinking dagger-legs into the hull of the *Garathol*, the cutters coming down to slice a clean hole, the tube crashing through, the temporary seal expanding around it.

And then the drop. She closed her eyes and the universe jolted as the transport's artificial gravity pulled the capsule down the chute like sucking a bean through a straw.

"Breach complete, seal is good," Sandpiper said into her ear. "You're clear to pop the hatch."

She unstrapped and looked momentarily over her squad. Each man and woman looked back at her with hard eyes.

"Release," she said.

In near synchronicity they popped their straps and thirty-two boots hit the floor. She hit the door release and it flipped down, creating a ramp into the room. Whether it had been occupied before was unclear, but it wasn't at that moment. She waved the squad in and they double-timed past her two by two.

It was some kind of mess hall, large enough to accommodate the drop-capsule, but not much larger. There were tables and chairs piled to either side, blow into disarray by the breach. There was only one exit.

"Barndoor, you and that scattergun are on point."

"Aye, Dava." The big man stepped to the door and leveled his barrel at it. His ink-black hair was tied in a loose tail for once. He nodded, and she hit the release.

The door slid away to reveal a large, empty corridor littered with the flashing warning of a red alert. She led them through and headed aft, toward the cargo holds.

They made the length of it without encounter. Jansen had insisted there would be a skeleton crew. It must have been an all-hands situation for them, all of them on the bridge or at other battlestations. The dead feeling the empty halls gave her was unsettling.

The corridor T'd into a perpendicular hallway. She had them check corners, and still nothing. There was a sign that indicated holds in both directions.

"Thompson-Gun, front and center," she hissed in her loudest whisper.

Thompson stepped through the crowd. "Here, Dava."

"Take half the squad," she said, then looking over them, pointed at the lanky B-fourean in the back. "Including Psycho Jack. You go starboard, I'll go port. Keep the comms open for now."

"Aye, Dava," she said. She marked Jack and six others and motioned them down the hall.

"And Tommy," Dava said, grabbing her arm before she left. "Try to keep Jack alive."

Thompson nodded and turned to Jack who was hesitantly following. "Come on, Psycho. Try to keep up."

Jack shifted the strap of his shotgun over one shoulder uncomfortably. The jacket he wore wasn't long enough and looked heavy, pulling his body forward in a slouch. "Right," he said, shaking his head and plodding after Thompson.

Dava felt a small pang of guilt, and it confused her momentarily. She knew Jack didn't belong in their outfit, but he didn't really belong anywhere, she could tell that. So why not use him? Why should she feel guilty?

She pushed the thoughts out of her head and refocused on the mission. Waved to Barndoor to head for the opposite corner. Followed closely behind.

* * *

The gangbangers jogged around the corner and Jax had to hurry to catch up. Half of his brain urged him to lag behind. What point did any of this have for him? If he was trying to just stay alive, participating in a raid on a ModPol transport was not the way to do it.

The other half of his brain reminded him that to be in ModPol custody was not going to do him any good either, and so he definitely didn't want to get left behind. He'd been desperately trying to think of a way out of the whole thing since they came out of Xarp, but he found it impossible to focus.

"Jack!" The one they called Thompson-Gun hissed at him and waved him over to a door the rest of the Wasters were crowded around. "You got those codes they gave us?" she asked as he approached.

"Yeah, right, of course." He looked at the panel and then at the expectant gangbangers. "This might take a minute, so um…cover me?"

Thompson nodded vigorously, then gestured to the rest. "Fan out and watch the corners."

He stared at the panel. It was another numeric pad, not too different than the one he'd managed to open back at the Space Waste base. There was a glaring lack of edges to the thing though, and his trick of popping it open didn't have any hope. They'd given him a list of codes to memorize – supposedly they were override codes – but he didn't much trust them. It was the one they called RJ that gave them to him. He seemed to be in charge, but knowing that Basil Roy had faked the detection software put Jax in a cautious mindset. Roy and RJ were close to each other and distant from the rest of the gang, almost as distant as Jax was.

But why would they want to fake a software interface? It made no sense to Jax, no matter how much he mulled it over. There on the bridge of the colossal command ship, he'd convinced himself the raid was effectively defunct. He was sure it wouldn't go forward because they'd fail to detect the transport on time. If that had happened, he'd know that for whatever reason, RJ and Roy faked the software to save the transport.

Then without warning, the all-hands alarm was raised. He'd been sitting in the mess hall at the time, trying to gather his thoughts and stay out of trouble. His hopes that the raid would be called off were dashed. They'd found the transport and were moving in on it. Which meant, what exactly? That the pre-recorded interface on the detector somehow revealed the target?

Not that he'd had much time to think about it. Before he knew it, he'd been shoved into an ill-fitting outfit heavy with leather and woven metal, awkwardly armed with a gun he was told was only for close encounters, and hustled onto a small ship that reminded him very much of the one he and Runstom stole when they fled the prison barge all those months ago.

He stared at the panel, willed it to give up some secret that would allow him to live through this goddamn raid. With a sigh, he gave one of the so-called override codes a try. The panel buzzed at him at an alarming volume and he flinched. He glanced over his shoulder to see the others looking back at him.

"Well, one down," he muttered to himself.

He tried another, received another buzz. From behind, he could hear hushed conversation and his paranoia wondered if they were discussing his disposability. Then his paranoia saw a wink of movement just above his eyeline. He squinted. Was that a tiny lens inside the bubble at the top of the panel?

It moved again, no more than a millimeter.

"Copy that," he heard Thompson saying.

He found himself unable to move. Someone was looking at him through a camera. He needed to call out, to warn them, but he couldn't get his brain to act.

The action returned to his frozen limbs when the door suddenly slid open. His flailing arms couldn't decide if they should grab for support or reach for the shotgun slung across his shoulder. His legs knew they wanted to move away from the door, but couldn't agree given one hundred and eighty degrees to choose from. Before he could completely stumble to the ground, he was yanked into the dark space beyond the door.

"Wait," Thompson called. "Jack, wait! What – eenn-naaahhh!"

With a flash of blue sparks coming from the end of a long black stick, she spasmed and collapsed, the sound of her strained howl clipped off behind the closing of the door.

* * *

Dava's team came to a significantly spacious corridor, one clearly meant for moving bulky cargo back and forth. There was a splotchy trail of dark-brown dust that ran almost all the way down it in an odd, meandering pattern. She bent down to get a closer look, then felt it with her fingers. "Dirt," she said quietly to anyone who might be listening. Must have been that some part of the cargo was plantlife. Food. Was probably loaded in zero-G and then sank to the floor when the artificial gravity was turned on, based on the odd way it lay.

At her best guess, all the soil-based cargo had gone to the inner holds along the left side of the massive corridor. She decided they should start the search for the weapons along the opposite side. She moved her team down to the first door, leaving two at the corner they'd come around to keep a lookout. Ahead, there was another corner further down that also turned inward toward the center of the ship. A small passageway, probably for moving between the larger halls, though only for moving people, not cargo. She put another Waster at that corner to watch the passage.

Jansen had given them a handful of override codes that he said may or may not work, according to his inside source. One of these days Dava would like to meet this mole of his, but she got the sense that she never would. She motioned for Barndoor to cover the door while she attempted some of the codes on the panel.

"This is useless," she muttered after the third attempt failed. Worse, she was uncomfortable with the unnecessary buzz the panel made on every rejection, which seemed to get louder each time.

She hit her comm. "Thompson, come in."

"Copy," the reply came back quickly.

"Any luck getting anything open?"

"Negative. Jack is trying to override one now."

"We're going to need him over here when you're done."

"Copy that." There was a pause, then just before Dava closed out, she heard Thompson's voice again. "Wait. Jack, wait! What—"

"Thompson?" Dava whispered. Nothing. "Dammit."

"I can probably blow it open," Barndoor said.

She looked up at him. It wasn't the stealthy method she was hoping for, but there was a finite amount of time before the transport became unstable due to the shelling and the breaches. Maybe it was time to choose expedience over patience. Her eyes fell to his scattergun. "Not with that thing."

He looked at his gun, then slung it over his shoulder. "No, of course not. I brought charges."

"I don't remember putting charges on the manifest." She wasn't against explosives, but preferred not to use them unless they were really necessary. Inside a spaceship, they seemed as unnecessary as it got.

Barndoor looked down uncomfortably. "I think Moses put them on there."

"Of course he did," she muttered. Moses and his boarding squad had breached on the starboard side, opposite the side Dava's team breached on. Right about then he was probably knocking on the door of the bridge, threatening to blow it down like the Big Bad Wolf. She nodded to Barndoor and then gestured for two of the Wasters to join the two at the corner of the main corridor. She took the last over to the corner at the smaller passageway. From there they watched Barndoor retrieve a charge from his satchel and carefully affix it to the door.

He jumped back and she flinched at his movement. The door began to slide upward, scraping the charge off like a barnacle as it did. He scrambled for his gun.

"ModPol!"

* * *

"Help!" Runstom watched Jax flail helplessly, losing his balance as he twisted toward the closed door and landed on his ass. He spun his head back toward the force that had yanked him in. "Wait – uh – listen, I'm not really—"

"Jax," Runstom said, putting his hands up, palms out. "Jax! It's me. It's Stanford."

"St-Stanford? Runstom? What – what the hell are you doing here?"

"What the hell are you doing here?"

He reached down to help the lanky B-fourean to his feet. He couldn't believe he was looking the operator in the eyes again, after all this time, and on this ship of all places.

"Believe me, I wish I knew," Jax said, brushing himself off. "I was hiding out on Terroneous, keeping a low profile, like you said—"

As Jax straightened up, Runstom realized he was wearing a caramel-colored leather jacket and matching brown pants. He grabbed the arm of the jacket where the bent circle-of-arrows logo had been sewn on. "What is this? Is this a Space Waste logo?"

Jax pulled away and looked down at his feet for a moment. "Yeah, I guess so. They kidnapped me – or saved me." He looked up and shrugged. "Depending on how you look at it."

"How do you look at it?"

"Fuck if I know," he said and broke into a familiar smile.

It made Runstom want to smile along. He thought he might never see this man again, or worse, would see him only in prison or dead. But he was too unnerved. How bad in the shit was Jax this time? Did he even know? "Let me guess: when they got you away from ModPol, they gave you the option to join them or walk the airlock."

"Pretty much." The smile turned sour. "You knew I was getting picked up by ModPol?"

Runstom sighed through his nose. "I found out too late."

"Oh." Jax looked past Runstom, around the dim room, feigning interest in its contents.

"Jax, I was on my way there." He took a step toward the operator and put a hand on his shoulder. "McManus got there first."

He huffed. "That guy is an asshole." He swallowed and lowered his voice. "Did he survive? I don't mean to – I didn't see anything."

"The asshole is alive and kicking."

"Good," Jax said with a nod, then he looked back at the door. "Shit. You zapped Thompson-Gun."

Runstom found himself caught between a shrug and a cocky twirl of the stun-stick, then he just holstered the damn thing into a loop on his belt. "Yeah, sorry. I didn't know if your friend—"

"She's not my friend." The silence that followed extended for a few seconds before he spoke again. "Stanford, you don't understand – I was good. I was fucking happy. All I want is to get back there."

Runstom squinted at his face in the dim light of the hold. "Back to Barnard-4?"

Jax was visibly agitated, his hands uselessly working around each other in front of his stomach. "No. No, not B-4. Terroneous. I have to get back there."

"Why?"

He dropped his hands, his shoulders drooping. "I've got… people. Friends."

"Friends?" Runstom wished he hadn't said it. Was he that desperate for the other man's friendship? Had he stopped to think about how empty his life had been in the months since they parted ways? He looked away, embarrassed by his own pathetic void.

"God dammit, Stanford," Jax said with an anxious laugh that bordered on pain. "Her name is Lealina."

"Oh." He shook his head at his own selfishness. "Shit. Listen, Jax: I'm not letting ModPol take you in. I'm not even with the Justice division any more. And I'm not letting Space Waste – well, you know. I mean…did you really think they would let you go?"

"I thought if I helped them I might be able to go home again," he said with a dip of his head. "You know, buy myself out with my cut of the – the uh – the booty?"

"But you know they don't work like that."

"I know." Jax took a deep breath and sighed it back out. "Sometimes they seem normal. As normal as anything else outside of the domes, anyway. I thought they might understand." His limp hands scrunched into fists and relaxed again. "It was the only hope I had."

They jumped in unison at the muted rumbling from

somewhere outside the room. Runstom's ears pricked and he listened hard. The walls were thick, but he could hear a distinct popping, unidentifiable except for its unmistakable rhythm. Gunfire.

"Jax, it gets worse," Runstom said, putting a hand out to steady the other man. "There are ModPol Defenders on board. Multiple squads. I don't even know how many."

"What? It was supposed to be a skeleton—"

"It's not. It's a goddamn army."

He took a step back. "Is that why you're here?"

"No," Runstom said with a vigorous shake of his head. "I was just hitching a ride. To EE-3. Public relations work. It's what I do now."

"I know."

Runstom was about to explain himself, but the response caught him off guard. "You do?"

"I guess you could say I've kept tabs on you. In the news and stuff." He paused, then added, "You know, just to see what was going on with the case."

Runstom wanted to say more, but the insistent popping of gunfire brought him back to the situation at hand. "When I found one of the assault squads, they decided to put me into 'active duty'. Which apparently meant coming to this hold to guard the excess ordnance."

"To make you stay out of the way." Jax failed to hide his smirk. It vanished quickly. "It's going to be a slaughter."

"How well equipped are the Wasters?"

"Armed to the goddamn teeth," he said, indicating the short-barreled shotgun slung across his shoulder.

Despite the light artificial gravity, Runstom felt a weight he'd been fighting off ever since that hold door came open and he laid eyes on the full-armored Defenders. It was going to be a bloodbath on both sides. And they could do nothing to stop it.

He started to pace, and his feet felt like they were moving through mud. "Stupid bastards are going to kill each other to death."

"Shit, Stanford. We need to get out of here."

"Yeah." He stopped pacing. Something was happening outside of his control. Well outside. Was he going to die for two bloodthirsty armies who wanted to duke it out in the middle of nowhere for a shipful of – what – food? It made no sense. "You're right. We need to get out of here. First, you need a change of clothes."

"Wait, where are you going?" Jax said as Runstom stalked toward the door.

"I have a small ship. Non-military, and fast. If we get you a uniform, I can get you on it. We can stroll away from here."

"Okay." There was hesitation, then he repeated his consent more quickly. "Okay, let's do it."

Runstom put a hand on Jax's chest. "You gotta wait here. I'll be right back. Here, take a look at the panel by the door. On this side you can see through the camera. You can lock from here and only you can open it. They taught me how to do that so no one could come in and go for their ammo."

He looked uncertain. "You'll be right back?"

"Don't open that door for anyone but me."

* * *

Bodies swirled, muzzles flashed. The air filled with smoke and the tearing sound of automatic gunfire. She could smell it, the burn of propellant mixing with the plastic-melting odor of hot projectiles trying to bore their way through the material in bullet-resistant armor on one side, alloy-mesh-lined leather on the other side.

Dava broke for the wall opposite the corner, the one that had the door, as soon as the shooting started. Despite being unprepared, Barndoor had fired first, after scrambling to unsling his scattergun from his shoulder. It was hard to say how many he'd hit with the series of short blasts, but the screams suggested more than a few. He'd backed his way up the corridor when the return fire started.

She flattened herself to the wall. Pollies – no, Fenders, by their armor and firepower – were bunched into the doorway, but the momentary confusion was melting and their training was kicking in. They were coming through the door in alternating pairs, covering and exiting, covering and exiting. How many there were in that cargo hold, she couldn't tell, but it was quickly becoming obvious her small raid team was outnumbered.

One of the Fenders came around in front of her, focused on the Wasters who were unloading clips at the door and slowly backing down the hall from where they came. There was no time for any thought but fight and flight. She plunged her blade into the distracted Defender's back and he instantly went rigid.

She'd been skeptical of the lizard-stomach-paralytic, but this was a good test. The knife was slower than a bullet, enough so that the high-impact-resistant armor split like bread, delivering the poison directly to the bloodstream. A few quick heartbeats and the nervous system rolled over, locking up the Fender faster than he could turn around. As he tumbled against the wall, she yanked a flashbang away from his belt and tossed it at the door.

They were all wearing helmets with visors, so she knew it wouldn't buy much time, but it did afford another second of confusion. Down the corridor, the Wasters were moving as fast as they could. There was a trail of at least four strewn between her and the rest. Closest to her, long black hair spread like spilled ink, a growing pool of dark maroon ballooning to one side. She knew there was no time, but she rolled him over anyway. Barndoor's sightless eyes turned up to stare through her.

"Shit." He was a terrible shot but she'd grown to like the long-haired grunt.

In his hands was a small rod with a button on the top.

She glanced back at the door. Several Defenders were shaking their heads and getting to their feet, using their hands to collectively steady one another and guide themselves through the door.

Among their boots, the charge lay like a gray lump, a red light on top blinking its own business.

She snatched up the detonator and ran for the nearby passageway. She didn't look back, but when she heard the first high-pitched shot from a military-issue semi-automatic pulse rifle, she pushed the button and dove for the corner.

The light gravity kept her in the air too long and the force of the explosion kicked her into the wall just inside the passage. She never wore a helmet, and she took the blow to the head hard. Staggering to her feet, bracing herself against the wall, she dropped her head, then picked it up far enough to look back at the hold. The explosion had done some damage, she could see that with just a glance: at the very least, a handful of missing limbs. It would slow them down but she'd come to realize that there was a very large unit inside that hold.

She needed to move. She shook the haze from her head and looked down the narrow passage. It was dangerous to use it – if they got there before she got to the end, she'd be easy target practice – but she had no choice. She needed to regroup with Thompson, who should be just at the other end of the passageway.

"Move," she growled at herself and took a dizzy step forward. "Move!"

CHAPTER 24

The longer Jax sat alone in the hold, surrounded by nothing but what his only friend had described as ammunition crates, the louder the distant popping sounds got. Were they were really getting louder or was he just becoming more in tune with them? His wandering mind wanted to turn them into a pattern, to decode their rhythmic tapping into a message. But for every second he spent chasing pleasant mathematical thoughts, he spent two more trying not to let loose his bladder.

He paced around the room, gripping the shotgun with both hands. Not that he could point it and fire at someone. If his life were threatened? He wasn't sure. And if he wasn't sure, he probably couldn't. But at least he was armed. It was a deterrent, wasn't it? If he thought too long about it, he feared he might conclude the opposite.

Then the noise was right outside the door. It was thick and nearly soundproof, but there was no denying the direction of the shooting had moved to the hallway just outside the hold. His heart climbed up his throat. He looked around the room for a hiding place. Stacks of boxes. Boxes of ammunition.

"Shit," he whispered.

They would come in – if ModPol was outside the door, surely they would come in. This was their ammo supply. Would the door hold? Runstom said not to open it for anyone but himself. Maybe he'd rigged it to only open from the inside. If that were possible.

Jax sprinted to the door mechanism. There was a tiny screen with a video, and he remembered the camera. He found the controls and panned it around. It was hard to follow the action on such a small screen. Bodies swirling, bright-white spots appearing as gunfire erupted. Who was out there? He hoped Runstom wasn't, even though he knew his friend could handle himself in a fight. But the fact remained: Runstom was his only way out of this mess, slim as their chances were. If something happened to him, there would be no chance.

Then a figure stepped back toward the camera. The lithe body and its reflexive, agile stance were unmistakable. He panned up and saw the back of Dava's head, her long braids of dark hair tied together in a tail. She stepped down and to the side, striking out with one hand, and Jax knew she was using a blade. She had insisted everyone bring one, even though no one would use one but her. The blue-coated figure in front of her stiffened unnaturally and keeled backward.

The ModPol uniforms showed brightly on the tiny screen. There was no reinforced leather out there. Only Dava and at least six opponents.

He felt time stop. It refused to budge, giving him an eternity to make a decision. He would have to let her die out there. He would have to consciously decide to let her die. He might as well pull the trigger himself.

"Fuck," he said aloud. None of this was his choice.

He stalked back to the crates. They were metal and secured with some kind of electronic locks, but there wasn't anything he could see in the way of authentication. Just a giant red button, the size of a fist.

So he punched one.

And it opened with the hiss of hydraulic hinges. It dawned on him: the room was secured, but the crates were meant to be opened fast. No one wants to tap in a lengthy secret code when they're under enemy fire.

Whatever he was looking at wasn't going to help him. Dozens of rectangular metal boxes, full of bullets. Magazines, he thought, remembering the short introduction to firearms that Barndoor had insisted on giving him a few days ago.

But the crates were all different sizes. He realized they must have contained different things. He sprinted around the room hitting red button after red button. And then he saw something useful: smokebombs.

Barndoor had given him a rundown of handheld explosives, which made Jax even less comfortable than the guns. The gist of operation was simple enough: pull the pin and throw. He thought back to that day on Sirius-5 when his introduction to Dava had been preceded by a room filling with smoke.

He grabbed one of the canisters and stopped thinking about how it might blow up in his hands and ran to the door. On the tiny screen he could see that four of the blue-uniforms were still upright, one of them having Dava's arm pinned while the others tried to aim their guns at her. She was twisting desperately to spoil their shot.

Jax hit the release and the door slid upward. He pulled the pin and rolled the canister into the hall. On reflex alone, he found the trigger of his shotgun and fired into the ceiling as the thick black smoke began pouring out in a rush like water spilling upward.

"Dava!"

As he squinted into the encroaching darkness, a ball of a figure rolled into the room, a trail of smoke billowing around it.

"Door!" she yelled as she extended her arms and aimed a pistol at the hallway.

He hit the mechanism and the door slid back down with a sigh, as though unconcerned about the chaos happening around it.

She remained in a crouch, eyes and gun aimed at the closed door, panting, for several seconds. Then she stood. "We're fucked," she said without looking at him.

"I gathered that."

"How did you get in here? Hacked the door?"

"Uh. Yes."

"You alone?"

"Yeah, unfortunately. I don't know what happened to Thompson and the others."

Dava lowered her gun and looked around the hold. "They were routed. Headed fore. Those that are still alive, anyway." Her face bunched up. "I saw Tommy on the ground out there."

"Shit," Jax breathed. Should he tell her that Thompson was only stunned? "Dava, I'm sorry—"

"When that smoke clears, they're going to get that door open." She started making her way along the edge of the long room.

He followed her cautiously. "What are you doing?"

She reached a corner and looked up. "There."

He followed her eyes to an inconspicuous grate. "You're going up there? We have no idea where it goes!"

"I know where it goes." She went to a nearby crate. "Help me move this over."

He did as she asked and with a grunt, they slid the crate a few meters to the wall. "Do you always make it your business to know where air ducts go?"

She stepped up onto the crate with her normal catlike grace, then winced and grabbed her leg at the top. "I make it my business to know where hiding places are."

He could see the blood welling through her fingers, and remembered that they'd given him a pack of all kinds of gear, most of which he didn't know what to do with. He unhooked the pack from his waist and opened it up on top of the crate. "Here," he said, finding a flat white package with a red cross on it. "This is a bandage, I think."

She sighed through closed teeth, and he felt pain on her behalf. She wiped blood from her blade and cut away her pant leg. She pulled the packet open and slapped the bandage on. It smelled terrible, like a combination of chlorine and sulfur, and it hissed against her leg.

"Get up here and hold it while the adhesive sets."

He pulled himself onto the top of the crate. As he moved to hold the bandage in place, she stood and reached for the grate with her blade. While he held her leg uncomfortably, she stretched up and unscrewed the four corners.

"That's good," she said, pulling his hand away and handing him the grate. "Come on." With a short hop, she pulled herself up into the vent.

Jax looked back at the door. Any second it could open and some very pissed-off ModPols would come streaming through it. These guys weren't cops either; Runstom had called them Defenders. They were soldiers. They wouldn't stop to read him his rights. They might accept surrender, but then again, they might not.

He sighed and looked up at the open duct. He was tall enough to reach it just by stretching his arms up. With a kick, he pulled himself up.

And got half his body through.

He struggled to find purchase with his boots against the wall but he couldn't get the leverage on his lengthy body that he needed to get all the way into the vent. Then he was yanked forward and looked up to see Dava there. She pulled him all the way in and then backed up a few meters to a place where she could turn around, at a circular hub where four ducts came together.

There they were able to sit up, almost, and stared at each other for a few panting moments.

"What now?" he asked.

"I need to find Moses."

"Oh." Moses Down. Jax hadn't spoken to the man since his first day in the mess hall. But he knew the leader of Space Waste was supposed to have been leading the breach-and-board mission. He would have come in on the other raider. "Where do you think he is?"

"His team was supposed to secure the bridge." She glanced around and he could picture the maps in her head.

"So you want to go to the bridge. That seems like a bad idea."

"I can't leave him."

The words made Jax think of Runstom. This was his chance to reunite with someone he knew he could trust more than anyone in the universe. He couldn't run off with Dava and go rescuing Space Waste bosses. He needed to stay and wait for Runstom to get back. He needed to know that Runstom *would* come back for him. That his friend wouldn't leave him behind.

"I've got someone on the inside," he said bluntly. "I have a ticket out of this mess and I'm going to take it."

She scowled fiercely and he stiffened, reading an attack on her face. Then she pulled it down into a frown and looked away. "Okay, Psycho Jack."

"You should call me Jax," he dared, now that the impending attack had vanished.

She looked at him, her eyes softer. "Jax. It wasn't right of me to bring you into this. I had selfish motives." She gestured at the room below. "You could have let me die out there."

Jax felt his face grow warm and he looked down. "Well, I mean, I owed you." He cracked a smile. "You know, for all the times you didn't kill me."

He looked up to see her return the smile. "Well, we're all gonna die now anyway. So get the fuck outta here."

With that she spun for one of the ducts and disappeared with no more than a swish. He blinked. She let him go, just like that, and he knew she was unaccustomed to letting things go. He felt like he should have said more to her. It was over.

After a week, he was no longer a gangbanger.

He turned back the way he came and slowly inched his way to the opening. He could hear the Defenders below, barking orders at each other. Then the barking faded. He dared to poke his head into the room. Empty. They'd searched and moved on.

Lying in the air vent, he deflated with a sigh of relief.

* * *

The network of vents gave Dava access throughout the ship, as long as she could remember which direction she was facing. She had the schematics on her pocket-sized handypad and she pulled them up in the small window, adjusting the brightness as low as possible. It was a bit of a maze, but it probably made sense to the engineers that designed it. She had to backtrack occasionally because there would be an unexpected fan that she couldn't bypass or residue that leaked from pipes and formed a sticky kind of mud. On her first attempt to crawl through the stuff she stuck to it like a rodent in a glue trap and had to leave behind a glove. She didn't know how much more she could stay in those ducts; their primary function was circulating oxygen throughout the ship, but they also provided heat, and she was sweating enough to feel a dryness in her mouth and throat. She swallowed away the tickle. Any kind of coughing, she could do without.

Finally she reached the section of the ship close to where the other raider would have breached. She was in a shaft that ran parallel to a main corridor, one that was identical to the first corridor her own team had entered after boarding, but running along the starboard instead of the port side. Every several meters there was a grate where the air flowed into the hall and she stopped at each, careful to get a good look through before passing.

She was at the fourth one along the main corridor when she heard the noise. Shouting, running, a few sparse shots

– the popping of pistol fire, which she guessed to mean Wasters who lost their long guns or ran short of ammo – and then the zapping shots of stunners. She flattened herself and crept close to the grate to try to get a look.

And almost choked when the floor of the hallway was blotted from her vision by the heavy slap of a head against metal. She held her breath and blinked slowly, willing herself into control. The face she saw was distorted, the surface shaped into little diamonds formed by the lattice of the grate. It was Jerrard, his helmet bouncing away and revealing his cornrowed hair, the gold hoop in his right ear poking through the grate like some kind of prize or lure. His black skin turning red in splotches. He was one of the few like her, one of the few "doomed to domed". His eyes glazed over in pain. He couldn't see her, but she could see the gray barrel of a gun pressed against the back of his head.

Then he shrank. Became not just a head, but a body. Flung against the far wall, his hands and feet shackled. She twisted her head, risking detection by getting so close to the grate, but desperate to see who else was out there. There were four, maybe five others also bound, leaning against the far wall, a dozen or more ModPol Defenders with weapons trained on them. Others marching down the hall. The zapping of stunguns drifting with them.

With the noise and the activity, she felt invisible and she hurried further down the shaft to the next grate. The same scene played out as her comrades were chased down, stunned or otherwise incapacitated, and then bound.

She tried to count them but lost track. Who was left? She could recognize most of them but some of their bodies were twisted away from her. None were Moses.

One more grate at the end of the corridor. She could see

the bottom of the heavy doors to the bridge. The last stand. Three of them, ammo expended, blades out. Moses in the middle.

They'd been unable to get through to the bridge. She could see the shadows in the distance on the opposite side. They were trapped. Moses was trapped.

She gasped.

Bit it back as quickly as she could, but the sound had escaped. And no one turned, no one looked down.

Moses raised his blade. It was no mere dagger, more like a machete that he'd modified years ago. It gleamed like a mirror. His right hand, farthest from her, brought it up high.

And in the reflection of the metal she saw his eyes. She saw his eyes look right at her. Hang there for a long, hard second. He put his lips together. Pursed them. Opened them just enough to blow slowly.

All those years ago, when he took her in. She was just a kid, a dumb kid looking for trouble. And he was more than happy to oblige: he had enough trouble to share with all. But he gave her rules. Nothing so hard and fast, not like the stick-up-the-ass schools in the domes. But there were lessons – and the lessons *were* always hard and fast.

Before the strike, he would tell her, whether it was to pull a trigger or to slice with a blade, before the strike, a small breath is necessary. Just blow, he would say. No huffing and puffing, just blow a kiss. Hold. Strike.

He brought the blade down, and she could no longer see his eyes. *Blow, hold, strike*. But there was more to it than that. The hard lesson learned was that the blow and the hold were necessary, but in that moment that followed, to strike was a decision. In that moment you knew if the strike was going to find its mark, and if it was not, then you did not take it.

As his blade came down, she saw its surface no longer as polished and bright, but instead muddied with drying and darkening blood. With a clatter, it fell to the floor. The other two Wasters glanced at him, then dropped their own blades. Moses folded his hands before him and put his shoulders back, straightening to his full height, towering over the cautiously advancing Defenders.

"You bested us," he boomed with the twinkle of amusement in his voice. "You beat us this time. Congratulations."

"On your knees!" one of the Fenders ordered, leveling his barrel.

"But be warned," Moses continued. His voice strong and rhythmic, and she had a childhood memory of her father, one that went all the way back to Earth. Her father who'd been a leader, both a spiritual leader and a community leader. She was too young to know how much power his words had in just keeping people living one day to the next.

"Be warned," Moses repeated. "Our forces will *re*group. They will *re*turn at another time. And when they do, we will have *re*venge."

They stunned him for an eternity before he kneeled.

* * *

For a time she'd lain prone in the hot, dry duct. Tamped down the emotions threatening to bubble up. Self-admonishment. Anger. Fear.

No. She would not abide fear.

She listened to his last words in her head. Regroup. She couldn't help him now, not while they were on their heels. If she was going to help him, she had to get off the *Garathol*, she had to get back to the *Longhorn*.

Breaking radio silence was a bad idea, but she needed to know the situation. Any messages she sent would be sufficiently encoded, but just transmitting a signal would give away her position. She decided to risk it.

DAVA: On the Garathol. Ambushed. Forces scattered. Moses captured. Sitrep?
COMMAND: Dava, Capt. T. responding. Incoming MP fighters have us outnumbered. RJ ordering Xarp-out.
DAVA: Running?
COMMAND: Tactical retreat.

She bit down on the curse that wanted to jump out of her throat. That sonovabitch Jansen. He was going to abandon them to save his own ass. Her pad buzzed again.

COMMAND: Dava – if you can get out, do it.

She took a breath. There was time to think, but how much, she couldn't say. There were the raiders; she could make her way to one of the breach points. They would be guarded, but maybe not heavily. If there were only a few, she had a chance at taking them out. The real problem would be once she detached. She'd have to fly it, which she was barely capable of. Flight systems were largely automated so she could get a ship from A to B, but to get it safely through an armada of ModPol fighters…even if she managed not to get blown away, she'd have to reach the *Longhorn* before it Xarped away. If she didn't make it, she'd be hunted down. The raiders had no more than subwarp capabilities and ModPol would have no problem tracking her.

She could hide, that was always an option. The massive *Garathol* was full of dark corners and air ducts. How long could she stay undetected? And where would it go? Straight to the ModPol outpost in Epsilon, of course. Still fucked.

For lack of a solid decision, she'd started to move through the shaft again, heading in the vague direction of the breach where Moses's team had come in. It was at least worth taking a look at what kind of guard was posted.

She froze when she got farther down the hall and heard the tramp of boots. From her floor-level vantage, she watched through a vent as the bottom halves of purple uniforms approached Wasters that had been bound and facing the opposite walls. She watched as the Fenders turned them around and marched them aft. They must have had a brig of some kind near the cargo holds at the back end of the ship. She held her breath as she watched them go.

One Waster remained against the wall. He slowly turned his head to glance over his shoulder. Then turned his body, his hands behind his back. Looked left and right and cocked his head.

She angled her head as best she could to see up and down the hall from behind the grate in the shaft. She couldn't see any Defenders and it had grown quiet.

"Sonovabitch," she whispered.

Lucky Jerk came away from the wall completely and leaned out to look down the corridor in the direction the rest had marched. He seemed to consider calling out.

"Lucky!" she hissed. "Lucky, down here!"

He flinched and glanced around, trying to find her voice. Finally he crouched down and peered at the grate.

"Hello?"

"Lucky, it's Dava."

He duck-walked closer. "Dava, what are you doing?"

"Lucky, you got a multitool on you? The screws are on the outside of this grate."

He blinked, then padded around his belt pouch. A moment later he was popping the grill away from the duct.

"Shit, Dava, you look like you've been through a gang-bang at a chainsaw factory."

She came out of the duct and stared at the empty corridor for three full breaths. "Lucky Jerk," she said quietly. "I think they forgot you."

"Where's the rest of your guys?"

She looked at him. "As fucked as your team. We should get to your raider."

"So we're all alone?"

"Yeah, we are. And we need to get out to the *Longhorn* before they leave without us, so let's move."

They hustled down the corridor. The chamber that Moses's team had boarded into was just a few dozen meters away. When they approached the door – which had been blasted off its mounts – she held Lucky back against the wall so she could peer in.

She pulled her head back and held up four fingers. She looked Lucky up and down. They'd taken all his weapons. She lost her rifle in her brawl with the Defenders and only had a pistol and her blade, which was out of poison cartridges. Lucky was lucky, but other than that he wasn't much use in a fight. Even if he could occupy one of them she'd have to take the other three on at once.

Unless she could break up the party.

* * *

Runstom's heart dropped into his stomach when he saw the cargo hold door open. It had taken him longer than he'd hoped to go find a disguise for Jax and now he was too late.

He'd gone fore to the midship crossway without encountering any trouble. From there, he could hear gunfire coming from the starboard-side main corridor. Instinctively, he'd wanted to get involved, to rush in and help out the ModPol Defenders. But he had nothing but a stun-stick. He was never issued a weapon or even armor, and he was just as likely to get clipped by friendly fire as he was by a Waster in all the chaos. So he'd repeated the mantra in his head: *Not my fight. Not my fight.*

Instead he'd gone up the port-side main corridor, the one that branched off to the living quarters. Along the way he'd passed the mess hall. The door was open and some Defenders had been looking after a boarding tube that had crashed down through the ceiling. He'd waved and moved on as quickly as possible.

He'd gone to the laundry after that in order to raid uniforms. The problem with Jax was that he was too damn tall, so Runstom had pawed through the small number of maintenance jumpsuits until he found the longest he could. It would have to do.

Then he'd made his way back, and the second time he'd passed the mess hall, one of the Defenders had stepped out to stop and question him. Runstom had all kinds of credentials in his WrappiMate and the antsy guard had felt a need to triple check everything. Oddly enough, he hadn't even asked about the jumpsuit. In the distance the occasional pratter of gunfire could be heard and Runstom could tell the guards were itching to be in the fight instead of stuck waiting to see if any Wasters would retreat to their ships.

Eventually they'd let him pass and he would have run back to the cargo holds if he didn't think it would attract unnecessary attention. He'd done a swift, quiet walk.

And the damn door was open.

He jogged to it, stepping gingerly around the broken bodies of fallen Wasters. The fight had come to the holds, and that meant someone opened the door: either gangbangers or Defenders. He wasn't sure what was worse when it came to Jax. Either one might want his skin.

He poked his head through the open door. "Jax," he whispered. He listened and heard nothing. If anyone had opened the door, it was probably Defenders looking for ammo. Maybe they knew a way to override the internal lock. "Hello?" he said out loud. "This is Stanford Runstom. I'm not armed."

He heard the pang of bending metal and a hushed curse from the back of the hold. "Stanford?"

He ran to the back to see Jax's head sticking out of an air vent. "Jax, what the hell?"

"Oh, uh." Jax squirmed forward and got half his body out of the opening but had nowhere to go except a two-meter drop to a crate below. "Can you help me down?"

Runstom climbed atop the crate and took Jax's arms and helped him in what ended up being more or less a controlled fall.

Jax picked himself up and stepped down from the crate, dusting off his leather. "I kind of got into a mess. But the good news is, I think I've officially resigned from Space Waste."

Runstom looked him up and down, instinctively looking for signs of injury. "Right, good. Put this on," he said, tossing the jumpsuit.

Jax frowned as he stripped off his jacket. "I'm going to miss this badboy."

"Really?"

Jax sighed. "No, fuck it. Turn around so I can take my pants off."

* * *

The jumpsuit was just a little too short but as long as Jax kept his arms folded, it wasn't too noticeable. Runstom led him to the aft of the ship where there was an elevator that went down to the hangar decks. They didn't encounter another soul along the way. Runstom thought he could still hear the occasional gunshot to the fore of the ship, but he knew it was too far away to be a possible threat.

Once at the hangar level, he took Jax to the port side where his OrbitBurner was parked. Two Defenders guarded the deck entrance.

"Yes?" one of them said as though Runstom and Jax were interrupting a very important standing-around session.

"Stanford Runstom, Public Relations." He showed his credentials and they barely glanced at them. "I'm going to check on my ship."

Jax looked down at the patch on his chest. "Rodriguez," he said. "Just a tech. Going to check out his ride. You know, make sure it wasn't damaged during the fight."

"Whatever," the guard said and waved them through.

The other stopped them. "Hey, you got that OrbitBurner in there, right? 4200?"

"Yes," Runstom said. "4200 LX."

He whistled. "Got the LX even, damn. Wish I could take a ride with you in that."

"What the hell are you talking about?" the first guard said. "It doesn't even have guns on it."

"Fuck you man, it's got a *rec room*. Hey," he said to Jax. "What kind of burn rate does the ion engine get on that baby?"

"Oh, uh," Jax said, glancing at Runstom who could offer him no help. "Dude. It'll make you weep."

The guard laughed. "Yeah, yeah I bet it would."

In an instant he seemed to lose interest in the conversation and after an awkward moment of silence and staring, Runstom and Jax moved on.

Minutes later they were on the small bridge of the OrbitBurner. Runstom sealed the doors and made sure the comms were all silent. He flipped on the contact map. Almost nothing but friendlies. And a lot of them. There'd only been a handful of fighters in the hangars on the *Garathol*. The rest must have come from somewhere else.

"Okay, listen, Jax."

Jax plopped into an acceleration couch. "Holy crap, what a week it's been. Are we really going to get out of here in one piece?"

"Yeah, we are." Runstom came over and stood in front of him. "But we need to talk."

"Uh, sure." The B-fourean waved his hand as if presenting a topic of discussion. "Public relations. What's that like?"

"It's…interesting."

"Back on Terroneous, I'm kind of known as the fix-it guy," Jax said wistfully. "Can't wait to get back there."

Runstom frowned and looked away. "Look, Jax. I'll get you back there, I promise. But…"

"But what?"

Runstom could feel pressure building inside his head,

countered by an emptiness in the pit of his gut. He needed Jax, and yet he wanted to protect him. And Jax was just an operator, none of this had anything to do with him. But who else could he turn to?

"I need your help, okay?" Runstom felt his face crunch together as he glared through his guilt. "Something is up. Something that doesn't fit. And...well..."

"What makes you think I can help?"

He sighed. "You're the only one I can trust."

"Well, same to you. I mean back on Terroneous—"

"Jax, you're the only one I can trust in the whole goddamn universe, okay?"

There was silence for a time and then Jax said, "What's going on, Stan?"

He waved a hand at the situation around them. "This. Space Waste attacks are increasing. ModPol Defense – it's growing. Justice used to be the ModPol mission. The Defense division was just there as a contingency. Now it's ballooning. I've never seen a force the size of the one they had on this transport, not since wartime."

"That sounds bad," Jax said. Runstom could see the tension building in his friend's face. "That sounds like I'm not going home."

"You will, I promise," Runstom said. "I just—"

The was an insistent beeping sound then, an incoming transmission request. Runstom looked at Jax and then walked to the front to turn on the comm.

"Runstom here."

"Lieutenant Commander Ploughy, on the bridge of the *MPP Garathol*. The captain would like to speak with you, Officer Runstom."

"Sure, go ahead."

"Runstom, this is Captain Yakimoto. We got word that you went down to check on your ship and I wanted to make sure everything is alright."

"Everything checks out so far," Runstom said. "We're going to warm up the engines and run some diagnostics to be sure."

"Excellent, good to hear it. You'll have clearance to launch in a couple of hours. The spaceborne enemy force is already dispersing, and our Defenders onboard are rounding up all the hostiles left behind."

Jax motioned for Runstom to mute the comm. "Ask her what will happen to them."

Runstom frowned, unnerved by the fact that Jax still cared anything for bloodthirsty gangbangers. But he complied. "What happens after the roundup, if you don't mind my asking, Captain?"

There was a pause before the reply came back. "The captain apologizes." Lieutenant Commander Ploughy's voice once again came back. "She's got her hands full, as you might imagine. As for the enemy combatants onboard, well, they *should* be POWs. However, your friends back at Justice are insisting on coming out to pick them up and return them to Barnard for trial."

"Trial," Runstom said flatly.

"Absurd, I know," Ploughy said. "We do all the fighting and Justice wants to treat enemy soldiers as mere criminals. Well, I suppose we can afford to throw them a bone once in a while."

"Yeah, I guess."

"Officer Runstom. This day was a great victory for Modern Policing and Peacekeeping."

"Of course, Lieutenant Commander," Runstom said, showing Jax his disgust with a frown.

"In just a few hours you'll be on your way to Epsilon-3, correct? Visiting the civilian domes under construction there?"

"That's correct."

"Be sure to give the administrators on Epsilon-3 all the details of the Space Waste attack. As I understand it, it's your job to convince them they would benefit from peacekeeping services."

"Yes, that's the reason for my visit," he said. He hadn't given the assignment much thought, what with the bullets flying around. Now that Ploughy had mentioned it, it was a good point to bring up when he met with the E-threers.

"Be sure to let them know then, Public Relations Officer Runstom. Be sure to let them know that had the Space Waste attack on this transport been successful, surely Epsilon-3 would have been their next target. After all, why else would they have come to Epsilon Eridani?"

"Right," Runstom said. He stared at the comm. Since when did ship commanders give a rat's ass about public relations? "Of course, Lieutenant Commander."

"Bridge out."

The comm went silent. Runstom looked around at nothing, too many questions circling his head to pin one down.

"Is it just me," Jax said from his sunken position in the acceleration couch, "or was that weird?"

CHAPTER 25

Dava watched the Space Waste pilot as he walked nonchalantly up to the door that led to some kind of massive laundry room. "Uh, hello? Oh, hi there. I think uh, someone left me behind. Can someone escort me to the brig?"

Confused voices drifted from the room. After a moment, Lucky Jerk stepped back slightly, hands in the air. He edged his way around the corner of the doorway but kept in view of those within.

"I'm not armed. They already took my guns."

Dava watched the barrel of a rifle poke through the doorway. "Just stay right there," came the voice behind it.

"No need to point that thing at me," Lucky said, continuing to slowly back away.

The Fender was forced to come all the way through the door. It took him a second to notice Dava flattened against the wall and he flinched, pointing his gun at her. By now Lucky was far enough down the hall so that the other three wouldn't be able to see him from inside the laundry.

He raised Dava's pistol at the Fender. "Ah ah," he chided.

"I wouldn't point that at her if I were you."

The Fender's barrel swung in Lucky's direction. The fingers on Dava's left hand hooked into the opening in the purple helmet, pulling the guard toward her. Then the blade in her right hand slid silently into the exposed neck.

There was a gurgle, but that was all her victim managed as hot blood washed over her hand. She left the knife in and pulled the rifle away as he slumped to the floor.

"Chaz?" A call from inside the room. "Chazzo? What's happening?"

She put the butt of the rifle to her shoulder and raised the barrel. She hated the noise and the sloppiness of such a weapon, but it was no time for finesse. She knelt on one knee and braced a shoulder against the wall, then motioned to Lucky.

He nodded and blew out a deep breath, then sprinted past the door, firing the pistol wildly into the room as he went.

The response took a few heartbeats, but then with a shout, a Fender appeared in the doorway. She wasn't wearing a helmet and Dava could see the tight braids of her red hair as she lifted her rifle and took aim at the retreating Lucky. Dava blew out a breath, held, then fired a single shot into the back of that exposed head.

The next Fender was close behind the first and he jumped as his comrade pitched forward. Before he could spin around to face her, Dava flipped the rifle to automatic and sprayed him into a messy lump.

She waited for thirty seconds in silence. Once the last Fender's body completed its slow-motion topple in the half-gravity, she could see Lucky poking around the corner at the end of the corridor, waiting for her signal.

Another half a minute of silence while they remained frozen. Then she inched to the doorway. Keeping low, she peeked in. Then she stood and lowered her weapon.

Lucky jogged up to the opposite side of the door. "What happened? Did the last one surrender?"

She nodded into the room. The last Fender was slumped against the side of the boarding tube, a small hole between the eyes of his helmetless face.

"Oh," he said, lowering his pistol. "Lucky shot, I guess."

"Come on," she said. "Pick up one of those rifles and give me my pistol back."

The raider that Moses and his team had come in on appeared to be in one piece. Within a few minutes, they were inside the cockpit. Lucky was shaking his head at the console.

"What's wrong?"

"Xarp wake," he muttered.

"The *Longhorn*?"

"Nothin' but Xarp wake."

"Jansen," she said. She knew the sonovabitch would run as soon as he could. "We need to get out of here."

"In this?" Lucky looked at her. "No way, Dava, no fucking way. We lift off in this raider and they're going to eat us to pieces out there. Look at this contact map. It's all ModPol fighters. Like a swarm of insects."

She watched the red glyphs dance around the map. Wasn't it Space Waste that was the swarm only hours before? "What's this?" she said when a small yellow blob appeared very close to the center of the map.

"Oh, uh." He zoomed in. "Looks like maybe it's a small ship on the hangar deck of the *Garathol*. I would have guessed all the fighters would have launched."

"But it's yellow."

He cocked his head in thought. "Right, so a civvy ship, not a fighter." He tapped at the console and some data spilled onto a nearby terminal. "OrbitBurner, 4000-class based on the ion drive sig. Definitely a civvy."

"What's it doing on the *Garathol*?"

He shrugged. "Not capable of interstellar jump, so must have hitched a ride. Diplomat, civilian contractor, whatever. Not police and not military." He looked at her. "That's our ticket."

"Does it have any weapons?"

"Probably not, which is a good thing if you're trying not to attract attention."

She sat back and folded her arms. "But if it's on the contact map, the engine is running. The hangar decks are on the aft end of this big-ass ship, way down on the bottom. And we have to get to it without getting noticed."

Lucky flipped a switch and the contact map blinked. The red swarms dimmed and tiny green dots appeared in the space between the *Garathol* and the spot where the *Longhorn* left its Xarp wake. "Countermeasures," he said. "Captain 2-Bit don't run from a fight without leaving behind a mess. ModPol's gonna have to clean 'em up before that OrbitBurner can go anywhere. Probably just running diags on the ion drive right now."

She nodded and stood. "Okay. We have time. Let's go."

They both flinched as their armpads buzzed. "Emergency all-call," Lucky said.

Dava looked at her pad.

THOMPSON: anyone out there?

Lucky gasped and started to speak but Dava waved him silent.

DAVA: where are you?
THOMPSON: some hold. Lots of ammo here.
DAVA: sit tight. Radio silence. I'm coming.

* * *

It took several minutes for them to make their way back to the cargo holds. There were no more guards in the main corridor that led fore to the bridge, but heading aft toward the holds, there were guards posted in the crossway. She thought about taking them out but there were too many – at least six – and she didn't want to risk detection. So she and Lucky backtracked and opened a duct. From there it was slow progress to the back of the ship, but eventually she was at the four-way break where she had parted ways with Psycho Jack.

They crawled through the still-open grate and dropped down into the hold.

"Tommy," she whispered. "Tommy, are you in here?"

"Dava?" Thompson, not whispering, came around a stack of ammo crates. "Holy shit, am I glad to see you!"

"Hey Tommy," Lucky said quietly, giving her a short wave.

"Fuck, I think I'm even happy to see you," she said and staggered toward them.

"Keep it down," Dava whispered. She braced Thompson as she nearly fell. Though she was scolding the other woman, she was swallowing back tears. "I thought you were dead."

Thompson panted and lowered her voice slightly. "Got stunned. Bad. Still coming out of it."

"How did you get in here?"

She cracked a short, unamused laugh. "Woke up lying in a pile of my friends, gunstripped and tagged," she said, indicating a kind of spray-on plastic stamp on her pant leg. "Door to the hold sitting here wide open. Last thing I remember is some Pollie opens the door, grabs Jack, zaps me. And then I come to and they don't even bother closing the door."

"Is this the weapon cache?" Lucky asked, peering at the crates.

"I wish," Thompson said. "Nothing in here but standard issue shit. Cartridges, stunpacks, flashbangs, smokebombs. Not even anything really explosive. I figured if I was the last one left I'd at least blow a hole in something."

Dava sighed. Her leg was throbbing and she was too exhausted to think, but it all sat wrong. "So much for Jansen's intel," she muttered. "There probably are no weapons. 'Cept those with Fenders on the other end of 'em."

"Yeah, where the hell did all those fuckers come from?" Lucky said.

"We'll figure that out later," Dava said. "Lucky, give Tommy that pulse rifle. Even in her condition she can handle it better than you can."

"Hey, I nailed a guy between the eyes," he said as he handed it over to Thompson without resistance. Dava gave him her pistol in return.

"Thanks. Those bastards took my Tommy-Gun," Thompson said. Then her face flattened and she looked from Dava to Lucky and back. "Ah fuck. We're it, aren't we?"

"Pretty much," Lucky said.

She nodded with mild acceptance. "So what's the plan?"

"Get off this ship," Dava said. "Come on. We need to move."

* * *

An hour had passed and Runstom and Jax were still waiting for a green light to launch. Runstom had been checking the radio chatter from time to time and said that the Space Waste command ship had left a bunch of counter-somethings around. The way he described them, Jax thought they sounded like small magnetic bombs: if a ship got too close to one, it would attach and then detonate with an electro-magnetic pulse. It was apparently more of a nuisance than a threat, but there had already been one incident where an incapacitated fighter lost control and crashed into a larger destroyer.

The conversation was heavy on Runstom mumbling about ModPol and Jax had a hard time following him. Had the man gone completely paranoid in the months since they'd been apart? Or was there some actual conspiracy that he was stumbling upon? And more to the point, what was Jax's role? He just wanted to go back to Terroneous and live peacefully and quietly. Was that so much to ask?

He offered to get them both something to drink and excused himself. Runstom was too busy sifting through electronic correspondence to give him directions, so Jax wandered off. The ship wasn't that large, but apparently big enough to have some kind of recreational room, or so that guard had said.

It wasn't hard to find. Once he left the bridge, there were stairs down to the embarkation chamber, which he'd come in through, and a passage in the other direction that wound down a spiraling set of stairs into a room at least four times the size of the bridge. That was his guess anyway, but the lights were off so it was hard to tell.

The stairs deposited him in the center of the room and there was a glowing panel on the wall directly across from them. He carefully walked through the darkness and poked through the interface until he found the light switch.

As the lights flickered to life, he felt cold metal against the back of his neck.

He raised his hands. "Uh, Stanford?" There was no immediate reply, so he added, "I'm not armed, you know." He had to leave his shotgun and his pistol back in the cargo hold when he changed into the maintenance uniform, and was thankful he never had the opportunity to fire either one.

"Turn around."

He did. Dava, Thompson, and another Waster stared at him, their guns lowered. "Let me guess," Jax said. "You're stealing our ship."

"Your ship?" Thompson said.

"Technically, it's Stanford's," he said, as if that would mean something to them.

"Whatever," she said. She frowned and turned away to pace around the edges of the room.

"Don't mind her," the man said. "She's just upset because she lost her favorite gun. And a bunch of her friends died." He was small in stature and young. He tapped at his name patch, which read, *"Lucky" Jerk*. In ink, an additional set of quotation marks had been added around the word *Jerk*. "Call me Lucky. You're Psycho Jack, right?"

In his head, Jax imagined drawing a sarcastic set of

quotation marks around the word *Psycho*. "How'd you get past the guards?"

"Well, there were only *two* of them," Lucky said with a twist of his hand that told Jax he didn't want to know the rest of the story.

Jax sighed. "Look, guys. All I want to do is get back to Terroneous."

"Then you're in luck," Dava said. "Because we just want to get back home too. We just have some business to take care of first."

Jax felt something he hadn't felt in a long time. There was a slow burn that rose up his chest and into his throat. "You do your fucking business somewhere else. Get the hell off my ship."

He felt the breeze of air that the movement caused before his eyes registered the sight of it, and then her blade was at his throat.

"Great, you going to scare me, Dava?" he said. "Threaten my life *yet again*? Do you have any idea what I've been through? For the past year of my life I have lived in constant fear."

The blade came away and she stepped closer. "Some day you and I are going to sit down and have a talk about what it means to live in fear. And then you will know that you know nothing about it." She turned away from him as the burn in his chest went cold. "And then you will understand why it is that I do the things I do."

She walked away and joined Thompson, who'd found the minibar.

"We don't have to steal your ship," Lucky said, drawing Jax's attention away from Dava. "We can just stowaway. I figure you're not going to the ModPol outpost. Not in this thing."

"No," Jax said. "We're supposed to go to Epsilon-3."

Lucky cocked his head and his eyes went upward like he was trying to decipher that statement. "Epsilon-3. Why?"

"I guess there is a new colony under construction there."

"Really?"

Jax scrutinized his face. "You didn't know about it?"

Lucky shrugged. "No. Did you?"

"No," Jax admitted. He raised his voice. "Dava. Did you know there was a colony going up on Epsilon-3?"

She and Thompson turned from the bar with drinks in hand and glared at him. "No," she said.

"Who the fuck would want to live all the way out here?" Thompson said, then went about refilling her cup.

Jax turned it over in his head. The officer that Runstom had talked to on the radio was very clear that Space Waste was here to target the new colony. Why else would they be here? That was the question he posed. But it made no sense. Space Waste had specific intentions of attacking the *Garathol*, boarding it and raiding its holds. There was never any talk of going to any planet, and certainly no one had mentioned a new colony.

"If there's construction going on, then there'll be interstellar flights," Lucky said. "Moving materials and people in."

Jax shrugged. "I don't know, I guess." Then his hopes rose. "Right, of course. We can probably find a way back to Barnard from there."

He stepped past Lucky and approached the minibar. He didn't know much about mixing his own drink, but he took a cup and an amber bottle and poured until it looked like something a bartender would hand him. He took a sip and swallowed fiery fruity sweetness, then finished off the rest and poured another helping.

"Psycho Jack likes his brandy," Thompson said.

"This is a shitstorm," Jax said. "What was the target? The rumor was experimental weaponry."

"Yes," Dava said. "That's what we came for."

"Okay," Jax said with a swallow. "Space Waste shows up to steal weapons. Supposed to be unguarded, or close to it. Right?"

"Yes."

"Only there's no weapons." He got another refill. "There's soldiers. A shit-ton of them."

"An ambush." Dava's face registered first shock, then frustration. Like she hadn't learned something new, only accepted something she already knew.

"And ModPol frames it as," Jax said. He spread his hands as if to present a headline. "Space Waste attacks Epsilon-3. Thwarted by ModPol Defense."

He drank and let the burn dance on his tongue before trickling down his throat. The rest looked at him distantly. They didn't see all the pieces, and neither did he. But Runstom's conspiracy wasn't just paranoia, he was starting to believe that. And as much as he wanted to go home to Terroneous, he knew that wasn't happening any time soon.

He locked eyes with Dava. "When did you finally stop being afraid?"

She returned his stare. "When I got angry."

CHAPTER 26

Once Jax had started to come around to Runstom's conspiracy theory, the other man didn't want to discuss it. It made for a frustrating subwarp trip to Epsilon-3. Jax spent the whole time trying to drop clues: things he knew about Space Waste, but without letting on that there were three Waster stowaways hanging out below in the rec room. It became clear that Runstom had reached the edge of his ability to cope with large amounts of untied threads. He was tired, burned out, and Jax, though fired up, had consumed too much brandy to properly move the conversation productively.

Runstom's plan was to do his job. It annoyed Jax, but he knew that his cop-minded friend sometimes needed to go into duty-mode in order to work things out in his head. There was a comfort to it, a shelter. He decided he'd go along and give Runstom the time he needed to process.

The job involved getting to Epsilon-3 and meeting with some of the new colony's administrators. Jax was able to get Runstom to talk about his work, at least. He was there to convince the local government that they were in need of ModPol's services; and not just the policing, but the peacekeeping as well. Conveniently, the staff of the *Garathol* had supplied Runstom with a plethora of battle footage. The first step after landing was to make a stop in the small ModPol office where a marketing intern would chop apart the footage and piece together the most terrifying clips into a sixty-second run.

Before that, while Runstom managed the paperwork at the dock, Jax went down to the rec room to have one last meeting with Dava and her pals. They all agreed that discretion was in everyone's best interests, and that Jax would accompany Runstom into town while the Wasters would lay low in the ship and look for an opportune time to quietly slip away. Then they could find their way to an interstellar port or whatever. Jax didn't care so much, just as long as they got off Runstom's ship. His friend had enough to deal with, he didn't need to find out that he'd inadvertently aided three murderous criminals in their escape from ModPol.

Then there were tours. Several of them. Runstom told everyone that Jax was a technical consultant, and when anyone asked too many questions, Jax went into technobabble mode until someone shut him up. It worked out well. The new domes were state of the art, like nothing he'd ever seen, even in the photos of Barnard-3 that his stepmother used to send him in an effort to convince him to visit. He kept asking Runstom under his breath, why wasn't the new colony all over the news back in Barnard? Throughout the day, he began to piece it together: it was under wraps because it was so expensive. Upon completion, the target audience was the wealthiest of the wealthy, those that would not seek it out but arrive by invitation only.

The hardest parts for Jax were the times when he could see the surface. Seeing the suited workers out there leveling out the terrain, scanning for mineral and ice deposits, putting together air processors, or whatever, every time it reminded him of his mother. It brought him right back to when he was younger and she took him to work on occasion. Showed him what the surface looked like. It was the only time he'd seen it, his whole life on Barnard-4. She'd ask, how can anyone live on a planet and never look out at its surface? And then that same surface had taken her away.

Finally there was a break for lunch, and Jax and Runstom had some time to themselves over a couple of meat sandwiches. Or what Jax hoped was meat. It was hard to tell, but the sauce made it bearable.

"Let me know if you need anything," the waitress said as she topped off their drinks, which were a mildly sweet carbonated liquid of some kind. She tilted her head as she looked at Runstom. "Okay?"

"Thanks," he said, his attention on his sandwich.

She had the beige-pink skin that Jax's stepmother had, and long blond hair that was woven into braids. She smiled broadly for a moment, then her mouth scrunched slightly and she moved on.

"I think you have a fan," Jax said when she was out of earshot.

"Huh?" Runstom mumbled between bites.

"The girl." Jax angled his cup in her direction.

Runstom's eyes went to her for a moment as she took an order from a table at the other end of the cafe. "What do you mean?"

Jax laughed shortly. "I mean she digs you, Stan."

"Oh," he said, then shook his head. "I doubt it."

Jax watched him eat for a moment. He was handsome and rugged and probably had women checking him out all the time. He was too used to being an outcast to notice. Jax could only imagine how hard it was for the green-skinned boy growing up. But that wasn't the only thing that kept Runstom in the dark. He watched the man's brow bunch as he chewed pensively through his sandwich. Whenever that mind of his latched onto a problem that needed solving, there was no letting go, and no room for much else.

Jax decided to broach the subject he'd held in for too long. "Stanford."

"Yeah?"

"Why hasn't X gone on trial?"

Dead silence floated between them and Runstom put his half-eaten sandwich down. "I don't know."

"We had the evidence."

"We had it, yeah. There was something…I just don't know. Some lawyer bullshit sleight of hand. Tied it all up."

"But there was enough to convict Jenna Zarconi."

"Yes."

Jax swallowed. "But does that exonerate me? Or will they try to link me to her? A co-something?"

Runstom nodded slowly without looking at him. "Co-conspirator. Until they get X…" he said, trailing off.

"Right, I know," Jax said. He'd never be free as long as Mark Xavier Phonson was free. "I need to stay hidden."

Runstom looked down. "I've talked to her, you know."

"To Jenna Zarconi?" Jax put his sandwich down as well, his appetite sucked away with his breath.

"Yeah. I know that sounds wrong. But she was the only person who knows the real story. Besides you and me, I mean."

Jax opened his mouth to speak, then closed it. He wanted

to understand that. He spilled everything to Lealina just to have someone else to talk to about it. But Zarconi was a murderer. Zarconi destroyed his life. But he never really knew how hard it was for Runstom. Maybe talking to Zarconi really was his only source of therapy for the whole mess. "Did it help?"

Runstom wiped his hands on a napkin and plopped it atop the sandwich. "Yes. No. I don't know. I suppose it helped some."

"I just don't understand why they're still after me," Jax said. "I mean, they got Jenna Zarconi. Even without X, they have their murderer. And I'm a nobody. They have to know I'm innocent, right?"

"Of course," Runstom said unconvincingly.

"Why couldn't they just let me be? Why did they have to come to Terroneous?"

Runstom nodded slowly. "It doesn't sit right with me either," he said. "First off, ModPol has no jurisdiction on Terroneous. They'd have to get the local government involved to extradite you. But they didn't. McManus was given orders to make the pickup himself."

"So who gave the orders?"

"There's that too. He didn't know."

"How could he not know?"

Runstom shook his head. "Sometimes orders come like that. Encrypted, verifiable as authentic, but no source. Rare, but it happens."

They both sat silently, and by the look on his face, Jax could tell that Runstom didn't like the idea of his arrest being some kind of secret order any more than he did. He didn't know what else to make of it in the moment, so he broke the silence.

"I guess this job is going well, anyway."

Runstom smiled faintly. "Yeah, so far it's a knockout. The threat of Space Waste so close to these fancy new domes – well, shit. It's like I don't really have to try. ModPol sells itself."

"That's good because you're not a very good PR officer."

They both had a laugh that died quickly. Runstom looked troubled. "I know I'm not."

"Hey, Stanford, I didn't mean—"

"No, no. I'm not offended. I mean, I really am not the right person for this job."

Jax thought about this. "But they put you on it anyway."

He nodded. "Yet another thing that makes no sense."

Jax sighed. "Where's that notebook of yours? I hope you're keeping track of all the shit that makes no sense."

Like a quick-drawn pistol, Runstom had his trademark notepad in hand. "I got a new pencil in the gift shop at the dock," he said, waving the utensil. Then he opened the pad and wrote. "Stanford Runstom is bad at PR. Check."

Jax laughed again. He wasn't safe at home, but he wasn't running for his life, he'd just eaten half a semi-meat sandwich, and his closest friend was sitting across from him. He decided it was okay to let himself unwind just a little.

"I think we're due for another meeting soon," he said.

Runstom glanced at the WrappiMate on his forearm. "Damn. We're going to be late."

"Who is this one with?" Jax asked, then forced a smile as an older woman in the white-suit uniform that the administrators all wore appeared behind Runstom.

"Assistant Director of Agricultural Systems," she announced.

Runstom stood up so fast his chair fell over.

"Mom?"

CHAPTER 27

Sylvia Rankworth of the Epsilon-3 Agricultural Systems Center cheerfully led Runstom and Jax to the railway that would take them on the scant fifteen-minute ride out to her office. It felt like the longest fifteen minutes of Runstom's life.

He smiled back as she rattled off facts about the self-sustaining AgSys facilities, and how they made use of local sources whenever possible. He couldn't follow any of it, and he could barely speak. He'd been in communication with his mother through d-mail over the years, but the address he had for her had always been an unknown destination. He hadn't actually seen her in person for several years.

So what the hell was she doing here?

He knew he couldn't say anything, not where someone might overhear, and it paralyzed him. Fortunately Jax kept up appearances by engaging her in conversation, asking questions about their farming methods and what processing was required out on the surface. Runstom heard him tell Sylvia that his mother had been a terraform engineer, until she was lost in an accident.

Finally they arrived at the AgSys headquarters, which was really just a tiny building at the end of the railtrack, sitting in the middle of a field of mud. Sylvia insisted that before they do anything, they go straight out to the fields so she could show the overly-interested Jax some of their farms in person.

They donned rubber boots and trudged along a dirty path no more than three meters wide, a clear plastic covering arching overhead and down to either side, another meter outside of the walkway. In effect, the mud fields were both outside and inside and the odor was earthy and salty and slightly musty.

"These are our muckbug cultivations," Sylvia said as they walked. "Epsilon-3 has an atmosphere, but it's very thin and primarily nitrogen, carbon dioxide, and carbon monoxide. Quite poisonous to humans, not to mention that the thinness of the atmosphere makes the surface too cold to sustain much life. There is water, however, and complex ecosystems that thrive in pockets of mud pools. The muckbug is one of these animals native to this planet. It's kind of like a fish, but lives in the mud."

She bent down to a spot where there was a handle protruding from the mud and pulled it up. A cage or trap of some kind came with it and inside were wriggling, slick, black worm-like creatures with multiple sets of fins running the length of their bodies.

"Ugh, that's uh..." Jax tried, then looked away and out at the fields of mud around them. "So those things are all over out there?"

"That's right," she said and returned the trap. "They are terribly repulsive to look at, but very high in protein, omega-3 fats, and a plethora of minerals."

"So you eat them," Runstom muttered, trying to control his disgust.

"You ate one at lunchtime, dear."

Runstom stiffened, unable to speak. Jax said, "The sauce made it bearable."

"Yes," she said. "We have chefs working around the clock trying to turn these tiny monsters into a delicacy. Once these domes are finished, only the richest of the rich will come live here."

"And you're going to feed them muckbugs," Jax said, clearly amused. "Why is it only for the rich?"

"Oh, some damn fool economists back on Barnard-3," she said with a dismissive wave of her hand. "They think there are too many poor people there."

"On B-3?" Jax said. "Give me a break, what poor people?"

"Poor is all relative, Mr. Jackson. You might have felt poor in those B-4 domes if you compared them to the domes on B-3, but how did dome life compare to that of those struggling folks on Terroneous?"

Runstom flinched and glanced around, but there was nothing to see but the plastic archway and fields of mud. They had walked far enough from the central facility that it was a hundred or so meters distant.

"Oh, don't worry, Stanley," she said. "We don't have eyes everywhere out here. Not yet anyway."

He tried to breathe but his chest felt like stone. "Okay. Well. Mother. It's good to see you."

She embraced him and after a moment of relief, he wrapped his arms around her slight form. When she pulled away, she wiped her face. "I miss you always."

Runstom felt his face growing hot. He glanced at Jax

who was staring at them in a kind of stunned silence, and then he looked back at his mother. "I miss you too."

She laughed to chase away the tears, then clasped her hands together. "I'm sorry, Mr. Jackson."

"Oh, uh. It's no problem," Jax said, trying to relax his stance. "It's just that um. Well – so wait, what do poor people on B-3 have to do with rich people moving here?"

She laughed again and blinked at Runstom and then turned back to Jax. "As I said, poverty is relative. Or so these economists believe. They think that if they shave off the top one or two percent, they move everyone else up."

"And to shave them off, you only need to move them to someplace more expensive," Jax said with a nod.

"For the capitalist, there's always one more new world to conquer," she said with a wry smile.

The statement jarred loose a memory in Runstom's head. His first meeting with Victoria Horus. Something to do with Horus moving on from the Zebra Corporation and into Modern Policing and Peacekeeping: that she'd conquered all of consumer electronics and needed to find the next world to conquer.

He wanted to mention it, but he saw Jax take a deep breath, as if preparing to ask a more important question, so he kept the thought to himself.

"Okay, Ms. Rankworth," Jax said, the false name sounding ridiculous in Runstom's ears. "How did you know my name was Jackson and that I've been to Terroneous?"

"Call me Sylvia, Mr. Jackson."

"You can just call me Jax," he returned after a slight hesitation.

"Boys," she said suddenly. "I have to show you something, it's just over here."

They followed her eager pace a few dozen meters to an intersection of tubes that ran through the mud. She pointed at a handmade sign hanging from some kind of mechanical pump in the middle. "I've been to Terroneous too, many years ago. I saw this and I had to have it."

Though unexpected rain
churns soil into mud,
the harshest of storms
births more green than blood.

She grinned as she watched Runstom read it. "The poet-farmer who wrote it was talking about the green of his crops, but I saw this and I just thought, oh how it reminds me of my little green baby."

"Mom, come on. I'm not a baby, I'm thirty-eight." Runstom had to turn away from Jax's laughing eyes.

"Ohh," she said, waving him off. She turned to Jax. "Did you two fly here? Who was the pilot?"

"Stanford was," Jax said. "He's a pretty good pilot. Not that I know much about that kind of thing."

"Yes, he always was a good pilot," she said proudly. "I started teaching him when he was twelve."

"Yeah," Runstom said. "But now I know how illegal that was, to let a twelve-year-old fly a freaking spacecraft."

She laughed again. "Oh Stanley, what, are you worried your young fugitive friend here is going to turn us in?"

"Oh, uh," Jax said. "So you know about that too."

"Yes," she said with a sigh. "I know pretty much everything these days. But I'm powerless to act on anything. And I can't share what I know with anyone. You know, I feel a bit like Cassandra. From Greek mythology? Do you know her?"

"Um, was that someone from Grecia, on B-3?"

"She means Greece on Earth," Runstom said. "Mom has a thing for ancient stories."

She went on then, prodding Runstom for information about his life, his job, his relationships (and questionable lack thereof), and she went about filling in the details of her own quiet existence. At some point Jax had the sense to excuse himself so that Runstom could be alone with her and they walked through the tunnels that ran between the muck and talked.

She told him all about witness protection. She maintained the connections she'd acquired during her undercover days, which provided a never-ending influx of information, which she could do nothing with. Through the local networks, she'd caught wind of a public relations officer from ModPol coming to visit Epsilon-3. When she learned it was going to be Stanford Runstom, she arranged to have herself added to the partnership committee.

Life for her had been smooth lately. Her mother – Runstom's grandmother, whom he'd never met – had been a farmer in the early days of settlement on Terroneous. Sylvia remembered her youth fondly and so when she went into witness protection and needed to find a cover job, she started to study up on agriculture. She'd taken to it quickly over the years. Assistant Director on some unknown project was as far as she would be allowed to rise, so as not to draw any attention to herself.

She claimed her spy network was underground, so far down that it was far below ModPol. She told him about a mole inside Space Waste, though whose allegiance he or she belonged to was unknown, nor what their agenda may be, but it was most likely a ModPol spy. Like she once was.

She also heaped warnings on him as they talked. There was a reason that he was moved out of Justice, and she could not be sure of what that reason was, but there was one possible explanation: someone wanted to keep him from the kind of digging he did after the B-4 murders. He hated to admit that he agreed with her on that point.

And it burned him that she was still looking out for him. Keeping tabs. But that was her nature, he told himself. She was being a detective, not just an overprotective mother.

"I know you went to see Miss Zarconi," she said. They were close to the center of the muck farm, the buildings in the distance nothing more than bumps on the horizon barely visible through the semi-transparent plastic of the arching walls around the path.

"Is she in your network too?" he said, then wished he hadn't been so defensive.

"She has her own network. Let's just say it overlaps with mine." After a pause, she asked, "What did she tell you?"

He struggled to remember the conversation. He knew Jenna wanted to say something, but she'd held back. The walls had been listening. "She knew I was going to the mining colony on Ipo. And she knew Jax was on Terroneous. She knew that McManus – from my old precinct – was supposed to go down and get him."

"Ipo," Sylvia said. "Also a moon of B-5. And how did things go on Ipo?"

Runstom cocked his head in thought. "I never got there. McManus's ship had been in a fight with Space Waste after he arrested Jax. They were on the drift, and I picked up the distress call. By that point, I got new orders to report to Outpost Delta and dock my ship on the *Garathol.*"

Once it had come out of his mouth, it sounded odd. "You never made it to Ipo," she said.

"Why would they send me there just to turn me around?"

She nodded in thought. "Someone suspected Jax was on Terroneous. And that you two are close, given the circumstances. What was your plan, when you headed to Ipo? Who went with you?"

"I was alone," he said. "I was – well, to be honest, I was going to make a stop at Terroneous and feel it out."

He sighed then as it crashed together in his mind. Someone had made sure he had an assignment close to Terroneous – so close that he wouldn't be able to resist contacting Jax. He would have led them right to their fugitive.

"Is Victoria Horus in on this?" he said. "She sent me to Ipo."

"I suspect Horus has her own agendas," she said. "And these games are long. Favors are traded. Horus has no interest in Jax, but someone else does."

"X," he said. "What of Mark Xavier Phonson?"

She shook her head and for the first time her face dropped in sadness. "He's gone deep. Too deep to find. Deep, but still inside ModPol, where he can keep his cards close. But you can be sure he has a hand in all this."

"He wants Jax caught."

She grabbed him by the wrist. "You have to be careful. If they'd caught you and Jax together on Terroneous…"

"Shit," he said. He'd have been arrested right along with Jax. Taken out of the picture. In a way, they were lucky that Jax had made the mistake he'd made. His public appearance in the documentary about the magnetic sensor disaster had forced their hand early. And so McManus had gotten there first, only to lose Jax to Space Waste. If Runstom had gotten there first, someone would have known it. They'd have both been cooked.

"It's worse than what you think," she said, her grip tightening. "Right now it looks like ModPol wants to arrest Jax for evading the law. But X doesn't just want Jax brought in. He wants Jax out of the picture. Listen, Stanley: the work you did made it so that X will never operate from anywhere except the shadows. He has his network, but his connections are weakened. A thorn like Jax can break some of those weakened bonds."

He looked at her eyes and felt her fear creep into him. "You mean they'll kill him? Even if they arrest him first?"

"They'll make him disappear," she said. "They'll try like hell anyway. As long as X is still breathing."

At this statement, Runstom felt his palms go numb. It was almost like his mother was suggesting that if Jax were ever to be safe in this galaxy, X would have to leave it. How much did he know her anymore? Or ever? Was it something she was capable of? Taking another life?

He shook his head and pulled away, loosening her grip on his arm. "If they hadn't taken me out of Justice, I would have put him in prison for life."

"I know, Stanley."

They continued walking and he took out his notebook. Flipped through it with each slow step along the muddy path, as though it would tell him what to do. Make the connections. But the damn thing was just paper. If he couldn't chase X, then what was his next move? What else was there?

"I need to find out who's on the inside of Space Waste," he said as they sat down on a bench. He flopped his notebook onto his lap. "If there's someone inside, the attack at Vulca was somehow linked."

"How's that?" she asked lightly. She probably knew something about it, but would give him a chance to work it out on his own.

He looked at the scribblings. Timestamps. Targets. Methods. "They knew how to disable the power in a way that cut off the observatory, which was the building they wanted to infiltrate."

"What were they after?"

He frowned. "Some kind of detection equipment. They bungled it though, got the old stuff instead of the new."

"Because you ran them off," she said with a smile. "Or so I heard."

He allowed himself to grin in pride for a moment, then pushed it away. "It helped that there was a trial unit there." He looked back at his notebook. "In fact, they were given specific orders to go on patrol that morning."

"Mmm." She lifted her chin slightly, folding her hands over one another. "Farmers on Terroneous used to say you could tell when a storm was coming because the leaves of the trees would turn over in the wind and expose their undersides."

"That's useful," he grunted, unsatisfied with her pontification. "If we found out who's undercover in Space Waste, could we contact them?"

"Possibly," she said. "I must warn you, Stanford: once someone goes under, they lose some of their allegiance. They become…well, almost an independent entity. Which means they may be in a position to negotiate with both sides, to force compromise. In fact, they may have to."

"Because they're both an ally and an enemy." Just spending time with her and he was thinking like her again.

"Precisely. So whomever this insider is, you can't trust

them to be ModPol any more. It takes a big sacrifice to get them to let you out."

"Right," he said, then stopped himself. "Wait, do you mean for Space Waste to let you out, or for ModPol to let you out?"

"I mean both," she said quietly, her eyes falling to her feet. "I did. Gave something up to get out before you were born."

"What?"

She put her hands on his and smiled faintly into his eyes. "Doesn't matter. It was all worth it because I have you."

He looked down and allowed himself to feel the warmth of her hands. "Mom," he said, but could manage no more.

"So," she said and stood. "We have an advantage in identifying this spy inside Space Waste. We don't have to go at it from the ModPol side. I believe your friend Jax may have actually met them, during his short stint as a gangbanger."

Runstom stood with her and they began walking back. "That's right," he agreed, buoyed by the realization. "He's probably been face to face with whoever it is."

"You've probably got a sketch-up app somewhere in that ship of yours. Get Jax to describe any Wasters he thought didn't fit in. Then we can run them through some databases that I still have access to. It's going to be grueling work, but that's espionage."

"Right," Runstom said with a smile. He hadn't felt so good in so long. Even with the thought that something ugly was working against them, he felt like a kid again, side by side with his mother, solving something.

When they got within sight of the office, she stopped and held him by the elbow. "Stanford, there's something I need to tell you."

He stopped and turned to face her. "What, Mom?"

"You're thirty-eight now. It's been hard to watch you grow up from a distance. I mean, I kind of forgot that you've turned into a man. It's hard not to think of you as my boy. But I'm proud of you."

He swallowed. "Thanks, Mom."

* * *

Jax ducked as he stepped through the pressure door and into the passage that would take them back to the main complex. "This place definitely wasn't designed for B-foureans."

"No, probably not," Runstom said distantly as he strode on.

Jax stutter-stepped to catch up, dodging light fixtures as he went. They'd taken the railway from the farms back down to the central city and during the entire ride, Runstom had spoken maybe ten words. "So, I guess you have some other meetings to take?"

Runstom didn't answer. He looked down at his WrappiMate for a moment, then selected a side door that led down yet another narrow passage. After a few more twists, they finally came to the main dome, and Jax felt like he could relax. He hadn't realized how tight those tunnels felt until he was free of them. It was an odd sensation, and he realized he was learning why Lealina had called the domes claustrophobic. Only he didn't know why all of a sudden he'd be feeling it too. He reflexively glanced upward to look for something – for what? Barnard-5, the gas giant that sometimes loomed on the horizon of Terroneous? He only saw the blue sky and a handful of drifting pure-white clouds. The dome-ceiling illusion. He looked away.

"Stan, maybe we could stop for a bite," he said. It'd been several hours since their half-finished lunch. The memory of it and those bug-fish-things made him second-guess his suggestion. "Maybe we can find a place that serves just veggies. Or at least beer."

"Later," Runstom said.

They were moving quickly across the dome, passing buildings both complete and incomplete in their construction. The population was minimal, but very active – everyone seemed to be going somewhere. "Where are we going?" Jax asked with a tug on Runstom's arm.

"Back to the ship."

"But I thought you had more meetings to take."

Runstom sighed. "Yes. I do. Tomorrow. I just need to do something right now."

"Well, what?" Jax said, gripping tighter and pulling his companion to a stop. "What's going on?"

Runstom frowned at Jax's grip, then turned a glare up at him until he released it. "Something's not right."

"Yeah, no shit, Stan." He sighed as he looked into the other man's thousand-yard stare. "Okay, whatever. I'm going to go get a drink. You can catch me up when you come out of orbit."

"No," Runstom said. "I need your help."

"With what?"

He looked over one shoulder, a movement Jax thought he'd never see Runstom be paranoid enough to make. Then he leaned close. "First, I want to check the ship for bugs."

Jax flinched at the thought of those squirming, slimy muckbugs sliding around the chambers of the ship. "Gross, what? You think those nasty things got in your ship?"

Runstom crooked an eyebrow and tilted his head, then shook it. "No, I mean *bugs*. Surveillance."

"Oh, right," Jax said. Maximum paranoia achieved. "Maybe you better tell me – actually, first things first. Before we go anywhere, you really gotta tell me who that woman was."

He frowned. "Sylvia Runstom. Well, Rankworth, now."

"Your mother."

"My mother." He seemed to deflate at the admission. "I didn't know she was going to be here. I didn't know she was going to be anywhere."

"Something tells me you caught up on more than just family matters."

He gave a slow nod. "Jax. We both may be in some bad trouble."

That Terroneous horizon grew fuzzier in his mind and he rubbed his eyes. "What did she tell you?"

"For one thing, she knew I was sent to Ipo," he said in a tight, quiet voice. "She knew that someone thought if I went to Ipo, I might make a stopover and contact you on Terroneous."

"Shit," Jax breathed. Ipo, one of the other moons of Barnard-5. Of course, he'd have been so close. "Would you have?" he asked, wishing he hadn't sounded so desperately hopeful as he did.

Runstom looked at him for a moment. "Yeah," he said with a sigh. "I would have tried. And then we'd have both been fucked."

"You'd draw me out and so they could arrest me. And they'd find a way to nail you too."

He shrugged and shook his head. "Who knows. It's

possible it was set up to be that way. Or she's putting paranoia into my fucking head."

Jax didn't know how to respond. He thought back to the events on Terroneous. If someone had suspected that he was there, sending Runstom to the nearby moon of Ipo was a sure way to draw him out without breaking jurisdiction – and it would have worked, because Runstom would have come looking for him. But because Jax had blown his cover, he'd forced their hand. They had to send someone else after him before he could disappear again.

And here he was, running around with Runstom on Epsilon-3. If anyone found out he was a fugitive, they'd lock him up right quick, and Runstom would be just as fucked. They'd be in the same stew they would have been in had they made contact on Terroneous.

"Maybe we should—"

"Jax," Runstom said, leaning in close again. "We're not splitting up. No one here knows who you are. No one anywhere knows who you are."

"Right." Jax took a deep breath. He was a nobody. An invisible B-fourean. "Of course not."

"Anyway, I need you," Runstom said abruptly. "So deal with it."

Jax released a short laugh. Fearing for his life and his freedom, somehow he felt relief in that simple statement. "Sure, of course." He gestured in a direction that may have been toward the docks. "You said *first* we're going to check for bugs. What comes after that?"

Runstom gave him another slow nod, his mouth scrunching in thought. "She thinks there's someone in...*Space Waste*," he said, whispering the gang's name.

Jax cocked his head. "Someone?"

"On the inside."

"Undercover?"

"Yes. Undercover." Runstom swallowed and looked around again. The handful of residents – all of them workers of some kind, as the domes weren't yet ready for their destined occupants – buzzed about their business paying no attention to the green-skinned, well-dressed man and his mutely-dressed B-fourean companion. They must have lingered too long for his tastes because he once again set off for the docks, gesturing for Jax to follow. "When you were…when you were with them…"

"Oh," Jax said, realizing what was being asked. Had anyone stood out? Anyone not quite belonging. An odd notion, since he'd considered himself the biggest outcast of the bunch. Though if he gave it any thought, he would have to admit it was the most diverse collection of men and women he'd ever encountered. Even the population on Terroneous – which had its fair share of immigrants – didn't match the range of backgrounds Jax had seen in his short time at the Space Waste base. Still. "I can think of one or two."

Runstom put a finger to his lips. They'd arrived at the hangars already. "We're not making any moves until we check the OrbitBurner."

The other man's paranoia seeped into Jax like stale dome air sucking into his lungs, and they walked stiffly through the yard until they came to the hangar where they'd parked the OrbitBurner.

It was empty.

Runstom tapped furiously at his WrappiMate, then at the wall panel outside the hangar. "Where the fuck is my ship?"

"Uh, Stan," Jax said, putting a hand on his shoulder to

try to calm him. It vibrated at his touch and he yanked it away. "Look, Stan. I think I know what happened to your ship."

Blazing eyes spun to face him. "What?"

Jax threw up his hands defensively. "I'll tell you, but if I'm going to explain, we might have to go get those drinks after all."

"Jax." Runstom looked as though he were going to explode, but at the same time was on the edge of collapse. He sighed heavily. "A drink."

"A few," Jax said. "Because I have a bit to catch you up on."

"And my ship?"

"Don't worry about it," Jax said, allowing himself a sly smile. "It'll be back. I can promise you that."

CHAPTER 28

The OrbitBurner ticked along at a nice pace and within a day they were back at the site of the battle. Only once did they see a ping from a distant ModPol patroller and then it was gone. The ship drew no attention, just a civilian out for a spin around the planets.

Dava managed to feel a little guilty about taking it, but it wasn't like she would keep it. They'd be back to Epsilon-3 within another day or two and Jack and his ModPol buddy wouldn't even notice it was gone. As for Dava, Thompson, and Lucky, it gave them something to do that kept them out of trouble. In a way.

"So you can scoop up the BatCaps in this thing?" she asked Lucky. Already, blips of debris were appearing on the proximity radar.

"Sure can," he said. "Even a civvy like this might come across a distress call. So there's a low-power tractor beam. Finding them is the harder part, but I know the pattern they went out in. I've done BatCap retrieval before. Every Space

Waste pilot has to at some point. You know how Moses is about those BatCaps."

"Right." Moses and his obsession with continuous improvement. He was probably drawing lines in the dust on the floor of a cell at that moment, trying to analyze what went wrong.

"Hey, do you think someone will come back out here looking for the BatCaps?" Thompson said. "Maybe that could be our ticket home."

Dava thought about it. "A lost battle. Moses would definitely come back for them. He'd want to know what happened."

They were quiet for a moment. Finally Thompson said, "Well, fuck that idea. If Jansen is in charge now, he's not coming back here."

"Here's one of them now," Lucky said.

After several minutes of patient navigation and course adjustment, he'd hooked the BatCap and pulled it into the emergency bay. She sent Thompson to go down to the airlock and retrieve the memory out of it. They wouldn't bother keeping the rest of the shell.

When Thompson came back up, she popped the memory module into one of the deck consoles. The camera array on it captured a full range of all the space around it, so they used the holovid display to see it in three dimensions. The video picked up at the point when the BatCap was deployed. It shot across space and then came to a rest just outside of the battle that had already started. A few fighters launched from the *Garathol* and the Waster fighters were making short work of them. This, Dava had seen from the raider. She scrolled forward.

To the point of the breach and board. She continued to scroll but at a slower pace. Where had it gone wrong? A wriggling sensation started in her neck and crept through the back of her head and into her brain. This hadn't just been a failed mission. This had been a clusterfuck. Trying to piece the events together, trying to make sense of it – how much did it matter? Wasn't it really a distraction from the loss? The grief?

"There," Lucky said. "Look, off to the upper right in this back corner. See those blips?"

There were two, then five, then twelve or more. Within a few minutes of realtime passing on the video, several dozen new ships had come into the battle.

"Can you get their origin?" she asked him.

"Sure, just a matter of reversing the trajectory." He tapped at the console. "I'm going to pause this and put the local system map up on the HV."

The video winked out and in its place was a zoomed-out view of where they were sitting in the Epsilon Eridani system. Epsilon-5, the gas giant, loomed off to one side. It was empty, so empty. The only asteroids were several AUs out.

"Did we have a BatCap closer to where those fighters appeared?" Dava asked.

"Should have," Lucky said, adjusting their course and accelerating before she could order it.

An hour later they were looking at another video. They scrolled forward to the timestamp when the fighters appeared on the first video. On this one, they were already in view, so they scrolled backwards and watched the fighters pulling back into their hiding spots.

"Asteroids," Lucky said. "That's weird."

"They're not real," Dava said. She bent close to the

holovid, but it was hard to see everything, even as she looked at it from different angles. "Right here. Pull this up on the flat screen, high-res."

"Okay," Lucky said. "Here we go."

The asteroids weren't asteroids at all. They were cubic shapes of metal, clumped together somehow. When the video played forward at slow speed, they could see the rocks break away as the fighters came through.

"Well shit," Lucky said. "I've heard of this. Some special kind of stealth tech. They magnetize all that shit to the hulls of the ships. Then when they're ready to go, they just turn off the magnet. The metal rocks there are just thin, empty boxes and just drift out of the way.

"Sonovabitch," Thompson said.

"Bring up the system map again," Dava said. "And show me the approximate location of the ModPol outpost."

He did, then flashed a point on the screen near the gas giant. "We believe it to be somewhere in this area."

"It's too far away," she said. "Too fucking far. These fighters are not defending that base. They were here before we got here, before the *Garathol* even got here."

"An ambush," Thompson said.

"They knew we were coming?" Lucky said.

"Yes," Dava said. "And they let us board anyway."

"Because on the *Garathol*, there was another ambush waiting," Thompson said. "What the fuck."

Dava stared at the empty space just outside the viewport. She couldn't see it, but right now there were pieces of Space Waste drifting away out there, spreading out into the nothing. Pieces of ships. Pieces of her friends. Pieces of her family. Now part of a fragmented sky.

It had been so well planned. Let the Wasters think they're

in control, let them board. There never were any weapons to steal. Just Defenders, in force. And while those Defenders were slaughtering Wasters onboard the *Garathol*, the stealth ModPol fighters came out of a cluster of asteroids, minced the Waster fighters to pieces and drove off the *Longhorn*.

And now Moses was captured, along with a number of others. Joining Johnny Eyeball and Freezer. Last she heard was that they were transferred to a new zero-G facility in the outer Barnard system. More intel from Jansen. Dava had wanted to go after them, but Jansen said the facility was too well guarded, too state-of-the-art. Her bosses had hinted that if they could lift some fancy new experimental weapons from ModPol's transport, they'd have a shot at going after the prison. And Dava had let herself believe that.

The wriggling sensation in her brain was back. It felt like failure – but not a mission failure. Another kind of failure. Failure to listen to her gut? Weakness, because she was trying to trust her team?

As she turned the players around in her mind she couldn't allow herself that excuse. She knew who to trust and she knew who not to. The skill was innate; like an animal, she could smell a liar, a deceiver, whether she could prove it or not. Trust – that never really was her issue. She hated working with a team *not* because she couldn't trust her squadmates.

Blips on a screen. Digital representations of a bloody fight, of lives snuffed out. Background noise.

She hated working on a team because she felt she had to *protect* her squadmates. Johnny and Freezer, when they were arrested, she felt like *she* had lost them. She had failed to protect them. Even for someone like Johnny who could handle himself, she felt responsible. She didn't understand why, but at least she understood what she felt.

And she lost Moses too. Tried like hell to convince him not to endanger himself. And when he insisted on coming, she was unable to protect him. When she saw him cornered, she was unable to rescue him.

Why was she so concerned with protecting them? It hadn't always been that way. Moses treated Space Waste like family and it must have finally sunk in, because that's what they were to her. After learning to be strong without anyone, going so long on her own, she'd found another family. It was painful to carry that weight again, but it was a pain she didn't want to live without ever again.

Things had gone beyond what her stubbornness could shelter. If she wanted to keep looking out for her kin, she was going to have to do more than seek solo missions. She was going to have to get them together to work as a force. She would use that force to break down those that had brought harm upon her family. And those that had betrayed her family.

She stepped away from the consoles, to the back of the bridge. The sound of Lucky and Thompson murmuring words like *ambush* and *bad intel* and *mole* and *setup* faded into the background. Out of her pocket, she pulled out the piece of paper that Psycho Jack had forced into her hands before he left the OrbitBurner.

Basil Roy faked the detector.

CHAPTER 29

"Do you know. How. Much. That. Ship. Cost?" Chief Suri Pattenbird slapped the table with each word. She raised her reddening palms and lowered her voice to a tremble. "First you get boarded. Then you abandon ship. Then—"

"But Chief—" McManus started.

"Then!" Pattenbird's voice rose again to full volume. "Then we go back to locate it and it's gone! Some moon-hick made off with one of our armored prisoner transports!"

"I know, Chief," McManus tried again. "It's just that—"

"What the hell were you even doing out there anyway?"

He took a breath, then cocked his head in confusion. "I had orders."

"What orders," she said flatly.

"Uh, well, to go to Terroneous and pick up Jack Jackson, the fugitive."

"Sergeant McManus," Pattenbird said with a wave of her hand. "What is ModPol jurisdiction on Terroneous, moon of Barnard-5?"

He swallowed. "ModPol has no jurisdiction on—"

"ModPol has no jurisdiction on Terroneous, moon of Barnard-5," she said, once again slapping the table. "So tell me again, what orders?"

McManus felt the sweat gathering under his arms. This particular reaming had been going on for almost twenty minutes. He didn't even have a chance to shower or change since landing at Outpost Delta and warping over to Outpost Gamma. He hadn't eaten except for rations back on the paddy-wagon. He sure as hell hadn't accepted food or any other accommodations from Runstom and his goddamn fancy-ass OrbitBurner.

This wasn't the first reaming of his career. Normally his mode of operation was to figure out whether the shit could roll uphill or downhill. Downhill was easiest, but he'd had such a sparse outfit and they were all too close to him to throw to the wolves. Except Katsumi. With the flight recordings lost along with the ship, he might be able to pin something on her. But the reality was, she was the only pilot he had under his thumb – and only barely so. And in fact she had done a damn fine bit of flying with that bloated space-tank.

Uphill was a no-go. He'd gotten the orders top-secret-like, direct from a terminal. He'd verified their authenticity, but there was no trail to the commander that logged them.

The only thing he knew for certain – maybe – was that he'd been identified specifically for the mission. He'd gotten the pre-order to check the mission computer, with a directive to follow security protocol: no one else should retrieve it but him. And he followed protocol. He did his job. Almost to completion. Almost.

With nowhere for the shit to roll, he'd have to take it himself. "There were secure orders," he said. "They may no longer be accessible. I accept responsibility for the loss of the transport."

"And the prisoner?"

He considered his answer for a moment. "No orders, no prisoner."

She stared at him long and hard, then swapped folders around on the table in front of her. "Since you're so interested in prisoner transportation, I've got another mission for you."

He did what he could to douse the growing fire in his chest. "Yes, Chief."

"Space Waste attacked an interstellar transport coming out of Xarp in Epsilon Eridani. One of our supply ships."

"Coming out of Xarp? How'd they manage that?"

She glared at him and he shrugged and waited for her to continue. "Defense was able to scramble a counter-force and rescue the transport. They took several prisoners. Now, you know Defense: they don't want prisoners. Especially Space Waste. Space Waste prisoners are like a pot of honey, just asking to get swarmed. I don't have to remind you that half the problem with Wasters is that they keep breaking each other out of prison."

"So Justice offered to give Defense a hand," McManus guessed.

"That's right," Pattenbird said. "So we need to go out there and pick them up. Bring them back to Barnard to the new zero-G maxi."

"When?"

"Now. More or less. And there's a lot of them. We're going to use the interstellar prison barge. As you know, we haven't used the barge since last year."

"Yeah," McManus said softly. It'd been out of commission since Space Waste tore it apart to break out some of their comrades. ModPol had lost a lot of personnel that day. He was still saddened from time to time about not having George Halsey to kick around anymore.

"It's been rebuilt and reinforced, and now it's time to bring it back into commission. Now since we don't want a repeat of what happened the last time we used her, we're stacking her up with triple guard personnel."

McManus nodded. A chance to bring some Space Waste scum across the galaxy to slam them into zero-G prison sounded like a vacation. And better yet, he'd be leading an army of guards. "So do you need me to help identify personnel?"

Chief Pattenbird gave him a wicked grin, one that made his skin crawl. "You think after all of your *fuckups*, you're going to lead the guard? I'm busting your ass *down* for this mission."

"Wait, what?" he blurted. "I'm a *guard*? But I'm a sergeant!"

"And if you want to stay one, you're going to do some time." She leaned over the table and practically growled at him. "And these motherfuckers are nasty. The worst of the worst of Space Waste. You better make sure you get your shots – and I don't mean that as a euphemism. Get inoculated, because you don't know where these sick fucks have been and they *will* bite."

He swallowed down the gag in his throat. "Yes, Chief."

"Glad we have an understanding." She stood and he started to get up but she put a hand out. "You're not dismissed yet," she said in a low voice.

And then she left. He turned his head and watched her leave the small, dark conference room. "What the hell?" he murmured to himself. Where did she go? He wasn't dismissed?

He turned around and stared at the blank wall. Absentmindedly glanced at the corners, looking for recording devices. An old habit, and useless: anything like that these days would be too small to see or protected by a cloak.

That's when he noticed the shimmer in the opposite wall. The room was so dimly lit, he was tempted to blame it on his eyes. But something in the air made him feel like he wasn't alone.

"Uh, hello?" he said. He felt dumb, but he'd feel dumber if there was someone there watching him twiddle his thumbs.

The wall shimmered for sure then, and a silhouette began to take shape. Then it was a shadow, and then it was a man.

McManus stood with a jolt. He didn't raise his hands, but his arms tensed. "Who the hell are you?"

"Really now, Sergeant McManus." The man was tall and toned under the tight-fitting chamel-suit, now deactivated into a muted gray. He pulled back the hood to reveal red skin and a hairless head. "I don't go through the trouble of hiding in dark corners just to give my name to every asshole who asks for it."

"W-what?"

He came around the table and got closer to McManus. "No, I won't give you my name. But since we're having a conversation, you'll need something to call me." He looked up and snapped his fingers, as if an idea just occurred to him. "I've got it – just call me X."

"X." McManus's eyes narrowed as he looked into the red-faced man's eyes. He searched his memory, but he'd never seen the man before.

"Yes. You've heard that pseudonym before, haven't you."

"Yes." Though what he'd heard wasn't much. Rumblings in the corners of the dankest cop bars. A man who played all sides, who had a hand in every pie and a taste of every take. A man who didn't get crossed. Except. "Right, X. I heard a rumor that you were connected to the B-4 murders," he said firmly, unwilling to be unnerved by some chump in a chamel-suit.

"Connected." He seemed to consider the word, then nodded slowly. "I suppose we're all connected, aren't we, Sergeant? In fact, I've heard a fair share of rumors about you."

McManus scowled. This X could be bluffing, but probably not. McManus had definitely taken his take when the opportunities had presented themselves. Individual incidents that were too small for concern. But enough of them added up – well, he tried not to think about it. He was just doing what most of the rest of ModPol did.

"Wait," he said. "*You* gave the order to pick up Jackson."

X smiled. "Yes." The smile flattened into anger. "And you failed to bring him in."

He threw his hands up. "Again with this. I was attacked by fucking Space Waste!" He jabbed a finger into the other man's chest. "And you're hiding in the corner while the chief reams my ass for it, telling me there was no order. What the fuck?"

There was a cold, almost wet feeling under McManus's chin. Then it sank in: it was hard, almost sharp. It was the barrel of a tiny pistol, and X held it there. He hadn't seen the move, some kind of sleight of hand, but there was no denying its sudden presence. He pulled his finger back and lowered his hand and tried not to swallow.

And then it was gone. Back into whatever fold it had come out of, X calmly staring him in the eyes, hands across his chest. "I chose you for a reason, Sergeant. It's not because of all the dirt I have on your ass. I have dirt on everyone. You, I chose you because you got the shit end of the deal when that sonovabitch Stanford Runstom chased a case that should have been done and dead."

McManus frowned. The shitstorm that followed Runstom's little pageant that played out on Sirius-5 had been hell for him and the other officers and detectives that were part of the Barnard-4 murder investigation. Non-stop interviews, both internal and external: superiors reaming his ass, Internal Affairs digging with all of their tentacles, and lead-hungry sensationalist journalists stalking them wherever they went. As though they were all in on this mass murder because they didn't go detective-crazy like Runstom did.

"Don't get me started," he muttered.

X nodded. "You are started, Sergeant. Now you need to end." He started to pace, waving a finger. "You were *supposed* to tie up a loose end."

"Jackson." McManus sighed in frustration. "Why did you have to do this secret order shit? Why didn't you just have him picked up officially?"

"Two reasons. As your chief reminded you, Terroneous is not under ModPol jurisdiction. But more importantly, no one in Justice gives a shit about Jackson. They got Jenna Zarconi. They got their murderer. Jackson is just a wrongfully accused sap. Bringing him in on a fugitive charge is more trouble than it's worth."

McManus played it out in his mind for a moment. X had a point: if ModPol brought Jackson in, the media would be back in their shit like predators on blood. "But he's worth the trouble to you?"

"Let's just say that when Zarconi came in, something came with her. Something I had to work. Very. Hard. To make go away."

"And Jackson makes it not go away." McManus took a deep breath before he said the next part, making sure he was ready for it. "You want Jackson, but you don't want him arrested. You want him to..." he trailed off.

X turned and gestured at the wall as if he could point at space itself. "Epsilon. Our illustrious Defense division bagged us an assload of Wasters. You remember how you lost Jackson?"

"Of course," McManus grunted. "Wasters raided the Black Maria and took him. It was the only thing they took. Didn't even pop him out of the Securitube. Why did they take him?"

"Recruitment."

McManus puzzled it over for a second and then shrugged. "Whatever."

"Yes, whatever." X circled the room until he was face to face with McManus. "I have intelligence that says Jackson was involved in the Space Waste assault."

McManus huffed. "We talkin' about the same Jackson? Skinny white guy from B-4?"

"He was brought on as a hacker. And he would have been captured along with the others." He grinned. "Believe it or not, one of Jackson's greatest strengths is being a nobody. No one knows who he is or what he looks like."

"I know what he looks like," McManus muttered. He heard himself say it and realized it was why he'd landed this job all along.

"And I hear you landed guard duty." X pulled the hood of his chamel-suit over his head and the fabric started to shimmer. "The prisoners will be loaded onto the barge at Outpost Epsilon. Then there's the Xarp back to Barnard, and a few weeks' subwarp out to the maxi, as I understand it." He walked to the back of the room, shadows bunching around him like he was sinking into mud. "Lots of time for a guard to spend in the company of those prisoners."

"I'll be sure to enjoy every minute of it." He swallowed and asked the question he barely dared to ask. "And what happens if Jackson isn't among the prisoners?"

"Then you find him, Sergeant McManus." Only a voice now, floating across the small room. "Jackson disappears and you might find yourself promoted to Lieutenant. Fail, and *you* become a loose end."

McManus couldn't remember leaving the room, drifting down the hall, and finding the precinct bar. The logic center of his brain was too busy trying to figure out exactly how fucked he was, while the baser functions were seeking refuge from reality as fast as possible. The latter had worked the dispenser on instinct and he unexpectedly tasted the sweet burn of liquor on his tongue as his own hands brought a bottle to his mouth.

The fire shocked him into consciousness. He was a survivor. He would do what he needed to do. And all he had to do was get to Epsilon Eridani, find Jackson somewhere in that largely uncharted solar system, and make one of the new worlds his final resting place.

Acknowledgments

A massive thank you to the hardworking folks over at Harper*Voyager*, especially my editor Rachel Winterbottom. I've thoroughly enjoyed the process and it's very exciting to be a part of this journey at a forward-thinking publisher that continues to make strides into the future of literature.

I'd like to thank all the people who have supported my writing in one way or another over the years. National Novel Writing Month (NaNoWriMo) helped me take a big leap forward, and I thank the NaNoWriMo organizers and community. We have so many great writer communities and organizations in Oregon and I want to thank all of them for their writing workshops, lectures, panels, networking functions, and other opportunities, especially the Northwest Independent Writers Association (NIWA), Willamette Writers, the Wordstock Festival, Literary Arts of Oregon, and OryCon (which is a sci-fi convention but I include it for their obvious dedication and support of the written word and authors).

I'd like to give a special shout-out to the friends I've made in the past couple of years in the other authors at Harper*Voyager*. A wonderful camaraderie has developed between us and I am so thankful for the support.

Cynthia: thank you again for always believing in me. You make me feel like a genius!

Jennifer: whenever I need to go to a blissful place in my mind, I inevitably end up with you. Sometimes we're off on one of our adventures, and sometimes it's slower, just you and I enjoying an everlasting moment. I love being with you like nothing else. You are my religion.